Dark Curtains

Cecil D. Nobles

Dark Curtains

To my family, especially my encouraging wife.

Table of Contents

Chapter 1

Peter Knowles slowly opened his eyes. The RV was still dark with only the faint, red light of the digital clock radio sitting upon the nightstand. As usual, he sat up and swung his legs over the side of the bed, let out a slight yawn, and stood up. Although retired, years in the military had tuned his body to a set circadian rhythm. Without even looking at the clock, he knew it was around 5:00 a.m. Peter was excited to get the day going, so he took a quick shower, got dressed, and prepared a cup of coffee. After making up the bed and ensuring everything was squared away, there was still one last thing he needed to do before hitting the road.

Grabbing his coffee, Peter sat down in front of his laptop to check his email. He had a few messages from the Department of Veteran Affairs, which seemed to always have a need to inform him of every little change they made which didn't affect him. He never knew if he would need the information, though, so he just kept them in his queue. The only other emails were from Goldilocks. These were of interest to him even though he didn't really know much about her. He virtually met her about a year ago while he had been searching online for information on the Wabash Trace Nature Trail in Council Bluffs, Iowa. He had read several reviews on the old train trail, which had been converted to a sixty-three-mile hiker's escapade. In one of the reviews, Goldilocks had described her experience and offered her email up for anyone that had questions. Peter took advantage of the opportunity and began to correspond with her. The first few back and forth replies hosted mostly insights of cool places to visit, things to see, and things to avoid. To Peter's surprise, he seemed to connect with her and began to ask her advice on a number of things, which led to a closer relationship over the next few months. He had kept it professional though, never asking her name, where she was from, or what she did. He simply enjoyed knowing someone to discuss topics of similar interests without pollutants which seemed to affect the rest of the world like drama, gossip, and other random nonsense.

After a quick review of the last email sent from Goldilocks, where they had been discussing black and white versus color photography, he clicked on the reply button and began to type. He opened up the letter as he always did with her:

"Hey Sunshine! Well, I've finally arrived at Alamogordo, NM. This October weather is great and I'm excited to climb the Sacramento Mountains today. I always swore I would return to this place and now I'm finally here! I know, I know...I should always take someone with me in case something happens, but you know me! Anyways, I just wanted to drop you a line to keep in touch and I'll be sure to let you know how the hike goes. By the way, I prefer B&W photos as I find them simple with less distractions. One can capture the intent and feeling of the moment without all the colorful distractions. But that's my opinion. Talk to you later. PK"

Peter clicked the send button, sat back and smiled. Being retired from the Air Force and only forty years old, he knew he had a good life. His pension, truck and RV provided him with everything he needed. Although he had become somewhat withdrawn from the social world, he liked it that way. The lack of social endeavors freed up his time to learn more, see more, and do more, which could be planned for. People, on the other hand, were unpredictable, full of emotions, and needy, which he could simply do without. He wouldn't label himself as an isolationist, but whatever he was had to be a neighbor to it. *No bills, no people, no worries*!

Peter stepped out of the RV and took in a deep breath of fresh air. He then did the usual walkaround to ensure the tires were good, nothing was leaking, and no damage had been done from another vehicle. He was very peculiar about his truck and RV and knew a little preventative maintenance would alleviate a breakdown on the side of the road. *An ounce of prevention is worth a pound of cure* he thought as he headed for the truck.

He knew his destination and knew there was only one road which led up to the mountains from Alamogordo. He would ascend up US Highway 82 towards the small town of Cloudcroft, situated on top of the Sacramento Mountains. Peter started the truck, gave it a minute to warm up, and then pulled out of the Texaco truck stop. *Thanks for the free Wi-Fi*! Adventure was at the top of the mountains today, and Peter drove head on to meet it.

Highway 82 was easy to find on the northern edge of Alamogordo. Peter loved roads which climbed mountains like a snake and the digital display of his GPS reflected such, putting a slight smile across his face. The growl of the truck's V8 engine purred as it wound its way towards the top. Joshua trees, some saltbush, and various other desert vegetation filled the landscape as he traversed the first six miles of the upward journey, but then gave way to more ponderosa and fir pine trees during the last four-mile stretch. The air was a little thinner at the top and the chill had him adjusting the heat in the truck. Peter knew he would have to dig out his old, green, military issued flight jacket for this adventure. He had taken off the name and service identification tags on it after his active-duty service, which meant he could still wear it as a civilian. The jacket was just too comfortable and had plenty of reliable pockets in it to part with. On top of that, it was paid for!

A little over halfway to Cloudcroft, Peter came across the small town of High Rolls. It wasn't much to look at, with several houses on both sides of the road and an occasional shop which sold local Native American trinkets. He noticed the High Rolls General Store and decided to pull over for a quick stop. Out of habit, he wanted to pick up a few bottles of water and some beef jerky to put in his backpack. Plus, he wanted to smell his truck's engine to ensure he didn't smell antifreeze or other signs of engine strain. It had been a steep climb, so a little rest for the truck wouldn't hurt anything. Approaching the venue, he could tell this was more of a local's store. There were two benches just outside the door situated on either side of a wooden, carved Native American statue. Peter took a moment to admire the workmanship as well as the expression the face revealed. He had always thought Native Americans portrayed a face of sadness and wisdom at the same time. He stood face-to-face with the statue. *What are you thinking about?* After a moment, Peter walked over and pulled the door open to enter the store. He grabbed a couple of bottled waters and a pack of beef jerky before proceeding to the checkout counter.

"Are you planning to stay up in Cloudcroft? I see you have an RV with you," the clerk asked, starting a casual conversation.

Peter thought for a second and then replied, "I've always wanted to check out these mountains! Do a little exploring, you know? Not sure if I will be staying the night or not."

"There's a lot to see up here. Most out-of-towners just head straight for Cloudcroft, rent a cabin, and rarely dare to venture beyond the campsite," stated the clerk.

Peter could gather from the man's physical appearance he had mostly Native American blood running through him. He imagined the complexity of growing up with Native American culture while trying to blend into mainstream American society during high school and even serving as a clerk. Peter decided to gather some information from this local, which seemed to enjoy random conversations.

"Any suggestions? I'm one of those non-typical campers," he said with a small smile. "I like to hike, but not on government carved trails. Rather, I prefer the unbeaten path to find a view unseen or discover something new."

After a brief moment of thinking with one brow raised up, the clerk replied, "Hmm...I'd recommend West Side Road. It's just across the street. It goes on for miles and miles with many rarely traveled trails." After a pause, he then added, "A few miles in, there's a couple of places large enough to park your RV. However, the road isn't maintained often and the ride there may be a little bumpy. Would probably be hard to turn that thing around too, since it's a narrow, dirt road. So, if you go, I recommend making it at least to one of those open areas." He raised his eyebrows after speaking and looked directly at Peter as if thinking, *are you that non-typical*?

Peter could feel the clerk's inner inquiry coming from those raised eyebrows. However, he had made the statement of being non-typical and he did enjoy a challenge. Why not?

"I think I'll check it out," Peter boldly responded. "Besides, I came here to see the magic these mountains hold and not just for the typical, picture perfect campsites and roadside kiosks selling imitation, Indian arrowheads." Peter realized his response may be taken as offensive, but he wanted the man to know he could dish it out as well as receive it!

The clerk's eyebrows lowered and a smile lit up his face. "Good luck out there. Drop back by on your way out and let me know how it went for you."

Before exiting the store, Peter asked one final question, "What's your name, if you don't mind?"

"Red Dog!" he replied seriously, but then began to laugh. "I'm just kiddin'!" he added while straightening up his face. "Visitors heading up the mountain ask me that a lot expecting me to say 'Tonto' or some other Native American name. I know they don't mean anything by it. I figure they have just been programmed to think such things through television and books."

"So, what is your name?" Peter asked again with an understanding expression.

"Ahanu!" he returned. "It means 'he who laughs'."

Peter could tell the clerk was holding back some serious laughter. He liked this clerk and his sense of humor! "Well, Ahanu, I'll be sure to stop by on my way out. Thanks!"

As he exited the store and began to walk to his truck, Peter realized the sun had crept up over the eastern horizon, though he couldn't see it yet. A sizable hill behind the store still cast its shadow over the area. After starting the truck and adjusting the heater a little, he pulled back onto the road and started looking for West Side Road.

To Peter's surprise, Ahanu was correct. West Side Road was across from the store about fifty feet east. He had come to realize, in the past few years, most people didn't give accurate directions. 'A mile down the road' may turn out to be three miles and 'just around the corner' may be five corners. At least Ahanu was accurate which, combined with his sense of humor, made him the type of fellow Peter would agree to have a casual conversation with. The road sign for West Side Road was awfully tilted, faded and partially hid behind some tree limbs. The lane was paved, but there were no white or yellow lines and potholes spotted the road giving even more credit to Ahanu as he had stated it hadn't been maintained. As he crept along, being careful not to bump his RV around too much, he realized there were several, sparsely populated houses just off the road. Some were nice, and he imagined some of the commanders and high-ranking officers at the nearby Holloman Air Force base probably had getaway cabins up here where they could get away from it all and just relax. The houses were tucked away behind fir pine tree limbs and mountain brush, and a lot of them would go unnoticed if you didn't catch the small driveway leading to them. After carefully maneuvering his truck and RV around four or five really tight curves, the houses began to disappear from the wooded landscape, and the paved road degraded into a dirt lane barely wide enough for his RV. Peter stopped to reconsider his course of action. Turning to his GPS, he realized it didn't offer much information. The road was depicted as a winding trail but continued on like a snake through the mountains. He did notice the name 'West Side Rd' on top of the GPS line after he zoomed in all the way. But then it dawned on him there was no place to turn around and backing the RV around those sharp curves would prove impossible! Forward it was.

The crumbling of rocks under the wheels and the occasional scratching of vegetation along the side of the truck seemed to magnify itself in Peter's ears as he eased along the road. Out of his left window, the pine trees climbed the terrain while his right-side view was mostly of the open sky sitting upon the Tularosa Basin area in the distance. The GPS informed him he was at an elevation of 6,780 feet and his view of the distant basin seemed to confirm it. He began to ponder Goldilocks and whether she had replied to his email by now. He imagined what she might look like before dismissing the thought. There was definitely no Wi-Fi to be found in this part of the world, and no way to communicate with her. He figured when he did get the chance, his message to her would probably start with his adventure of getting stuck in the Sacramento Mountains!

The sun had inched higher in the sky and the mountains were no longer tall enough to mask its light. The truck's radio display told Peter it was already approaching 10:00 a.m. Although the sun had conquered the mountains, the temperature seemed to remain a cool fifty degrees or so, as he gradually made his way further south along the mountainside and further from civilization. He began to weigh the risks of getting stuck or having something break with no way to call anyone due to the lack of cell towers. Although Peter wasn't one for carrying a cell phone around with him, he always kept one of those prepaid, flip phones in the truck's glove compartment for emergencies. He chuckled a little as he thought if he finally did need to use the phone for help, it would be to no avail since there was no signal up here. He decided to take a chance and continue along the road.

Eventually, Peter came across a fork in the road. The GPS told him West Side Road continued on to the left while a new one, Forrest Road 90A, branched off to the right. Of course, he noticed the misspelling of the word '*forest*' right away, but dismissed it attributing the error to some random high school dropout probably paid minimum wage to make digital maps. But why blame the poor kid for the error when his or her supervisor should have caught the mistake before putting it out for the world to see their incompetence? Peter wondered if he was too hard on the world. Did he think himself superior to other humans? Were his expectations of people too demanding? He quietly sat in his truck and thought about it for a few moments. He wasn't a mean person, but he was a straight to the point type of guy. In the military, he had to receive feedback often which wasn't always flattering. Rather, it served to point out his weakness and address improvement areas. His commanders and peers would provide this feedback with the intent to help him. However, in the civilian world, Peter quickly realized society did not accept such honest feedback and, more times than not, took such advice as offensive when it was truly meant to help the person. He rationalized his honesty to others as a good thing and would never resort to sugarcoating words to help someone feel better about themselves. If the baby was ugly, then call it ugly!

Thinking the view of the Tularosa basin would be better, Peter turned the steering wheel to the right and proceeded westward slowly along Forrest Road 90A. Eventually, after about two miles of careful maneuvering, he noticed an open area to his right large enough to circle his truck and RV around a tree rooted in the center. It was a beautiful area! Several larger trees on the perimeter had grown long limbs which provided shade over a clean, level ground. Most of the sky was viewable, and Peter already knew he would be looking up at the stars on this night while sitting in his collapsible lawn chair. He figured he could cut up some onions, jalapenos, ham and cheese for the perfect omelet, a personal favorite. As he pulled up and parked beside one of the trees, he realized walking around in the wooded area would be fairly easy as there wasn't much underbrush. He exited the vehicle and stood up tall with his arms lifted high towards the sky. He bellowed out a loud "HELLO!" as he slightly leaned backwards to give his back a good stretch. And there it was...peace and quiet! No one answered his greeting and there were no noises from manmade contraptions. The only sound was the occasional chirp from a curious bird hiding somewhere in a nearby bush. As he walked around the truck and RV to assess any damage suffered from the clawing vegetation West Side Road had to offer, he spotted a closed gate off to the west. A faded, rusty sign read: WARNING! GOVERNMENT PROPERTY! NO TRESPASSING! Peter knew whatever this gate once protected was no longer active due to the dilapidation of the gate and sign. "I'll have to check that out," Peter said out loud as he returned to get his RV setup for the night.

After setting up and out of curiosity, Peter pulled out an old book which had detailed maps of each state. They were in alphabetical order so he quickly found New Mexico and began to drag his finger across the page till he was pointing at Alamogordo. He then traced his route from there to High Rolls and then along what he believed was West Side Road. He inspected the area he thought he was at, but found no identifying marks. No government facilities or other structures were noted, nor anything else to indicate what was behind the gate and rusty fence. He placed the book back and stepped out looking at the gate. "If they wanted to keep people out, they should have secured it better," he mumbled to himself. He grabbed a camouflage backpack from the back seat of the truck. Just like the flight jacket, he had acquired it in the military and found its durability and efficiency a must. Peter then reached into the front seat, grabbed the two bottles of water and beef jerky, and placed them in the sack. Some ace bandaging, duct tape, survival knife and a green lighter also filled the pack in the main compartment. He knew there was a compass in the small, left pocket and twenty feet of cord in the larger, right pocket. There was always enough space in the rucksack to house any keepsakes Peter might find along his adventures. Another inner pocket contained several zip tight plastic bags, some matches, pen and some paper. Placing each arm through shoulder straps, he pulled the backpack snug against his back and then fastened two straps together around his waist. All the hiking and his previous military lifestyle kept Peter in shape. He was 6'1 weighing two hundred pounds, so hauling around a backpack wasn't a problem at all. Walking around to the driver's side, he opened the door and removed a small, digital camera from the door compartment. After placing it in one of his many jacket pockets, he locked the doors on the truck and headed for the gate.

Peter easily scaled the gate and began to trek west. Old gravel covered the trail he assumed was once a road. Tree limbs had encroached over the path now, so driving a vehicle through here surely meant a new paint job! Although he was heading west, the Tularosa basin was hidden behind the hill he began to ascend. He figured that once he reached the summit, the vast basin below would reveal itself once again making for a nice photo. He knew he would go for a color shot rather than a black and white to amplify the vast blue sky contrasting with orangish, tan basin desert. Goldilocks popped into his mind at that moment, and he began to ponder what she looked like again. Was she tall, short, skinny, or overweight? Would her hair turn out to be blonde, given her name was Goldilocks? He decided to imagine her as an attractive lady, labeling her a seven out of ten on the man scale. If she was too pretty, other men would bother her and pose a threat to Peter. Any less attractive meant she would probably be out of shape and he wasn't very fond of ladies who didn't take care of themselves that way. A seven was perfect!

After walking about a thousand feet and around three slight curves, the horizon started to lower ahead of him. He knew he was approaching the top. Ahead, and to the left, he noticed a structure through some tree limbs on the left side. As he continued, he noticed it appeared to be a house based on the door and window positions. It also had a couple of venting pipes extending above the roof, and an old, rusted clothesline hung between two metal poles on the south side. A horizontal, cylindrical gas tank was nestled beneath one of the windows on its east side which Peter was facing. The old, army green paint had faded and chipped which exposed rotting boards beneath. He could tell there was a significant downward slope behind the house just beyond the clothesline as he could see trees sinking beyond his view. He continued along the road examining the unfolding exterior of the house till he came to a stop directly in front and north of it. Peter stood still and listened. He wasn't sure if it was the dilapidated fence and gate, the abandoned, army colored house, or the overgrown vegetation around a once habitable area which made a post-apocalyptic feel come over him. Perhaps it was multiple factors giving him the feeling of being a lone survivor exploring an abandoned military complex after a nuclear war. Whatever it was, it excited Peter and he reveled in the exhilaration it gave him.

Taking a few steps forward, he placed his right hand on the old, wooden door and gave it a shove. It swung open on rusted hinges with popping metal sounds. The structure's awakening seemed to aggravate the floor as it threw up dust particles into a circular dance. Several floorboards had popped out of joint over time, and most of the glass panes had been broken out of the back two windows. Hints of yellowish paint on the interior walls were mostly covered by dust and spider webs. A dirty, wooden chair and a tri-level shelf with three rusted cans atop seemed to be the only remaining residents in this room. Cautiously, Peter placed his hands behind the door frame and pulled himself up. He could see exposed ground through the floor where the boards had popped out in some areas. To the left, there was an open door revealing a counter with a sink and several wall cabinets with their doors partially open or altogether missing. The right-side wall had two doorway entrances equally spaced but neither had doors. Two equally sized rooms, approximately a hundred square feet in area, were behind the doorways and Peter deduced these were probably used as sleeping quarters. He took a few steps to take a better look into both rooms, which revealed nothing interesting, and then noticed the cans placed atop the shelf he had previously noted. Curious, he reached for one of the cans and brushed off the layer of dust which had accumulated over who knows how many years. The yellow and blue design of the old can revealed itself with a label reading *Cowbell Powdered Whole Milk*. Examining it more closely, he found what he was looking for! The year 1947 was in small print on the backside and was almost undecipherable.

The other two cans on the shelf were extremely rusted and lacked any labels. Peter thought about placing the can in his rucksack to keep as a souvenir, but instead placed it back on the shelf. Turning around, he headed for the kitchen area only to find empty cabinets and a rusted sink. One of the walls contained an alcove which could have contained a refrigerator at one time.

Peter began to imagine life in this house back in 1947. An Army soldier was in uniform having just gotten off duty and was in the kitchen preparing his evening meal. Two more men in casual, civilian clothes sat in the living area puffing on cigarettes while reading about President Truman's latest initiatives. In one of the bedrooms, another soldier was stretched across his bed writing a letter to his girlfriend. With only four guys, Peter imagined this place was probably a really good assignment. Most would probably avoid it at all costs, but not him. The solitude this remote location provided would allow any soldier to focus on their work without worldly distractions and, having only a few other men, would reduce the chances of conversational drama. Yes, this would have been a great assignment! But what was the assignment or mission assigned to this location? He exited the house and proceeded further along the path.

Peter was on top of the hill now as he continued down the path, which had begun to curve to the right until he was heading northeast. From this view, the Tularosa basin was in full view with the White Sands National Monument awkwardly appearing in the distance amid the tan, desert landscape. Holloman Air Force Base and the town of Alamogordo were also visible. Far in the distant west, the San Andres Mountain range formed a jagged horizon. He took a minute to take it all in, even taking a deep breath and holding it for a second before exhaling good, clean mountain air! Moments like these were what he lived for.

After viewing the basin for several minutes, he walked further along the trail to come across another building. This wasn't a typical structure! It was metal and painted white with no windows. There was a thick, concrete foundation which extended beyond the building. It formed a platform someone could use to walk around the entire building. As he faced the building from the north, there was a closed, metal door to the left and a huge, sliding door in the center portion of the wall which extended from the foundation to the top. The large door wasn't closed and Peter stood there for a moment hardly believing what he saw. Beyond the door, and situated in the center of a large room, was an enormous telescope! It had to measure at least twenty feet long with an attached seat and cranks to its rear area. There was a circular base plate holding it up. The telescope pointed towards the western sky. Peter always had an affinity for science and space since he was a little boy. *What a find!* He headed to the built-in steps leading up onto the concrete platform. Peter noticed large, steel rails extended from the bottom east side of the building as he stepped up and after a moment realized their purpose. The entire building was built upon these rails and could be slid back to reveal the open sky for the massive telescope! He was excited and continued on inside through the large doorway. However, as excited as he was, Peter remembered to be safe, taking a moment to survey his surroundings for any potential hazards. Not noticing any, he slid his backpack off and placed it to the side on the floor. Smiling, he began to climb up to position himself in the astronomer's seat. This closer look and feel revealed the telescope was no longer functional. As he peered into the tube in front of his face, there was only the hollow shell of a long tube. The lenses had been removed and patches of rust had begun to eat at it. No matter. Peter already had his eyes closed as he sat there and imagined those same Army soldiers before performing their duties back in the 1940s! One was calling out astronomical coordinates from a clipboard intended for the guy sitting in the driver's seat of the telescope. The other two leaned over a table pointing at constellations on a blue star chart. What an exciting assignment Peter thought as he opened his eyes and began looking around the large room.

There was an old wooden desk in the far corner and three refrigerator sized devices with metal panels containing reels, buttons and lights. He thought they must have been used to record data or calculate settings for the telescope. He climbed down from the astronomer's seat and started towards the wooden table. There was nothing on it, but there was a drawer with a small, metal handle. He gave it a tug only to discover it was locked, or stuck. He almost walked away but then realized this place had been abandoned. After retrieving his survival knife from his backpack, Peter began to work at the drawer prying the left side and then the right side of the drawer until it cracked open. Opening it further, its contents consisted of two wooden pencils, a tin reel without tape, and a calendar. Interested, he pulled out the calendar and blew off the settled dust. Oftentimes, military personnel wrote down key events on calendars as reminders and even wrote notes along the edges. The date of the calendar was 1947 with the month of March on top. He could tell the previous two months had been torn away and no handwriting was noticed. Losing interest, he quickly fanned through the remaining months when a sheet of paper fell out onto the floor. Peter tossed the calendar back onto the desk and bent down to retrieve it. As he stood up pulling the paper closer, he suddenly froze! The words TOP SECRET//UGEN were stamped on the top and bottom center. He recognized this type of classification marking but realized he had never actually observed classified information outside of a secure facility. The Air Force had placed him in an intelligence career field when he first entered service which required a top-secret clearance. The job came with intense training on properly marking, caring for, and storing classified information. Someone had obviously made a huge mistake! Peter's instincts told him to burn it right there on the spot, but his curiosity got the best of him as he decided to read further:

TOP SECRET//UGEN
Classified by: Multiple Sources
Destroy in accordance with AR 380-5
Date: 26 Feb 1947
(TS//UGEN) SUBJECT: UGEN Test Successful

(TS//UGEN) Remote site WATCHFUL EYE successfully completed its PROJECT UGEN mission between the hours of 0130L and 0800L on 25 Feb 1947. All tracking equipment was calibrated properly and performed as expected. The experimental craft was detected at 0146L by radar tracking equipment. As expected, the craft successfully obscured radar tracking at 0200L and remained undetected until 0415L when the radar reacquired its position above White Sands Missile Range. At 0646L, our optical tracking equipment detected the craft and proceeded to track it until 0700L when it became cloaked as planned. Although not visible, the radar tracked the craft until 0715L when it then became undetectable via optical or radar methods. Craft was once again acquired at 0745L until the end of the test at 0800L.

(TS//UGEN) Apart from the successful test, Dr. Boyd is performing above expectations. No indications of side effects observed after the introduction of the UGEN into his system. Will continue to monitor and record his progress.

PAGE: 1 of 1

TOP SECRET//UGEN

Peter stood in silence as he lowered the paper and looked over at the large telescope. What had he just read? Although he had never heard of Project UGEN, he acknowledged to himself the document had been written in a military style and followed proper formatting guidelines. He knew the military had incorporated stealth technology, but it wasn't revealed until the F-117 flew over Panama in 1989! Moreover, he had never heard of an aircraft which could disappear from optical viewing and, on top of that, this letter had been written in 1947! Was this a legitimate document? As he looked around, he admitted there was evidence to support its validity. This was once a secured, government facility and there was a large telescope which could be used to track an object visually. Who was Dr. Boyd and what exactly did he have injected into his system? Peter realized he had begun to let his mind wander with questions, which would accomplish nothing. He folded the document in half, carefully placed it inside his backpack and then slung the pack over his shoulder. He marveled one more time at the large telescope before exiting the building.

Chewing on a piece of beef jerky he had recovered from his sack, Peter continued down the trail. After rounding another corner about a hundred yards east of the telescope building, another building on the right side of the road came into view. He realized he was making a loop which would put him back on the entrance trail and could even see the army green house through the trees. He decided to explore the newly found building before returning to the campsite. It wasn't as large as the previous two buildings and lacked any windows. The greenish exterior paint was chipped and faded with the entrance door hanging crooked on one hinge. After three hard pushes, he managed to loosen the door from its last hinge as it fell against a wall and then onto the floor. It was the loudest thing he had heard since exploring the outpost, which caused him to instinctively pause for a second to see if there would be any response. Nothing. The walls inside were bare and dust had saturated the floor. Six evenly spaced, electrical conduits emerged from the floor along the back wall. Based on the exposed number of wires, Peter imagined this building to be an electrical building of some sorts which either supplied power to the other buildings, or housed quite a bit of electronic equipment possibly used for recording data. Either way, the room was empty of anything interesting, so he decided to exit. *Who was Dr. Boyd?* He followed the path till it did in fact dump him on the trail from which he had entered.

After taking a final look around, Peter headed back towards the campsite. *UGEN?* He walked the length of the trail and carefully climbed back over the gate. He scanned the area quickly to make sure no other visitors had arrived and to make sure his campsite hadn't been touched. As he walked around the area, the contents of the discovered document kept swirling through his mind. *Experimental craft?* There was only about an hour of daylight remaining so Peter decided to go ahead and prepare the campfire. Retrieving some of the gathered wood, he placed it within the boundaries of the fire pit before settling down in his chair. Quietness was all around him with the exception of a gentle breeze blowing through the local pines. The shadows began to stretch across the ground as the sun crept towards the horizon. As the evening passed, the air began to chill, persuading Peter to get a fire going. Before long, a warm fire illuminated the area and cast shadows on the side of the RV which seemed to dance with the flicker of the flames. Hungry, Peter decided it was time to prepare his omelet. *Top Secret.* He cut up some onions, jalapenos, and a bell pepper before placing them in a bowl. Two eggs were cracked and added along with some bacon bits. He placed a frying pan on the stovetop, added a little non-stick oil, and then poured the contents in. A few minutes later, he was sitting in his chair again beside the fire enjoying the fruits of his labor. This was a great day! Great exploration, a mysterious document and a delicious omelet had Peter smiling as he sat back staring at the stars. Normally, in a moment like this, he would void his mind of any thoughts and enjoy the peace. But the peace escaped him as he continued to contemplate the document. Should he tell the government he found it? Perhaps he should throw it on the fire. His instincts had him uneasy, as he knew the consequences of having classified information outside of a secure facility. But could he be held accountable? Could he forget about the contents? How he wished he had Dr. Boyd beside him now to answer all of his questions and satisfy his curiosity. Night settled in. Peter extinguished the fire with dirt and water until there was no more smoke. He secured his belongings, locked the truck doors, and climbed into the RV for the night. Lying on his bed, Peter deduced he had two choices concerning the document. Destroy and forget about it or investigate the contents to satisfy his need for answers. Would curiosity kill the cat?

Chapter 2

It was still dark outside when Peter cracked open his eyes. *WATCHFUL EYE?* Usually, he would get up immediately and put on a pot of coffee, but he found himself just lying there in the dark and in the middle of nowhere. The document had already invaded his mind. He leaned over to the nightstand beside his bed and switched on a lamp. After rubbing his eyes, he leaned over towards the foot of the bed and flipped open his backpack to retrieve the document. Laying back down, he began to read the letter again. He knew he would not be able to forget about the letter. Until he researched the contents, it would continue to invade his mind. Peter was like that. Once something grabbed his attention, he had to find out as much as he could about it. Caution would have to be taken, though, since he knew the government had eyes and ears on almost everything including phones and the internet. The last thing he wanted was trouble or the government getting involved in his life more than it already was. Realizing there would be future opportunities for hiking and exploring, he decided to wrap up his trip here in order to learn more about this place and the document.

As the sun began to light up the sky, he enjoyed a cup of joe in the chair near the fire pit before packing everything up. More dirt and water were added to the fire pit to ensure it was extinguished and would pose no threat to the area. Peter converted the RV back into travel mode and walked around the area once more to ensure he was leaving this place as he found it. He took a final look at the old gate and fence before climbing into the truck. Once again, he began to carefully backtrack along the dirt road which would lead him to West Side Road and then on to the town of High Rolls. He loved the flexibility his life offered, being able to alter his plans without obtaining input from others. *No bills, no people, no worries* echoed in his mind. Several hours later, Peter began spotting houses and obscure driveways as he approached High Rolls. He knew he was going to stop at the local store again to fill up his truck with gas and maybe take in a quick conversation with Ahanu.

After filling up his truck, he walked towards the store and noticed the old, Native American statue was still there with the same look on its face. Peter smiled softly as he opened the door and entered.

"That was quick! What did you think?" Ahanu asked, grabbing Peter's attention.

"I thoroughly enjoyed it! It was exactly what I was looking for," Peter responded. "That is some beautiful country up there, and I didn't even come across another human being."

Smiling, Ahanu stated, "I thought you would have stayed a few days out there. Didn't expect you back so soon."

Peter thought about his discovery and his decision to leave earlier than previously planned for. There was no need to explain to Ahanu why he was leaving early and no need to bring up the document. However, he figured he could possibly glean some information about the abandoned facility he had found.

"You were right about that road," Peter chuckled out. "It hasn't been maintained in a long time, and I don't think my RV cared for it too much."

"Yeah, not many people venture beyond the paved area except for the occasional four-wheeler or hiker. But they don't go very far before turning around," responded Ahanu.

"I did manage to go quite a distance. As a matter of fact, I came across a couple of gates and old fencing with government warning signs on them. Know what that's all about?" Peter asked as he attempted to look interested in a bag of chips on one of the aisles.

Nodding with understanding, Ahanu replied, "I've come across them before. I think the first one guards some communications towers. No one works there that I know of, but I do occasionally see one of those green government trucks heading that way. They're probably just going to check on the place or make a few repairs."

"Yeah, I saw the antennae on a hill behind that gate. What about the other gate? The one that looks old and rusted? What's there?" Peter questioned once again as he turned to look at Ahanu.

"Don't know. I tend to obey signs warning me to stay out, you know? Some of the older residents around here make up ghost stories about what could be there, but that's just to keep the kids from going around the place," Ahanu replied. "They refer to it as Mule Peak in their stories, though I have no idea why."

"Interesting," was Peter's only response as he grabbed a can of Vienna sausages off the shelf. He walked over to the refrigerators and pulled out a red Gatorade before heading to the counter to pay.

"Think you'll ever make it back up here?" Ahanu asked as he rang up the items.

"No idea. It is beautiful and I'm sure there's plenty more to see. But right now, I've got my mind on other things," Peter stated.

"Two dollars. Where are you heading to now?" Ahanu asked as he took money from Peter and placed it in the cash register.

Picking up his Vienna sausages before Ahanu could place them in a plastic bag, Peter responded, "Wherever the road takes me. It was nice to meet you, Ahanu!" He then walked out the door. He heard Ahanu bid him farewell as he headed for his truck.

The descent down Highway 82 was as enjoyable as the ascent. As he weaved down the curvy road, Peter was careful not to overuse the brakes. He placed the transmission in fourth gear to let the engine assist his brakes. As the temperature climbed back into the seventies near the bottom, Peter rolled down his windows and threw his left arm over the door. It was a beautiful day, and he knew exactly where he was going. Over the past few miles, he thought about where he may find more information on Mule Peak and decided the local library may be his best chance. As he entered Alamogordo, he began scanning both sides of the main road. A couple of minutes later, he spotted a light tan, brick building on the right side of the road. A sign out front identified it as the Alamogordo Public Library. Peter pulled into the parking area looking for the best place to park. There was only one other car, so he decided to take up two parking spots with his truck and RV versus parking along the curb beside the building. Before going into the library, Peter pulled off the flight jacket and tucked it away in the back seat. The air was a lot warmer at this elevation, and the jacket had begun to get uncomfortably warm.

"Good morning!" caught Peter's ear as he entered. It had come from a typical, gray-haired lady with blue rimmed glasses. The skirt she was wearing was gray while the button up, collared shirt was the same color blue as her glasses. Peter didn't like to stereotype, but this lady fit the part!

"Good morning," he responded as he walked towards the counter she was standing behind. "I was wondering if you could help me with some information."

"What would you like to know?" she answered as she raised her left eyebrow.

"Ever heard of Mule Peak?" Peter asked.

"I have! It's located up in the mountains overlooking Alamogordo. There used to be an old Army outpost or something there, but that was ages ago. Let me see if I can find more information for you!" the librarian replied as she walked from behind the counter and headed towards the 'Local History' section.

Peter decided to let her do her job, and he lingered near the front desk. After about five minutes, she returned with a book which she held open in order to keep her place. He wondered how long she had been working here, and was quite impressed with her customer relations. So many times, Peter got the impression people hated their jobs and reluctantly performed tasks for customers. If it hadn't been for a paycheck, they would probably care less whether you got helped or not!

"There's not much, but I did find an article and a photo!" she spoke out as she placed the opened book on the counter. Peter leaned over the book with her as she began to point at the article.

"This was taken from the Alamogordo Daily News on 20 October 1945. Says here the White Sands Missile Range base was establishing a remote location on Mule Peak situated in the Sacramento Mountains. Its mission would be to track newly designed rockets and missiles during flight tests. It would also test acquired German rockets," she finished.

"Interesting," was Peter's response as he leaned on the counter with his hand under his chin. "What about the photo?"

The photo was a five by seven print and was in black and white. There were seven men in Army fatigues with the front three kneeling while the rear four stood. An eighth man, dressed in a suit and tie, stood to the left of the group. This photo was obviously taken from the Sacramento mountains as Peter could make out the Tularosa basin and White Sands National Park in the background.

"The only information is on the back which reads 'The Mule Peak Crew', '1946' and 'Dr. A. Boyd' written in black ink," she responded.

"Can I get a copy of that photo?" Peter inquired.

"Of course. There's a copy machine in the corner. You'll need a dime. Return the original photo to me before you leave, please," she stated as she walked back behind the counter. Peter noticed she walked with more of a bounce in her step now, indicating the pride she took in her job. *If everyone was as excited to help someone as this lady is, the world would be a better place.* He walked over to make a double-sided copy of the photo.

Hints of the green laser lights of the copier moved along the edges of the machine as Peter waited for his copy. Standing there, he began to ponder whether or not to make a copy of the classified document. According to federal regulation DOD 5200.01, any piece of equipment used to make a copy of classified material became classified itself! His workspaces, when he was in the military, used to be scattered with computers and copiers which had red stickers on them indicating at what classification level they could be utilized. When the equipment became outdated, they couldn't just give it away. There were sanitization procedures that had to be met and, even then, they were declassified and shipped off to some warehouse on base. Also, if one was unsure if a particular document was still classified, they were to treat it as classified. But Peter was a civilian now, and he figured the information was outdated. Besides, who would know? Retrieving his copy of the photo and the original, he returned to the counter librarian.

"Here's the original," Peter spoke to the librarian and then added, "I need to make another copy of something. I'll be right back."

"No problem!" was the response.

After a quick trip to the truck, Peter was standing at the copier once again watching the green lights. He was doing it! At least now, he would have a backup just in case he lost the original document. As he exited the library after making the copy, he realized he was walking and breathing a bit faster. He was sure his heart rate had elevated, which usually came with nervousness. Although he had rationalized making a copy, years of adhering to the rules to avoid prison had him almost sweating as he climbed up into his truck. Peter sat motionless for a few moments trying to calm himself. Leaning over, he opened the glove compartment to place the copy inside, but then hesitated. Was this a safe place to keep it? He quickly closed the compartment and sat back up. Where should he put it? Peter reached beneath the driver's seat and pulled out a small, black gun case. Popping open the two tabs, he opened it to find his .45 caliber pistol. He folded the copy twice and then placed it on top of the gun before closing the case. Sliding the gun case back under the seat, he started the truck.

Where to? Peter was still in the library parking lot with the truck running. For the first time, he didn't have a plan for a destination. Usually, he knew exactly where he was going and even planned for the next few trips. He reached behind the steering wheel and cut the truck's engine off. The discovery of this document had put a wrinkle in Peter's plans. He knew he wanted to investigate it more, but how? His first thought was to find a Wi-Fi hotspot and get on his computer but he knew if the document was still classified, the government's intelligence agencies might discover his inquiries. He knew certain agencies intercepted words like TOP SECRET and compartmentalized titles on the internet. Sometimes, it wasn't a word, but a group of words that would ping their attention. Searching for 'Mule Peak' may not interest them, but searching 'Mule Peak, stealth and tracking' together just might! Peter knew he needed more time to think about it.

Pulling out of the library parking lot, Peter turned right and headed towards Holloman Air Force Base, where he would get a good meal and spend the night. Holding over at the base would also give him time to think about his next step and let him catch up on laundry. Peter smiled as he drove thinking he was lucky not to have someone around nagging him about when to do his laundry or other chores. A lot of people might find happiness with relationships, kids and a job, but not Peter. Those things brought bills, people and problems!

The entrance gate to the base wasn't busy during this time of day. As usual, he followed proper entry procedures and only briefly conversed with the guard on the whereabouts of the RV parking area. Many military members didn't like the idea of wasting their hard-earned cash on rent, so they instead bought a mobile home which they moved from assignment to assignment. It was mostly single men that lived this type of life, but the savings were usually worth it.

Before proceeding to the RV lot, Peter decided to swing by the lodging building. Walls didn't stop Wi-Fi signals, so he thought if he parked close enough, he may just pick up a good signal. Finding a good spot to park, he exited the truck and entered the RV. He sat down on the sofa and powered up his laptop to find there was actually a Wi-Fi signal! A minute later he had his email opened. There was only one email for him and it was from Goldilocks! She began as she always did:

"Hey Mister PK! My sentiments exactly on the black and white photos! Thanks for sharing your opinion. Hiking again huh? Yes, you should take someone with you! Hiking can be dangerous even if you do have a military background! I can only imagine the view and look forward to hearing from you about it. I'm actually heading to Meteor Crater in Arizona this weekend. I know it's just a big hole in the ground, but I find it interesting how a big, old rock from outer space slammed into the Earth and left such an impact. Plus, it's been a while since I've had an adventure and your trip spurred me. Anyways, thanks for the reply and I look forward to hearing more about your trip! Goldilocks"

Peter read it three times to ensure he didn't miss anything. *Meteor Crater?* She was only one state away! He pondered the idea of driving there to meet her and began to imagine what their first face-to-face encounter would be like. What if she had a husband? Peter realized he didn't like not knowing more about her. He would have to find out more about her without asking her directly. He pressed the reply button:

"Hello Sunshine! Meteor Crater? That's right next door to where I'm at! I stopped by there a couple of years ago and it is quite an impressive hole in the ground. I'm sure you will enjoy it. Is it a long drive? Do you ever get bored driving? I kinda enjoy driving. I get to see a lot of the country that way.
        As for hiking, ..."

Peter stopped typing. He did enjoy his trip in the mountains and his stroll around the abandoned government outpost. What should he tell her? *Hey, I found a top-secret document!* He contemplated what he would say and then began to type once again:

"It was very nice! The mountains were beautiful although the road leading to my campsite was in serious disrepair. There's a lot of cool places up there and I even found an old observatory complex from the 1940s. Plus it had a large telescope. It was a little eerie, but I plundered around it a bit. Some letters left behind indicated they used to track missile tests fired from the White Sands Missile Range. I bet the assignment there would have been awesome! If you are interested, here are the coordinates of my campsite so you can look at it on a map to get a feel for it: 324831N 1055241W.

Wish I had more information on that place! Anyways, I'm not sure what my next destination is. Thought I may take some time and do some research on this area. Talk to you soon! PK"

Peter pressed "Send" before he changed his mind. He threw his arms up and placed his hands behind his head as he leaned back onto his sofa. Staring at the ceiling, he felt a sense of relief after writing a little about what he had found. Goldilocks was the only person he had contact with consistently, and it was nice to have someone to talk to at his leisure. She always opens with "Hey Mister PK!" and he always replied with "Hello Sunshine!" which was something that started after the first few email exchanges. Peter began to ponder his feelings for her. *What feelings?* He had to admit there was an attraction towards her, although he couldn't place a finger on why. How crazy it must be to be attracted to someone you've never met face-to-face or know hardly anything about! Whether his thoughts were logical or illogical, Peter didn't care. He enjoyed writing to and thinking about her!

A bang on the RV door startled Peter as he opened his eyes. He had dozed off. As he stood to answer the door, he noticed it was evening through the windows. Opening the door, he was met by a tall man with a beard. He was unusually skinny with his arms covered in tattoos.

"Sir, you can't park this thing here," he told Peter.

"Sorry, I stopped briefly and must have dozed off. I'll move it immediately," he responded. He let out a fake yawn to convince the skinny guy of his story of dozing off.

The man turned around and headed back towards the building. Realizing a couple of hours had passed, he decided to check his email a final time before leaving the parking lot. He pressed the power button on his computer to awaken it from sleep mode. The screen lit up with his email still open. And there it was! A response from Goldilocks. Peter clicked on it and began to read:

"Hey Mister PK! Was glad to read about your adventure and that place you wrote about sure sounds interesting...especially the telescope! If I get the time in the future, I will definitely have to check it out! I took a look at the coordinates you gave me on an online satellite imagery website. For sure, it was a remote location. I did a search online for old observatories near Alamogordo and got two results. The first one was a place called Sunspot which is further east along the mountains and the other was called Mule Peak. Supposedly, it was operated by the government in the 40s and 50s but I couldn't find anything else on it. I would venture to say you were at Mule Peak! You wished you had more info, so hope this provided some.

Wow! You are asking questions about me now? That's a first. It's usually just questions to gather information on locations or to get my opinion on travelling equipment. I don't mind though! No...I do not find driving boring, even though I have no one riding with me. I live and work in St. George, Utah, so it will not be too bad of a drive.

From our conversations, you seem pretty private. I know you are retired military and travel around a lot. Anything else you would like to share? I don't want to cross any lines, but have you ever thought about us meeting...in person? Goldilocks"

Peter felt a little uncomfortable and he could tell his heart was beating faster. Was he actually getting to know someone? Was Goldilocks wanting to meet? There was much to think about as he closed his laptop and exited the RV. The sun was already halfway below the horizon when he pulled out of the parking lot and headed for the RV parking area.

Peter quickly found a good spot and began to set up his RV for the overnight stay. Taking a break from thinking about Goldilock's email, he started thinking about his next course of action to find more information on Mule Peak and the classified document. Goldilocks had already informed him there wasn't much information on the internet regarding Mule Peak. He definitely wasn't going to search the words 'TOP SECRET' on the open internet. That left Dr. Boyd. Was he still alive? After all, if he was a doctor in the 1940s, he would have been at least in his thirties given his employment by the government on such a classified mission. The government wouldn't take just any young doctor and throw them into a program of this caliber. If that were the case, Dr. Boyd would have to be in his nineties now or deceased. Peter retrieved the copy of the photo he had made and began to examine the guy in the suit and tie. Why was he in a suit and tie in such a remote location? The man appeared to actually be in his late forties and, if this was Dr. Boyd, that would mean he would be over one hundred years old. Surely, he had passed on since then.

Peter turned out the lights in the RV and settled down in his bed. What a day it had been! He couldn't remember the last time he had so many thoughts running around in his head. Furthermore, his thoughts were not of routes or destinations, but rather on his curiosity of the classified document and of Goldilocks.

Chapter 3

*D*r. *Boyd!* It was Peter's first thought of the day. He reached over from his bed and grabbed the photo off the nightstand. He looked closely at the nametags of the seven men in army fatigues but couldn't decipher any of them. His eyes moved slowly across the photo looking for any clues, and then stopped once again on the man in the suit and tie. As he stared at the man, there was something vaguely familiar about him, but Peter couldn't put his finger on it. Had he seen this man before? Perhaps Dr. Boyd, if this was Dr. Boyd, was just one of those guys with a familiar face. He placed the photo back on the nightstand, stood up, and headed for the shower.

Although the shower was small, he enjoyed it and the base's RV parking area had a water connection which allowed Peter to connect his tanks. The one thing Peter didn't have in his mobile home was a washer and dryer! As he showered, Peter began to dread the thought of having to do the laundry, but he had put it off too long. Reluctantly, he figured he could swing back by the lodging building which had plenty of laundry machines and a connection to the internet! While waiting on the laundry, he would have plenty of time to email Goldilocks and answer some of her questions. At least he had a short-term plan. Finishing his shower, he got dressed and brewed a cup of coffee. A peek through the window let Peter know the sun was about to rise as its rays were already cresting over the Sacramento Mountains. By the time he converted the RV back to travel mode and started his truck, the sky was filled with morning light as the sun began to crest from behind the mountains.

This time, Peter parked in a normal spot rather than pulling close to the building. He would take his laptop with him to the laundry room versus having the tattooed guy knock on his door again. He assembled his laundry, which barely fit into the bag, and headed in after securing his vehicle.

Peter found a chair and table in the corner of the laundry room after he started the first load. Peter smiled as he realized the military still used the same chairs and tables he had used when he first entered the military and moved into a dormitory. It was the standard setup with one wall lined with washers while the other had dryers. Several tables were placed around the room so residents would have a place to fold and stack laundry on. On top of that, the military was nice enough to place a few, hard plastic chairs around just in case you got tired of standing. Peter connected his computer's plug-in to the wall outlet and pressed the 'Power' button. He had thought a lot about his response to Goldilocks email and was eager to get it started:

> *"Hey Sunshine! Thanks for the research you did on my adventure. I'm sure you would enjoy it, should you ever choose to visit here. I'm at Holloman Air Force Base where I stayed last night and am currently enjoying the chore of laundry.*
>
> *I admit I am a private person. Moving around a lot in the military and now in my civilian life doesn't really accommodate close friends or relationships. It always seemed that once I had made a good friend, it was time to leave for another assignment. With that said, I don't mind at all sharing more information with you."*

Peter stopped typing. She already knew he was retired from the military and he travelled around a lot. What more was there to tell? Although his truck and RV were dear to him, she definitely would not want to read about his affinity for them. He then realized just how simple his life had become. Not the simple lifestyle he enjoyed, but simple in there wasn't much to him. He couldn't discuss work, pets, or love life like most. The night before, he thought about whether or not he would let Goldilocks know more about himself and decided to do so. But now that he was actually typing his response, there wasn't much to tell. How boring would she think he was? Peter continued to type:

> *"My name is Peter. I'm forty and stay fit. Not fit as in lifting weights and having a six-pack, but fit as in eating healthy and hiking. I'm very self-reliant. I analyze things quite a bit (something I picked up in the military) and sometimes enjoy "people watching", as long as there doesn't have to be interaction with them. No, I'm not a Unabomber :). I guess I just prefer to see the good in the world rather than dealing with other people's problems, complaints and selfishness.*
>
> *As for meeting each other, the answer is yes. I have imagined it, but thought the suggestion might scare you or something. I would hate to be an inconvenience as well, as I am sure you are probably a very busy lady."*

The washing machine buzzer interrupted Peter. He moved the wet clothes to the dryer and then loaded the washer with the remaining laundry. The photo crossed his mind. *Dr. Boyd!* It was almost as if his mind was trying to tell him he recognized the guy in the suit and tie but he just couldn't recollect a memory of him. At that moment, Peter figured if he had seen the guy before, he was probably famous and had been on television or something he saw in passing. Maybe Goldilocks would be able to recognize him! He could take a shot of the photo with his camera, and then load it into his computer with a thumb drive. She might even find it interesting and fun, which was more than Peter was providing writing about himself. He was going to do it! He thought about shutting his computer down and taking it with him to the RV to make sure no one would take it, but then he realized he was on base where there was rarely any theft. Besides, it would take him less than a minute to retrieve the camera, photo, and thumb drive.

Upon his return, Peter carefully placed the photo on the laundry table and lined his camera up for the best shot. Satisfied with the digital display of the photo, he captured the image and then transferred it from the camera to the computer. A few clicks later, he had a digital copy of the front of the photo attached to the email. He began to type once again:

> *"On another subject, I came across this old photo. Do you recognize the guy in the suit and tie? He looks very familiar to me, but I just can't place him. Any ideas? Anyways, I thought I would ask.*
> *"Well, I have to finish my laundry. Look forward to hearing back from you. PK"*

Peter clicked on the 'Send' button. There was still a good hour remaining for his laundry to finish, so he left his laptop on just in case she decided to reply. He sat back as comfortable as possible in the hard, plastic chair while listening to the rolling laundry.

About an hour later, and after folding the remaining laundry on the table, Peter placed the neatly stacked piles of clothes into the bag. Before he could move over to shut down his laptop, he heard it indicating he had received a new email. Three quick steps and a look at the screen revealed Goldilocks had responded:

> *"Hey Mister PK! Or should I just say Peter now? Wow...You're funny! Thanks for sharing more about yourself with me. My name is Samantha but I go by Sam. I'm in my late thirties and have blonde hair. I enjoy long walks on the beach!*

LOL! I'm just kidding...thought I would be funny and respond how you did. You make me laugh!

You really don't know who that guy is in the picture? Have you ever heard of 'Gen6'? You know, the company that made billions by creating computers and cell phones? Their icon consists of a green fruit tree inside a black triangle. That guy looks like the founder who happens to be Alfred Boyd! He used to be on television years ago advertising his products but he mysteriously disappeared in the early nineties. People figured he was the typical billionaire who got tired of making all that money and moved away to some private island.

We should meet. Let me know the next time you're near my neck of the woods and we'll arrange it. Sounds exciting! Talk to you later. Sam"

"She thinks I'm funny?" Peter said out loud. She obviously didn't know him that well. *Funny?*

Peter knew of Gen6 and the memories of the television commercials from years ago returned to him. He glanced at the photo again and realized his brain had been trying to tie the guy in the photo with the television commercials. Although he now recognized the face, the name Alfred Boyd wasn't ringing any bells. He didn't follow current events, famous people, or other menial interest items most people found interesting. Had Dr. Boyd started his career with the government and then started his own business? More questions began to formulate in Peter's brain.

Before shutting the computer down, he opened the web browser on the laptop and searched for 'Alfred Boyd'. If this guy was famous, there were probably millions of searches for his name and no intelligence agency would track each of those. Sure enough, there were plenty of online pictures and news articles covering Boyd. As he scrolled through the search results, most discussed his connection with the Gen6 corporation while the newest results were people pondering his mysterious disappearance. The words 'conspiracy', 'faked death' and 'insane' seemed to appear quite often in the search result titles. There were several video links as well to old Gen6 commercials and Alfred Boyd interviews. One in particular was titled *'Boyd's Last Interview'* dated 18 August 1992. *Last interview?* Peter stared quietly at the video icon as it showed Boyd in a suit sitting on a green sofa across from a dark-haired lady in a blue dress. The setting appeared to be a one-on-one interview between them. Peter picked up the photo and meticulously compared it to the video icon. Something wasn't right! Based on his estimations, Alfred Boyd should be in his late eighties or possibly early nineties when compared to the date of the photo. But the Boyd sitting on the green sofa in this video looked to be more in his early fifties with a little gray hair starting to show. Curiously, Peter clicked on the video icon and began to watch the interview. He maximized the video to full screen to re-evaluate Boyd's appearance but his assessment remained the same. Perhaps with all that money, Boyd had undergone some serious cosmetic surgery. Peter knew some people, especially men, aged well and would actually begin to look more distinguished as they grew older. As the video continued, the host asked Boyd questions mostly pertaining to the latest technology Gen6 was developing. She threw a few nonchalant questions about relationships, which Boyd smiled in response while explaining he had never really explored that area of his life. Near the end of the interview, the host asked Boyd what his retirement plans were. Boyd's response seemed typical to most but rang in Peter's ears:

"When I retire? Oh, I don't know. Perhaps I'll move to the west side. I'll keep a watchful eye open and let you know when I decide!"

Peter paused the video and replayed Boyd's response to the host. *West Side? Watchful Eye?* Those words echoed loudly in his mind. Was it a coincidence? The road leading to the abandoned observatory complex was named West Side Road. The classified document referred to the complex as a remote site named WATCHFUL EYE. Was there a double meaning in Boyd's response? Peter's head became even more saturated with thoughts and questions. Was he reading more into this than what was actually there?

Gathering his belongings, Peter grabbed the bag of fresh clothes, his laptop and the photo and headed for his RV. Although he had no plans, there was plenty to think about. The mid-morning sun was shining brightly now as he exited the lodging building and walked across the parking lot. He glanced to the east to view the Sacramento Mountain range. It was beautiful this time of year, with the trees starting to change colors. There were patches of yellow and gold along the range which the local people called sunspots. Perhaps that was why the other observatory Sam had found on the internet was named Sunspot. Peter felt refreshed outside. Sitting in a laundry room with no windows for a few hours wasn't his idea of a good time. The outdoors was where he belonged. He placed his clothes and laptop inside the RV and returned to the parking lot to gather his thoughts. He noticed numerous personnel in Air Force uniforms walking along sidewalks with the occasional vehicle slowly driving by. There was no speeding on base since there were always security forces patrolling the roads for anyone who even thought of driving over the speed limit of thirty-five! Order. Discipline. Peter enjoyed those attributes of military life. Service men and women looked after one another. They didn't litter, as it meant someone else would have to go out of their way to clean it up. The grass was always kept groomed and the road cleaners were observed frequently. It was a different world on base, and Peter found it comfortable as his mind tackled the many thoughts in his head. He walked over to a curb and sat down resting his arms on his knees. He stared at the pavement between his legs as he thought about his next move.

Was Alfred Boyd still alive? Based on his appearance in the video, Peter believed it was possible. Had he given a clue to Peter of his whereabouts when he mentioned 'West Side' and 'watchful eye'? There were many cabins tucked away in the woods up near High Rolls and Cloudcroft which would serve as a good location for anyone wanting to disappear. But someone as famous as Alfred Boyd? Surely, someone would recognize him. Peter began to ponder why he was even thinking about this man and what was he even trying to discover? He could care less if some billionaire had escaped the world and decided to disappear in a mountain range. Why couldn't he control his own thoughts, forget about what he had discovered, and return to his simple life of travelling and exploring? *No bills, no people, no worries.* How had he let this classified document and his own curiosity take control of his life? Peter removed his arms from resting on his knees and leaned back placing his hands on the grass behind him. He closed his eyes and tilted his head upwards toward the sky focusing on the sun's warmth. For a brief moment, he escaped his own thoughts as he sat there thinking a reboot of his thoughts might provide some clarity.

Peter spent the next few hours walking around base. He stopped at the dining facility across the road for a hearty, inexpensive meal. Although he didn't miss standing in line to get food on a Styrofoam plate, the order and efficiency of the service was welcomed. And even though he didn't interact with the service members in uniform, he did enjoy the overheard discussions of work and weekend plans. It reminded him of his past. He glanced over at a corner table and recollected how he had actually sat there years ago enjoying a meal with coworkers.

After Peter ate, he walked over to the morale, welfare and recreation center. This was where airmen went to relax. Rows of books and relaxing chairs lined the walls while several tables were in the middle which provided room for board games. Near the rear, there was an alcove with several computers lined up along the side. The military had always considered it a priority to provide email and video capability to families with deployed members. Peter stood in the middle of the room deciding whether to pick up a book or just sit and relax. It wasn't working! As much as he tried to relax and get his mind off of Alfred Boyd, his curiosity would take over plunging him into deeper thoughts. He headed straight for the computer area.

As he sat in front of a computer, he realized the odds of finding a billionaire who didn't want to be found were astronomical. But Peter possibly had information no one else had. Opening up the internet browser, he typed in the address to open an online search tool. Once opened, he typed in 'Alamogordo, New Mexico' and 'satellite imagery'. A few seconds later, he had a bird's eye view of the town of Alamogordo. He zoomed in and panned east until he found the small town of High Rolls and then West Side Road. Following the route, he had previously taken, he scanned the wood lines on both sides of the road. He noted the cabins nestled in the forest along the first part of West Side Road. They were easier to spot from this satellite imagery than they were when he first began his trek down that road in his truck. He continued to pan south along the road. After about a mile, there were no more cabins observed. Only the mountains, trees and the dirt road filled the screen but Peter kept panning. As the minutes and miles of road crept by, he realized he was getting closer to the abandoned observatory complex. Other than the road, he hadn't noted any signs of civilization since the last cabin near High Rolls. He almost closed out the internet browser when he spotted what he was looking for! Off to the east side of the road, about three hundred feet, there was a structure. Peter zoomed in on the spot. It was a large house! Based on its distance from the road and the trees between the two, he realized how easy it would be not to have noticed it during his trip. From the satellite imagery, he noticed it was gated and only one, white SUV was parked near it. This house, if it was a house, would have taken a lot of resources to build. *Could this have been or still be the residence of Alfred Boyd? Who would build a house so far away from society?* There was no cellular reception in this area and the only road leading to and from it was in serious disrepair. Peter began to wonder if his analysis was sound? Could he be sure the Dr. Boyd in the classified document was the same person as the Gen6 billionaire with the same name? Sure, they looked similar in appearance, but many people looked similar to others. Had he read more into the billionaire's interview response to his retirement plans than what was actually there? Perhaps this nicely built home in the mountains served as a retreat for some rich guy wanting to get away from the city. On top of these thoughts, Peter questioned whether he believed Alfred Boyd was even still alive based on the estimation of his age. Peter leaned back in the chair, placed his hands in his lap, and took a deep breath. What was he going to do now?

Walking back to the RV, Peter remembered camping on Mule Peak and how he had wished Dr. Boyd was there with him to answer his questions. Of course, he never considered the guy could still be alive, nor did he expect to find out further information on who exactly this doctor was. What exactly would he ask Boyd if he were to find him? *Hey, are you the billionaire who wanted to disappear from society? Surprise! I found you! What top-secret aircraft were you all tracking that night in 1947? What did they inject you with?* Regardless of how preposterous the questions seemed, they were exactly the reason he had been looking to find more information on the classified document. There were unanswered questions which dug far into Peter's curiosity, and he couldn't just forget about them. Moreover, there was a chance, just a chance, answers could be found down West Side Road.

Peter hopped into his truck and pulled out of the parking lot. Instead of heading for the main gate to exit, he drove back to the RV parking area. There was no need to pull the RV back down West Side Road, and it was too late in the afternoon to head up there now. Upon arriving at the RV park, he unhooked the RV from his truck and began to set it up for another overnight stay. Whether he found the Dr. Boyd he was looking for or not, he would at least be able to satisfy his curiosity and hopefully move on with his normal life.

Chapter 4

The coffee was good and hot. After the morning routine of showering and eating, Peter had not changed his mind. He was going to once again travel down West Side Road. This time, he knew exactly where he was going and no hiking was planned. Either Alfred Boyd was alive and living in the mountains, or he wasn't. Besides, Peter had nothing better to do at this point, so why not go visit some random stranger? *I've lost my mind!*

The drive up the mountains along route US Highway 82 was still enjoyable. By now, the sun was peeking over the mountains, and the desert vegetation once again gave way to mountainous pines. Peter had his window down until the air began to chill once again, reminding him of his jacket in the back seat. This trip, however, Peter didn't have a clear mind to enjoy the views or the hum of the truck's engine. He was thinking of a house down a dirt road. Who would be there? What would he say? As he entered the town of High Rolls, he thought of Ahanu! Perhaps Ahanu could answer some of his questions concerning who lived in the house! A few minutes later, Peter pulled into the parking lot of the High Rolls General store. Not hauling around a mobile home-made parking so much easier. Stopping, he peered through the windshield and made out the old, Native American statue solemnly standing near the entrance of the store. *We meet again, my old friend!*

Peter locked his truck's doors and entered the store to find Ahanu down one of the aisles. He was stocking the shelves with fresh loaves of bread when he noticed Peter walk in.

"I didn't expect to see you again!" Ahanu exclaimed.

"That would make two of us then," Peter replied with a smile. "Thought I would come back up here and buy some more of that beef jerky from 'he who laughs' before I head out."

"You must surely enjoy that jerky then!" Ahanu cackled back as he stood up and headed for the counter. "Keep hanging around here and you'll soon see just how cold these old mountains can get."

"I'm for sure not going to be here that long!" Peter said as he walked over and grabbed a bag of beef jerky. Besides, it would be rude not to buy something after entering a store for information.

"Does it get busier up here in the winter months?" Peter asked as he placed the merchandise on the counter.

Ahanu flipped the jerky package over to scan the barcode before responding, "Not really. The skiers like it better. But overall, traffic slows down a lot. The snow has a tendency to pile up, and those desert people down the hill don't like slippery roads, you know?"

Peter realized he had started a conversation about absolutely nothing important. Talking just to be talking was how the world was, though, and he had to play the game sometimes to get what he was looking for.

"I've got a question for you Ahanu," Peter stated as he placed a five-dollar bill on the counter. "Who lives in the large house way down West Side Road? I noticed it the other day when I was leaving."

Ahanu slightly nodded as he took Peter's money and exchanged it. "Some dude," he answered. "His name is Eugene, or so I'm told. Keeps to himself. People around here say he's gay because there's a man that lives with him named Tony. I see Tony every once in a while, when he comes to buy a few items, but he doesn't talk much. Why do you ask?"

"Just curious," Peter replied. "Figured it was probably some politician or Hollywood actor that used it as a getaway."

Once again, Ahanu nodded and asked, "So, am I going to see you again?"

"Who knows, but I plan to enjoy this beef jerky!" Peter replied laughing as he exited the store. He gave a final glance over at the statue as he walked to his truck contemplating this latest information.

Eugene. Eugene. "You've got to be kidding me," Peter whispered out loud as he entered the truck and shut the door. *Eugene and UGEN.* This couldn't be a coincidence! Who was Tony? More determined than ever, Peter pulled out onto US Highway 82 headed for West Side Road. Today, he was going to find answers. Today, he would determine if he was insane or not!

Every bump and scratching shrub was still in place as he wound his way southward along West Side Road. The trip was faster this time without the RV. Peter had already passed the cabins recessed in the forest closest to High Rolls, and was once again in the middle of nowhere with mountains to his left and the Tularosa Basin to his right. Bouncing along down the road, he thought of Sam. He hadn't thought of her much since the last email and realized his quest to discover more about Alfred Boyd had taken priority. *Should I plan to meet her? When?* He didn't get much further in these thoughts, though, as he refocused on the task at hand.

Peter rounded yet another curve along West Side Road which opened up into a rather long, straight section. He recalled from the satellite imagery the house he was looking for was along a straight section and, based on his estimation, he had reached the point where it should be. Slowing down, he began to look ahead and to the left for an access road. There it was! He turned left and gently pulled forward along the road. After about three hundred feet, the trees gave way to an open area which had a dilapidated shelter situated beneath a copse of trees. The road turned left and continued along the tree line until it once again became obscured by trees on both sides at the back end of the open area. Peter continued. Trees were on both sides now and obscured any view except for the road in front of him. After driving another hundred feet up the road, it brought him to a closed, black gate with a no trespassing sign attached. *I'm actually here!* Peter slowed the truck and crept closer to the gate before stopping. He noticed a camera was attached to the top of the left gate post and was looking directly at him. Switching the truck off, he opened his door and started to exit, but paused. Leaning over to the back seat, he opened his backpack and retrieved the classified document he had discovered. He knew he had a copy stashed away in his gun case beneath the seat, so he decided to bring the original just in case he needed it. Peter then exited the vehicle and closed the door behind him as he stared into the camera. *What now?* Feeling a reminder from the air, he opened up the rear door and grabbed his jacket. After he put the jacket on, he folded the classified document and placed it in the right pocket while taking a quick look around. There was no perimeter fence attached to the gate. He pondered the thought of just walking around the gate and then on to the house, but thought it may be a little intrusive. Instead, he let out a loud "Hello!" Peter raised both his arms above his head and started to wave them back and forth as if trying to get someone's attention. Nothing. Maybe no one was home or perhaps the residents just didn't want any visitors. Peter walked to the front of the vehicle and looked at the road to see if there were any fresh tracks but to no avail. As he began to stare into the camera again, he heard footsteps approaching from the other side of the gate.

"Can I help you?" came a voice from behind a tree as the footsteps grew louder.

Peter paused a few seconds as a tall, lanky man wearing jeans and a light brown jacket came into view. It was not Alfred Boyd. The fellow appeared to be in his late forties with parted, dark hair. Beneath his brown jacket, he wore a black, collared shirt which Peter could tell was tucked in based on the length of the jacket. This man was very neat looking.

"Hi!" was all Peter could think of to say.

"Yes?" the neat man asked. "Can I help you? Are you lost?"

"Lost?" Peter responded. "No, I'm not lost." Peter decided to get straight to the point rather than belabor the point. "My name is Peter Knowles and I was wondering if I may have a word with Mr. Eugene."

"Eugene isn't taking any visitors at the moment. Give me your message and I will be sure to deliver it to him for you," the neat man replied with a smile. "Does he know you?"

"We've never met. I was hoping he could answer some questions for me regarding the old, abandoned observatory further down West Side Road," Peter answered truthfully.

The neat man raised an eyebrow quizzically before stating, "I doubt he knows anything about that old place. He never leaves the house except for an occasional walk around the garden. Besides, he's only lived up here since a few years back, and I've never heard him speak of the place."

Pulling his lips in a bit, Peter added, "I see. Well, I've driven a long way for the chance to ask him some questions. Are you sure there's no way I could speak with him? Could you at least ask him?"

"Sir, I've already informed you he wasn't taking visitors, and he would be unable to help you with your inquiry. I must bid you a safe trip home," the neat man shot back at Peter before turning to depart.

Peter had come too far and his curiosity had grown even more since talking with this man. He couldn't leave just yet and decided to give it another try. This time, he would have to put the right words in the right order.

"I hate to bother you further, but could you please give him a message then for me?" Peter asked.

The man stopped and turned around, "Sure. What is your message?"

Peter thought quickly and said, "Tell him I've kept a watchful eye open and I'm curious if he spells his name U-G-E-N. Tell him we have something in common, and I really need some questions answered, if you don't mind. I'll wait here for a response."

The neat man turned back around and headed for the house. Peter walked over and leaned back on the hood of the truck. He folded his arms in front of him and rested them on his chest. The warmth of the truck's hood felt good. While he waited, he began to think of Sam once again. Depending on how this situation turned out, he may have something interesting and exciting to write about! Perhaps resolving this situation would unclog his mind, freeing him to determine his next destination. Of course, his future destination would probably accommodate a meeting with her on the way there. The thought of heading to Denver to explore the Roosevelt National Forest crossed his mind then which put a small smile on his face. Pausing from his thoughts of Sam, Peter realized the conversation with the neat man had already begun to free his mind again. It was amazing how speaking a few words could lift such a weight off his chest. He even felt as if he was breathing easier.

Peter's thoughts were interrupted when he noticed the neat man walking toward the gate once again. He stood up straight from his lean on the truck, as he noticed the neat man digging some keys out of his front, right pants pocket. Unlocking and swinging the gate open, the neat man threw one arm out towards the house with an open hand indicating for Peter to proceed to the house.

"Eugene asks if you would care to join him for tea on the back patio," the neat man relayed. "Right this way!"

Peter walked through the gate and waited for the neat man to close and lock it. Afterwards, he followed the man towards the house as both of them walked in silence. A minute later, Peter found his eyes marveling at the large, exquisite house. There was actually a lawn with green, manicured grass which was a rarity in the southwest. On it, several marble fountains trickled water and were sculpted in the form of old, Greek gods. The house itself was white with a large entryway supported by two marble columns. Whoever lived here had plenty of money! Gold colored trimming ran along the edges of the roof and windows which made the house appear to shine! *Impressive!* Peter continued to follow the neat man around the right side of the house. As he rounded the rear corner of the house, he noticed the back of a gentleman with gray hair sitting on the patio. The patio was made of stone with red bricks outlining the edges. It accommodated four metal chairs with red and gold cushions arranged around a glass table in the center. A beautiful, colorful garden filled the backyard consisting of several fruit trees, flowers and exotic shrubs. The neat man threw his arm out towards a chair opposite the gray-haired fellow indicating Peter should take a seat. Without looking at the gray-haired man's face, Peter walked around the glass table and sat down on the comfortable, patio chair. After taking a deep breath, he lifted his eyes to come face-to-face with the gentleman. *Oh my God!* It had to be Alfred Boyd!

The neat man entered the rear of the house after seeing Peter take a seat. The gentleman wore an expressionless face as he looked Peter in the eyes. Even with his gray hair, he appeared to still be in his sixties! He was intelligent looking, wearing a green polo shirt tucked into tan khakis. His legs were crossed and both arms rested on the chair. Peter had noticed the man's brown, leather shoes through the glass top of the table when he sat down. He knew he could never afford such. But there he was, probably sitting across from a billionaire who didn't want to be found. They both sat motionless staring at each other. A short time later, the neat man emerged from the house with two white cups and a pot of hot water. After placing the cups on the table, he carefully placed two pouches of tea in each cup which he then filled with hot water.

"Will there be anything else, Sir?" the neat man asked of the seated gentleman.

"That will be all, Tony," was the reply as the gentleman sat still without losing eye contact with Peter.

"So, Mr. Knowles, Tony tells me you have a few questions for me. But first, who are you?" asked the gentleman, raising his eyebrows questioningly.

"Sir, first of all, thanks for allowing me to join you and please, call me Peter," was Peter's response. "As for who I am, well, I'm just a normal guy whose curiosity has gotten the better of him!" He leaned forward and began to steep the tea bag in the cup. "You have a very beautiful place here."

"An ordinary guy with curiosity, you say? Well, Mr. Knowles, it seems as if we both find ourselves curious today. However, I think I shall have my curiosity satisfied first. What do you think you know?" the gentleman inquired, stressing the 'think' and getting straight to the point.

"I think you're Alfred Boyd! I think you used to work up here in these mountains back in the late 1940s. I think you were part of Project UGEN," Peter shot back after picking up a little condescension. He was an ordinary guy in ordinary clothes, but he had dignity and could hold his own. *Let the verbal jousting begin!* "Does that satisfy your curiosity?"

The gentleman raised an eyebrow and slightly tilted his head down and to the right as if questioning Peter's boldness. Easing his look, he then leaned forward, picked up his hot tea, and took a sip. "May I ask why you think such things?"

His question seems a little nicer now. Peter was able to fluctuate his conversation intensity depending on the level the other person wanted to keep it at. A display of competence had always been the forefront of his conversations, something he picked up as a military leader. He preferred casual communications versus intense, but with his competence, he was able to deliver either.

"Look, I'm not here to expose you. I believe anyone should be able to live how they choose, even if it's in hiding. I'm a retired, military vet with a pension who travels across the country pulling an RV with my truck. I don't work for anyone, and no one works for me, which is the way I like it. I don't bother people, and I don't like to be bothered. If I'm bothering you, let me know and I'll leave. Hiding away up here in the mountains, that's your business, and I'm not going to tell anyone. Like I said, I'm just an ordinary guy with curiosity." Peter placed his cup down on the table and leaned back in a relaxed posture. He knew words were not the only form of communication, so he hoped the relaxing stance would also relax the conversation, which would probably benefit him more in the end.

The gentleman also assumed what appeared to be a relaxing posture before responding, "I appreciate your honesty, Mr. Knowles. But that still doesn't answer my question of why you think those things."

"Fair enough," Peter said. "I was exploring West Side Road a few days ago and stumbled across an abandoned observatory which was active in the 1940s. I found a Top-Secret document left behind which mentioned a Dr. Boyd and a secret aircraft, which spurred me to research it further. After all, I was in the military, and a super-secret aircraft grabbed my attention. After a little digging at the local library, I discovered an old photo of a man in a suit and tie which looked remarkably like the Alfred Boyd who started the Gen6 corporation. A little more research, and seeing your last interview with a talk show host, I was able to piece some things together, so here I am."

"Yes, you are!" the gentleman replied. "But if I worked up here for the government in the forties, wouldn't I be dead by now or at least nearing a hundred-year-old? Do I look that old to you Mr. Knowles?"

"Mysteriously, no," Peter answered. "I would probably say you're in your sixties. Or, at least, you appear to be in your sixties."

"Hmmm!" was the response. The gentleman took another sip of his tea as he pondered his next words. After what seemed like an entire minute of silence, the gentleman added, "Mr. Knowles, as I am sure you are aware, there are some things in this world which should remain hidden. Unspoken things! Things the world isn't ready for. Yet, here you are wanting to take a look inside Pandora's proverbial box. The human need to satisfy curiosity! How many times has it led to destruction, I wonder?"

Peter knew the gentleman's words were more of a statement rather than a question. Furthermore, he agreed with the man that some things should remain hidden from the public. Peter tackled the thought of which was greater, his understanding some things should remain hidden or his curiosity.

"You know," Peter started, "they say curiosity killed the cat. We assume it's the cat's curiosity, but that isn't necessarily so."

The gentleman smiled as he responded, "How right you are, Mr. Knowles!" The gentleman took another sip of his tea and continued, "Curiosity! It has always gotten the best of us since Adam and Eve ate the forbidden fruit."

Peter nodded slightly in agreement as he gathered his thoughts. He hadn't received confirmation or denial of any sort to satisfy his curiosity. Answers had already been given to the gentleman, but no answers had been received. The man knew exactly what Peter was looking for, but up to this point, he had provided nothing. He decided to press further.

Peter was blunt, "Sir, I've answered the questions you've had of me and, hopefully, satisfied your curiosity as to why I am here. I've been very truthful and have tried my best not to waste your time. My assumptions of your identity are either correct or incorrect. I only ask you to return the favor now, and satisfy my curiosity."

The gentleman placed his cup back on the table top and folded his arms across his chest. Peter could tell many thoughts were being pondered in the man's head. Peter knew if he didn't get any information out of the gentleman now, he would probably be wasting his time if he continued to stay.

After a few moments, the gentleman responded. "You seem to be a good man, Mr. Knowles. I gather you are a content person in life, choosing to live a life free of worries and uncertainty. If you knew the answers to your questions would change your life as well as your view of reality, would you still want to know the answers?"

Change my view of reality? The man's question was unexpected. Why would finding out more about a classified mission, which happened in the 1940s, change his life? Sure, it might divulge insight into outdated, top-secret experiments on stealth aircraft, but change his life? As an intelligence analyst during his service, he had come across information which could place people's lives in jeopardy or cause embarrassment to the government, but nothing that would change someone's view on reality! Peter's curiosity grew.

"I would," was Peter's response.

"Will you join me for a walk through my garden? It's beautiful this time of day!" the gentleman asked Peter as he stood up and walked to the edge of the patio.

Following the gentleman's lead, Peter stood and slid his chair up to the table. As the man stepped off the patio, Peter walked up to his left as they both began to slowly meander through the garden.

"Have you ever wondered, Mr. Knowles, why it took humans almost six thousand years to evolve past the use of horses as transportation? And then, within the span of the past one hundred years, they discovered the knowledge and created amazing technology such as engines, aircraft, computers and even spacecraft which could travel outside of our solar system?" the gentleman asked.

Peter responded, "No, not really. I guess, thinking about it now, it does seem rather odd, though."

"So much knowledge! Who knows what they'll create in the next hundred years?" the gentleman added. "Where did the knowledge come from? Surely, thousands of years and time didn't enlighten them, so why now? Supercomputers, cellular phones, stealth aircraft, night vision! The list of achievements is vast and all developed within just a short time span when compared to man's existence on Earth."

Peter thought about the gentleman's words before he responded, "Sounds like you're implying the knowledge came from somewhere else? You're not going to tell me little green men from other planets enlightened us, are you?" Peter chuckled a little but quickly realized the gentleman wasn't smiling back.

The gentleman continued, "Based on statistics, Mr. Knowles, most believe there are superior beings from other worlds. Their belief stems from their need to justify their existence and independence from some all-powerful 'God' who created them for his pleasure. How little humans would feel if there was a creator. What do you believe?"

"About life on other planets, or God," Peter asked.

"Both!" came the response.

Peter smiled as he thought and said, "Well, I know a lot of people think Roswell and Area 51 are related to aliens. Many people even say they have been abducted. But as for what I think? I think Area 51 is just a secret military base testing top-secret aircraft, and I believe a lot of people have very creative imaginations to hide their insecurities! As for a god, I've never seen one."

"Then where did all that knowledge come from?" the gentleman asked.

"It didn't come from anywhere. It was just a leap in evolution which scientists say happens every few million years," was Peter's answer. "If you are Alfred Boyd, you were directly involved with a lot of these technological accomplishments. You tell me where it came from!"

The gentleman stopped walking and smiled at Peter. "I guess I would be able to answer that question, if I were Alfred Boyd!" He continued to walk and added, "Let's change the subject! I take it you are not a religious man, Mr. Knowles, but have you ever read the Bible?"

"The entire thing? No. I used to go to church when I was a little boy and remember the main idea of what they were trying to tell me. I believe it's a good book with stories loosely based on historical events, and tries to teach people kindness and love," Peter answered honestly.

"It's a good read," the gentleman stated. "One of my favorite parts is found in Genesis, chapter six. It's a great story of how God's angels disobeyed him and bred with the human women. This, of course, was followed by the deluge to wipe out all of the abominations created from their union. Most preachers don't preach about them, you know?"

Peter stopped walking this time and looked at the gentleman, "Genesis six? That wouldn't happen to be related to the name of a certain, multi-billion-dollar computer company, would it?"

The gentleman smiled and said, "If I were Alfred Boyd, maybe so!"

Peter realized they were heading back towards the house. He wasn't sure if the gentleman was trying to tell him something indirectly, or if he was just wasting time. This conversation was not what Peter had expected, and he still had nothing concrete to quell his questions. Up ahead on the patio, Tony had cleared the table and was heading back in the house. To Peter, it seemed as if this meeting was coming to an end.

"So, do you ever leave this place?" asked Peter.

"I'm happy here for now, Mr. Knowles. People have become so dependent on technology these days, and the world is moving so fast. I'm old now and prefer to just sit by and watch it happen. Think about it, no one leaves his house anymore without his cell phone! They have a need for the internet and all that instant knowledge it offers, you know? They run around going to doctors and the gym trying to stay healthy to prolong their lives. Yes, the world is a busy place!"

The gentleman walked with Peter to the front of the house and said, "Funny, isn't it?"

"What's that?" Peter asked.

"The human desire for knowledge and immortality! Since Adam and Eve, humans have been tempted to gain those two things over and over. The desire to be gods!" the man answered with a smile.

"Basic instincts!" Peter simply replied while throwing a smile back.

He held out his hand in an offer to shake, which the gentleman replied in kind with another smile. "I truly appreciate your time," Peter said kindly. "Although I was entertained, I think you managed not to answer a single question regarding my curiosity. Maybe you are, or maybe you aren't, Alfred Boyd."

Peter turned to depart and had gotten a few feet before he paused and turned around to ask a final question. "So, tell me, do you believe in superior life forms on other planets?" He was smiling and saw the gentleman was too.

"On other planets?" the gentleman asked as he scrunched his face. "Of course not! If there were some superior, unknown genetic lifeforms, I think it would be much closer to home!" The gentleman threw his hand up in a wave and then entered his house.

Peter watched the man enter his house before proceeding back to his truck. What an interesting conversation he'd just had. Even though he found no concrete answers to his questions, he rather enjoyed conversing with the man. If that was Alfred Boyd, he was obviously intellectually sufficient to start a billion-dollar corporation!

Peter found his truck right where he had left it near the gate. While pondering the conversation he had with the gentleman, he began to make the trip back to Holloman where his RV awaited. He knew the man had controlled the conversation. What information had Peter gathered, if any? Could he for sure say the man he just met was Alfred Boyd? He had driven up the mountainside with questions and was now returning with no concrete answers. However, he knew what he saw, and the man definitely looked like the Alfred Boyd he had seen on the video. The only piece that didn't add up was the age! If the gentleman had been over ninety years old, Peter would have had no problem truly believing he had met with Alfred Boyd. But he wasn't that old, so Peter was unable to make the connection for sure. He decided to assign 'probable' to the evidence he had found. In his former life as an intelligence analyst, he was trained to assign one of three confidence levels to his assessments. 'Possible' meant there was little evidence. 'Probable' meant there was a lot of evidence to support the assessment and was usually the confidence level needed before leaders would take action. The 'Confirmed' level was extremely rare, meaning all questions had been answered. The old saying in his line of work was if you waited till you had confirmation, it was usually history, and the need for the information had passed. *The gentleman I just met was probably Alfred Boyd!*

As Peter descended further down the Sacramento mountains, something the gentleman said stuck out. *Unknown genetic lifeforms!* He had never heard that phrase before, but there was something familiar about it. A smile crossed Peter's face as he recollected the conversation of little green men! For a moment during the conversation, he had thought the gentleman was going to tell him the government had actually recovered an alien aircraft which had led to the development of sophisticated technology and top-secret aircraft. He was glad the gentleman answered his last question about whether he believed in life on other planets or not. Still, 'unknown genetic lifeform' is not an everyday phrase.

Something else stood out to Peter about the conversation. The Bible! The gentleman seemed to randomly bring up topics which had absolutely nothing to do with why Peter was there. First, the idea humans had to have obtained knowledge from somewhere, possibly 'unknown genetic lifeforms' as he put it, and then a story about angels breeding with human women! Peter began to come to the conclusion the gentleman he had met may have been Alfred Boyd, but the time spent in seclusion had taken its toll on the man and made him delusional!

The road had come to an end. Peter had met with a man whom he believed to be Alfred Boyd, even though he couldn't prove it. There was nowhere else he knew to look for answers he had about the top-secret document. It was time to return to his journey through life again just the way he liked it...no bills, no people, no worries!

Chapter 5

After a long day up and back down the Sacramento mountains, Peter sat comfortably in his unfolding lawn chair. The sun was setting and created a magnificent canvas of blue, pink and purple colors across the western sky. He found it amazing how nature could paint a beautiful canvas every day without ever repeating the same one. A few other travelers, a man and woman with two children, had set up their RV nearby. They too, were sitting outside admiring the sunset. Peter enjoyed the simple things in life.

The thought of swinging by the lodging building to use their Wi-Fi crossed Peter's mind, but he figured he would wait till morning. Besides, he needed to think about his next email to Sam. Was he going to tell her about his adventure back up the mountains to meet with a complete stranger, whom he believed to be Alfred Boyd? Was he even sure he wanted to arrange a meeting with her? As the evening rolled by, Peter relaxed, enjoying his usual omelet filled with jalapenos and then took a hot shower. As he laid on his bed, he thought about the gentleman's story of Genesis, chapter six. He had never heard of angels breeding with women or at least no preacher he had ever heard talked about it. Peter stood up and walked over to open a cabinet which served as his own, little library. There were only a few dozen books within, but he remembered placing a Bible inside a few years back. Finding what he was looking for, he grabbed the Bible and laid back down on his bed.

Although he wasn't an expert on the Bible, he knew Genesis was the first book, so he easily found chapter six and began to read. Being older now, Peter found he could understand more of the verses. Before, when he was young, he thought the word 'know' in the Bible meant a familiarization with someone rather than a carnal knowledge. As he read, he found the gentleman's tale was truthful. The verses revealed 'the sons of God' found human women beautiful, took them as wives and 'knew' them. Their offspring were described as 'nephilim'. Then, the story continued with how God was displeased and repented he had made man because of the wickedness, which began to spread across the world. The decision to destroy all living things, because of corruption, was made. The only exception was a man named Noah, who would be spared along with his family. Why had the gentleman brought this topic into discussion? Peter found no resolution other than the gentleman was truthful about this strange chapter in the Bible.

Early the next morning, Peter attached his RV to the truck. He wasn't planning to spend another night on base. But before leaving, he planned to swing by the lodging building to check his email and send one to Sam. His continuing thoughts of her during the morning had led him to the conclusion he needed to arrange a meeting so they could finally meet in person. He was going to offer to meet her at Meteor Crater since he knew she was headed there and it wasn't very far away!

On the drive over to lodging, he figured after he met Sam, he could proceed on to Red Rock Canyon National Park which was situated a few miles west of Las Vegas. Even though he had explored Red Rock Canyon years before, while stationed at Nellis Air Force Base, it offered beautiful hiking trails, many of which Peter had never ventured down. Also, he was familiar with the Las Vegas area, so there wasn't much advance planning needed. The fact he was starting to plan ahead again pleased him.

Obeying the rules, Peter pulled his RV and truck into the lodging parking lot and found a suitable place to park. He knew it wasn't close enough to intercept a Wi-Fi signal, so he retrieved his laptop and headed to the laundry room. Once again, he found the laundry room empty which was just the way he liked it. He pulled up a chair to one of the folding tables and powered up his laptop. The date on the computer reminded Peter it was Friday, and he began to wonder if Sam would receive his email since she was supposed to leave for Meteor Crater over the weekend. Maybe it was too short a notice to arrange a meeting, but he quickly dismissed the thought, realizing he was just trying to talk himself out of it. Once the email program was opened, he realized he hadn't received any from her. He clicked on the 'Create' button and began to type:

"Hey Sunshine! Well, I'm still at Holloman but not for long hopefully. I've decided to head to Red Rock Canyon National Park near Las Vegas. I've been there before, but there are trails I've yet to tackle. As a result, I have a proposal for you! What do you think about me stopping by Meteor Crater on my way so we can meet? Don't worry about it if you can't accommodate as I know it is short notice. I just figured it would be nice and convenient since I'm headed in that direction. Since I'm leaving Holloman after sending this, I should arrive in the Meteor Crater area later this evening, where I will stop and spend the night. Let me know if tomorrow morning at 10:00 a.m. will work for you. If so, let me know how to identify you and where to meet. I admit I'm excited about meeting you!

On another subject, I can hardly wait to tell you about my adventures here! So much has happened and you're probably not going to believe me. Nonetheless, I think you'll find it intriguing! Hope to tell you all about it tomorrow.

I would give you my phone number, but would you believe I don't have one? I do have one of those prepaid cell phones, but keep it in my truck for emergencies. Anyways, I hope you get this before you leave for your trip. If not, I'm sure there will be more opportunities to meet. Until next time...PK."

Peter read over the email a couple of times before he clicked on the 'Send' button. He leaned back in the chair and took a deep breath. *I'm actually going to meet her!* Thoughts about the future began to flood his mind. Could this be the beginning of a romantic relationship? Would they both find each other attractive and want to spend more time exploring a relationship? How could this all affect Peter's way of life? He imagined himself exiting the front door of a two-story, white house with a future wife. A kiss goodbye was given to her as she entered her vehicle to head for work. Before returning inside the house, he walked out to the end of the driveway in his housecoat and retrieved the daily paper, where he threw a wave over to the neighbor.

Peter was always intrigued by how imagination worked! It could be completely random while serving as a focal point for gathering thoughts. Could they be controlled? Sure, someone could imagine anything at any time they wanted, but where does the brain synapse which spurred the thoughts and imagination originate from? At that moment, Peter thought of God. He had never invested serious time into religion dismissing it as a ruse to distract and lead people. It was a civilized society's greatest tool for controlling people. It kept them from serving the less desirable, natural instincts such as theft, murder and rape. People may not listen to other people, but if you tell them 'God' said it, they would fall into compliance! Peter wondered if there was a divine being who created the human brain and its complexities such as thoughts or dreams. Or was it as the scientists theorize? Did millions of years, dirt and water serve as a spawning pool for single-cell organisms which formed from organized chaos? How lucky humans must be! Being honest, Peter didn't know the answer and knew he never would. Why spend time pondering things you will never know the answer to? *Curiosity!* There it was again, the thing that compels people to search for answers. Peter began to think of the conversation with the gentleman again.

Peter opened up a web browser after closing his email. The thought of a god reminded him of the previous night's reading. He typed in 'Angels Humans Genesis Six' and clicked the search button. *Curiosity!* Numerous pages of results showed up, letting Peter know others had been curious as well. Browsing over the results, they mostly related to the story in Genesis. However, many results referred to the Book of Enoch. He clicked on one of the links which spoke of Enoch. After a little reading, he discovered the Book of Enoch wasn't in the Bible, but was discovered with the Dead Sea Scrolls in 1947. A little more reading revealed the biblical Enoch had written quite a bit on fallen angels and their judgement. Peter glanced over to the bottom right corner of the computer screen and realized the time. It was time to hit the road and head to Meteor Crater! After shutting down the computer, he headed back to his truck.

The sky was overcast with thick, gray clouds as he headed north on US Highway 54 through Alamogordo. The streets were busy with people heading to work or taking their kids to school. It was Friday, and he noticed how everyone appeared to have a little more energy knowing the weekend was just eight hours away. Unfortunately, Peter found himself driving slowly behind a school bus which seemed to stop every fifty feet! He wasn't in a rush, but he was excited to get to Meteor Crater, and the bus was serving as a nuisance. After at least five, excruciating stops, the bus turned right and cleared the path to Peter's destination. Or so he thought. He was almost out of town when he noticed an auto accident ahead. He immediately began to look for a turnoff which could navigate him around the jam, but realized he had just passed the last street turnoff, and a U-turn wasn't possible with the RV. He crept up to the rear of the line and came to a stop. Up ahead, several police officers were standing around two cars which had collided. Peter could tell one of the cars had pulled out ahead of the other and was responsible for the holdup. "Just great," he grumbled as he placed his left elbow on the door and propped his head against his fist. Looking out the left window, he noticed a shopping plaza. Since traffic was stopped in both directions, the lane to his left was clear and provided an open path to the plaza's parking lot. He thought about turning around in the plaza parking lot to head back to the street he had passed, but saw the line of traffic was already blocking it too. Looking back at the plaza, he noticed the word 'coffee' in a shop window which captured his attention. Refusing to just sit in line and waste time, he cut the wheels sharp left and pulled into the plaza.

Peter took a sip of satisfaction as he exited the mom-and-pop coffee shop. Looking towards the road, he realized a tow truck was just arriving and knew he wasn't going anywhere just yet. Turning left and right to see what other stores were available at the plaza, he noticed a franchised bookstore. *Book of Enoch.* He hadn't read a book in some time, but knew reading was good for the brain. Besides, he had a few minutes to kill. Walking over, he opened the door, walked in and headed straight to the first worker he noticed.

"Excuse me, Sir," Peter spoke, getting the worker's attention.

"Yes? Can I help you?" was the reply from the young man. He was wearing tan slacks with a tucked in, green shirt provided by the franchise. Hair that hadn't been combed topped him off, and was saturated with gel giving him a modern day, grunge appearance.

"I'm wondering if you could help me find a book. The Book of Enoch," Peter tasked him.

"Follow me and I'll punch it in to see if we have it or not," the young man replied as he headed over for a computer not far away. Peter followed.

A few keyboard and mouse clicks later, the worker informed Peter, "We do have a copy of it in the store, and it's located in the religion section."

Peter followed the young man over to the section. A minute later, the worker pulled out a book and handed it over. "Here you go!"

"Thanks!" Peter smiled and followed the young man to the cash register. As he was paying for the book, he flipped through the pages briefly and gathered it was mostly compiled in a verse format with numbers before each sentence. There were several unnumbered paragraphs, also, which probably served as discussion points on the verses. He knew this wasn't going to be a straight read through like most books, but figured it would be entertaining nonetheless. Besides, he would have some time this evening after setting up his RV, so why not pass it with reading? Completing his purchase, he headed for the door and noticed through the window the traffic jam had been cleared. Time to get on the road once again!

Peter's GPS led him north to intersect with Interstate 40 in Albuquerque. After a quick stop there for food and fuel, he headed west along I-40. Not long after passing through Albuquerque, he realized he probably should have checked his email to see if Sam had responded. The gas station he had stopped at probably had Wi-Fi, but it was too late now. For sure, there would be a place to connect to later and closer to Meteor Crater. Peter relaxed and settled into his normal travel routine of sipping on coffee and glancing at the GPS, while keeping his eyes on the road. The miles rolled by.

About an hour before sunset, Peter exited I-40 via exit 233. It had been a long day of driving, and he was glad to see the Meteor Crater RV Park just south of the interstate. The southwest desert in this area was extremely flat, with only a few hills observed on the horizon. Small desert brush saturated the landscape which made the RV park stand out like a sore thumb with its taller trees and white RV campers. The trees had obviously been planted years before to provide shade and a more pleasing environment for travelers. The park wasn't more than a few hundred yards off of I-40, so Peter just eased along Meteor Crater Road till he saw the white, domed structure he remembered that served as a welcome center and gas station. It reminded him of a large golf ball which had been buried halfway. A small blue sign on the right side of the road read: 'TUNE TO 1610 AM FOR LOCAL INFORMATION' but he knew if he did it would just be a repetitive broadcast stating the operating hours of the tourist attraction. Besides, there was nothing else around for miles except for desert, so how much could possibly be broadcast? Peter turned right off the road into the RV park and pulled up next to the welcome center. Switching off his truck, he stepped out and took the traditional stretch of raising both arms into the air and leaning slightly back till he felt his muscles tighten. *I'm here!* After locking his truck doors, he entered the welcome center and paid to park his RV for the night. He noticed nothing had changed inside since his last visit. The same type of t-shirts and postcards of the crater were still for sale. Even the male cashier behind the counter was the same man sporting unforgettable mutton chops which hadn't been trimmed. Exiting the store, Peter smiled softly at the recognition he truly enjoyed the diversity of human appearances as it made his mind imagine how someone's life experiences could shape such a look. *Mutton chops!* Before the door closed behind him, Peter swung around and re-entered the building. He had forgotten to ask about Wi-Fi access. After a short inquiry, he had the password to it which was only provided to travelers staying overnight. Returning to his truck and RV, Peter pulled further into the park and found a nice camping spot under one of the taller trees. He immediately began to set up his RV knowing the sun would be down soon. Moreover, he had to check his email!

It only took Peter about thirty minutes to have his RV ready for the night's stay. By the time he finished, the sun had already disappeared behind the horizon and only dark purple hues remained in the western sky. Other campers already had their lights on, and some were even setting up chairs and tables outside knowing the desert sky would present a brilliant display of stars. He always loved how the sky in the southwestern United States would come alive at night. Places like this RV campground provided optimal conditions for stargazers, as there was no light pollution from homes or towns. No forests or structures blocked the horizon, and there was practically no humidity. It was in the middle of nowhere. Peter used to own a small telescope and would peer through a tiny hole to see the rings of Saturn and an occasional comet if he was lucky enough. However, he had given up the hobby realizing once he had seen the rings of Saturn and the moon's craters, there wasn't much left to see except small white lights. One could only find temporary interest in looking at the same thing over and over.

Peter switched on his computer and prepared a peanut butter and jelly sandwich as it cycled through the bootup process. He was enjoying the anticipation of an email from Sam! Spreading the peanut butter, he whistled an old cadence tune he had marched to in basic training. Even though he knew the computer was finished with powering up, he prolonged the excitement as he walked slowly to the refrigerator and grabbed a soda. A few seconds later, he took a bite out of the sandwich as he sat down in front of the glowing screen. Keeping the sandwich in his left hand, he grabbed the mouse and clicked on his email. There it was! She had responded a couple of hours ago which relieved Peter that he hadn't checked it in Albuquerque. He knew if he had, the absence of a reply would have troubled him a little. No need to worry about that now, though, as he clicked to open the email:

"Hey Mister PK! I type this email realizing you are probably on your way to Meteor Crater. The proposed meeting for tomorrow at 10 a.m. sounds great...but I will be unable to make it. I'm not even going to make it to Meteor Crater this weekend.

I'm in the hospital. Nothing for you to worry about as I'm sure I'll be fine in a few days. I have Leukemia and every so often, my symptoms flare up and yell at me for overdoing it. That's life, I guess. I really don't talk to anyone about it, but figured I at least owed you the truth as to why I would be unable to meet you. I really wish I could! I hope you aren't upset. I'm sure we will get the chance to meet soon.

Switching subjects, you really don't have a phone? I admit I have stereotyped you as a loner with not much interest in society, but I at least figured you had a phone. I actually laughed when I read it, but then came to admire the beauty of your simplicity...and I mean that with the highest regard! You said in your last email you had something 'intriguing' to tell me when we met. Since that's not going to happen this time, and since I have at least another day sitting in this hospital bed, why not tell me about it in an email? I could really use the read as watching game shows on television isn't my idea of fun.

Again, I'm sorry I couldn't meet you. Please enjoy Red Rock in Vegas and don't gamble too much! Sam"

Peter sat there. Something wasn't right. His chest felt constricted and his breaths seemed like they had to be forced. His throat felt as if it was tightening. He laid the sandwich on the table beside the laptop and sat back. This was unfamiliar territory for Peter. He knew he was sad Sam was sick, but these feelings were not from sadness. No, he had been sad before, but his chest and throat were not affected like this. This was something new. It couldn't be heartbreak since he wasn't in a romantic relationship. As Peter sat there, he realized he cared about her. Not the caring he once had for his troops or the caring he had for his truck, but a new kind of caring. One that could physically affect him.

Leukemia. Although he didn't know much about it, he knew enough to know it was potentially fatal. He remembered watching a movie once where a woman fell in love with a man diagnosed with it. It ended with the man dying and the woman crying. It was obviously something personal to Sam and figured it was something she didn't want to talk about since she changed the subject in the email quickly. He would respect that.

After consuming the last bite of his sandwich and a few minutes of deep thought, Peter began composing an email to her:

"Hey Sunshine! Sorry to hear you have to watch game shows over the weekend! I'm sure you'll be back on your feet in no time. I appreciate the trust and respect you provided me by telling me something I know is personal. Hang in there!

Well, it's night time here at the Meteor Crater RV Park. As usual, the sky out here is beautiful and bright. I have to admit, I'm kinda glad to be out of Alamogordo and back on the road.

I experienced something different there, and I found it intriguing. Since you asked for it, here it is:

Remember the B&W photo I sent you in which you identified who you thought was Alfred Boyd, the billionaire? Well, I picked it up at the public library in Alamogordo where I was researching something special I found at Mule Peak's abandoned observatory. I didn't send you the backside of the photo as I had to be careful for certain reasons I care not to discuss over the internet. Anyways, there was a date '1947' and a name 'A. Boyd' on the back, so when you informed me you thought it was Alfred Boyd, the pieces started to fit together...with one exception! The photo was from 1947! If the man in the suit and tie in the B&W photo was the billionaire Alfred Boyd, he seemed to defy aging effects! After your email, I searched him on the internet and found the video of his last interview in 1992. In the video, he appeared to be in his 50s which wasn't possible if the guy in the photo looked like he was in his late 30s. The guy in the photo, if still alive, should be at least in his 70s or 80s in 1992. I almost dismissed the Boyd in the photo and the billionaire Boyd in the video as being the same person based on the ages. However, near the end of the video, the billionaire Boyd said something which sparked my interest even more. Again, I care not to discuss it over the internet and I apologize for being cryptic. Let's just say it led me to a house up in the Sacramento Mountains, where I found an older gentleman who looked like the Boyd in the photo and video! Although the gentleman never confirmed if he was Alfred Boyd or not, we had an interesting conversation. I do know he was rich based on his house and appearance. Plus, he lived secluded in the mountains wanting to escape the world. In the end, I believe I found the billionaire Alfred Boyd. I can't prove it and his age and appearance defies it, but I believe it to be him. By the way, the gentleman I met looked to be in his 60s. Crazy huh?

Anyways, I don't plan to tell anyone else this information since I respect his privacy, so I ask you to keep it secret. What do you think? Maybe I'm just crazy, huh? Hope you found this intriguing, and I hope we can schedule another meeting soon. PK"

Peter sent the email and figured it should give her something to occupy some of her time. Sure, she may think he's crazy, but at least he thought it would be entertaining if nothing else. Besides, it felt relieving to divulge some of what he found. He didn't mention, directly, the top-secret document nor key phrases like 'Watchful Eye' and 'UGEN', which kept him at ease in regards to classification security. Furthermore, and he didn't know why, but he trusted her not to tell anyone else. Even if she did, who would believe her?

There were still a few hours left before Peter needed to sleep. Wanting to clear his mind a little, he grabbed the Book of Enoch he had purchased earlier and laid on his bed. He wasn't sure what he was going to find in the book, but at least it would make him tired if nothing else. The first few pages served as commentary explaining the discovery with the Dead Sea Scrolls. Finding the commentary boring, Peter flipped through until he came across 'Chapter 1' and began to read the verses. The format and use of words were very similar to reading the Bible. However, unlike the Bible, the first chapter went into great detail about fallen angels, known as 'The Watchers', and their fall from heaven. It was written from Enoch's point of view describing how he served as a mediator between the fallen angels and God. Enoch explained how there were two hundred angels of which there were twenty leaders responsible for the care of the Earth. The leaders became attracted to human females, took them as wives and began to have children with them. These children became known as nephilim and grew to extraordinary sizes. They dominated all of creation. Enoch wrote how they corrupted all flesh from humans to animals. They were evil and tormented mankind for being unable to sustain them. All the while, their fallen angel fathers were teaching mankind forbidden knowledge. They taught them knowledge of how to read the stars, mining, forging weapons and applying eye makeup for the women to be more beautiful. Wars erupted and evil spread as man and Earth cried out to God. His judgement was swift and severe. He tasked archangels in heaven to bind the fallen angels in the valleys of the Earth for seventy generations until the day of judgement. There, they would remain in darkness and isolation until the seventy generations had passed. For the offspring, or nephilim, God was going to flood the whole Earth to eradicate all corrupted flesh. They were not in his image and were an abomination. The only humans to be spared were Noah and his family. The rest of the world would be destroyed to make way for a new start.

Peter was surprised he read as much as he did before growing sleepy. He had to admit he found it interesting and compared it with Greek myths about titans, minotaurs, and the like. He never understood how people in today's age could still believe in such fantasies.

Peter got comfortable on his bed. There was no interest in seeing Meteor Crater again, since it was still just a big hole in the ground and had nothing else to offer. Peter figured once he woke up tomorrow, he would head on to Red Rock Canyon which was about another day's journey. He knew he would think of Sam during the drive and when their next meeting could be arranged. He decided not to worry about her leukemia, but rather continue on as he had before with her. However, deep inside, Peter did feel a sense of sadness. He wished he could rid her of it and take it on himself. Besides, she was amazing, and he was just a loner who no longer contributed anything to the world. Yes, she was more amazing than he was!

Chapter 6

Morning came early! Peter had laid awake most of the night thinking of Sam and his feelings towards her. How could it be possible for him to feel such a way about her when he had never even met her? Was there some unknown force drawing him to her, or was he entering a new stage in life where he felt he needed companionship? He knew he didn't have the answers and would probably never find them. Not finding the answers to his questions seemed to be more frequent these days. Continuing to think and trying to rationalize it all, Peter took a quick shower and got dressed. He still had a way to travel before reaching Red Rock, and he intended to get on the road as soon as possible since he preferred driving with the sun to his back.

After getting ready and before leaving the RV, Peter powered up his laptop. He knew Sam probably hadn't responded yet since he had just sent the email last night. But he was going to check to make sure. Besides, he probably wouldn't be able to check it again until after he reached Red Rock. After a couple sips of coffee, the laptop was ready. He opened up his email and found no replies from her. Peter began to explore another feeling inside. He wasn't sure what emotional label to attach to it, but he knew he missed having an email from her. Tonight would provide another opportunity to check his email and hopefully suppress this new feeling.

Peter opened the RV door and stepped out into the cool, morning air. The desert had a way of cooling at night which surprised most people, as they think the desert is just always hot. The sun, which had recently awakened from the horizon, had already begun its daily battle against the chill and threw warming rays on his face. His eyes closed; he threw both arms straight up into the air, slightly leaned back and then widened his arms out wide to complete his stretch. Relaxing, he opened his eyes and looked around. An expensive, black sedan caught his attention and was parked near him on the edge of the camping area. The windows were tinted and the car's engine was still running. The analytical side of Peter noticed its lack of 'travel smudge' as he called it. This place was in the middle of nowhere, so driving for many miles would have added a layer of dirt and dust on it. Furthermore, there wasn't a hotel here, so why was this nice car parked in an RV park? It was definitely out of place!

The driver's side door opened and a man stepped out wearing a black suit and tie. It was Tony! *What the heck?* This couldn't be a coincidence, could it? Noticing one another, Tony began to walk over to Peter who just stood there in surprise.

"Good morning, Mr. Knowles!" was the greeting.

Peter looked all around in a nonverbal way to let Tony know he was surprised to see him way out here. "Good morning to you! What brings you out here?"

"You!" replied Tony. "Eugene wishes to have a word with you," he stated as he motioned towards the black sedan.

Peter didn't know how to respond. This encounter had caught him off guard with no time to process the many thoughts going through his mind. *How did he know where I was?* Not seeing any threats, he nodded to Tony and began walking towards the car.

Still confused, he asked Tony as he followed, "How did you know I was here?"

Tony took a few more steps without replying and then opened the right, rear door. Peter could see the gentleman sitting in the back behind the driver's seat. *What's going on?* Hesitating, Peter stopped near the door with a puzzled look on his face.

"Please, Mr. Knowles, won't you join me?" the gentleman encouraged him.

Peter, with the puzzled look still on his face, entered the car. Tony shut the door before walking to the front of the car and stopped as if he was posting guard. Peter looked to his left at the gentleman who looked comfortable in a pair of gray slacks and blue, button-down shirt which was tucked in.

"Talk about the unexpected!" Peter stated. "Never thought I would see you here."

"Yes, well, I must admit I don't get out often, so my being here should tell you something," the gentleman replied.

"How did you know where I was?" Peter asked.

"Seeing as to how you don't own a phone, your truck was kind enough to let me know your position," the gentleman told Peter truthfully and with a smile. "Surely you know vehicles these days have GPS, and they don't just tell you where you are! How I found you is not important. Rather, why am I here?"

"Okay. So why have you illegally tracked me down? I'm sure you didn't travel this far to talk about aliens or human characteristics as before," Peter asked.

The gentleman let out a slight chuckle before responding, "Mr. Knowles, during our last meeting, you stated you had no desire to expose me to the world. I believe your exact words were, 'Hiding away up here in the mountains, that's your business, and I'm not going to share it.' Am I correct in my recollection?"

He was. Peter remembered the conversation well. Of course, he was referring to not letting the media know in efforts to become famous. He hadn't told anyone, except in an email to Sam! *Am I being spied on?*

Nervousness began to creep over Peter. Who was he really dealing with here? What had he gotten himself into? Once again, the gentleman was controlling the conversation and Peter felt defensive this time. It was time to think before he spoke.

"I do remember saying those words," Peter replied. "What makes you think I've told anyone? Besides, I don't even know for sure who you are! All you gave me was the runaround and talk about nonsense when I did ask."

"Don't play me for a fool, Mr. Knowles. We both know you know exactly who I am, even though you can't prove it. And with that, you should know I have vast resources at my disposal. Have you forgotten how I made my billions? Do you think I would create computers and phones without an intimate knowledge of how they work? Or better yet, how email works?" the gentleman asked sternly.

There it was! The gentleman, now confirmed as Boyd, had spied on Peter. Not only did he illegally track him using the GPS on his truck, but he had intercepted a personal, private email. Peter didn't like the situation at all!

"You read my private email?" Peter asked with an angered look on his face.

Boyd let out a sigh and peered through the left window. "Do you know what you have done?" he asked looking back at Peter. His face was more solemn now.

"What I've done?" Peter retorted. "You've illegally spied on me when all I did was ask a few questions about some dumb, top-secret document I found. I asked them out of personal curiosity. Not out of malice! I actually enjoyed our conversation and meeting you, even though you told me nothing. Now, I'm angered over your blatant invasion of my privacy. Who do you think you are?"

"I, too, enjoyed our conversation," Boyd replied calmly. "It was the best talk I've had in many years. Like you, I don't make friends, and I dare not socialize. Talking with you that day was a breath of fresh air. And honestly, I figured once you left, your curiosity would be abated and nothing more would come from our meeting."

Peter recognized the tactic. Boyd was empathizing with him to get him to calm down. Moreover, he was massaging Peter's ego in efforts to open up receptiveness.

Boyd continued, "Look, I recognize my invasions into your privacy are disturbing, and I do apologize. However, after our meeting, you left me with little choice. I couldn't take a chance on you telling anyone. There's more to this story, Mr. Knowles, than just some old guy wanting to get away from society. Surely, you must see that?"

Frustrated, Peter replied, "How can I possibly see that when you have told me nothing?"

Both men sat in the back seat and stared at one another. Peter could tell Boyd wanted to tell him something, but the words were not coming out. After a few quiet seconds, Boyd turned left to peer out of the window again.

"There are others out there who wish to know my whereabouts. Men who have unlimited power and will stop at nothing to get their hands on me," stated Boyd continuing to peer out of the window. "I fear it will not be long, now, before they find me," he continued while turning his head to look back at Peter.

"What are you talking about? Why should it concern me if your old business partners are looking for you? If you came all the way out here to tell me you're mad because some Gen6 board members are going to track you down, then fine! Maybe you'll understand what it's like to have someone invade your privacy. You're mad at me and I get that. Why not just hack my email again and send me a message? It would have saved you a lot of time!" Peter exclaimed.

"The men I speak of are not board members, Mr. Knowles!" Boyd exclaimed, getting more frustrated. After relaxing a little after the outburst, he continued, "I came out here to warn you that if they picked up on your knowledge of me, then it's not just me they will be looking for."

Peter raised his eyebrows showing his mounting frustration. "Warn me? Warn me of what exactly? Why would anyone be looking for me? I don't know anything!"

"Sure you do! You know there is something different about me, do you not? You know about a top-secret project named UGEN, too!" Boyd offered.

What's happening! Peter found himself in just the place he never wanted to be. He was right smack in the middle of worry which just so happened to involve people. He wanted to get in his truck and continue on to Red Rock forgetting he had ever ventured to Mule Peak! But he knew this was something he couldn't escape. There was no 'EXIT' sign or door showing him a way out. He had no choice but to deal with it!

Once again, both men stared at each other. Peter finally fell back into the seat as a sign of defeat. Besides, continuing to argue with Boyd wasn't going to help the situation. He began collecting his thoughts as he looked around trying to find something to focus on. Boyd, too, assumed a relaxed posture leaning back in his seat as he let the thoughts settle in Peter's mind.

"Okay," Peter finally spoke. "Help me try to understand what is going on. I know you are older than you appear. I know you were part of Project UGEN. What was, or is, Project UGEN?"

"Mule Peak was a beautiful place," Boyd started. "We achieved so much success, in regards to technology, which propelled our country leaps and bounds ahead of everyone else. Unfortunately, it didn't stop with technology. It was something new and exciting, and we didn't realize what we were really getting into. I do wish I could elaborate more on the project, Mr. Knowles, but telling you more at this time would just make it more difficult for you to understand."

"Once again, you've told me nothing," Peter replied, shaking his head.

Changing the subject, Boyd asked, "Did you ever read that story in the Bible I spoke of? The one of angels intermingling with humans?"

Peter was about to ask what that question had to do with anything. He didn't want this conversation to end leaving him with more questions and curiosity as before. He decided to play along, for the time being, in an attempt to relax Boyd. Even more, a small break in what was happening was welcomed.

Peter kindly replied, "Believe it or not, I did. I had never heard of it before you told me about it. I even learned of a book, the Book of Enoch, after a quick search online and have read a little of it. Fantasy isn't my strong suit though."

"Really? Enoch, you say? You know it was rediscovered in the late 1940s. Seemed a lot was happening during that time. What an amazing read it is! Tell me, Mr. Knowles, did you read the part about God's punishment on them?" Boyd asked excitedly.

"From what I understood, he had the archangels place them somewhere hidden in the Earth bound and chained. Then, he flooded the entire Earth," Peter responded. "I don't see why he didn't just have them all killed and leave the humans out of the punishment."

"Yes! And what was the length of their sentence before they were to be released?" Boyd asked more interestingly.

The thought of dementia started to enter Peter's mind. This old man really liked to talk about weird things. He had enjoyed the pause in the real conversation, but it was time to get back to reality.

"I think seventy generations, but let's get back to what we were discussing before," Peter urged.

"I didn't realize we had left it," Boyd emphasized, raising an eyebrow questioningly. "You're an inquisitive and curious man, Mr. Knowles. Don't you find that story interesting?" Boyd's face grew extremely serious then, "I do!"

The serious look on Boyd's face caught Peter off guard. Was Boyd trying to tell him something?

"Are you trying to tell me something?" Peter asked.

Boyd looked down at his watch and let out a sigh. After two taps on the window to get Tony's attention, he said, "My time is up, Mr. Knowles. I would like to leave you with two bits of advice, if I may. First, I would forget you ever met me, which I doubt you will. And second, I recommend you find another vehicle!"

Peter's door opened then which had been opened by Tony. Peter didn't exit.

"Wait!" he demanded. "I'm not finished with this conversation. Once again, you have provided no answers. You came all the way out here to warn me of mystery men, which has definitely sparked my concern, and now you are just going to leave?"

"In the future, you will not find me if you try. My West Side residence isn't safe anymore for me, as I'm sure your email and truck's GPS history had led them straight to it," Boyd replied as he looked straight ahead. "Either do as I say and forget it all, or follow your instincts, Mr. Knowles. The choice is still yours."

With a stern look, Tony said, "I recommend you exit the vehicle, Sir."

Peter's expression was one of amazement. He had no doubt Tony could drag him right out of the vehicle. Furthermore, Boyd had filled his head with so much to digest, he didn't know if he was coming or going. Numbly, he exited the black sedan. Tony closed the door and walked around to enter on the driver's side. Confused, Peter stood there as the black sedan pulled away and headed for Interstate 40. *What just happened?*

After returning to his RV, Peter sat down and began to think. What was happening? How did his life take this turn? Before he continued to worry about it, he knew he had to analyze the situation in order to come up with the best course of action. He already knew his two choices. He could continue on to Red Rock and forget all about what just happened, or, dissect Boyd's conversation and possibly take precautions if warranted. He stood up and headed to make some coffee which always helped him think more clearly. Doing so, he started delving deep into his thoughts in efforts to rationalize the meeting he just had.

First, although indirectly, Boyd had confirmed his identity. Second, Boyd knew where to find him using his truck's GPS. Peter hadn't told anyone where he was going, except Sam, so tracking his GPS was the only possible answer. Next, Boyd had somehow read his private email. How else would he know Peter had sent an email to Sam. Unless, that is, Sam knew Boyd and was informing him of Peter's whereabouts. That was extremely unlikely and was quickly dismissed from his thoughts. No, the man he spoke with this morning was Alfred Boyd who obviously was good with computers, or knew people in key positions to help him. With those facts gathered in his mind now, Peter decided to believe Boyd's story of how he found him.

Next, who were the others out there searching for Boyd, and possibly him too? During his conversation, he believed they were money hungry, board members. However, Boyd had dismissed that assumption quickly. Peter recollected the sense of fear in Boyd when he spoke of these men. Could it be the government? Whatever the reason these 'others' had to want to get their hands on Boyd, Peter couldn't imagine how it concerned him. But wait! Boyd had stated he knew Peter was aware there was something different about him. Besides being a billionaire in hiding, what was different about him with the exception of his age not matching his appearance? Was that why the others were looking for him? Peter's mind began to piece ideas together. Mainly, he remembered the top-secret document and how it noted UGEN, whatever it was, was introduced into Boyd's system. Could that be the answer to why Boyd looked so young for his age and why the others were after him? Peter realized his mind had hit science fiction mode as he took a sip of coffee and sat down. *That's crazy!* There was no believable option to choose from as to why the others were after Boyd.

One more piece of the conversation remained for Peter to ponder. *The Genesis story.* Once again, and possibly out of delusion, Boyd wanted to discuss the fallen angels. At first, it appeared as if they were going to take a break from the real discussion and talk about something on a lighter note. But then, Boyd got all serious when he stated he found the story interesting. His seriousness alerted Peter there was possibly something more to the story. Was Boyd trying to tell him something indirectly? Peter knew a form of indirect conversation and referred to it as 'talking around' something. While in the military, members couldn't say certain words or talk about missions outside of a controlled environment. When the need arose to talk about something classified outside of a controlled environment, members would 'talk around' the subject. The conversation would make absolutely no sense to those who were not read into the program, but was understandable to those who were. But what could Boyd possibly be 'talking around'? Peter reluctantly let out a small smile realizing his brain was in science fiction mode again. Unfortunately, this was another part of the conversation Peter was unable to figure out.

After an hour of exploring his thoughts, it was time for him to make a decision. To him, it was an easy one to make. Worrying about and taking action on what Boyd said was a road filled with uncertainties. Heading to Red Rock and forgetting about it all was a certainty. Climbing into his truck after putting the RV in travel mode, Peter pulled out from the Meteor Crater RV Park and headed west on Interstate 40. *Red Rock...here I come!*

Chapter 7

According to the road signs, Flagstaff was only a few miles away. Always keeping a watch on the gas needle, Peter knew he was going to have to stop for a refill. Since Flagstaff was a larger town, he planned to find a truck stop which usually offered the best services. After he had left Meteor Crater, he wondered if there was a way to disable the GPS on his truck and even if he could. He enjoyed his truck's GPS system and actually relied on it. The days of reading maps while driving were over and some of the newer gadgets had spoiled him. With the latest revelation though, he didn't like the idea of being tracked. In addition, he would have to take the time and sign up for a new email account, seeing as to how that was hacked as well. He hated that idea, knowing signing up for a new one meant answering dumb questions and coming up with a complicated user name never used before. He began to think of how much an inconvenience Boyd had placed on him. Now, he had to notify his bank, the Veterans Affairs office, and others of the email change. *Change!* After the military, Peter hated change and thought of it as an inconvenience.

About halfway through Flagstaff, Peter noticed a truck stop just south of I-40. Slowing down, he took Exit 198 which led to East Butler Avenue and then on to the truck stop. It was called Little America Travel Center and must have been pretty popular seeing the number of tractor trailers parked around it. Peter pulled in and found a suitable place to park. Stepping out, he took a breath of fresh air and stretched. The smell of pine trees was strong in Flagstaff and reminded him of Christmas time while growing up as a kid. He enjoyed how smells could invigorate his mind to match old memories to them. The desert landscape he had been in for days had disappeared, and now pine forests were the dominant feature around. Peter had travelled I-40 several times and realized the forests only spanned around this part of Arizona and would eventually lead back to more desert. He welcomed the momentary change of scenery.

Inside the travel center, Peter took time to let his legs walk around the aisles to loosen them up. Of course, he stopped in front of the beef jerky and was about to grab some when he noticed a sandwich shop in the corner. Changing his mind, he headed that way and ordered the thickest roast beef sandwich they had. Walking over to find a seat after paying, he noticed a religious man in black clothes with a white collar around his neck. He identified the man's religion as Catholic, since they were the only ones he knew of to wear such attire. He chose a table just across the aisle from the priest. Unwrapping his sandwich, he threw a glance over and saw the priest glancing back. Both men gave a nod to one another.

"How's it going?" the priest asked.

"As good as can be," Peter lied. He knew it wasn't appropriate to start a conversation by telling the other person all about your problems. Even though this was a priest who probably spent a lot of time listening to people's problems, Peter didn't know the man.

After the formal exchange, the priest returned to his food. Something was itching in Peter's brain, though, and he had to scratch it. The opportunity had presented itself, and even though that something wasn't very important, he figured it best to go ahead and scratch it. He gave the priest a few minutes till he had taken the last bite of his meal.

"Excuse me," Peter said, grabbing the man's attention. "You're a priest, right?"

The man smiled and asked, "How could you tell?" He let out a little chuckle which made Peter chuckle back.

"Dumb question! Please, forgive me!" Peter replied, causing both men to chuckle even more.

"Why do you ask?" said the priest.

"Well," Peter started, "I'm doing some research and figured you may be able to help me with it, if you have a couple of minutes?"

"Sure! What's your research on?" answered the priest.

"The fallen angels in Genesis, chapter six. From what I understand, they bred with the human women and had offspring. The next thing you know, God floods the entire Earth. Is that how you understand it?" Peter asked.

"Wow! Wasn't expecting that one," the priest said with a surprised look. "I'm not too familiar with it to be honest. It's not something we really focus on."

Peter expected as much. He then asked, "How long is a generation in the Bible or does it just refer to how many grandfathers someone had?"

The priest thought for a minute and then answered, "A generation is seventy years. That one I do know!" The priest's smile revealed he was happy he at least could help with something.

A thought then entered Peter's mind. "When did the flood happen? I mean, what year? Do we know?"

The priest thought for a second and then responded, "Based on our best estimates using Biblical genealogy, around 1650 BC. However, that date is debated quite often. But 1650 is what I learned at seminary and what we teach at this point."

"What do you know about the Book of Enoch?" Peter then queried.

"Well, it's not in the Bible for starters. However, it is referred to. In the book of Jude, the author speaks of an Enochian prophecy about

Jesus returning with ten thousand of his angels. The prophecy isn't in the Bible and is only found in the Book of Enoch. Some religious scholars believe his book should have been included in the Bible. I mean, if he walked with God for three hundred years and was then raptured, he probably has something important to say. That's about all I know," explained the priest. "If you are researching the fallen angels, you should read the Book of Enoch and the Book of Jubilees. Both have quite a bit to say about the fallen angels!"

"Your answers to my questions will serve me well! I do appreciate your time," Peter said with a smile as he gathered his trash and stood up.

"No problem! Always glad to be of assistance. I wish you the best in your research and God bless you!" the priest stated as he waved at Peter.

A thought had begun to develop in Peter's mind. He knew it was absurd, but so was the last encounter he had with Boyd. Exiting the travel center, he walked over to his truck to reposition it for gas. *Seventy generations.* The pumps were open which allowed him to quickly fuel his vehicle. *Book of Jubilees?* Within a few minutes, Peter was back in his truck. He started it and was about to depart when he decided to pull over and park on the edge of the travel center's parking lot. Thoughts were once again running through his mind. Sitting in the truck with the engine still running, he leaned forward and placed his forehead against the top of the steering wheel. In his mind, he replayed the conversations with Boyd who seemed infatuated with the fallen angels. It seemed to Peter as if Boyd wanted to tell him something and was using these angels to 'talk around' a classified matter. Had the seventy generations of imprisonment passed, and now these fallen angels had been released? Were they teaching humans once again forbidden knowledge? Peter began to laugh out loud. The thought was so preposterous! His laughter began to mix with frustration. Trying to relieve himself somewhat, he sat in the truck and laughed as hard and loud as he possibly could. There was nothing funny anymore, but he continued to laugh hysterically. *I'm losing my mind!* All he wanted to do was control his thoughts enough to forget about Boyd and their conversations. He wanted to continue his simple life of travelling. But the itch of curiosity had settled deeply in his mind, and he knew he was going to have to scratch it!

Peter lifted his head from the steering wheel and took a deep breath. Looking around, he was glad no one had seen or heard his outburst. Looking through his right window, he noticed a suitable parking location which was closer to the travel center which he knew had Wi-Fi. It was time he paused his life, once again, and analyze the thoughts swirling around in his head. He pulled into the parking spot and cut the engine off. Within a few minutes, he was inside his RV sitting in front of his computer which was now connected to limitless information. Beside him, a piece of blank paper and a pen to help organize his thoughts.

During the last conversation with Boyd, Peter had thought they had taken a break from the main topic when Boyd had asked if he had read the story in the Bible contained in Genesis chapter six. After a discussion of the subject, Peter wanted to return to the main conversation and suggested as much. Boyd had replied he didn't know they left it. Boyd's look was serious. Afterwards, Boyd had asked Peter if he knew how long the fallen angels were imprisoned for which he responded with seventy generations. *Seventy generations.* Peter recalled the priest's answer to how long a generation was. He picked up the pen and wrote **70 x 70 = 4900** on the piece of paper. The fallen angels, according to the Book of Enoch, were to be imprisoned for 4,900 years. He also wrote down the date of the flood according to the priest which was around **1650 BC**. On his laptop, he typed in the search words: *Jubilees Fallen Angels.* Numerous results came up and Peter began to search for the date he was looking for. *When did the fallen angels get judged and imprisoned?* Two minutes of reading later, he found what he was looking for. The Book of Jubilees revealed the fallen angels, or Watchers, had descended to Earth and mated with human females shortly after the Biblical figure Jared was born, which was 3543 BC. Remembering information from the Book of Enoch, part of their punishment was to watch their offspring, or nephilim, war with one another for five hundred years. Peter picked up the pen and wrote down **3543 - 500 = 3043**. The result of the equation would be the date of imprisonment in BC time. He then continued to write an equation on the piece of paper: **-3043 + 4900 = 1943**. *You've got to be kidding me!* Peter began to shake his head as if in denial of his calculations. According to what he had read in the Book of Enoch and the Book of Jubilees, the fallen angels' imprisonment would end sometime in the 1900s based on his calculations! Peter placed the pen back on the paper and leaned back in his chair. He began to recollect pertinent parts of his conversations with Boyd: *There are some things in this world which should remain hidden...unspoken things! Would you want to know the answers if you knew it would change your life and view of reality? Within the span of the past one hundred years, we've discovered knowledge and created amazing technology. Where did all that knowledge come from? If there were some superior, unknown genetic lifeforms, I think it would be much closer to home.*

Complete absurdity! Peter had not seen angels walking around or giant offspring for that matter. Armageddon had not happened! It was all nonsense! It had to be just coincidence the numbers added up. It had to be a coincidence that Boyd, who didn't appear to age normally, was stationed at Mule Peak working on a top-secret program in the mid-1940s! It had to be a coincidence Boyd created a multi-billion-dollar computer company which brought about the internet and instant access to knowledge!

Peter didn't know what to think. His analytical skills told him the data was adding up and there were multiple pieces which fit together. He might not be able to *confirm* this hypothesis, but it was *possible* or even *probable*! There would have to be proof if this hypothesis was true. But, how could anyone possibly prove such a thing? The only one Peter knew who could confirm or deny the hypothesis was Alfred Boyd. But where would he find him, especially after telling Peter not to look for him anymore?

For the first time in a long time, Peter felt alone. Although he enjoyed the solo life, he never felt lonely as he moved from one destination to the next. His lifestyle didn't require anyone else. He was content with his own thoughts and the occasional, short interaction with others. But this was different! He needed someone to talk to. He needed someone to tell him if he was crazy or not. In the end, if he didn't have anyone to listen, he was going to have to figure it out for himself. He was a trained intelligence specialist with all the skills to figure out problems and answer questions. It was time Peter Knowles took the gloves off! It was time to turn caution into a calculated process with countermeasures. Peter's previous look of frustration transformed into one of excitement. This challenge to discover the truth behind Alfred Boyd and his mysterious conversations might prove to be the most difficult Peter had ever faced.

Red Rock Canyon was no longer the destination. If Peter was going to really look into this mystery, he needed to really think carefully about his future actions. If Alfred Boyd had tracked him and intercepted his email, then what would stop him, or anyone else for that matter, from doing it again? A game plan had to be designed and he needed a little time to figure it out. He needed a place to park and at least spend the night, which would provide enough time to come up with a course of action. He knew where he needed to go.

It only took a few minutes to arrive at an RV park just across the road from the Little America travel center. Peter had noticed the business sign "Black Bart's RV Park" when he had pulled into the travel center earlier. After paying the fee at the office, he pulled his truck and RV over to the east side of the lot and found a suitable camping area. Within the next hour, he had his mobile home completely set up and was sitting comfortably in front of his computer, which was now connected to the internet. A freshly brewed cup of coffee, a pen and some paper were placed close by. He was ready.

On a blank sheet of paper, Peter jotted down the intelligence cycle which he had used many times in the military: *Planning, Collection, Processing, Analysis/Production, Dissemination.* This was the process the intelligence community used to answer questions and would now serve as a guide for him. He wasn't sure if there would be a dissemination step, but there was no need to worry about that now. He was in the planning stage. To begin the planning, he had to determine what question needed to be answered. After carefully thinking about it, he knew the question. It wasn't one of the random questions which would pop into his head, but the root question behind everything. It was the question that was always there, but he didn't know how to ask it. *What was/is Project UGEN?* Peter knew if he could answer this question, then most, if not all, of the other random questions would be answered.

Knowing that Project UGEN was a classified program, he had to be careful. Certain precautions would have to be taken so nothing he did would point back to him. A quick sip of coffee kept Peter focused. He knew one of the first things he needed to do was acquire a new computer. The computer he now used had his 'fingerprints' all over it. His real name, credit card information, emails, IP address...it would all point directly to Peter Knowles if he used it. He needed a new one! He would pay cash and wouldn't input any truthful, personal data into it when setting it up for use. This would allow the search for anything without identifying himself.

A sudden knock on the RV door disrupted Peter from his planning. Figuring it was the park overseer, he got up and opened the door. To his surprise, a blonde-haired man in a black suit and a redheaded woman wearing a black business skirt and jacket stood outside the door. Both were professional looking. Seeing the door opened, the man reached inside his jacket and pulled out a black wallet. The woman threw the right side of her jacket back and placed her hand on a pistol as if ready to pull it out!

"FBI! Place your hands out in front of you and step out!" the man demanded as he flipped open the wallet to reveal an identification card. The letters F B I were predominant on the badge, but that was all Peter was able to make out. He placed his hands out in front and exited his RV as ordered. *What is going on?*

The man grabbed Peter behind the arm and walked him over and placed him face first against the side of the RV. He then quickly frisked Peter.

"No weapons!" the FBI man stated to the woman. He then turned Peter around to face him.

"What's going on?" Peter asked, still surprised at what was happening.

"We got a tip about a truck and RV matching your description. Someone reported they saw a little girl being dragged into it while yelling for help. The description of the little girl matched a missing persons case we have been looking into. My partner and I were assigned to search this park."

"I can assure you it wasn't me!" Peter exclaimed.

The FBI man and woman glanced at each other before the man responded, "Then you won't mind if my partner searches your RV and truck."

"Not at all! I have nothing to hide and will cooperate fully!" Peter stated.

The FBI man nodded to the woman who then pulled out her pistol and slowly entered the RV. Peter heard her identify herself as FBI as she entered further into the RV.

"Sir, please step over here with me," the FBI man directed as he once again grabbed Peter by the back of the arm. He escorted Peter away from the RV until it was no longer visible.

"Can you please show me your ID?" the FBI man requested.

"I don't have it on me," Peter truthfully answered. "It's on the table inside."

"Okay. Just wait here with me then, for now," was the response.

Both men stood there as several minutes passed. Peter felt enough time had gone by for the woman to search the RV for a little girl. Furthermore, a few other nosy campers began showing up to see what was going on. Just when Peter was about to inquire on why it was taking so long, the FBI woman appeared walking towards the two men.

"The truck is locked. I need the key!" she said as she came to a stop in front of Peter.

"It's in my pocket," Peter replied as he slowly slid his right hand inside to retrieve the key. He then produced the key and handed it to the woman. "You can look through the windows and tell there's not a little girl inside."

Without responding, the FBI woman grabbed the key and disappeared again as she headed for Peter's truck.

"We appreciate your cooperation, Sir. I hope you understand we have to take tips of this nature very seriously," the FBI man told Peter as they stood waiting.

Nodding his head in agreement, Peter replied, "I do! I do! I hope you all find her, but I assure you I don't know anything about it."

A few more minutes had passed when the FBI woman returned. "I didn't find anything," she said looking at her partner.

The man nodded back towards her and then looked over to Peter. "I'm sorry for the inconvenience and your loss of time, Sir. We were not just looking for the little girl, but also any possible signs that she could have been inside, which takes time. Again, we thank you for your cooperation."

The FBI woman handed Peter the keys to his truck back before they both started walking away. Peter glanced around to see several fellow campers whispering. *People!* Now that the ordeal was over, he headed back towards his RV. When the truck came into view, all four doors were wide open. *She didn't even close my doors!* Peter walked to the truck and peered inside to make sure nothing was damaged or missing. After closing the doors and locking them again, he re-entered the RV and looked around. Several objects were out of place, but he easily put them back where they belonged. No damage was noted either. Inside, Peter was glad he had cooperated with the agents. He imagined the distress the missing little girl must be feeling and felt compassion for her and her parents. *I hope they find her.*

With everything back in order, Peter grabbed a bottle of water out of the fridge and began to drink it. Standing there, he began to refocus.

Approximately thirty minutes had passed since the agents had arrived. The whole ordeal seemed like a dream and happened so fast to Peter. But it was over, and now he needed to get back to what he was doing. The question was still there and needed to be answered. Finishing the bottle of water, he returned to the table and laptop.

The computer screen was blank! Peter wiggled the mouse and made sure everything was still plugged in. Nothing. He unplugged the computer, counted to ten, and plugged it back in. Pressing the 'Power' button, Peter watched as the red light came on indicating his computer was booting up. Just as he leaned back into his chair to wait for it to finish, a message came across the screen: **HARD DISK ERROR - DISK NOT FOUND.** Peter let out a low, guttural growl of frustration. He figured the FBI woman must have jarred the computer or something which dislodged the internal hard drive. Reluctantly, he powered the computer down and began to disassemble the laptop. Once the back was off, he located the hard drive, removed it and looked for any external damage. Not finding any, he re-inserted the drive and put the back cover on. Once again, he powered the computer back up and waited. After a few seconds, the same error message appeared! *You've got to be kidding me!* After a minute of sitting with a scowl, Peter began to chuckle. "Good thing I was planning to buy another one," he said to himself, remembering his previous plan. He closed the lid of the laptop and unplugged it.

Peter walked outside and stretched. He needed the fresh air. Computer problems always had a way of frustrating him to the point of stress. After a deep inhale and exhale, he looked around and noticed all the nosy people had dispersed. He could hear the traffic on the nearby Interstate 40 and quickly contrasted it to the quietness the desert could offer. Peter didn't care much for cities with all the noises, traffic and concrete. Moreover, they were filled with people. Nosy people, mean people, selfish people...the city was full of them. As he stood there, he realized the irony of campers set up in the middle of a city. He smiled as he looked down and kicked a few rocks.

The visit by the FBI, and his now broken computer, had disrupted Peter's planning process. Although he knew he was going to continue with it, he wasn't in the mood now. He grabbed his wallet and headed for the park's office where he knew a cafe was. It wouldn't hurt anything to take a while to relax and enjoy another cup of joe! Besides, he knew he had to clear his mind in order to focus it once again on planning.

Entering the office area, Peter headed straight over towards the cafe and ordered a black coffee. While waiting, he walked back over to the main office, where an older man with gray hair sat behind the counter.

"How's it going?" Peter started the conversation.

"Good! What can I do for you?" the gray-haired man asked.

Peter smiled and inquired, "Just wondering if those agents had any luck at other RV parks?"

"Don't know what you're talking about!" the man replied. "What agents?"

Peter raised an eyebrow quizzically, "The ones looking for the missing little girl. Said they had gotten a tip and were on the lookout for an RV and truck which looked similar to mine. They were checking RV parks in the area."

"Sir, I still don't know what you are talking about, and I ain't heard of no missing girl," the gray-haired man stated.

Peter had assumed the agents would have stopped by the office to ask them to keep an eye open for a matching description. Or, at the least, let the office know they were present. Peter didn't know the FBI's protocols on matters like these. At least he had asked about the little girl, which somewhat quenched his compassion for her. He really did hope she was safe.

"Thanks anyways. I guess they didn't stop by here," replied Peter as he headed back to pick up his cup of coffee.

He chose a small table by a window and sat down. The coffee was good and welcomed. A front must have been passing through this part of the country, because the air outside had become a little cooler. That, with the elevation of Flagstaff, provided for a cool day which was more enjoyable with a warm drink. Peter peered out of the window and could see hints of moving traffic through the tree line. He was beginning to relax. *Sam.* The thought of her was welcomed. Hopefully, she was out of the hospital and back at her home where she could be comfortable. He had no way to check his email. He was anxious to hear about what she had to say about his intriguing story he had sent to her in the last email. He thought about how nice it would be if she was with him now enjoying a cup of coffee. Although unusual for Peter, her company would be welcomed no matter what she wanted to talk about. Thinking about her let him know he needed to get a new computer quickly. He needed her correspondence. It comforted him.

The sun had already dipped lower in the sky and would be kissing the horizon soon, as Peter exited the park office and headed back to his RV. It was time to continue planning or, if he couldn't do that, try to enjoy the rest of the evening. *What were their names?* Peter realized he couldn't recall the FBI agents' names. For that matter, he couldn't recall them even telling him. Although the man flashed his badge, it was quick, not giving enough time to examine it. *Flashing lights.* Peter stopped walking. In every child kidnapping situation he had seen on TV, or read about in the paper, the police and federal agents were usually in mass with flashing police lights when approaching a suspect. There were no lights or police cars when the agents came to check him. In the back of Peter's mind, something started to tingle. His instincts were sparking! *The others!* Peter began to walk at a brisk pace towards his truck. The thoughts racing through his head had him questioning whether the man and woman were federal agents at all. The park's office had no clue of what he was talking about when asking about them. His brisk pace turned into a jog. What if they were the 'others' Boyd had told him about? Although thinking it was absurd, there was only one way to be sure. The only reason the 'others' would search his vehicle would be to retrieve any hard evidence that could point to them. His computer had contained emails and search histories which were related to Boyd and other information loosely related to Project UGEN.

Now, the hard drive was destroyed. The only remaining, real evidence was the classified document!

Reaching the driver's side door, Peter unlocked and opened it quickly. Reaching under the seat, he pulled out the gun case and placed it on the seat. Peter paused, took a deep breath in, and opened it. The copy of the classified document was gone!

Chapter 8

Opened drawers and strewn papers was the predominant sight in Peter's RV. The copy of the classified document had been taken! Now, Peter was in a frantic search trying to remember where he had placed the original? For the past hour, he had rummaged through his RV. His heart was beating fast and his eyes darted around nervously. The 'others' were real! Boyd had tried to warn him. And if not the 'others', then Boyd himself had sent the man and woman. *This can't be happening!* After a thorough search of the RV, Peter flopped down in the chair near the table. He ran his fingers through his hair which left an appearance of a frazzled man. *Where is it?* Peter closed his eyes and began to piece together his actions over the past few days. He began to control his breathing and forced his mind to slow down. Suddenly, his eyes opened wide. In a dash, he exited the RV and headed for his truck. There in the back seat was his old flight jacket he remembered wearing to Alfred Boyd's house. Unlocking the doors, he opened the back door and grabbed the jacket. A folded document met his fingers as he reached inside the pocket. A smile crossed his face as he pulled it out. His memory had served him well as he remembered placing the original document inside the pocket before the initial meeting with Boyd. Carefully, he unfolded the paper. He stopped breathing. All thoughts, emotions, cares...everything fled his mind! Neatly written in the center of the paper was one word: **STOP!**

Peter knew now, more than ever, he needed to think carefully about the events which were unfolding. He needed to consolidate everything which had happened. Locking his truck doors, he walked back to the RV and went inside. *Is it safe?* Ingrained in Peter over the course of his military career was the principle of safety first. He may not have known exactly who the FBI, or posing FBI man and woman were, but he knew they didn't hesitate invading his privacy and even stealing from him. Furthermore, they were armed. What if he had not allowed them to search his property and insisted they produce a search warrant? *Worries!* Who had sent them and why did they have a need to steal the document? *People!* Peter realized his world had changed. Instead of travelling and enjoying retirement, he was now imprisoned to some unidentified problem which was taking all of his time. *Drama!*

The light was fading quickly outside. Peter needed to make a decision to either leave or spend the night. Realizing whoever was behind the recent invasion could probably track his truck's GPS, he didn't see a need to pack up and leave. *Tomorrow.* Peter realized he was considering making rash decisions, which wasn't like him. No, he would not give in to fear and worry. He had always tried not to interfere in other people's lives and tried even harder not to bother anyone. What gave them the right to bother and invade his life? His thoughts of worry and fear started to subside giving way to thoughts of determination. Peter exited the RV and headed for the truck to retrieve his pistol. He wasn't going to be afraid, and if someone wanted to pay him another visit in the middle of the night, well, he would be ready!

Lying in bed, Peter was calm and collected. His mind had gained control over the irrational emotions which had plagued him earlier. Now, he was back in control and in planning mode. His thoughts were well organized and efficient, his breathing was relaxed, and his plans were evolving. Falling asleep, Peter felt comforted with his head against the pillow, through which he could feel the outline of a loaded, ready to fire weapon.

The sun's rays slowly creeped down the wall beside Peter's bed until they landed on his eyes. Before he even opened them, he knew he had slept later than normal which meant he slept peacefully. Opening his eyes, he took a moment to analyze his mindset before starting the day. Yes, he was still in control. Peter reached beneath his pillow and pulled out the pistol, which he then examined while still laying down. He knew his weapon, how to use it, and planned to keep it close by.

It was already mid-morning when Peter pulled out from the RV camp. Instead of getting on I-40, he headed towards the south side of Flagstaff as he knew he would probably find what he was looking for there. Most cities were similar in that the more north and west you went, the nicer the neighborhoods were. To the south and east, you would more than likely find the shadier parts of society. It only took a couple of minutes once he reached the south side to find what he was looking for. Peter turned on his right signal light and pulled into Murrell's Mechanic Shop. It wasn't one of the fancy, franchise mechanic shops you would find advertised on television. Numerous wrecked vehicles were parked close together on the north side of an old, gray cinder block building with two large bay doors open. One of the bays was clear while the other had an old Toyota jacked up one side with the right rear wheel missing. Oil stains covered the concrete inside and outside the shop. This was definitely the type of place he was looking for. Pulling up in front of the open bay, Peter switched off the ignition and exited the vehicle.

"Nice truck you got there!" came a voice from a man walking out of the bay. "That thang's hemi engine is a beast!"

Peter knew immediately he had found the right place. The man was wearing old blue jeans badly stained with oil and both knees were worn out. Over his red and black plaid, button up shirt, he wore an unzipped, dark green jacket which had more stains than the jeans. His face was skinny and worn with dark sockets surrounding his eyes. The dirty, blonde hair was shoulder length which had been pulled back and placed in a ponytail. A hard life was written all over this guy.

"It is!" replied Peter. "Best vehicle I've ever owned."

"What 'ya need me to do 'fer her?" the mechanic inquired as he took an old oil rag from his rear pocket and began wiping the grime off the tips of his fingers.

"Know anything about GPS?" Peter asked.

"I know it'll git ya somewhere if you can 'figger out how the dang thang works!" the mechanic replied through a raspy laugh. After a few seconds he added, "I also know them no-good dealers can use it to repo the thang if you're late with a payment."

Without a doubt, Peter was at the right place. "Well, it's paid for," stated Peter. "But I just don't want Uncle Sam to be able to track my every move. The government's already trying to take our guns away, and the last thing I need is for them to be tracking my every move. You know what I'm talking about?" Peter knew he was stereotyping the mechanic and was even playing to his obvious political views. The rebel flag draped across the back wall in the garage was a clear sign.

The mechanic nodded in agreement accompanied with another raspy cackle. This guy had obviously smoked way too many cigarettes. "Well, since ya own it, I'd say everything on it's yours. You needin' me to take out the GPS?" he asked.

Peter smiled. "Please do! Need me to unhook from the RV?"

"Nah! I can do it right there. Most of 'ems under the steerin' wheel. Take me about fifteen minutes is all. Let me get my screwdrivers," the mechanic said as he walked back into the garage to retrieve his tools.

Thirty minutes later, Peter pulled back out onto the street. He hoped the forty-five dollars he gave to the mechanic had fixed the problem. He looked over where the GPS display usually relayed his position on a scrolling map, but there was nothing to look at now except a blank screen. Headed north, Peter began looking for an electronics store.

A huge mall area welcomed Peter on his left as he drove eastward through Flagstaff on I-40 Business. Looking around, he saw the franchise computer store he was looking for which had a large yellow sign out front. He needed to buy a new computer, but he knew he had to be careful not to have the purchase traced back to him. Peter was cognizant not to use his credit card anytime soon, knowing any use of it would reveal his location. Although he knew the 'others' were aware he was in Flagstaff, he didn't want them tracking bar codes associated with his credit card purchases. Bar codes could be utilized to identify the specific computer he bought and would give others the information needed to access it. Peter knew a thing or two about tracking computers and cellphones from his past.

There was plenty of space in the parking lot to pull his truck and RV in. Before entering the computer store, he visited the RV to get some cash he had stored for emergencies. It wasn't much, but there was enough to get a new computer. Reaching beneath the RV's kitchen sink, he retrieved a white envelope which had been taped to the back wall. Getting enough cash, he then secured his property and headed inside the store.

One of the first things he noticed as he browsed through the computer section was the Gen6 icons splattered across most of them. The green fruit tree inside a black triangle was catchy. For a moment, Peter considered Boyd's choice to use a fruit tree. It was a fruit tree in the book of Genesis which opened the eyes of Adam and Eve and granted them knowledge. Even the name of the company, Gen6, had to be in reference to the book of Genesis. It had to all be tied together somehow, and Peter knew he would scratch the itch of curiosity soon enough. With a smile, he quickly wondered why Boyd didn't use a fruit with a bite taken out of it instead of the fruit tree if he really wanted to point to the book of Genesis.

Peter's choice of a new computer didn't have the Gen6 logo on it, but it could perform the tasks he needed it to. Walking to the counter to pay, he took notice of the many cameras hung along the ceiling rafters. *Always watching us.* He wondered if facial recognition had advanced far enough to identify him. He wouldn't put it past the government! He knew himself of the vast, covert network the government had to spy on citizens through electronic surveillance. The same cellular networks, computers, cameras and other classified equipment the intelligence community used to spy on foreign nations was also present in the United States. Why wouldn't the government spy on its own people?

"Buying a new computer, eh?" greeted the female cashier as Peter placed the computer box on the checkout counter. "Did you find everything you were looking for?"

"Yes, and I did, thank you," replied Peter. "I'll be paying cash today."

"No problem. Telephone number?" the girl asked as she stood waiting to press numbers on the checkout computer.

"Sorry, don't have one," said Peter as he smiled knowing his response was unusual.

"No problem," she smiled back, still waiting to input information into the computer. "Can I get your name and address?"

"Is it necessary? I'm paying with cash," Peter stated.

"No, not really. The store just likes to keep track of your purchases so we can better assist you in the future. Plus, if you ever lose your receipt, we can pull up an electronic copy in case you want to return something," she explained as she then scanned the barcode on the box and told Peter the cost.

That's what you've been told! Peter handed her enough money to cover the cost and waited for his change and receipt. How conveniently the store had placed the location, date and time on the receipt. He wondered what his country would really look like if someone took a deep look behind the curtain.

"Thank you very much and please come again," she said to Peter as he grabbed the box and headed towards the door. He nodded back kindly before walking out through the doors.

Peter knew he needed to find a Wi-Fi hotspot to get his new computer up and running. It would take at least an hour to get through the initial setup phase and multiple reboots. Then, he would need to establish a new email account. *Sam.* How would he communicate with Sam without Boyd or anyone else being able to find out his new account information? If his email had been intercepted before, then they would know he corresponded with Sam. They would know her email address, her real name and personal information on top of that! Any email Peter sent to her would reveal his true identity. He would have to think of something!

Peter felt a sense of freedom knowing he had resolved two issues which could have led the 'others' to know of his location. With the truck's GPS removed and the acquisition of a new computer, he could now pursue his mission of finding out exactly what Project UGEN was, or is, without feeling like someone was about to knock on his door. Although he knew it was possible for the government to track almost anyone, he had never imagined he would be the target himself. Considering the ones which tracked him down may not even be associated with the government, concerned him even more. Precautions had now been taken, though, and he would be more careful not to leave bread crumbs which could lead back to him.

There was one more thing to accomplish before leaving Flagstaff. He gave his right signal and pulled off the road into a gas station. It didn't take long talking to the attendants before he had directions to the public library. Peter was glad the old-fashioned way of getting directions still worked. Peter smiled as he climbed back into his truck. He enjoyed the sense of achievement every time he garnered a new piece of information when he was on a mission. Whether it was a big or small piece of information, it was satisfying, as it let him know he was still moving forward.

Twenty minutes later, Peter sat in front of one of the library's public use computers. It took a little sweet talking the librarian since the rules stated you needed a library card in order to use one and there was no way he was about to apply for one. After explaining he was passing through and complementing the library's vast assortment of books, she had given in. Once again for Peter, he had put the right words in the right order to get what he wanted. Peter was tempted to search for information related to Project UGEN, but he knew better. The computer he was using had a unique IP address which meant any information accessed on the internet would lead directly back to it and provide a time stamp. If someone wanted to, they could correlate the overhead camera footage, which this library had, with the timestamp and quickly identify the person sitting at the computer at the time the information was accessed. the 'others' wouldn't be too happy if he continued to investigate Project UGEN after they warned him to stop. However, Peter didn't feel they wouldn't feel threatened if he just accessed his email.

A few keystrokes and mouse clicks later, Peter had opened his email account. As expected, and hoped for, Sam had replied to his last message he had sent a few days earlier:

> *"Hey Mister PK! What a story! I did indeed find it intriguing and imagined what the conversation between you and the 'maybe' Boyd must have been like. You always have the best adventures, though this one seems a little out of your realm since you mostly adventure down trails and not looking into hermit billionaires! I bet a lot of media outlets would pay good money for that info.*
>
> *I'm thinking you are now at Red Rock? How are/were the trails? You know I enjoy hearing about that kind of stuff, so please fill me in. Besides, the doctors say I'll probably be here a few more days, so I could use the reading material. I told them I could rest just as easily at my home, which is a couple blocks away, but they just smiled and said a few days wasn't that long. Well, it is when you are in my position. Oh well! Look forward to hearing from you. Sam"*

After reading the message a couple of times, Peter sat back and relaxed in the chair. He was happy to hear she would be back home soon and that she enjoyed his story. Before leaving the library, there were two emails he needed to compose and send. He had already planned what he was going to write. He clicked on the 'Reply' button and began the first one:

"Hey Sunshine! Glad to hear you will be out of the hospital soon and glad you enjoyed my 'intriguing' story! I haven't made it to Red Rock Canyon yet, as I decided to stop and enjoy Flagstaff for a few days. It sure is beautiful here. However, I'm leaving after I send this email, so my next one probably will not reach you until after I've hiked a few trails there. After Red Rock though, I'm heading north up to Seattle to hike around Mt. Rainier National Park. The elevation is pretty high up but I'm hoping I'll be able to handle it. Maybe after that, I'll head back east towards the Dakotas, but I'm not sure yet.

You be sure to get your rest and I'll try to write to you in a few days. PK"

Peter read over the email and then clicked on the 'Send' button. He hated the lies he sent her, but decided not to view them as lies to her. Rather, they were lies to anyone intercepting his email. For a while, he thought about deleting his current email account and creating a new one. Then he realized he only ever emailed one person. On top of that, this email account could prove to be useful as it just had!

Next, Peter clicked on the 'Create' button to begin writing his second message. This one wasn't intended for Sam. He entered his own email address on the 'To' line and began to create the simple message:

"You were right. I trust my instincts."

Peter sent the email and within a few seconds, he received the same email. Content, he logged off the computer, informed the librarian he was finished, and exited the library. Walking across the parking lot to his truck, he couldn't be sure the last email he sent would reach the intended recipient. However, his instincts told him Alfred Boyd would be receiving those seven words soon enough. Further, they told him others may receive it as well, but it would only serve as confusion for them.

Peter knew he was still in the planning process with regards to the intelligence cycle. He knew he needed to complete the first phase before he could move on to the collection phase. If he was going to truly find out what Project UGEN was, he needed to be methodical in his approach and avoid the urge to solely rely on instincts. He had already taken the necessary precautions to prevent people from tracking him and had misled anyone interested in his personal email account. Now, he needed to plan on how to acquire new information on Project UGEN without sending red flags out. Searching for it on the internet would surely be one of those red flags. On top of that, he knew searching for it online would probably lead to zero results since it was a classified program. He didn't have the access to classified information systems he once had, and couldn't enter a secure facility without credentials. Attempting to do such would be a one-way ticket to prison. Peter knew he had to be careful and knew finding out more information would be difficult. Currently, he knew of only two sources which could provide information and possibly even answer the root question. Alfred Boyd and the 'others'. Even if he wanted to talk with Boyd again, he didn't know how to contact him. Boyd had told Peter during their last conversation not to try to find him in the future, and he wouldn't be returning to his home on West Side Road. As for trying to reach the 'others', that course of action seemed dangerous to Peter. Although he didn't know exactly who they were, his instincts told him they were dangerous. Even Boyd had fear in his eyes when he spoke of them. Peter had to think of more options.

It was time to get out of Flagstaff. Peter didn't have a destination just yet, but he knew he wanted to change directions away from Red Rock Canyon. He could head back east on I-40 towards Albuquerque, which would give him some time to think about his next step. He quickly considered heading north or south, but figured staying near an interstate would be the most efficient choice once he decided on a destination. Pulling onto I-40 East, Peter kept watch in his side view mirror to make sure no one was following him. He knew he was a little paranoid, but it wasn't everyday someone posed as the FBI and invaded your home! He drove about five miles beyond the eastern city limit of Flagstaff before he was sure no one was following him. Setting his truck on cruise control, Peter let the miles roll by.

It was evening and the sun was to Peter's back as he headed towards Albuquerque. His mind hadn't stopped planning his next move. Several ideas had come to mind, but one interested him more than the others. When he had searched for Alfred Boyd while using the laundry room at Holloman, and when he had searched for fallen angels, he remembered one word which repeatedly popped up in the results. *Conspiracy*! He didn't even consider clicking on those links as he figured it was some lunatic who believed the world was ending. But now, given his current situation, it may be time to look into some of those conspiracy theories. If nothing else, it may provide some important clues he could use to further his plan.

As Peter pulled onto Exit 233, he began to see the white, dome-shaped building at the Meteor Crater RV Park. After a short trip down Meteor Crater Road, Peter was right back where he had been a few days earlier. The day still offered a couple of hours for daylight travelling, but he thought it best to use that time setting up his new computer using the park's Wi-Fi connection. Furthermore, he wanted to stock his RV with some food and other supplies he needed. There was no rush anyway, as he didn't have a destination yet. He was out of Flagstaff, and no one knew where he was!

The guy with the mutton chops was working. After a quick exchange of pleasantries and payment, Peter found a suitable location and pulled his RV into a camping spot nestled near one of the older, taller trees the park offered. Completing the setup routine for an overnight stay, he entered into the RV and took his new laptop out of the box. Pressing the 'Power' button, Peter leaned back and waited for the setup burden to begin. A few moments later, he began creating an imaginary user, complete with an imaginary phone number and address. He was careful not to use any information which could lead back to him should anyone try to track him down. By the time he was finished with the initial setup, he realized just how much personal information had to be entered before the computer would let him use it. *No wonder they could hack my computer!* Personal information, likes and dislikes, choice of colors and sounds...pretty much everything needed to create a psychological profile of the user! Of course, he randomly answered all the setup questions and took caution not to enter his own preferences. Now that all the personal data had been collected, the computer let Peter know it needed to download the latest updates. After inputting the RV park's Wi-Fi information, he clicked on the 'Begin' button and watched the computer communicate to the outside world for the first time. *Who are you telling all that personal information you just gathered to?* Watching the download bars, Peter felt as if his eyes had been opened. Sure, he knew computers could be hacked, but after speaking with their creator, Alfred Boyd, and after this setup, he wondered how vast the information gathering on Americans was. All this time, he figured computers were there to make our lives easier. He never imagined there was an ulterior use for others.

Knowing the downloads would take some time, Peter secured his truck and RV before heading to the welcome center to purchase food and supplies. As he walked across the parking lot, he looked towards the spot Boyd's black sedan had been parked the day prior. *Wonder where he is now*? The sun had already landed on the horizon and began to sink even more. Taking a moment, Peter knew the world was still a beautiful place. The gentle breeze, evening sky and fresh air made him feel alive. He would have to remember to stop every day, regardless of what he was doing, and enjoy nature's beauty. Continuing on, he bought enough supplies to last for an extended period of time. On his way back to the RV, he couldn't help but glance over again to the spot Boyd had parked.

Peter still had enough time to eat and complete a couple of tasks before the computer had finalized the setup process. After enjoying some stir fry and rice, he cleaned up his kitchen area and then wiped over the rest of his furniture. Although a man, he knew he still needed to keep a clean dwelling. He knew it wouldn't be long before he was going to have to do laundry again, too. Just as he finished wiping off the last table, he heard the familiar sound of a computer reboot. He put away the cleaning supplies and then returned to sit in front of the laptop. He really wanted to open his email account, but knew it would immediately be linked to the new computer. He was going to have to wait to use a public computer to check his old email. Opening the web browser, Peter inserted the words he wanted to search for: 'Conspiracy, Fallen Angels'. As usual when searching for anything, the web threw at him a host of responses. Meticulously, he began to click on each one to decide if any could be taken seriously. Several websites had made the link between the seventy generations of imprisonment for the fallen angels and the 1900s as the completion period. Some sites had pictures of giants which had obviously been photoshopped. *Quacks*! More than a few pointed to secret societies such as the Freemasons and Illuminati as the powers behind the conspiracies. Peter soon realized there was no hard proof anywhere to be found, rather, a bunch of coincidences which made for a good read. However, after an hour of searching, he found something that piqued his interest. One man, Dristan Cavenaugh who lived down in Texas, had done a good job of weeding out the fake stories and had compiled a theory based on factual data. Furthermore, he expounded on how big businesses were in on the conspiracy and how their trademarks and icons secretly revealed their involvement. He believed sections of the government, Hollywood, and big businesses were covertly preparing citizens to not only accept, but welcome a type of new world order. Really grabbing Peter's attention was Dristan's belief that superhuman DNA would be combined with human DNA to create superhumans. *Alfred Boyd's defiance to aging*? Dristan argued one of the same ideas Alfred Boyd had shared from the beginning. He noted how humans always strived for longer life and increased knowledge. Peter sat back in his chair and thought about the Adam and Eve story he had heard so long ago. Lucifer, a fallen angel, had tempted Eve with those same two things, knowledge and immortal life! Again, though, there was no hard evidence to prove any of it. Was Alfred Boyd, and the top-secret document Peter found, evidence to prove such a conspiracy? Less than a week ago, Peter knew he would have signed off such conspiracies as absurd, but after talking with Boyd and after the unwelcomed, fake FBI visit, he figured there might be something to it. *Where will the rabbit hole lead?*

Before getting off the computer, Peter created a new email account. Of course, he didn't use his personal information, but inserted the same information he had used when creating the fake user for his computer. After some thought, Peter started to compose an email addressed to Dristan Cavenaugh who had provided an email on the website:

> *"I found your website interesting and would like to discuss a few things with you. I assure you it will not be a waste of your time...trust me! RweDecieved@email.com"*

Peter left his computer on as he laid down for the night. If the computer beeped to indicate a new email, then it could only be from one person since he had just created the new account. Thoughts of fallen angel conspiracies danced in his mind as he eventually let slumber take control.

The next morning, Peter realized how hard he had slept when he noticed the new email waiting for him. Although the new email beep didn't wake him, he was glad he slept well and was rested. Before opening the new message, he walked over and peeked out the RV window towards the spot Boyd had parked before. *Nothing.* Taking the time to brew a cup of coffee, Peter then sat down and opened the new email:

> *"Hello RweDecieved. My telephone number is 888-567-4623. Call me anytime tomorrow. Dristan"*

The time stamp on the message was from late last night. Peter considered the offer to call Dristan. Even though he didn't have a personal phone, he could probably use a pay phone somewhere. He didn't want to use the prepaid phone in the glove compartment of the truck either, as it was for emergencies. Furthermore, Peter realized a phone conversation wasn't what he needed. After a quick search on the computer, he downloaded and set up a free video chat client called Live Chat Now! He used the same title for identification as he did for his email. Prepared, he clicked on the 'Reply' button and sent a message back to Dristan:

> *"No phone. Please download the Live Chat Now! video client. My profile name is: RweDecieved. I will wait for your call."*

After sending the email, Peter laid across the sofa and relaxed. He wasn't exactly sure how a conversation would go with Dristan Cavanaugh, but it was worth a shot. Best case scenario, he would provide some valuable information Peter could use. The worst case would result in Peter wasting time with a complete lunatic. Time would tell.

Chapter 9

Peter jumped a little when he heard a ringing sound from his computer. Realizing he had dozed off, he took a quick look around inside the RV and then sat up on the sofa to view his laptop. There was a green, vibrating phone icon on the screen which bounced to the ringing that had startled Peter from his nap. The identification tag of the caller read "Sheeple1947". Excited, Peter moved his mouse over the answer button and clicked. The bouncing phone icon disappeared and the Live Chat Now! window depicted two people in a voice conversation.

"Hello?" was the greeting from the computer. "Anyone there?"

Peter replied, "Yes, I'm here. Is this Dristan Cavanaugh?" Peter wanted to confirm he was speaking to the right person.

"It is," Dristan replied back. "You said you wanted to talk. I'm assuming you visited my website?"

"I did. You seem to be knowledgeable in some areas I'm interested in, so I'm hoping you can provide some more insight for my research, if that's ok?" Peter spoke back.

"Perhaps. You also said it wouldn't be a waste of my time, so I'm hoping you have information to share as well. What is your name?" Dristan inquired.

Peter thought for a second before responding. There was no way he was going to give this guy his real name. "You can call me John," he offered.

"Okay, John. So, what would you like to talk about today?" Dristan replied emphasizing the 'John' to let Peter know he knew it was a fake name.

"Well, no need to beat around the bush, I guess," Peter started. "Do you believe the fallen angels of Noah's time have been released from their seventy generations of imprisonment and are somehow influencing our world today?" It sounded like lunacy as Peter heard his voice ask the question. He was actually shaking his head as he asked the question.

"You definitely don't beat around the bush!" Dristan replied with a chuckle. "I've never had anyone ask me so bluntly before. As for my answer, the evidence would suggest so."

"What evidence do you have?" Peter quickly asked.

"Maybe evidence isn't the right word. However, one could put a finger on the things which would indicate such. To start with, there's ancient texts, including the Bible, which speak of these fallen angels. It's not just in Christian religion either! Most cultures and religions in the world today speak of giants and a great flood in their history. Take Greek mythology, for example, where you have titans roaming the earth. They were giants who were imprisoned in Tartarus, which happens to be the same name of the place where the biblical fallen angels were kept and mentioned in the book of Peter. The English Bible interprets it as hell but the original Greek reveals it is Tartarus. When they bred with human women, mighty men were created such as Hercules and Perseus which sound a lot like biblical nephilim. Sure, there are variances in names and events, but such is to be expected as the stories pass down from generation to generation over thousands of years," Dristan stated with earnest.

"I can see the coincidence," Peter replied. "But you're right, it's not evidence."

"Well, there's more than just historical similarities! How do you explain the great pyramids, Stonehenge, and all the ziggurats around the world? These pyramidal shaped structures are enormous and are found on almost every continent. They were constructed before man had the ability to sail around the world, so how do you explain the identically shaped structures around the world? The Mayan and Aztec cultures were centered around these structures. Iraq has a huge one in An Nasiriyah which is called the Ziggurat of Ur. They all seemed to have served as temples, usually dealt with human sacrifices and are astrologically aligned most of the time. Hieroglyphics on their walls depict giant-sized humans walking amongst the humans. Ever wonder who gave the Mayans the knowledge to create the Mayan calendar?" Dristan asked enthusiastically.

"I've actually seen the Ziggurat of Ur when I was deployed to Iraq," Peter responded. "That thing is enormous and it did serve as a temple where human sacrifices were offered."

"Their construction is amazing as well! Some of those stones couldn't have been moved so far of a distance by man. Even our largest crane couldn't move the stone in Baalbek, which is estimated to weigh over 1,650 tons which equates to over three million pounds! I'm just saying humans didn't have the strength to move such stones or knowledge to even construct them," Dristan added.

Peter could tell Dristan was knowledgeable and passionate about the topic. Already, the information he provided had Peter rethinking ancient history and how some of the oldest megalithic structures may have been built. *Has proof of giants and fallen angels been around this whole time and we, as humans of today's age, failed to realize it?* Peter realized he could discuss archaeological finds with Dristan all day but, in the end, there would be no definitive proof or information he needed. Rather, a lot of speculation!

Peter then asked, "Is there anything in today's world that points to fallen angel existence?"

"I think so!" Dristan quickly responded. "Where do you want to start? Hollywood, the government, secret societies, alien grays? There's more pointing to their existence today than anything archaeologists have discovered from the past."

"How about genetic alterations or modifications," Peter snuck in. "Any hybrid people walking around out there?" He couldn't help but think of Alfred Boyd!

Dristan took a moment and then replied, "The disciples in the Bible asked Jesus what the end times would be like. Matthew, chapter 24, states he told them it would be as in the days of Noah. Well, according to what we know, the days of Noah were filled with hybridization. Angels and humans mixing to create creatures God viewed as abominations. In the book of Enoch, it states the nephilim even defiled the animals and the Bible says all flesh had become corrupted. I guess when the book of Genesis stated Noah was perfect in his generations, they meant his lineage hadn't been polluted with cross breeding. These abominations were not created in God's image and were destroying the Earth, which is why I believe God flooded it. He wanted to get rid of all things not in his image. If it was just because of human sin, then why hasn't he already destroyed it again?"

"I never really looked at it that way," Peter replied.

"If the end times are going to be like the days of Noah, I'm thinking we are going to see those same things. We're already cloning animals and I'm pretty sure scientists have already experimented on humans. Ever heard of the Liger? Scientists have successfully crossed the DNA of a male lion and female tiger. The thing is enormous and they are not sure how large the thing can get as the crossing inhibits the growth regulator in their DNA. In all honesty, I believe the government, along with Hollywood, is preparing us for a hybrid race of people. For example, look at the exponential increase in movies and television series which depict mutants or superhumans as the heroes. Makes you want to be a mutant when you see what they can do, huh? Seriously, it's one superhuman after another on television! On top of that, who knows what substances people are taking into their own bodies. How many people do you know that are not on some type of medication? Flu shots, vaccines, steroids...the list goes on and on man! A lot of these vaccines come from cloned sheep and cows. To encourage people to take these vaccines, the government now restricts children from going to school if they don't have the mandatory shots, or they will not let people work in certain places unless they do the same. I don't know! Maybe I'm just paranoid, but I refuse to take all those vaccinations!"

Peter listened to everything Dristan was ranting about. Before all of this, Peter would have automatically labeled him as psychotic! Now, however, he wasn't so sure. The more he learned about fallen angels and conspiracies, the more he was able to put a finger on. If all these things were actually occurring, what would it mean? That was a question Peter wasn't ready to answer yet.

After some thought, Peter asked, "But humans have intelligence. Perhaps they have just discovered all of this on their own in efforts to enhance society. I don't see where fallen angels have secretly told humans to start creating such things...do you?"

"That's a good point," started Dristan. "But have you ever wondered why the sudden burst of knowledge and control after 1947? That's the year most things started getting weird in my opinion. Think about it! Our government started the National Security Act of 1947 which restructured our entire military and intelligence agencies. Secret bases were built and high-tech weapons created. The United Nations even! Where did they all of a sudden get this insight and knowledge? People often think Roswell was where a UFO crashed. I believe that what happened there has to do with what we are talking about. Ever heard of Aleister Crowley? He started the occult religion known as Thelema in the early 1900s and he was reportedly a Mason. Supposedly, he summoned a demon which dictated he write The Book of the Law. Crowley drew the image of this demon which looks identical to an alien grey, as we call them. We usually consider UFO abductees as crazy, but most of them tell the same story about how they were abducted and experimented on. Human egg fertilization and embryonic removal are the common themes in abduction cases. Anyways, Crowley influenced a lot of well-known Americans such as Jack Parsons who started the Jet Propulsion Laboratory and Ron Hubbard who started the Church of Scientology. Somehow, all of these things are woven together, and it would take years to figure it all out. I'm just saying I think this stuff is real! And don't even get me started on how all of our government buildings in D.C. resemble ancient Greek structures built for the gods or why NASA names most of our rockets and satellites after Greek gods. There's just too much out there for it to be a coincidence, in my humble opinion."

Peter was blown away! So much information, and he hadn't had time to process it all. If all these things Dristan was telling him were true, then society had a huge curtain pulled in front of them from seeing the truth.

"There's so much you have told me, and it's going to take time to think through all of it," Peter told Dristan.

Before Peter could end the conversation, Dristan quickly interjected, "You said this wouldn't be a waste of my time. What do you have for me?"

Peter sat quietly for a few seconds as he thought about what he would tell Dristan. After all, the man had taken his time to answer Peter's questions and had actually provided some valuable information. He had to be careful what he told Dristan, since he knew the guy would probably start searching the internet for information which could have the fake FBI knocking on his door. With all of Dristan's knowledge and information, they may not be as nice to him.

"I have to be very careful what I tell you, and I hope you understand. But I feel I do owe you something. Have you ever looked into the Gen6 corporation and its founder? I suggest you do that. Maybe we can talk again another time. Have a good day!" Peter responded before disconnecting from Live Chat Now! He knew the information he gave Dristan would just spark curiosity and a lot of questions, which is why he abruptly disconnected.

Immediately, he went into his computer settings and shut the Wi-Fi connection off. Although he didn't get any definitive proof of anything,

Dristan had provided so much information which somehow lined up with some of the thoughts that had been swirling in Peter's mind. Peter knew he was falling further down the rabbit hole. He was starting to see the world with new eyes. The problem was his uncertainty of whether to trust his eyes or not. *Do crazy people know they're crazy?*

The coffee had cooled down quite a bit before Peter remembered he had a cup. Taking a sip, he continued to relax on the sofa while contemplating the conversation he just had. He was confident no one, like the 'others', was listening. He had a new computer with new identification tags and false information. Furthermore, he had insisted on a voice over internet conversation since it wasn't easy to intercept like phone calls and typed messages. At that moment, Peter realized even though his computer wasn't being tracked, Dristan Cavanaugh's might be! If that were the case, outside agencies intercepting his computer communications could easily identify a computer he was conversing with. Peter's heart began to beat a little faster before he realized he was being too paranoid. Yes, it was possible Dristan's computer was being tracked, but the actual likelihood was slim. Peter decided not to worry about it anymore.

The information Peter gathered from the conversation seemed logical, aside from the fact it seemed crazy at the same time! Peter leaned up on the sofa and reconnected his computer to the Wi-Fi. Automatically, Live Chat Now! reconnected and, sure enough, he had already missed two calls on Live Chat Now! Both were from Dristan. Quickly, before another call could come through, Peter closed out the program but not before disabling the auto connect feature. Programs like this one were imposing, and it irritated Peter. Although they were useful, they shouldn't automatically think the user wants them running.

Opening up a web browser, Peter typed in the name Aleister Crowley and clicked 'Search'. After a cursory glance at the returns, he realized Dristan proved truthful. Crowley was involved in all sorts of occult activity and did have connections with affluent Americans. Next, he typed in the words "Baalbek stone" and searched. Once again, Dristan's description of this stone was accurate, which added to his credibility. Since his military days, Peter had come to rely on the "trust but verify" course of action.

Peter closed the web browser and shut the lid on his laptop. Leaning back on the sofa, he placed his hands behind his head and stared up at the ceiling. *Is there really a God out there?* That was the million-dollar question! Thoughts of mistakes, career choices, good deeds and other life impacting decisions began to flood Peter's mind. He quickly shut them down, though, since dwelling on such thoughts would lead nowhere. He was a man of data and facts, not feelings and opinions! He surmised he could admit there was a god, but only if he could prove it!

After a few hours and lunch, Peter stood outside the RV staring off in the southern sky. It was a nice day, full of sunshine. Feeling the slight cool breeze on his face, he contemplated his next course of action. Only one thing kept coming to mind. *Sam.* Was she still in the hospital? How was he going to contact her? When was he going to get the opportunity to meet her? There was uncertainty in all his answers, and Peter didn't like it! He felt like it had been forever since he had last conversed with her. He was having the same feeling he had felt days earlier when he was thinking about her. Was the current road he was on going to prevent a continuing relationship with her? That thought didn't sit well with him. Peter continued to think.

Peter wasn't exactly sure what he should do. After thinking about things, he realized he had garnered some enticing details which only served to tickle his curiosity even more. But to what extent? Would he be able to solve every riddle this conspiracy had to offer? How long would he chase the tail? Would he ever get a better chance to meet Sam? He had no concrete proof of anything he had discovered. Even if he did, what would he do with it? Was he even in danger from these 'others'? Peter didn't figure it was likely they were searching for him any longer. Perhaps he should try and continue on with his life.

It was around two o'clock when Peter climbed into his truck. The camper had been placed back into travel mode and he was ready to hit the road. Carefully, he pulled out of the parking spot and onto the road leading to I-40. A glance in the side view mirror showed the white, dome-shaped building at the Meteor Crater RV Park fading into the distance. Giving a left turn signal, Peter turned onto the on-ramp and accelerated to merge with the interstate traffic. With the time of day, the sun was almost straight overhead and wouldn't be a nuisance for him yet. He had decided to head back west. He knew his destination and somehow knew it was overdue. After setting the cruise control on his truck and taking a sip of coffee, Peter spoke the words which provided a sense of comfort. "Sam... here I come!"

Chapter 10

Flagstaff was about thirty minutes behind Peter now as he headed north on US Highway 89. The cruise control was set, and the driver's side window was about halfway down as the miles flew by. A few larger hills in the distance made up the western horizon, but the rest of the view was mostly flat, desert landscape dotted with sparse vegetation. Every once in a while, Peter noticed how large, lattice towers used to connect power lines were equally spaced in a straight line and spanned the entire landscape. There wasn't much to look at on this drive, but that was fine. Peter's thoughts had him occupied thinking about where he was heading, why he was heading there, and if the decision to do so was wise.

Since leaving Meteor Crater RV Park, Peter had used the time to contemplate his actions. The first real concern was whether or not he felt the entities involved with Project UGEN posed a danger to him or anyone he had contact with, like Sam. They had retrieved the classified document from him which was the only real evidence he had of the existence of Project UGEN. Were they even interested in Peter anymore? Even if Peter went to the press and told his story, society would label him as 'crazy' or a 'conspiracy nut' without any evidence. At that thought, Peter started to shake his head as he realized social engineering had been at work. Society had been programmed to automatically dismiss conspiracy theories. No one bothered to investigate them either because doing so would indicate they were crazy. As he thought about some of the better-known conspiracies in recent times, he realized how effective social engineering was. He thought about the Kennedy assassination and the World Trade Center bombing. When the word 'conspiracy' was added to them, almost everyone dismissed any evidence which was contrary to the story mainstream media had put out. Peter admitted it was a genius tactic as it could work in any situation where the real truth tried to come out. He imagined a group of scientists going public to tell the American people there was a cure for cancer, but the government didn't want them to have it. All it would take to shut them down would be for the media to label it as a conspiracy! No one would touch those scientists or listen to them because doing so would mean they were crazy as well. Peter couldn't help but wonder how many truths had been revealed to the world only to be dismissed because they were labeled as a conspiracy. Through these thoughts, Peter figured he wasn't much of a threat to those involved in Project UGEN, which ultimately meant they weren't a threat to him either.

The next thought which concerned Peter was how to approach Sam. As far as she knew, he was in Red Rock hiking the trails. Furthermore, there had been no correspondence to arrange a meeting. Sure, they had both expressed interest in meeting one another, but that was the extent of the existing relationship. Should he walk right up to her in the hospital, if she was still there, and introduce himself? What reason would he give her for the unannounced visit? *Hi! I'm Peter and I think I may have feelings for you on a personal level!* Better yet, another introduction entered his mind. *Hi! Wish I could have emailed you but some people have been tracking me and I didn't feel it was safe to contact you over the internet!* Regardless of the numerous ideas he had, Peter couldn't find a valid one he felt wouldn't surprise her in a negative way. He realized he felt a need to meet her, but needed to make sure she was ready to meet him as well. Besides, would he want to meet anyone if he was in her condition, laid up in a hospital room? At the end of his contemplations, he decided he would continue on towards St. George, Utah. However, he wasn't going to make contact with her until she agreed to it. Coming to that conclusion allowed Peter to relax a little and breathe easier. *You only get one chance to make a first impression.*

Sam had told Peter she lived in St. George, Utah. Peter had figured she was in a hospital there, since she had asked the doctors to let her rest at her house just a few blocks away. It wouldn't have been hard to find her. All he had to do was walk into the hospital and announce he was there to see Sam who was being treated for Leukemia. The city wasn't very large, which meant there would be a limited number of medical centers which could help with that specific cancer. Peter was confident he could have found her.

The miles rolled by as Peter continued towards St. George, which was only about two hours away at this point. He was now heading west along US Highway 89A and the sun was staring him right in the eyes. The landscape had started to change ever since he started heading west, giving way to a rusty, orange hue with large plateaus and a few mesas. A sign on the side of the road let Peter know he was coming up on the town of Fredonia. This would be a great time to stop for a meal, stretch his legs, and fill up the gas tank. A few minutes later, he noticed a Chevron station on the right and pulled in.

There were only two pumping stations as Peter pulled beneath the overhang. He knew his truck and RV would take up all the space on the right side of the pumps, but this was a small town where gas stations weren't busy and the people were usually nicer. In the larger cities, people would often blow their horns or yell expletives at him when he took up all the space near the pumps. Peter liked small towns.

While filling his truck with gas, he took a walk around it and the RV to check for damage or other maintenance needs, but didn't notice any. About the time he completed his walk around, a young man, of about thirty years, exited a building off to the north and began walking towards Peter. The man was wearing jeans with a red t-shirt that had a Superman emblem across the front. His dirty blonde hair hung to about his shoulders and hadn't been combed. The bottom half of his shirt was trying to hide the beer belly, but failed, as Peter could see some belly hanging over the top of his jeans.

"That's a nice setup you got there, Sir!" was the greeting the beer-bellied man shot towards Peter. "Need any servicing? I got a garage just behind the store."

Peter smiled as he replied, "No thanks! Everything seems to be in good working order." *My responses always sound so military!* When the man didn't walk away, Peter knew the guy was probably bored and wanted to start a conversation. Peter looked back towards the pump and grasped the nozzle.

The tactic didn't work as the beer-bellied man continued, "Where are you heading?"

"North. Probably going to stop in St. George if they have an RV campground," Peter reluctantly replied.

"We have a place to park your RV here in Fredonia!" offered the beer-bellied man. "It's just around the curve there on the right. Only costs 'bout thirty bucks for the night too!"

The nozzle clicked and Peter removed it from his gas tank and hung it back on the pump before turning to face the guy again. After a few thoughts, Peter asked "Is there a library in Fredonia?"

"Sure is," was the quick response from the beer-bellied guy. "It's just down the road a bit, too!"

"I appreciate the information. Maybe I will spend the night here in Fredonia," Peter concluded as he gave a slight nod and smile to the man before walking inside the station to pay cash for the fuel. Exiting the store, Peter noticed the beer-bellied man lingering around. Ignoring him, Peter walked directly to his truck.

As Peter pulled out from the gas station and headed through the small town, he surmised spending the night here wouldn't be a bad idea. It would cost less and was smaller than St. George. As long as the public library offered internet, he didn't see any reason not to stay the night. Not too far through the town, Peter noticed the word 'library' attached to the side of a tan, single-story structure with a clay tile roof. A single flag pole with a raised American flag was in the front. After looking around a bit for a place to park, Peter decided to park along the street near the curb.

Once inside, Peter noticed there were a couple of computers along the back wall. The collection of library books wasn't impressive, but what could anyone expect in a small town? As he looked around, he realized there was no one in the building. With a quizzical look, Peter slowly walked around the room in an attempt to find someone.

"Hello?" broke the silence as Peter sounded his presence. No response. Looking back through the glass entrance doors, he noticed a lady walking fast across the street headed in his direction. Her hair was black and curly and she wore blue rimmed glasses. Although a little hefty, she trotted across the street giving a quick glance left and then right. Sure enough, she entered the library and Peter could already see a little perspiration forming on her forehead. She was neat looking, wearing a pair of black slacks and a buttoned up, blue shirt with white flowers all over it.

"Well, hey there!" she greeted Peter as she walked by him and around the other side of the counter. "Sorry it took me so long to get here, but I was looking at the new trinkets Martha got in over at the gift shop across the street."

Peter's smile was genuine. Already, he could tell this lady was nice and probably laughed a lot. "No problem at all. Did Martha have anything you liked?" Peter asked nicely.

"Nothing yet, but I'm not finished looking," she laughed back. "Anything I can help you with?"

"I would like to use your computer, if you don't mind. How much does it cost?" Peter asked.

"It's free! Mr. Cartrette was kind enough to petition the state for a grant. I'm sure it took some finagling…" she continued on, but Peter tuned her out. Rather, he started thinking about what to type in the email to Sam, until he realized the lady had stopped talking.

"That's nice!" Peter responded knowing those two words would be a great response to anything she had been talking about. As he started to head to one of the computers, the lady started following him. *Please don't follow me!* Once again, Peter saw a coming conversation which he really didn't care to entertain. Even though the lady was nice and the computer was free to use, he dreaded chit chat conversations about absolutely nothing important. He quickly thought of a tactic to get her away without offending her.

"Just got to check my personal bank accounts and stuff, and then I'll be off," he expressed to the lady.

"Do you bank around here?" she asked with a smile. She was definitely wanting a conversation.

What in Hades does that have to do with anything? How, in any way, shape, or form will that information be of any assistance to you? "I don't," Peter said to the woman as he raised both his eyebrows high and smiled big through closed teeth. He knew his body language was communicating to her his sarcastic thoughts. *Is that it? Will there be anything else?*

"I still use my bank back in Denver. I'm originally from Denver..." she continued as Peter realized that, unless he wanted to seriously offend this lady, he was going to have to give her some time to talk about nonsense. Peter knew he wouldn't have to partake much in the conversation as the woman didn't stop talking. Inside, Peter was on fire!

Fifteen minutes later, Peter finally got the opportunity to log onto his email account. Although he felt drained after hearing the librarian go on and on about nothing, he was excited once again. He paused as his hands touched the keyboard. If he logged on to his account, his location would be known. His previous email sent from the Flagstaff library was meant to mislead any would-be viewers. Logging on to this computer with his email would foil the misdirection. Peter removed his hands from the keyboard. Leaning back in the chair, he wasn't sure what to do. He didn't know what the next course of action would be to find out more about Project UGEN. If he didn't continue on to see Sam, then he had no destination planned. The one thing Peter knew for sure was that he wanted to see Sam. He had to take a chance.

As his email opened, he didn't see an email from Sam. It had only been a couple of days, though, since he last wrote her back in Flagstaff. Peter slid the mouse over the create button and clicked. Taking a minute to memorize her email just in case he might need it later, he manually typed it into the 'To' line and began to compose:

"Hey Sunshine! How's it going? I hope you are out of the hospital and resting comfortably on your own bed. I was heading to Red Rock but just couldn't stop thinking about you and how we almost met. As a result, I didn't go to Red Rock. Rather, I turned around and stayed in Arizona. I propose, if you are okay with it and feel like it, that you let me drive to St. George so we can have dinner together or something. If not, I understand and it's okay. We can try again at a later time.

If you agree, I can be in St. George tomorrow (Tuesday). If that is okay with you, let me know a place and time to meet you. Again, if you don't feel up to it, I understand. I look forward to hearing from you soon. PK"

After reading what he had typed, he clicked the send button. Something inside him was relaxing. If he liked communicating with Sam this much over email, he couldn't imagine what a face-to-face talk would be like.

On another thought, Peter knew he had just logged into his old email account. For the first time since Flagstaff, someone could now pinpoint his location based on his account and the computer's IP address. Peter rested, however, on his belief he was no longer of interest to the 'others' since they had stolen the only evidence he had. Without evidence of Project UGEN's existence, he was just another crazy, conspiracy theorist!

"I'll be right back! I'm just going to head over to Martha's to finish looking at her stuff," the lady shot Peter's way and she departed through the front entrance. *Small towns are great!* In no hurry, Peter opened up a new internet browser and began searching for RV parks in St. George. There were several to choose from. As he clicked on the links to ascertain prices and commodities of each park, he heard the familiar sound indicating a new email had arrived. Moving his mouse over a tab, he clicked to bring up the browser he had opened with his email. Sure enough, there it was! Sam had already responded and Peter's heart began to race. In a matter of seconds, he was reading what she had sent:

"Hey Mister PK! I was just checking my mail when yours popped up! I have to admit I was a little surprised when I read it. Surprised in a good way! Honestly, I have been eager to meet you as well, but figured you would propose a meeting on your own time. I would hate to be a nuisance to anyone, you know?

I've been at home for about an hour now. The doctors say I'm doing fine, now, and there's no reason I should stay in the hospital. Frrreeeedddoooommmmmm!!!!! Yes, I'm happy to be out! Even more, I would love to see you tomorrow. I'm already starting to think of what to wear and all, but I'm sure you don't want to hear about all that girly kinda stuff. I'm not planning to work for the rest of the week, so I need something to occupy my time. Maybe we'll have time for me to show you around the great city of St. George!

Anyways, meet me at Cliffside Restaurant at 1pm. It's easy to find! Just find Airport Rd on the west side of St. George and head south. It's across from the airport...you can't miss it! I'll be sure to get there a little early so you can find me. I'll be wearing a dark green, long sleeve shirt with a single black line running down each arm from the shoulder to the end. Don't forget I have blonde hair too! Look forward to seeing you. Sam"

There were bubbles inside of Peter. Bubbles wasn't exactly a word in Peter's vocabulary, but there were no other words to describe the feeling. His smile extended from ear to ear as he stood up with elation. He almost jumped, but contained himself. After a few paces back and forth to get some of his energy out, Peter sat back down and replied:

"Hey Sunshine! I'll be there and look forward to it! PK"

It was a short reply, but he refused to show his giddiness. Before he logged off the computer, he brought up a map of St. George and found the airport. From there, he easily located the restaurant and then determined the best directions to get him there.

Peter wasn't sure if he should wait for the librarian or not, but decided to go ahead and leave. Just before entering his truck, he heard a shout from across the road.

"Come back anytime!" she cried while waving at him.

In a slight yell, Peter gave her a big "thanks!" before closing his door and starting the truck. For the moment, he was on top of the world and no one, nor thought of his own, was going to steal his joy!

Peter found a good place to turn around and then headed back through town looking for the RV park the beer-bellied man had told him about. It was evening now, and he was ready to set up for the night, enjoy a quick meal in the RV, and take a shower. Afterwards, he would choose something to wear for when he met Sam the next day. Several thoughts entered Peter's mind that didn't have anything to do with meeting Sam, but he dismissed them quickly. He was going to enjoy this time and set worry aside. Peter was clinging on to this moment with everything he had.

Chapter 11

Peter had spent most of the morning relaxing with a cup of coffee before putting his RV back in travel mode. He had been thinking of Sam all morning and was happy to be focused on something else besides everything that had happened over the past few days. Peter knew his life was changing in ways he didn't understand yet. Sure, he had become set in his ways travelling around the country and living the solo life, but lately, he had allowed outside influences to affect his life and his decisions. He had become more instinctive, changing his mind from one day to the next. The more he allowed the change to happen, the less stressed he felt. Although his conscience would tell him to plan and prepare, his actions were based more off of emotions rather than logic. In all honesty, he was a little afraid of the change. Peter felt meeting Sam would help bring more stability to his life. If things between them went well, then he would have something, or someone, to focus on. If the two of them didn't hit it off, well, he could always go back to travelling and the solo life.

It took less than two hours for Peter to make the drive to St. George. Once he drove through the city to the west side, he found a large parking lot near a shopping plaza and stopped. It only took him a couple of minutes to wash his face, brush his teeth and double check his hair in the RV. Satisfied, he jumped back into his truck and headed for the Cliffside restaurant.

Driving south along Airport Road, the view was incredible. He was driving near the eastern edge of an elevated plateau which provided an excellent view over St. George. The usual rusty, brown hues painted the distant mesas and plateaus while the green trees painted the St. George valley. Sam had been wise in her selection for a meeting place. Up ahead, and off to the right, Peter noticed a fence line which surrounded the airport. Across the road from the airport, there was a two-story building which seemed to be some type of lodging. Beyond that, Cliffside restaurant sat on the edge of the plateau. He had arrived and was excited knowing Sam was in the restaurant!

Peter parked along the far side of the parking lot to make sure his truck and RV didn't get in the way of other vehicles. Stepping out of the truck, he took a minute to make sure his red, button-up shirt was tucked neatly into his blue jeans. He had rolled the long sleeves up a little, about midway between his elbow and wrist. Although he had worn his brown, leather hiking boots, they went well with the jeans and shirt. Plus, they matched the brown, leather belt he was wearing. He felt physically comfortable but couldn't say the same about his mental state, as his nerves were jumping around everywhere! Peter headed for the restaurant.

The number of vehicles in the parking lot let Peter know this place was pretty popular. Furthermore, he could ascertain the food inside was going to cost a pretty penny by the make and model of expensive cars present. As he arrived at the entrance door, he took a deep breath of outside air, and then entered.

The inside of the restaurant was nice. The walls were white, the wood floor was polished, and the entire east side wall had floor-to-ceiling windows which provided a spectacular view of St. George. A nice fully stocked bar was situated along one of the walls and several green plants were strategically placed throughout the place. This was definitely the right choice to meet someone!

Peter scanned over the restaurant slowly looking for blonde hair and a green shirt. And there she was! Across the restaurant and sitting at a round table-for-two near the large windows, was Sam. She was staring directly at him. A big smile covered her face as she motioned with her left arm for Peter to come join her. Returning a genuine smile, he walked over as she stood up to greet him. Neither one of them spoke as they embraced in a quick hug before sitting down at the table. Both still had smiles they couldn't control.

"You are Peter, right?" Sam asked laughingly. Her blonde hair was naturally curly and extended just below her shoulders. A couple curly sprigs fell down in front of her eyes as she laughed. She casually brushed them back with her hands.

"Yes! Yes, I'm Peter!" he answered. "Did the haircut and tucked in shirt give me away?"

"See! I told you before you were funny. It's so nice to finally meet you!" she said.

"Likewise!" Peter replied.

Peter remembered thinking about what Sam looked like when he was on the mountain at Mule Peak observatory. Even his best imaginations of her didn't come close to portray just how beautiful she was. Her hair accentuated the beauty of her light-colored eyes, which had captivated his attention. There was no number to rate her beauty on the man scale.

"Did I pick the right place?" she asked.

"Oh, yes! This place is amazing and the view!" he answered while nodding his head.

Sam smiled even more when she realized Peter's eyes never left hers when he responded. "You're more handsome than I imagined," Sam stated honestly.

Peter raised his eyebrows as if in surprise. He could tell he was blushing. *I feel like a high schooler!* He really didn't know how to respond to that statement, but managed to let out "thanks" in return.

Sam continued to smile and seemed to enjoy Peter's innocence. She had learned quite a bit about him through their correspondence and knew he was more of a logical thinking type of guy who shied away from more personal emotions.

"Are you hungry?" she asked Peter, deciding to transition from flattering statements to allow for more logical responses. It was important for her to make him feel comfortable. She sat down at the table and motioned for Peter to sit also.

"Yes. What's good here?" he asked as he sat and reached for the menu a waiter had placed on the table sometime during their conversation.

"Oh, my goodness! You've got to try the butternut squash soup. It's absolutely amazing!" she offered. "If you are wanting to try something a little heartier, then I would suggest the farm burger. A lot of people love that one."

"You seemed more emphatic talking about the butternut squash soup, so I'll go with that and, if I'm still hungry, I'll try the burger," he replied while still smiling. *Why will this smile not go away?*

"Awesome! Think I'll have the soup and salad combo today," she stated as she motioned for the waiter. "Do you want water with that?"

Peter nodded in agreement. As he watched Sam order their meal, he realized she was very confident. Moreover, there was a glow about her. Even though she had a terminal illness, he could tell she was filled with joy and not just because she was meeting him for the first time. No, Sam had something genuine! Her love for life was sincere. After ordering, she turned to look back at Peter.

"So, what do you do for a living?" Peter asked.

"I own a bicycle shop, believe it or not. I've always enjoyed the outdoors and take fitness seriously. I figured why not do something I enjoy while helping others as well."

"I can see that," Peter stated. "Owning your own business is admirable and beats sitting in an office somewhere working for someone else."

"It pays the bills and allows me to meet new people. Plus, biking is pretty popular in this part of the country with all the trails around," she said. She then continued with a smile, "My turn! Do you have a permanent residence or do you truly live in an RV? I've been dying to ask you that!"

Peter chuckled before responding, "I live in an RV. Why pay for maintenance and taxes on a home I don't live in? Maybe there's a house for me in the future when I'm done travelling and seeing the world."

With a quizzical look, Sam then asked, "Then how do you get your mail? Where does Amazon ship to? Can you have a credit card without a permanent address?"

After a slight nod indicating he understood the questions, he responded, "What mail? I don't have the usual bills like utility, telephone and cable. If anyone ever needs to send me a letter, they can use email. I don't order things online, as I'm one that prefers to handle something before I buy it. As for a credit card, I got one back when I was in the military and rented a house. I still use that same address on it. I rarely use the thing anyways."

"I find that interesting," she said. "I admire your way of life, to be honest with you. I think you're brave to carve your own path through this life. Okay, your turn!"

"Think you could ever live like I do? Travelling around and all?" he asked.

"I wish!" she replied quickly. "Unlike you, I don't have a military pension to support such a life. Maybe one day though, who knows?"

Peter noticed her change in demeanor. The smile had given way to a more weighted look and Peter then realized her leukemia probably limited her time away from a medical center which could provide the care she needed. Undoubtedly, her life was tethered to medical care and would be like that for the rest of her life. He felt a lump of sadness somewhere in his chest.

"Well, living like this isn't always a bed of roses. Sure, I get to see a lot of things and all, but, there are consequences too. For example, you're the only friend I have," he admitted.

Somehow, Sam knew Peter was telling the truth. Moreover, she knew that was probably a choice on his part and couldn't be blamed on travelling. However, she didn't see the need to point that out to him since he already knew the truth of it himself.

"My turn. Have any family?" she asked.

"No... not really. I'm sure there's probably a great uncle out there or something, but I don't know any of them. Neither of my parents had brothers or sisters and I'm an only child," he answered. He then stated with a smile, "At least I get to save money by not having to buy Christmas and birthday presents."

Sam chuckled as she nodded. Her eyes then popped open wide and Peter could see a fresh thought had entered her mind.

"Oh, my goodness, I almost totally forgot! You've got to tell me about meeting Alfred Boyd!" she said with excitement. "How did you find him?"

Peter froze! For the first time in a while, his mind went blank. He had been trying so hard not to think about Boyd and Project UGEN since he planned to meet Sam, but now it was the topic up for discussion. Peter realized his smile faded into one of seriousness.

"Uh..." was what Peter managed to get out. "Well..." he tried to continue. *Can I please press the pause button?*

"Oh, come on and spill the beans!" she pleaded. "I've anticipated hearing this story for a while now. I'm not going to run out and broadcast what you tell me to the world!"

"He's a strange fellow, for sure," was Peter's response in a quieter voice. "I'm not sure we should talk about this."

"You shouldn't!" came the words from a man that stood up from the table behind Sam. Within two steps, he was standing beside their table with a phone in his hand which he extended towards Peter. "It's for you."

Sam's eyes were wide open as she looked from Peter, to the man, and then back to Peter. *What the heck?* It only took Peter a second to realize who the man was. It was Tony! *Not now!* Peter stared up at him in amazement and unbelief. He had been so fixated on Sam since entering the restaurant, he hadn't even noticed anyone else.

"Take it!" Tony said more forcibly.

Slowly, Peter took the phone from Tony and brought it to his ear.

"What's going on?" Sam asked in a soft voice. Her face showed concern.

"Hello?" Peter whispered into the phone.

"Mr. Knowles! Nice to speak with you again. Listen carefully as we don't have much time. I'm sorry to interrupt your lunch and all, but there are a few guests among you who don't have your best interests in mind. You have to trust me on this. I need you and Miss Fisher to get up right now and go with Tony. He knows what to do."

Peter knew the voice! It was Alfred Boyd. If it hadn't been for his military experiences dealing with stressful situations while deployed in combat zones, he imagined he would probably have fainted. He looked over to Sam with a serious face, who was obviously surprised by what was happening. What was he going to say to her? Although he wasn't completely sure what he thought of Alfred Boyd, something inside of him told him to listen.

"Is your last name Fisher?" he asked her.

"Yes!" she replied with a questioning stare.

"Listen," Peter whispered to her in a low voice. "I need you to trust me. This is Tony, and we are going to go with him. I'll explain everything once we get outside." He then slid his chair back and stood up.

"I don't know about this!" Sam exclaimed as she continued to sit. "What's going on, Peter?"

All of a sudden, one of Tony's arms slung around and slammed Peter hard enough to make him fall over the chair he had been sitting in and against the wall. Peter looked back at Tony in shock just in time to see Tony holding an extended pistol! Bang! A loud explosion erupted from the gun! A man standing on the other side of the room took the bullet straight in the face as the blood splattered against the wall behind him. Another casual looking man, standing beside the man who had been shot, quickly pulled out a pistol from beneath his jacket and started to aim it in Tony's direction. Bang! Another shot rang out from Tony's gun and impacted the other guy directly in the forehead.

Screams of terror erupted all around the restaurant with the patrons falling down to the floor and trying to find cover. Sam was in shock and couldn't move. A look of pure horror covered her face as she just sat there.

"We have to go now!" Tony exclaimed to both of them. He reached out, grabbed Sam by the arm, and forced her up. "Let's go!"

Tony forcibly led Sam towards the door as Peter frantically stood up and followed. Two dead bodies were on the floor and the other people were all scrambling. Peter faintly heard someone yell to call 9-1-1. The ringing in Peter's ears, from the gunshots, made it hard for him to concentrate as he pressed forward after Tony and Sam.

The bright sunlight almost blinded Peter as he exited the building behind the two. *This can't be happening!* He stopped and confusedly looked around as if expecting to wake up at any time.

"Get in the car now!" Tony yelled at him while shoving Sam into the backseat of a black sedan. "More will be coming!"

Peter ran over to the passenger side of the car and entered the front seat. Jumping in the driver's side, Tony slammed the door, started the car, and sped off!

"Sam! Are you okay?" Peter asked frantically while turning around to look at her. There was no reply.

"She's in shock," Tony responded after he quickly glanced back at her.

"Where are you taking us?" Peter demanded from Tony. He looked Tony directly in the eyes.

"Away from here, for now!" was the answer. "I need you to just stay calm."

"Stay calm! Are you kidding me?" Peter asked in surprise.

Tony gave Peter a quick glance but then put his eyes back on the road. He seemed calm. Sam had leaned her head over and had it leaning on the window through which she was blankly staring out. Peter's heart was still racing as he tried to get control over his emotions. Experience and training had taught him poor decisions were usually made when emotions were high. He reached back to her, after he took a few deep breaths, and pushed Sam's hair back to get a good look of her face. He needed to check to make sure she was okay.

"We need to pull over and check on her," Peter said sternly to Tony.

"We will," Tony answered. "Just give me a few more minutes to get us to a safe place."

Peter gave a slight nod and continued to look back at Sam. He was mad at himself! *She hasn't done anything to deserve this!* This was definitely not the way he wanted this day to go. His selfishness, in that he rushed their meeting, had gotten her into this predicament. Right now, she could have been at home resting and recuperating instead of being involved in a shootout and having her life in jeopardy. *What have I done?*

A few minutes later, Tony pulled off of Interstate 15. He then pulled into the parking lot of an old motel which obviously hadn't been in service for a while. No other cars or people were in the immediate vicinity. As soon as the car stopped, Peter jumped out and carefully opened Sam's door. At the realization, her eyes opened wide as if in terror and started flailing her arms at Peter! He did his best to try and calm her.

"Sam! Sam! It's me...Peter!" he intently spoke to her trying to focus her attention on him. He knew many people who had experienced shock had similar reactions when coming out of it. "It's okay!"

The tears started bursting from her eyes as she finally focused on him. She stopped flailing her arms and slumped back against the car seat as if in defeat. The crying and tears tore at Peter and he knew he had caused it.

"Look, I know you don't know what is going on. Heck, I don't even know for sure," he calmly stated to her. "I do know it's my fault and I'm so sorry." His expression was one of deep sorrow.

Tony exited the vehicle and walked over to where Peter was kneeling down between the car and Sam's door. He extended a half bottle of water to him and said, "She needs to drink this."

Looking back, Peter grabbed the bottle of water and unscrewed the lid before holding it out for Sam. He could tell she was trying to figure out everything which had happened from the way her eyes were jerking around.

"Drink this," he said to her while grabbing her hand and placing the plastic bottle into it. "Please! Take a few sips of water while I tell you what is going on. It'll help."

Sam focused her eyes on Peter. Her crying had stopped, but the trail of tears glistened brightly along her cheeks.

"Peter?" she finally managed to get out.

"Yes! It's me, Peter. Please, drink some water. Everything is okay now," he replied as he once again pushed back her curly, blonde hair so it would hold behind her ears.

"She's okay. We need to go," Tony stated plainly as he walked back to enter the car.

Peter looked directly into Sam's eyes before saying, "Listen. We are safe now, but we can't stay here. I'll explain all I can on the ride." Standing up, he waited for Sam to position herself before he shut her door. Walking around to the other side, he too got in the back seat beside her. Tony put the car in drive and pulled back onto I-15 heading south.

"You shot those guys," Sam stated as she looked up at Tony. He didn't reply or acknowledge the fact, but just kept his eyes on the road.

"Can you please just take me back to my vehicle," she asked as she peered blankly through her window. She was doing her best to stay calm, but Peter could tell she was barely holding it together.

"Before all this happened, you asked me about Alfred Boyd," Peter spoke to her. Just from the tilt of her head, he could tell she was probably wondering what that had to do with anything. "Well, all of this has to do with him and, even more so, it has to do with something I found on top of Mule Peak."

Through his peripheral vision, he could tell Tony gave him a long, hard glance through the rear-view mirror. Although he had always wanted to tell her about what he found on Mule Peak along with his endeavors, he had always chosen not to tell her for fear of getting her involved. But now, she was involved, and he saw no reason not to tell her everything. Now that he had decided to tell her everything, the next question was whether or not she was going to believe any of it.

"Peter," she started and then paused about what she was going to say next. "I don't know anything about what is going on. What I do know is that we have corresponded for a while now and I looked forward to meeting you. In the restaurant, you were exactly the person I thought you would be. Now, all of this is happening, and to be honest, I don't know what to think about you." She looked at him with a confused look while slightly shaking her head. "I also know that I have been kidnapped by two men and have no idea where I'm going!" she yelled.

"You're right!" Peter said to her solemnly as he looked over at her. "Believe me, I never imagined this was going to happen. As far as our meeting, you were more than I thought you would be, and I have always thought very highly of you. Enough so to drive all this way just to get the chance to meet you." After a brief pause for thought, he continued, "Let me tell you everything, and I mean everything! Then, if you want to go back to your car or house, I will make sure it happens."

Sam began to contemplate his offer. Did she even have a choice? After considering her current predicament and seeing that Peter was trying to be sincere, she gave a slight nod and added, "Alright, Peter. I'm listening."

Peter knew Tony was going to hear everything. However, if Boyd had wanted to harm Peter, he probably would have done so by now. The fact Boyd had sent Tony to protect him from the others said a lot too! As powerful and elusive as Boyd seemed, Peter didn't feel any threats from him. As a result, he looked at Sam, took a deep breath and started.

"Tony works for Alfred Boyd. He was with Boyd when I first met them up in the Sacramento Mountains. Do you remember the email I sent telling you about the meeting?" he asked with a raised eyebrow.

"Yes. But you said you thought it was him, but you couldn't be sure," she replied, raising an eyebrow back to Peter.

"Right! But then something else happened. When I went to meet you at Meteor Crater, I spent the night there in the RV park. The next morning, and since you were unable to meet me, I planned to head on to Red Rock. However, Boyd and Tony were outside of my RV. Tony, being the nice guy he is…" Peter paused to throw a slight smirk towards Tony in the front seat, who paid him no attention. "Well, let's just say he insisted I get in the sedan and have a little chat with Boyd."

Peter took a brief pause and saw Sam was listening as she promised, so he continued. "Come to find out, he had hacked my email account and knew I had told you about him. I was furious, but then he told me he had also tracked me to Meteor Crater using my truck's GPS, which made me even more furious!"

"You never told me that," Sam interjected.

"I didn't, but it's because of what I found out," he continued. "Boyd was upset I had told you about him. But that wasn't the only reason he had tracked me down. He started telling me about these 'other people' that were after him. I expressed to him none of that concerned me, but he then said they could be a threat to me as well."

Sam noticed how Peter made quotation signs with his fingers when he had mentioned 'other people' which made her ask, "Who are these 'other people'?" while also making quotation signs with her fingers.

Peter thought for a second while looking around blankly. He then refocused his attention to Sam, "I found a top-secret document at that place I explored on Mule Peak. For obvious reasons, I chose not to tell you about it. Anyway, it seems the people that were stationed there back in 1947 were conducting classified tests on secret aircraft I've never even heard of. It also mentioned a Dr. Boyd and that he was performing great after some type of injection. Having a name and location, I chose to research it at the Alamogordo library which is where I found that old black and white photo."

Again, Sam interjected with the question, "Why am I getting a weird feeling you are about to tell me something straight from the looney farm?"

Peter told Sam everything. He told her about how Boyd always alluded to the Bible and talked of fallen angels. Boyd's age, Peter's discussion with the priest about the book of Genesis, and his research into the book of Enoch also was explained. He told her about his conversation with Dristan Cavanaugh after he had bought a new computer and had the GPS removed from his truck to keep people from tracking him. He told her about the visit from the fake FBI agents who had stolen the top-secret document. He told her everything, even about Project UGEN, up to the point he had met her at the restaurant.

The time and miles flew by as Sam listened intently to Peter as he explained everything. She didn't know what to make of his story. How could she? The one thing she did know was how serious Peter was about it. She didn't know whether to laugh or take it seriously. Once Peter finished, she could tell he felt a weight off of his shoulders by the way he settled in the seat.

"Peter," she said as she looked at him. "I'm a Christian and have been for a good while now. I've never heard about these fallen angels." She couldn't think of anything else to say.

"Neither had I," he responded. He had done everything he could at this point to try to explain it all to Sam. He knew she was either going to trust him or think he had completely lost his mind. "I'm not a Christian, but I grew up in church. I would have remembered a story about angels breeding with human women."

"Is that Vegas?" Sam asked surprisingly as she leaned up to get a better look through the windshield.

The miles had rolled by as Peter was telling Sam his story. Neither one of them had paid attention to the road.

Peter leaned up too. "It sure is," he said in a concerned voice. "Tony, where are you taking us? Don't you think it's about time you tell us?"

"Mt. Charleston," was the simple reply from Tony as he continued to focus on the road.

"Is that where Boyd is?" Peter asked.

After a few moments anticipating Tony's response, which never came, Sam asked, "Isn't Mt. Charleston a ski resort area in those mountains over there?" while pointing through the windshield at the distant, snowcapped mountains across from Las Vegas.

Peter leaned back in his seat after he, too, realized Tony wasn't going to answer his last question. He turned to Sam to answer her question, "It is. I used to live here when I was in the military. Mt. Charleston is a small town near the top and has a ski resort. As hot as Vegas gets, there's usually snow up there most of the year."

Both Sam and Peter settled in the back seat as Tony circumvented Vegas on the north side. He continued on and eventually headed north along US Highway 95 through the desert away from Vegas. Peter realized they were on the last leg of their trip when Tony took a left off the highway and headed up Lee Canyon Road.

"Not bad for a first date, huh?" he jokingly asked as he looked over at Sam. He needed to lighten the mood.

She looked back at him with a look indicating he had lost his mind. Looking back forward, she answered, "Sure. You sure know how to win a girl's heart!" as sarcastically as she could manage.

Peter noticed her eyes rolled as she answered. *At least she didn't ask us to take her back!* Peter closed his eyes and relaxed the final few miles. *Boyd had better be here!*

Chapter 12

They had entered the town of Mt. Charleston, and the views were spectacular. The landscape of the mountains was significantly different from what they had been driving through in the Mojave Desert. In the flat of the desert and surrounding the Las Vegas area, prickly gray limbed bushes with green tips dotted the desert landscape with an occasional Joshua tree sticking up in the midst. As the three of them ascended up to Mt. Charleston, the number of Joshua trees increased significantly but then started to fade away as they climbed giving way to bristlecone and ponderosa pines, quaking aspens and even some cedar trees. The land itself was still mostly rocks and stones, but the increased amount of rainfall the mountains received allowed for the support of these larger trees. The town of Mt. Charleston was nestled in a valley surrounded by a huge forest and massive mountains all around. Many of the homes, nestled in crevices and along winding roads up the mountains, served as getaway houses for the rich. Peter wouldn't be surprised if Alfred Boyd had a home here.

"At least it is beautiful up here. A lot of my friends travel here to ski. I've always wanted to visit here, but this is my first time. Good thing I wasn't expecting to work for the rest of the week," Sam said nonchalantly.

Neither Sam nor Peter had spoken much since heading up the mountain. Both seemed to be pondering their thoughts about everything that had happened, as well as what or who would be at the end of this trip. Tony just drove and kept his eyes on the road. After a few twists and turns, they pulled in the driveway of one of the mountain homes. It was separated from the other houses and surrounded by trees. A good view of the place wasn't offered until they had finally parked the car. When Tony opened his door to get out, the mountain air rushed in confirming they had climbed quite a distance. The temperature had dropped about twenty degrees and was significantly cooler than the desert basin.

"Wish I had brought my jacket," Peter stated to Sam before opening his door and exiting.

"Well, it's kinda hard to plan for being kidnapped and taken to the top of mountains in Nevada," Sam sarcastically stated as she exited the vehicle also.

Closing the door, Peter did a slow three-sixty to take it all in. It was beautiful and the air was crisp. He closed his eyes, leaned back slightly and raised both arms to stretch. After a deep breath of fresh air, he opened his eyes and looked at Sam. She was standing on the other side of the car staring at him as if in amazement.

"Make sure you take the time to get that stretch in! Never mind the fact that we're on top of a cold mountain and may be dead soon," she said bluntly.

Peter's instincts told him impending death was not looming around the corner. He was actually eager for Sam to meet Boyd, if he was even up here. At least there would be another person to bounce opinions off.

"We'll be fine," Peter answered her concerns.

"Follow me if you will," Tony encouraged both of them as he turned and walked toward the house.

Both fell in behind Tony as they stared up at the house. The roof was a light gray and topped a dark, gray wooden house. The two-story entrance had a peaked covering and was supported with four gray columns. Through two large windows near the entrance doors, a large room was lit with a large staircase leading up to the second floor. A grand chandelier hung from the ceiling and was an indicator that whoever lived here had lots of money. Walking up to the doors, Tony unlocked them. Opening them, he took a step back and threw an arm towards the door while looking back to Sam.

"Please, after you," he calmly said to her.

With no notable expression on her face, she entered. Peter and Tony entered afterwards and shut the doors. It was warm inside, and the room was large. To the right of the staircase which was centered in the room was a large open area with floor to ceiling windows along the back wall which overlooked the entire basin north of Las Vegas. The right-side wall housed a large, brick fireplace complete with a warm fire burning in the midst. In front of the fireplace was a large, leather couch which formed a large semicircle and faced the fire. Another large chandelier, this one wooden, hung directly over the couch and magnified the high ceilings and large, wooden beams spanning along the top. The area was elaborate, yet simple. To the left of the large staircase, a long, wooden dining table spanned most of the length with twelve ornate, wooden chairs pulled up to it. More large windows were along the back wall while an astonishing, and really large, saltwater fish tank was built into the far-left wall. Expensive fish lazily swam inside. The blue light emanating from the tank filled the area and made it feel relaxing.

Peter threw a glance over at Sam and realized she was impressed, even though she was trying not to show it. An expensive design like this wasn't the norm for ordinary people like Peter and Sam, who only saw the likes in magazines and television.

"If you would, please, take a seat over by the fireplace," Tony encouraged them.

After both Sam and Peter headed to sit on the large couch, Tony departed up the stairs. Sam walked behind Peter, but when he turned to head for the right side of the couch, she turned left. Peter noticed her action but continued on around and sat on the right side. *Women.* Sam, now sitting calmly on the left side, just stared into the fire. She knew Peter was looking at her. *Men.*

Both sat on the couch quietly. Sam was obviously still upset she had been kidnapped. She had crossed one leg over the other and was bobbing it up and down. Peter didn't know what to say in a situation like this. He didn't want to make Sam angrier and he didn't want to say something to make her think he wasn't considering her feelings. The crackling of the fire was the only sound.

Finally, Peter looked over to her and let out an "I'm sorry" as sincere as he could.

Sam stopped bobbing her leg and looked over to Peter.

"I'm sorry," Peter stated again, solemnly.

Sam knew he meant it. She was about to speak when footsteps coming down the staircase echoed through the room. Both turned to look. It was Alfred Boyd! Without saying a word, he descended the stairs and headed toward the far corner of the area where they were seated. Once there, he stood behind a wooden chair which had a white seat cushion and backing. Three royal blue stripes ran top to bottom along the back and the cushion. Gently, Boyd tipped the chair back a little and began to drag the chair over the floor. The scraping noise filled the room as he dragged it directly in front of the fireplace and centered on the couch. After turning it to face the couch, he walked around it calmly and sat down. Peter threw a glance over to Sam and saw she had her eyebrows raised as if wondering 'really?' He couldn't help but smile a little.

All three sat in silence with Sam sitting on the left side of the couch, Peter on the right, and Boyd in the chair between the two. They took turns just staring at one another. Who was going to be the one to speak first? What were they going to say or ask?

"Mr. Knowles is quite an interesting fellow, wouldn't you say, Miss Fisher?" Boyd spoke first, grabbing both their attention. Boyd let out a slight smile her way.

Sam glanced over at Peter, who had put on a face of confusion, before looking back at Boyd. Then, she asked the question, "Can you please tell me what the heck is going on?"

"I've always wanted to sit in this chair," Boyd replied as he tapped both hands on the chair handles. "You know, the head of the Food and Drug Administration sat in this very chair back in 1955 when he signed the license for the Polio vaccine. I fancied it, so after a brief conversation with him, I was allowed to take it with me. Of course, a sizable contribution helped encourage him to part with it." A small smile was still on Boyd's face.

Peter didn't know how to respond. *Yep! This is Alfred Boyd!* However, he had figured a few things out about Boyd over the past few conversations. Boyd doesn't answer questions directly, or not yet at least, and seems to talk about nonsensical stuff often. Peter looked over to Sam to see how she was handling what Boyd had said.

"Wow! That's nice! I'm sure that has something to do with the price of tea in China and all, but it doesn't answer my question. What the heck is going on?" Sam responded sarcastically before throwing the question once again at Boyd.

He's not going to answer that. There was something satisfying to Peter seeing Sam interact with Boyd. Perhaps, on some level, he was hoping she would be able to empathize with him better or at least have a little more understanding. Peter decided to stay silent and watch the exchange.

"Miss Fisher, there's no need to be rude. I've welcomed both of you here, which seems to be quite safe. Surely, we can have a civilized conversation," Boyd replied to her without a smile.

"Welcomed us? How about you had two people murdered and then kidnapped us? If we are welcomed, as you put it, then we should be able to walk right out the front door," Sam responded matter of factly.

"And so you can, Miss Fisher," Boyd said to Sam as he threw up his left hand toward the door. "It's getting late out, though, and I would encourage you to stay the night. In the morning, Tony will take you wherever you want to go. Or, if you insist, I'll alert Tony so he can do so now."

Peter wasn't expecting the conversation to take this direction. Although he wasn't happy how things had evolved during the day, there were questions he needed answers to. Boyd presented that opportunity.

"I insist!" she quickly stated before standing up. "Are you coming?" she asked Peter before moving to a position behind the couch.

Get answers or go with Sam? The thought disappeared in Peter's mind as quickly as it entered. His response to her, in his opinion, was going to make all the difference to her. As much as he would love to figure out what Project UGEN was all about, he loved the feelings he had felt for Sam over the past little while.

Standing up, he replied, "I'm coming with you." He walked around the couch to meet her as they both headed for the door. He noticed the ever so slight tilt of Sam's head and glisten in her eye and knew he had made the right choice. There was nothing more important than Sam.

"Very well!" Boyd stated as he remained seated. "It was nice to see you again, Mr. Knowles."

That's not going to work. Peter knew Boyd had mentioned his name as enticement to play on his curiosity. He had to admit it probably would have worked, but Sam was here now, and she was stronger than any enticement Boyd could offer. He continued to head for the door with Sam.

Both thought Boyd would probably follow after them and try to get them to stay. However, it didn't happen and, in a few seconds, Sam and Peter were standing outside and beside the car waiting for Tony.

"He's quite eccentric, wouldn't you say?" Peter looked over the car and asked Sam.

"The guy is a lunatic, if you ask me!" Sam responded frantically.

Peter thought for a little bit, and then asked, "What if all the stuff I told you is true? What if Boyd did actually save us from these other people? We don't have the answers we need, and the guy that can provide those answers is in that house."

"We need to get back to St. George and go to the police. People were killed! Let the police take care of all of it. We'll tell them what we know and then go about our business," she replied back to Peter.

"Aren't you just a little bit curious? I mean, you just met Alfred Boyd! A guy that should be at least in his nineties! What if all the stuff I told you is true? What if our lives are in danger? Going back to St. George may be the last thing we want to do!" Peter asked Sam sincerely.

Sam looked over to Peter as if surprised by his words, but didn't speak. Peter knew she was thinking hard about what he had just said.

"I know you are still upset at what happened earlier today," Peter said, understandingly looking Sam in the eyes. "Believe me, this is not how I imagined the day turning out and I'm truly sorry it has turned out like this. But I'm not convinced heading back to St. George is the best thing to do right now."

Sam listened and considered what Peter was saying. She couldn't deny one of the dead men in the restaurant had a gun and was trying to use it. Further, Peter seemed sincere and honest in everything he had told her. Plus, he stood with her in the decision to walk out of the house.

"What are you suggesting, Peter?" she asked.

Seeing that Sam was calming down and being a bit more rational, he responded, "I think we should go back inside. It's safe as far as we can tell. And, even though Boyd is a weirdo, I think we can get the answers we need out of him."

"You mean the answers you need!" Sam retorted.

Peter sighed a little to show frustration, but then realized she was right.

"Maybe," he started but then paused for a brief second. "But maybe we'll also find out who these others are and if they really do pose a threat to us."

Sam felt Peter was a good guy. She had come to know him better through their email exchanges and honestly felt the day's events were just a series of unfortunate events for Peter. Within a few minutes at the restaurant, her girl instincts had let her know he was fond of her. She found that pleasing at the time. She looked over to the entrance doors and then back to Peter ready to respond.

"Are you suggesting we stay the night here, too?" she asked, giving in to Peter's logic.

"I don't see why not. After all, the place is nice and I'm sure he can accommodate," Peter replied looking over to the house.

"Fine!" she said and turned to head for the doors. Peter fell in step behind her. He was amazed when Sam didn't knock on the door, but rather just opened it and walked right in. Once inside, he closed the doors and started to walk towards the couch which was the direction Sam headed. As he turned to head that way, Boyd was still sitting in the same chair. *He never moved!* Tony was nowhere in sight either. Sam showed no hesitation as she continued and sat on the left side of the couch again. Peter continued on as well and sat back down on his side of the couch, but this time he sat just a little closer to Sam and was almost directly in front of Boyd.

"Have you changed your mind?" Boyd asked calmly while looking at Peter.

Peter was once again intrigued with Boyd. *You knew we would come back.* Boyd was a superior communicator. On top of that, Boyd had the ability to almost see into the future just by reading people's physical and verbal responses which also revealed his vast understanding of the human psyche. And now, instead of addressing Sam, he spoke to Peter as though he knew the tactic would probably lead to whatever desired outcome he wanted. Now, Peter had to decide which tactic he would take. Should he try to joust and get the upper hand on wit, or should he placate Boyd to try and get the answers he desired?

"We need some answers," Peter replied in a calm voice. He looked over to Sam, and then back to Boyd. "I need some answers." Peter stressed the 'I'.

"Then I make you two an offer," Boyd said with a honeyed voice. "Stay the night and let's make conversation. As you know, Mr. Knowles, I love to converse when I have the opportunity. Tony will prepare us a meal, and both of you will enjoy a good night's rest in your own rooms. If you agree to stay, I will, in turn, provide you some of the answers you are looking for."

Peter looked over to Sam who looked back at him. Sam shrugged her shoulders in such a way to indicate she was okay with it. He then looked back at Boyd.

"Sounds like a good deal. But I want to test you first to make sure you will hold up your end of the bargain and not just talk around the answers to show us how smart you are," Peter spoke to him plainly.

"I never said I didn't have an ego, Mr. Knowles. But I am a man of my word. Give me your test question," Boyd replied.

"How old are you?" Peter asked bluntly.

Peter knew if Boyd answered the question honestly, it would answer a whole slew of questions he had in relation to Project UGEN. It was also one Boyd had talked around before without ever giving an answer.

"How old do I look?" Boyd asked in response.

"That's it, let's go!" Peter said in a sharp tone as he stood and looked over to Sam.

"Seriously? Of all the questions you could have asked, and you want to know how old I am?" Boyd asked surprisingly.

When Peter saw Sam stand up and head for the door, he fell in beside her. He was taking a gamble hoping Boyd would see the sincerity before they walked out the door. Confidently, he continued to walk towards the door without any hint of hesitation. As Peter reached for the handle, he heard Boyd's tense voice.

"I'm one hundred seventeen," were the words that stopped the two in their tracks. For Sam, it confirmed Boyd's lunacy. But for Peter, it confirmed his suspicions. The two looked at each other.

Hardly moving her lips, Sam whispered, "Told you he was a lunatic."

Peter smiled back at her statement before responding, "I don't think so."

Sam stood in disbelief as Peter walked back towards the couch. *He actually believes that crazy!* Reluctantly, Sam walked back to the couch with loud footsteps obviously wanting the two men to notice her frustration. As she rounded the couch, she noticed Peter had sat down and was leaning forward with his elbows resting atop his knees and his hands clasped together between his legs. To Sam, he looked like an elementary student waiting for the librarian to read his favorite book!

As Sam plopped down on the couch, she decided it was time to stop the craziness. "So, you're one hundred seventeen years old? That's a lie! You look like you may be sixty, but no cosmetics or plastic surgeon in the world could take off that many years. Why are you stringing Peter along on some fantastical story?" she shouted at Boyd.

"He's not lying," Peter replied without taking his eyes off of Boyd. "Are you?"

"Prove it!" Sam aimed at Boyd.

"I can't now, can I? Sure, I could present you with a birth certificate, but you would only say it had been fabricated. How can you prove your age, Miss Fisher, without a possibly forged document?"

"He's not lying," Peter stated again, still enamored.

"This is crazy!" Sam retorted, throwing her arms up in disbelief. "Top-secret documents, fallen angels, ageless men! You've really gotten him to believe this nonsense. I'm a Christian, so why haven't I ever heard about these fallen angels? The only fallen angels in the Bible were the ones God cast out of heaven with Satan."

"You haven't heard of them, Miss Fisher, because you obviously haven't read your Bible," Boyd answered looking at her. "And because your pastor never told you about them!"

"Okay, then, give me a Bible and let me see it for myself!" she sharply returned.

Peter sat back a little on the couch. He was interested to see where this was going to go. Meanwhile, Boyd quietly stood up and walked towards the backside of the large staircase where he retrieved an old book from a shelf. Walking back, he kindly handed the Bible to Sam and then returned to his seat and crossed his legs.

"Genesis chapter six, verses one and two," Boyd stated.

Sam thumbed through the first few pages until she found the text. She was glad he had said Genesis because, in all honesty, she wasn't too familiar with the Bible, but knew Genesis was the first book. As if almost on cue, Boyd began quoting the second verse as she read it:

"That the sons of God saw the daughters of men that they were fair; and they took for them wives of all which they chose."

"Doesn't say anything about fallen angels to me!" Sam spurted.

"Ben ha Elohim," Boyd spoke softly. "That's Hebrew for sons of God. It's used to describe those created directly by God. The same phrase is used in the book of Job, chapter one and verse six and again in chapter two, verse one when the sons of God came to present themselves, and Satan came also." Boyd paused to consider her reaction. "Angels, Miss Fisher."

Boyd gave Sam a moment to digest what he told her before adding, "Why don't you go ahead and read verse four where it speaks of giants being born as a result of the ben ha Elohim mixing with the women. These giants were abominations and not in the image of God, which is why the next few verses discuss how God was going to destroy all flesh with the flood."

Sam took the time and read the whole chapter while Boyd and Peter waited. Boyd was right in that she had never read it before. She didn't know how to respond as she looked over to both men. Closing the Bible, she placed it on the couch beside her. In her mind, and with this new proof, she began to recall the story Peter had told her on the drive to Mt. Charleston. Although nowhere near convinced, she decided to listen just to see how the night's conversations would unfold.

Both Boyd and Peter saw the slight submission in her demeanor.

"To a lot of people, a person reading and studying the Bible is a dangerous thing, Miss Fisher. Many think it's best if people just attend church and listen to the pastor as he takes the scripture and makes it fit into man's religion," Boyd explained as he emphasized the word "man's".

Social engineering at its finest. Peter realized just how broad religion had grown. There were so many denominations, and each one claimed to be the inheritors of God's promise. On top of that, they used the same Bible to justify their religious views by explaining what the verses meant, often out of context, to their congregations. *Sheeple. The blind leading the blind.*

Turning his attention back to Peter, Boyd decided to introduce a new topic. He enjoyed the fact he had captured Peter's undivided attention and yet, no proof of anything had been yielded.

"You know, Mr. Knowles, a plane once crashed up here in Mt. Charleston back in 1955. Did you know that?" Boyd asked Peter.

"I didn't," Peter replied, showing interest.

Boyd went on, "Thirteen passengers died in addition to the pilot. The government secured the entire top of the mountain while it investigated the crash, while the Air Force told the locals there were top-secret documents on board justifying their need for everyone to stay clear during the recovery. The names of the deceased were not released to the press, nor any information related to the flight, including its destination."

"Sounds like the government to me," Peter said agreeingly.

"I was supposed to be on that flight. Me and five others. However, at the last minute and just before boarding, we were assigned to a different flight. Strange, don't you think?" Boyd asked.

"Should I guess where the plane was headed?" Peter asked instead.

"Groom Lake, Mr. Knowles. Ever heard of it?" Boyd answered with a smile.

Peter gave a look and slight nod like he wasn't surprised to hear the answer. "So you used to work there?"

"Where's Groom Lake?" Sam cut in.

Peter looked over to Sam and clarified, "Area 51. Groom Lake, S4, Dreamland, the Ranch. There's many names often used to refer to it."

"Work? I guess you could call it that. I would probably use the term 'plan' instead," Boyd replied.

"Plan? I'm almost scared to ask," Peter queried.

"So much knowledge, and all gathered in one place. So much was going on and happening then, and all by design. Not every one of us agreed with how fast things were evolving. Some, thirteen to be exact, thought we should stop what we were doing."

"I'm listening," Peter urged.

"After the crash, the six remaining of us decided to continue along with what we had started. I say started, but I would be lying if I said we didn't have predecessors. Besides, the wheels were turning and there was nothing anyone could do to stop them."

Boyd stood up and began to pace as if pondering his next words. He knew he had both Sam and Peter's attention. After a moment of thought, he continued.

"In 1955, the Polio vaccine was licensed, as I stated earlier. Everyone had to have it. The plan was so successful, more vaccines followed and were once again forced on the public."

"No one has ever forced me to get a vaccine!" Sam interjected.

"Are you sure about that, Miss Fisher? Did you ever go to public schools? Ever tried to work somewhere only to be told you had to have received certain immunizations?" Boyd pushed the point. He stopped his pacing and looked directly at her, "Ever had the flu shot?"

Sam sat back on the couch.

"Alright, then! So, you're saying the lot of you were designing drugs to help the American people. Sounds admirable," she stated with a slight smile. "But something tells me you're not finished with your story. Right?"

Boyd smiled in return to her question. "It was also in 1955, that a certain scientist correctly identified the number of human chromosomes which was a monumental breakthrough." Boyd began pacing and thinking once again as he continued, "A huge amusement park was opened in California, nuclear warheads were attached to intercontinental ballistic missiles. I could go on and on. And that's just in 1955!"

Peter was in deep thought. Boyd wasn't just spouting off historical facts for no reason. He was trying to tell them something.

"Control," Peter whispered loud enough the other two heard.

Boyd stopped pacing, raised both eyebrows at Peter, and then placed his right index finger on his nose. Boyd then returned to his seat.

"And preparation," Boyd announced with a more serious tone. "The world today is oblivious to what is going on all around them."

"So why don't you just come out and tell us what is going on all around us?" Sam asked with a little anger in her voice. Obviously, she had been listening and digesting everything Boyd had been saying.

"You wouldn't understand it, Miss Fisher, with mere words," Boyd sadly responded. "Words can't show you, which is the only way to really understand it all."

After a moment of silence in the room, Boyd turned to Peter and asked, "Mr. Knowles, you were in the military. What's the best way to get large masses of people to change?"

"Make them feel like they need it!" Peter responded.

"Precisely! But you have to set the stage before they think they need it, and when they do, you have to make sure they are prepared to receive it," Boyd added.

With that, Boyd stood up, walked across the large room and beyond the huge staircase before disappearing down a hallway. Sam turned to look at Peter, but neither one of them knew what to say. After a minute, Boyd returned with two cans of drink and a bottle of water. He set the two cans down on a wooden table in front of the couch.

"Thirsty?" he asked.

"I am!" Sam replied as she leaned forwards and grabbed one of the cans. Peter followed her action and grabbed the other. Popping the tops, both began to take a sip. Peter wasn't thrilled with Boyd's selection, but he was a guest and took what was offered. Of all things, and probably as an indicator, Boyd had given them popular energy drinks called Nailed.

"You must think we're going to be up for a while, huh?" Sam asked before taking another sip.

"Do you like that drink, Miss Fisher?" Boyd asked.

"Well, I'm not one of those crazy energy drink people, but Nailed happens to be my favorite one when I do choose to drink one," she responded. In actuality, she was just happy to take a break from listening to the history lesson.

"It's quite an interesting design on the can, wouldn't you say? Three bright neon nails on a black can?"

"Sure," she responded. "They gotta make money so why not advertise with something to catch our eyes, right?" After another sip, she stopped as if surprised and asked, "Wait! You're not going to tell me the government put control ingredients in it, are you?" before letting out a little laugh.

"Of course not! Don't be absurd," Boyd returned with a little laughter himself before glancing over to Peter and then back to Sam. "There's nothing harmful on the inside of that can," he finished.

Sam and Peter caught how he stressed the word 'inside' and moved the cans further away from their mouths. As if on cue, they both started looking at the cans they held.

"What do you see on the can?" Boyd asked.

"It's black," Sam started. "And it has three old-style nails highlighted in neon. Almost looks like the type of nails you find holding rail lines in place. They are placed parallel to one another which makes them resemble the Roman numeral three on the can."

"Are you sure those are nails," Boyd asked as he walked over to the bookcase behind the staircase once again. He returned with another book and handed it to Sam. "This is a book on the Hebrew language. One of their letters is the Vav. Look it up, if you will."

Sam began to get a little worried but wasn't sure why. Placing the energy drink on the small table, she began to flip through the pages. The two men waited patiently. Peter actually stood up and moved to sit beside her to get a look at what she found. She gently pulled her finger down a page and stopped when she found it.

"The Vav. Okay...I found it," she said.

"Tell me, Miss Fisher, does it resemble one of those nail marks on the can?" Boyd asked.

"Sure," she admitted, not knowing where the topic was going. "It almost looks like our number seven, but the top horizontal line is shorter. Kinda looks like a peg as well. It says here it means 'hook' or 'hooked' and represents the number six in Hebrew."

"A peg? You mean like a nail?" Boyd asked as if surprised.

"Yes," Sam replied.

"Now, look at the can again and tell me what you see," Boyd requested with a more serious voice.

Sam and Peter picked up their cans and looked again. *You've got to be kidding me!* Peter saw it immediately. He turned to look over at Sam who had started shaking her head slightly but then stopped when her brain made the connection. Both looked back up to Boyd who was sitting emotionless.

"Three nails on the can. Three nails were used approximately two thousand years ago to hang someone upon a tree. I'm sure you are familiar with that story. Three sixes. Surely, I don't need to expound on that," Boyd stated. "Don't be surprised, Miss Fisher. Rarely does anyone see things for what they truly are."

"I remember this company's motto," Peter added. "Release the monster inside! Goes right in line with what I'm seeing now!"

"Coincidence?" Sam asked shyly.

"Hardly!" Boyd responded quickly. "The human subconscious is a powerful tool for those who wish to take advantage of it. What better way to prepare people for something than subliminally? Hollywood, the music industry, videos, logos! They're all around you and you never even notice. Subconsciously, these images program you to accept change that others may want to impose on you."

"Sheeple!" Peter said as he looked down between his feet. "People, myself included, just blindly believe whatever they hear or whatever is put right in front of their face. The fact we trust others without question." Peter's face expressed anger and even outrage. More than anyone else, he hated being taken advantage of or the feeling he was being controlled!

Sam didn't know what to think anymore. When she had walked through the doors into Boyd's house, she had thought it was all nonsense, and poor old Peter had been taken advantage of. But now, she found herself contemplating the possibility of all of it. Could there be some all-powerful group of individuals controlling the world? And for what purpose? To bring about the end spoken of in the Bible? Her thoughts were daunting and scary. Inside, she wasn't feeling too well. She could feel her body getting weak and she knew why.

"Hungry?" Boyd asked the two as he stood up and headed for the large, wooden table on the other side of the room. "Let's eat! Tony has been preparing quite the meal for us!"

Peter stood and walked in front of Sam holding out a hand, "Let's eat."

Looking up, she placed her hand inside of Peter's and allowed him to help her up. Together, they walked over to the table and sat across from each other and adjacent Boyd who had seated himself at the head of the table.

Chapter 13

Tony had prepared an astonishing meal! Peter couldn't help but wonder who Tony was and how did he know how to do so many things? He was a butler, bodyguard, driver, killer, and now chef! He rarely spoke, and facial expressions to show emotions were nonexistent. With everything Peter had observed, Tony was very loyal to Boyd.

The part of the large table the three sat at was covered with a variety of dishes. This was not a one course meal like Peter was used to in his RV, but was rather complete with a salad, bread, side dishes and a main course. For sure, there would be dessert at the end too and maybe even a cup of coffee. The entree was roasted duck breasts neatly sliced and piled on a large, ornate plate. On the same dish, and around the duck, were sliced squash and diced red potatoes. Another plate was filled with grilled onions, bell peppers and orange slices. The aroma was delightful as the three waited for Tony to finish the final phase of setting up the meal.

"Shall we say grace?" Sam asked, indicating she was ready to partake. She extended an arm out across the table to each of the two men.

Although Peter never said grace before he ate, he would participate during formal events while serving in the military. He reached his right arm out and held hands with Sam who then turned her eyes to Boyd as if waiting for him. Boyd looked at both of them and then extended his arm as well to Sam. Peter could tell this was a bit odd for Boyd as well, but figured he should oblige a lady sitting at the table. Sam bowed her head and said a prayer to bless the meal, the lives of the three sitting at the table, and finished by asking for wisdom and understanding. An 'Amen' was given and the two men pulled their arms back. Sam smiled and thanked both men for the opportunity.

"Bon appetite!" Boyd said as he motioned for Sam to start.

"So, is there anything Tony can't do?" Peter asked as he smiled.

"Not that I have discovered," Boyd replied with a chuckle. "He is a loyal man who has earned my trust."

Sam filled her plate and passed the utensils over to Peter before saying, "You know, he killed two men at the restaurant today."

"If he did, it was because he felt there was no other choice, my dear," Boyd answered.

"Who were those guys?" Peter asked as he continued to assemble his plate of food.

"The same people I spoke of at Meteor Crater. They are not the sort you want to make friends with, Mr. Knowles," Boyd stated as plainly as he could.

"Yes, but who are they and why did they come after Sam and me?" Peter asked, stressing the "who".

"Dristan Cavanaugh is dead, Mr. Knowles," Boyd replied in a serious tone.

Peter was about to take a bite of duck, but then froze and looked at Boyd in surprise.

"He had always been a curious fellow, but he seemed to have come across a bit of information recently which spurred him closer to the truth. It was only a couple of hours after he typed in my name before these other people we have spoken of got to him. It didn't take a genius to link his computer transactions to an IP address at Meteor Crater," Boyd informed Peter. "Seems someone else also has the same level of knowledge as Mr. Cavanaugh had."

That's impossible! Peter knew he had spoken with Cavanaugh while at Meteor Crater, but there was nothing to link Peter to the IP address there. He had taken steps to remove his truck's GPS and had purchased a new computer which had no personal information linking it to him. How could anyone, Boyd or these others, link Peter to Dristan Cavanaugh? Regardless, Boyd seemed to know somehow.

"How did they know it was me at Meteor Crater? I took measures to prevent anyone from tracking me," Peter asked.

"Mr. Knowles, come now! You should know there are many ways to track someone. I would think you knew that, especially with the specific set of skills you acquired in the military," Boyd replied with a wry grin.

Peter was growing angry inside. Once again, he had been tracked, and it made him furious. He clenched his fist tight around the fork he was holding as he began to ponder. Obviously, they hadn't tracked him with the computer, and he had removed the GPS from his truck. *How?* Surely, they didn't have a drone flying overhead to track him the entire time. It only took a few moments for Peter to ascertain a possibility.

"A bug!" Peter whispered but then his voice grew louder. "They put a tracking device on my vehicle, didn't they? Those two agents?" he asked, turning to look at Boyd.

Boyd smiled as he saw Peter come to the revelation.

"But they don't know where you are now," Boyd quickly put out there looking at Peter and then over to Sam. "You are safe here."

"Are they after me too?" Sam asked with a serious look on her face.

"Do you not have the same knowledge as Mr. Knowles?" Boyd answered with a question.

"Great! Just great!" Sam exclaimed as she lost her appetite. She slid her chair back and stood up placing the backside of her right hand against her forehead. She really wasn't feeling well.

"So how do we fix this?" Peter asked with frustration. "How do we let them know we are not a threat to them? We aren't going to tell anyone!"

"We've got to go to the authorities and explain everything!" Sam immediately answered, turning around to face Peter.

"That's the last thing you want to do!" Boyd interjected.

No one was eating at this point. Sam continued to stand while the two men just sat at the table. Boyd could tell by looking at them both they were in deep thoughts.

"An ordinary man with curiosity," Boyd let out.

Peter looked at Boyd, "What?"

"Isn't that how you described yourself when we first met, Mr. Knowles? An ordinary man with curiosity?" Boyd reminded Peter. "As a matter of fact, if I recall correctly, we were talking about how curiosity killed the cat, weren't we? And of course, you pointed out how it doesn't say whose curiosity killed the cat and that we only assume it's the cat's!"

Peter remembered the conversation. *Why did I have to be so curious? Am I the cat?* Once again, thoughts flooded his mind. *Whatever happened to no bills, no people, no worries?*

"Why are you helping us?" Peter finally asked after a few quiet moments. He looked Boyd straight in the eyes.

"And there it is! I was wondering when you were going to ask that," Boyd informed Peter. Sliding his chair back, Boyd stood up and began to pace near the table thinking of his answer.

Sam was obviously interested in the answer as well turning around to look at Peter and then Boyd.

"Computers, entertainment, restaurant chains, medical, money and government," Boyd let out spacing each word from the other. "Care to guess which one I was?" he asked rhetorically with a quick smile.

"What are you talking about? Stop with all the stories for once and just answer us, please!" Peter pleaded.

"Mr. Knowles, I am answering you. I just already know the additional questions my answers will instigate, so I prefer to answer them all at once, if that's okay with you!" Boyd retorted.

Peter threw both arms up in the air indicating his frustration and acceptance together. Sam moved back over to her chair and sat. Meanwhile, Tony brought in cups of coffee for the guests and placed them on the table before departing.

"The six of us which were absent from the flight that crashed up here," Boyd continued as he paced. "We each had our orders in relation to the six areas I just stated. Mine was computers, of course, and what an endeavor it was! The others often referred to me as simply 'John', since I was to make way for two others to carry on after me. The name was in reference to John the Baptist in the Bible, who made ready the arrival of a certain messiah. Anyway, newly acquired knowledge in relation to human chromosomes made it possible to, let's say, engineer the two who were to carry on after me. Two mothers were identified and prepared, unknowingly of course, to give birth to two boys who would grow up to revolutionize the computer and internet industry. Both were programmed before birth and both were born in 1955. They promised instant access to worldwide knowledge, and boy, have they provided it! It doesn't take a genius to figure out who those two men are today. I tell you this information so you can grasp the level of planning and dedication we all had invested. Hollywood and radio were revolutionized and entertained the masses, all while subliminally programming minds to accept the inevitable. Food chains flourished with every family enjoying access to quick, tasty meals. Oh, the hormones they took in! Ever notice how high school students have been getting bigger and looking older over the years? Most boys these days are over six feet tall and sport full grown beards around high school. The young ladies of yesteryear are full grown women by the time they graduate now." Boyd paused to ensure both Sam and Peter were paying attention.

After the pause, Boyd continued with his story, "Medicine! Now there's something worth mentioning. It's sad how people have trusted the medical community. No one wants to die and will do anything to prevent it. In groves, people stand in line at hospitals and doctors' offices ready to be injected with anything that can prolong their life without ever asking what's in the medication they are taking or, more importantly, where it's coming from. It's hard to meet anyone, nowadays, that's not on some sort of prescription medication. Their lives depend on it, you know? And then we have government and money. I will not belittle your intelligence, as you can see more clearly now. Society completely depends on the government now to meet nearly every need from money, security, food...all of it!"

Boyd stopped talking and walked back over to stand behind his chair at the dining room table. Sam and Peter, both seated, were looking at him as if the curtain had been pulled from in front of their eyes. Then, Boyd summarized what he had been trying to tell them.

"Previous generations used to walk to their churches and fill the house of the Lord with prayers. They depended on God for everything. Now, they walk to their mailboxes waiting on their checks from Uncle Sam. They go to the doctors to extend their lives. They surf the internet to receive all the answers they need. All the while they are distracted from the void in their lives by listening to music and watching television which is far more entertaining than reading some old book sitting on the shelf. In essence, they no longer depend on God to provide what they need. Rather, they depend on these new, false gods as some people used to put it," Boyd finished and sat down.

Peter took a sip of his coffee. His brain was numb. For the first time, he had received more information than he could process. There were no words. All these things had been right in front of his face, but he never saw them. There was a weird lump, never felt before, somewhere inside his gut.

Sam, also, sat quietly in her chair. Somehow, deep inside, she knew Boyd was speaking the truth. It couldn't be just coincidental. Had her spirit been quenched all this time? She tried to remember how many times she had heard passages from the Bible about not being deceived in the end times. *Have I been deceived?* She felt sick. As she looked across the table at Peter, the room began to spin. She stood up.

"Can you please show me to my room?" she asked as she walked away from the table. She knew she was walking but could longer see anything. Everything went black.

Peter noticed Sam's face was pale as she sat across from him. When she stood up from the table, there was a blank expression on her face before she asked to be shown to her room. It was then his instincts kicked in and told him she was in trouble. As fast as he could, he jumped out of his chair knocking it over, and ran around the table to her. At the last second, he was able to catch her as she fell face first. He held onto her and helped her to the floor. Boyd wasn't far behind and knelt beside the two.

"She has Leukemia!" Peter cried out to Boyd. "Help her!"

Boyd saw pain in Peter's eyes. "Of course! Tony! Tony!" he yelled.

Peter could feel Sam's heartbeat and knew she had fainted. *It's all too much for her!* He gently brushed the hair out of her face and continued to hold her head in his lap. He felt as if his insides were being shredded and it was painful. This was Sam. His Sam!

"Take her upstairs," Boyd told Tony as he entered the room in a hurry. "I'll get help."

Tony knelt beside Sam and placed both arms beneath her. With no problem at all, he lifted her out of Peter's lap and slowly carried her up the stairs. Peter was right behind them, not knowing exactly what to do. If nothing else, he was going to stay right beside her.

At the top of the stairs, Tony turned left and headed down a hallway. Paintings lined the white walls and several doors were across from one another.

"Second door on the left," Tony voiced to Peter who ran ahead and opened the door.

Inside, Tony placed Sam on a large bed. Peter walked around to the other side and continued to look at Sam who was unconscious. Then, he looked around the room and headed for a door he thought would lead to a bathroom. Sure enough, there was one, so Peter turned on the faucet and grabbed a washcloth from a shelf. Once he doused the cloth in water, he wrung it a couple of times and then hurried back to the bed. As calmly as he could, he began to wipe her face with the cool rag while telling her everything was going to be ok. Tony had grabbed a thin book and was fanning her face as well.

Within a minute, Sam slowly opened her eyes, regaining consciousness. Dark blue rings had already encircled her eye sockets and she looked sick. Peter smiled at her.

Looking up at Peter, Sam moved her right arm and placed her hand against Peter's leg just to make contact. "I'm sorry," she whispered to him as she took slow, shallow breaths.

"The sorrow is all mine, Sam," he returned to her softly.

At that moment, Sam could see Peter's heart. She noticed the thin line of water along the lower edges of his eyelids and the difficulty he had breathing. *He loves me.* With that, she closed her eyes and fell asleep.

"She needs to rest," Tony said as quietly as he could.

Peter nodded and then carefully got up from the bed and sat on a sofa near the wall. All the while he kept his eyes on Sam. A couple of minutes later, Boyd appeared outside the open door of Sam's room and motioned for Peter. Quietly, Peter stood up and went to the hallway.

"I've called a doctor we can trust. He's in Vegas, so it's going to take him about thirty minutes to get here. How is she?" Boyd inquired.

"She's sleeping. Everything that has happened today has been too much on her. She had just gotten out of the hospital too," Peter answered. "She wouldn't be in this condition if it hadn't been for me."

"This is not your doing, Mr. Knowles. There's no way you could know the day's events were going to unfold as such," comforted Boyd. "Besides, I think Miss Fisher is quite fond of you."

"I doubt that after today," Peter returned shaking his head.

"Tony will escort the doctor up once he arrives and will pay him for his services and discretion. As for me, I prefer not to be around as I'm sure you can understand," Boyd informed Peter as he turned to walk down the hallway.

"Thanks," Peter voiced after him to which Boyd just raised his right hand and waved in return as he continued to walk. *What do you want from me?*

As Boyd had said, Tony escorted the doctor up to Sam's room once he arrived. The doctor immediately went to the side of Sam and measured her pulse. Next, he pulled out a stethoscope and listened to her chest. He did a careful visual exam of what he could see. Satisfied, he stood up and motioned for Peter to follow him into the hallway.

"Is she ok?" Peter asked.

"She is, but she needs plenty of rest. You told me over the phone she had leukemia?"

At first, Peter was surprised, but then realized Boyd would not have provided his identity and, instead, probably used his name. "Yes, she does."

"I would have to look at her complete record to give you a full diagnosis, but for now, I can tell you she is okay and recovering. Tell me, what led to her collapse?" the doctor asked.

Peter looked at the doctor. He was short and bald on top with the exception of a crown of black and gray hair surrounding his head. A brown, sleeveless cardigan was neatly pulled over a black, buttoned up shirt. His dark rimmed glasses accentuated Peter's stereotype of a doctor.

"She just overdid it today, I think. All the travelling and conversation must have gotten to her," Peter answered.

The doctor reached inside his pants pocket and retrieved an orange bottle of pills.

"When you told me she had leukemia and had fainted, I decided to bring these. Give her one after she wakes and then twice a day after a meal. They will help her recover more quickly," the doctor prescribed as he handed the bottle to Peter.

"Will do," was Peter's response.

The doctor turned to leave but then hesitated to say, "Listen, I know you told me this was a discreet matter and all. But my advice is to admit her into a hospital, so she can be afforded the care she needs. Just my advice." He then walked over to Tony who was waiting for him at the top of the staircase. Both men faded from view as they descended down the stairs.

Peter walked over to a nightstand and placed the bottle of pills on the nightstand before returning to the sofa. Sam was still sleeping peacefully as far as he could ascertain. The emotional pain he felt when Sam fainted was slowly dissipating and he was able to breathe easier. He closed his eyes and began to think of Sam and eventually dreamed of her.

Chapter 14

It was still dark when Peter awoke. A tight, dull pain echoed in his lower back as a result of how he had slept on the sofa. As he leaned forward to stand, so he could stretch the pain out, he looked over at Sam still sleeping on the bed. Obviously, at some point during the night, someone had turned off the lights in the room, but left the bathroom's light on with the door partially open. The little bit of light entering the room was enough for Peter to see Sam's face. *She's beautiful!* On his feet, he bent over to touch his toes and stretch his back muscles. He didn't know exactly what time it was, but his body told him it was probably just before daybreak. He decided to quietly head downstairs.

The hallway was dark, but towards the stairs there was a faint light emanating from somewhere downstairs. Peter walked slowly to the stairs and looked down into the large room with the couch and large table. The fireplace was still burning and dimly lit up the couch area. On the other side of the room, the large table had a blue glow about it from the large aquarium lights. Seeing no one, Peter continued down the staircase and then looked down the hallway to where he believed the kitchen to be. He could discern a room at the end which had a little light shedding throughout, so he headed in that direction. As Peter had guessed, the hallway opened up into a kitchen area which was somewhat lighted by a stove light. The kitchen was just as impressive as other parts of the house and was complete with black trimmed, silver appliances, a large marble-topped island in the center, and wooden cabinets galore. Peter walked over to the refrigerator and retrieved a bottle of water. Peter noticed it was fully stocked with new items confirming the fact Boyd hadn't been at this house too long. Shutting the refrigerator door, Peter walked over to the middle island and sat on a bar stool. As soon as his thirst was quenched, he took in the silence all around him and began to think.

Peter's first thoughts were of Sam and her condition. As the doctor had stated the night before, she needed to be in a hospital. However, his instincts told him admitting her into a nearby hospital might put her life in greater peril than she was already in. He wondered if she had family members or friends worrying about her and where she had disappeared to. Surely, people in St. George would have heard about the killings at the restaurant. If she did have family and friends, they had the right to be worried! For now, though, she was safe and sleeping.

Next, Peter thought about his truck and RV. Had the others vandalized it again, or had it been impounded by the local police? It had only been a day, so maybe it was still sitting there untouched, but Peter realized that was highly unlikely due to the events which unfolded at the restaurant. What about the little bit of money hidden away beneath the sink, his pistol...everything? It was at that moment Peter realized, without his truck and RV, he had absolutely nothing! It was a profound moment for him to see just how simple a life he had been living. He had no friends or family to speak of, no permanent address, and nothing he could really put his hands on. He only had things he could carry with him. Without his truck and RV, that was nothing! Perhaps that was the reason he had been longing to meet Sam. *Sam.*

What was I thinking? A humble feeling swept over Peter as he moved on to think about his actions over the past several days. Out of anger and curiosity, he had decided to not forget about Boyd and these others, but rather delve into trying to figure out just who they were. The intelligence cycle planning, the measures taken to prevent anyone from tracking him, and his thoughts of discovering the truth behind Project UGEN. Had he just been fooling himself? Did he really think he was smart enough to tackle these people? He thought of a junior varsity football team going up against a professional team. *I'm an idiot.*

"Good morning, Mr. Knowles. Am I disturbing you?" came a familiar voice. It was Boyd. He was dressed casually wearing black, cotton pants and a black pullover shirt. It must have been the socks he was wearing that allowed him to sneak up.

A little startled, Peter turned to respond, "Good morning. Not at all. Just needed a bottle of water." He took another drink.

"Was the sofa kind to you?" Boyd grinned as he asked.

"Not really," Peter answered.

Boyd walked over to the coffee pot along the far wall and began to prepare it. "How is Miss Fisher this morning? Still sleeping, I take it?" he asked as he loaded the machine with coffee and water.

"She's still sleeping. As far as I can tell, she slept through the night. She had to be exhausted," Peter said and then decided to add, "Wait, you know how to make coffee? I figured you would have woken Tony up for that task." He chuckled as Boyd turned around to throw an evil eye his way.

Boyd pressed a button on the coffee machine to get it brewing and then walked over to take a seat on a bar stool near Peter.

"I knew you were a morning person. The military has a way of doing that to people," Boyd continued to make conversation.

Peter nodded. Even though he was a morning person, he wasn't normally one for having conversations so early. However, this was Boyd and the situation dictated otherwise.

"I find that mornings help me understand who I am. The breaking dawn, cooler air and the peace it brings help me collect my thoughts, you know?" Peter added.

Enough coffee was brewed to make a couple of cups as Boyd got up and headed that way. Retrieving two cups from a cabinet, he poured them and carried both back to the island.

Placing a cup in front of Peter, he said "We never got to finish our conversation last night."

Peter put the cap back on the bottle of water and then took a sip of coffee before responding, "We didn't, and you were just about to tell me why you were helping us."

Boyd caught the sarcastic grin Peter made after he made the statement. "You forgot to mention coffee!" Boyd smiled.

Peter threw a questioning look at Boyd but then realized Boyd was referring to his previous comments about how the morning time affected him. Acquiring a face of realization, he responded "Ah yes! Coffee helps too."

The two men sat silently for almost a minute. The coffee was refreshing, and both men seemed to appreciate the moment. It was Boyd who broke the silence.

"They're all dead," he started and then paused for a thought. "The other five, that is."

Peter looked over at Boyd to indicate he was listening.

"We all knew the time would come, but we never figured it would be so soon. After I discovered they had all died within a week of each other, I knew I was next," Boyd continued and then paused for a sip of coffee. "It was back in the mid-nineties when I decided to disappear. I had mentored my two apprentices, the two I spoke of yesterday, and was amazed at their progress in revolutionizing the computer and internet industries. However, their success inevitably led to my obsoleteness."

Boyd noticed a confused look on Peter's face so he elaborated, "I was a tool, Mr. Knowles, nothing more. My direction always came from somewhere else. We were all told we were going to reshape the world with the added benefits of fame and fortune. But, when the time came, they didn't need my expertise anymore." Boyd paused for another sip of coffee, smiled, and then added, "I'm not ready to go, just yet, Mr. Knowles!"

"Why do I have a feeling you need me to help you stay around a while longer?" Peter asked through inquisitively squinting eyes.

"Because your instincts serve you well," Boyd answered smiling. He placed his cup of coffee on the counter and stood up. After glancing through a window, he turned to Peter and said, "Day is breaking. Take some time to freshen up and then we can talk again. Upstairs, second door on the right is your room in which you can shower and find a change of clothes. If you need anything, don't hesitate to ask."

Peter nodded as Boyd walked out of the kitchen. After finishing his cup of coffee, he headed up to his room to prepare for the rest of the day. As promised, his room had a change of clothes lying on the bed. He wasn't surprised to find they fit perfectly. *Is there anything Boyd can't find out?*

A couple of hours had passed, and fresh sunlight began waking up the house. Sam opened her eyes and looked over to the windows in her room which provided a beautiful view of the mountains to the south. Although she had slept all night, she still felt completely exhausted. The feeling was too familiar to her. Normally, when she felt like this, she would be lying in a hospital bed back in St. George with an IV in her arm. Doctors and nurses would periodically check on her, but the rest of the time she just watched horrible television, looked blankly out of a window, or just slept to pass the time. She hated the leukemia which had invaded her body. But this time, she wasn't in a hospital, and no doctors or nurses had come in to check on her. No IV was plugged into her arm. She turned her head to examine her environment more thoroughly. The walls were blue with white trim, and the ceiling was white. It was the expensive furniture which sparked her remembrance of where she was! *I thought I was dreaming.* In a split second, her memory recalled the previous day and the prior evening's conversations with Boyd and Peter. Her heart started to pound, but then she realized she was safe. With a bit of effort, she pushed the bed covers off and then sat up. She was weak, but managed to slide her legs off the bed and place her feet onto the floor. Sitting on the edge of the bed, she needed to rest a minute.

"Peter," she spoke out inaudibly at first but then tried a second time. "Peter." No one replied.

Looking over at the nightstand, she noticed the orange pill bottle. Squinting her eyes a little, she was able to make out the familiar name of the drug contained within, but decided not to reach for it. Taking as deep of breath as she could manage, she forced herself up on her feet. Slowly, she dragged her feet across the floor as she began to make her way to the door. Once at the door, she leaned against the frame and closed her eyes to regain the quickly fading strength she had.

"Peter," she spoke again, but this time it was even quieter than before. Stepping out into the hallway, she placed her right hand against the hallway wall to help her keep balance. One step at a time, she made her way to the staircase railing and peered down into the large, open room. Peter was sitting on the couch staring at the fireplace while Boyd walked across the floor and placed two fresh cups of coffee on the table in front of Peter.

"Peter," she tried to call out to him. This time, it worked.

Peter thought he heard his name and turned to look across the room behind him. He was about to dismiss it, but then glanced up the stairs to see Sam leaning against the railing.

"Sam!" he let out, alarmed, as he jumped to his feet running to and then up the stairs.

Boyd turned to look her way surprised as well to see she had managed to make it that far. He knew a few things about leukemia as well as the effects it had on the body during an episode. He remained where he stood, though, letting Peter handle the situation.

Peter placed Sam's arm around his neck to support her as he mentioned, "Sam, you shouldn't be up. Let me help you back to your room."

Sam managed to give a slight, single nod. The two slowly made their way back to her room with Peter doing most of the work. Inside, he placed her back on the bed and pulled the covers back over her. He brushed the hair away from her face with his hand and then sat on the edge of the bed beside her.

"Can I get you anything?" Peter asked in the sweetest voice he could manage. He couldn't remember ever using such a tone before now.

"Water, please," Sam responded.

"No problem. Be right back," smiled Peter as he quickly walked out of the room.

Within a minute, he was back and handed the water to Sam who, in turn, took a few sips.

"How are you feeling?" Peter asked sincerely.

"Like I've been run over," she replied. Seeing the sadness on Peter's face, she added, "Nothing a little rest can't remedy."

"A doctor came last night. He left those pills on your nightstand and said I should give you one when you woke up and then two every day," he stated as he reached for the bottle.

Sam nodded and managed to sit up a little. She took the pill Peter handed her and followed it with some water. After handing the bottle of water to Peter, she laid down flat.

"Has the world ended yet?" she said quietly with a little smile.

The smile made Peter feel better which made him smile back. "No," he answered. "Not yet."

"What were you two talking about downstairs?" Sam asked quietly.

"Nothing. I had taken a shower, put on this change of clothes and had returned downstairs to ask Boyd what he needed from us. When I asked, he decided we should have some coffee during the conversation and was just returning with it when I heard you," Peter replied truthfully.

Sam closed her eyes knowing she needed to rest more. Peter reached out to cup both his hands around her right one. "I'm so sorry, Sam. For everything. I'm going to make it right, I promise."

Even with her eyes closed, she could feel Peter's emotion. *He does love me.* She didn't respond, though, but laid there. Before long, she let her eyes close and let the dreams succumb her conscience.

Peter headed downstairs. He stopped as he descended the last step and looked over to Boyd who had sat back down in the chair.

"I need some time to think," Peter threw at him

"Take all the time you need, Mr. Knowles," Boyd responded and smiled.

Peter exited the front doors. Nature leapt on him like a lion as the cool, sharp mountain air made his hair stand up. The smell of pine saturated his nostrils, and the brilliant sun's rays illuminated his face. Just a couple steps outside the house, Peter closed his eyes and extended his arms way above his head as he slightly leaned back to enjoy the routine stretch. This time, though, he extended it for a few seconds more. Refreshed and alert, both physically and mentally, Peter opened his eyes once again and began to walk along the winding, mountain road.

Peter had just made a promise he intended to keep. These 'others' out there wanted to harm not only him, but Sam too, and he wasn't going to let that happen. He was going to walk until he was sure of what he needed to do. With his mind abuzz, he started down the narrow street which led away from Boyd's house. The question Peter had to answer was how to stop these 'others' from coming after him and Sam. Should he expose them, and if so, how? What evidence did he have? Even if he could convince Boyd to expose himself to the world again, what purpose would it serve? Even if Boyd told them about everything, including how everyone had been deceived, the public would quickly dismiss him as a lunatic. Rather, they would just say he was wanting to get back into the spotlight and had made up crazy conspiracies to accomplish just such. Going through the many thoughts of exposing these others, Peter realized such attempts would probably be futile. He had to think of something else.

Could he and Sam hide? Boyd had successfully managed to avoid these others for many years. He had kept his identity off the grid, safely tucked away in a private home in the Sacramento mountains. And now, he was safe here in Mt. Charleston. Peter knew he could easily go into hiding having no attachments to the world. He was simple and self-reliant. The only big change would be his need to acquire money somehow, knowing he wouldn't be able to use his pension money anymore as withdrawals could be tracked. A cash paying job somewhere in Small Town, America would suffice though. Peter let out a sigh as he walked. He realized hiding wasn't plausible either. *Sam.* He could never ask her to hide. She hadn't done anything to anyone and was innocent of it all. She was free spirited, kind, and gentle. People in the world needed people like Sam. She gave them hope and warmth for the soul.

An hour of walking and contemplating ideas, Peter was still no closer to a solution. Every option he considered wasn't viable. Was finding out what Boyd wanted with him the only choice to possibly escape the predicament he and Sam were in? He knew the situation was larger than what he could handle. Perhaps Boyd had the solution. Reluctantly, he turned around and headed back to the house. For the first time in a long time, Peter faced a dilemma he didn't have the answer to.

There was no need to prolong the walk back as Peter was ready to hear what Boyd wanted. He hoped whatever it was, it would help Sam and him return to their normal lives. Several thoughts of what Boyd could possibly want entered his head, but he dismissed them realizing there was really no way of knowing. Turning into the driveway which led to Boyd's house, Peter stopped a moment and looked around. The mountains were beautiful and the sun was shining brightly on his face. He took a deep breath and then headed for the door.

"Welcome back!" Boyd greeted him from the chair near the fireplace.

Peter finished closing the front door behind him before throwing an affirming nod back towards Boyd. He headed for the couch.

Boyd sat still as he watched Peter walk across the room to sit on the couch. "A penny for your thoughts?" he asked Peter.

Peter, sitting comfortably on the couch, shook his head before getting straight to his question, "What do you want with me?" After a quick pause, and before Boyd could respond, he added, "I hope it includes a way for Sam to get her life back."

"In more ways than one, Mr. Knowles," Boyd answered with a smile. "As for what I want, I need to tell you and show you a few things before answering."

"I'm listening," Peter replied.

"Do you know who Osiris was?" Boyd asked.

Peter wondered why Boyd could never just get straight to the point. Always, there had to be a story or history lesson. He was about to get frustrated, but realized he was in need just as much as Boyd. Deciding to play along, he answered, "Yes. He was an ancient Egyptian god, or something like that."

"Yes, he was! God of the dead. He was the brother and husband of Isis and father of Horus. He was actually known by many names, depending on which culture's perspective you take. Isis, and Horus too, also had many names," Boyd stated. "You know, legend has it that Osiris' brother killed him and cut him up into pieces in order to claim his throne. Isis searched for and found the different pieces of Osiris with the exception of the phallus. She crafted one out of gold and then reassembled the body and brought it back to life long enough for the two to make a son, Horus. Of course, Horus is best known for having one eye."

"The all-seeing eye, right? A friend of mine referred to the eye on the back of the dollar bill as the eye of Horus. Any truth to that?" Peter asked.

"Perhaps. That eye on the dollar is placed atop a pyramid like the ones in Egypt, if I'm not mistaken. Ever imagine the Washington Monument as a phallus? Mr. Knowles, certain organizations have been around for a long, long time. They plan events which span more than a single lifetime. But let's save that story for another day, shall we?" Boyd pleaded.

Peter nodded, anxious for Boyd to get to the main point.

"Now that you have had your history lesson on Osiris, let's move on. Do you remember the 2003 Iraq war? What was the first thing the United States soldiers secured?"

"I have no idea," Peter replied, shaking his head slightly as if thinking to remember.

"The National Museum of Iraq. Quite strange for a military force to secure a museum to start a war, don't you think?" Boyd asked.

Peter shrugged and replied, "Depends. Maybe Saddam's fighters were there."

Boyd stood up from his chair and began to pace in front of the fireplace. "Perhaps there was something else there they wanted," he stated with an intriguing eyebrow raised. "They held the museum for a couple of days before looters went in and ransacked the place. Funny how armed soldiers couldn't stop looters. Regardless, after the war, a lot of the stolen artifacts were recovered. However, there were about five hundred pieces that haven't been found. The missing artifacts were part of the hidden treasures of Nimrod."

"Nimrod. I've heard that name before, but I don't remember where," Peter chimed in.

"Maybe at church," Boyd surmised. "Nimrod is spoken of in the Bible as well as other historical records. He is described as the son of Cush, grandson of Ham and great-grandson of Noah. He was a 'mighty one' and a 'mighty hunter before the Lord'. The Bible explains further that he was the king of Shinar. Read forward a few chapters and you find the tower of Babel was constructed by this king of Shinar. Later, this king of Shinar and a coalition of other kings made their way in conquest around the area known as the Fertile Crescent and engaged in battle against Sodom and Gomorrah. He was called Amraphel during this battle. Outside of the Bible, some believe this same king was also known as 'Hammurabi' to some, based on the timeline. Hammurabi and Nimrod's stories seem to be similar when comparing historical records. The name 'Gilgamesh' also surfaces when reading about Nimrod. I guess it depends on which culture was writing the history and which language they used. By the time Nimrod had reached Egypt, many referred to him as 'Pharaoh' or 'Osiris'. Following me so far, Mr. Knowles?"

"I'm not sure," Peter said with a serious expression. "I think you're saying Osiris and Nimrod were probably one in the same. And, you believe the United States military had something to do with treasures stolen from a museum in Iraq. You presume they took treasures which once belonged to Nimrod, or Osiris. You tell me, am I following you?"

"Seems you are," Boyd smiled. "One last bit of information, if I may, before I get to what I want from you?"

"Go for it," Peter said nonchalantly as he leaned back on the couch to listen.

Boyd continued, "In the last days of 2014, a Spanish-Italian archaeology team in Egypt discovered the legendary tomb of Osiris in the necropolis of Sheikh Abd el-Qurna on the west bank of Thebes in Egypt. It contained multiple levels with chambers and shafts. Inside, a wall relief with carvings of Osiris and demons holding knives was found. Want to guess what else was found inside this tomb?" Boyd raised an eyebrow with excitement as he waited for Peter to respond.

"Well," Peter started, "if it was a tomb in Egypt, I imagine they found a mummy inside." He couldn't help but smile at his answer.

"One would think they would," Boyd answered and began to pace back and forth over a short distance. "However, the archaeologists never revealed if they found a body. As a matter of fact, after they announced the discovery and released a couple of pictures of some of the rooms, everything went quiet, for the most part." Boyd went quiet and paced a few steps more before sitting down in his chair across from Peter. He appeared to be in deep thought.

"Okay," Peter chimed up. From his experience with Boyd, he surmised his time wasn't being wasted on history lessons and archaeological discoveries. If Boyd was telling him all this, it probably tied into the bigger picture somehow, but he just couldn't figure it out.

Peter decided to spur the conversation along, "So what do you think? Think they found a body? Think they are trying to hide something? I'm assuming you think these 'others' you talk about had something to do with all of this?"

"Oh," Boyd answered with a serious face, "I'd stake anything on it."

Boyd examined Peter's face and then sat back in his chair before stating, "Would you like to see the picture they took inside the tomb?"

He stood up after Peter nodded and retrieved a photo from the shelf behind the staircase. Upon his return, he handed the photo to Peter for examination. Boyd walked casually over to his chair and sat to give Peter some time to analyze what he saw.

Peter carefully examined the photo hoping for some insight as to what Boyd was trying to tell him. A carved-out room was dimly lit with a couple of light sources. The walls of the room were too dark for Peter to make out anything on them, but showing what was on the walls was not the purpose of this photo. Rather, this photo's purpose was to capture what the room contained in the center. Four blackened columns stood in the room and were spaced about ten feet apart from each other to form a rectangular shape. The columns themselves were square shaped with four flat sides which had hieroglyphics carved on them from top to bottom. On the floor, and within the rectangular area the four columns formed, a large rectangular area had been neatly excavated and was half filled with water. A dark, stonelike sarcophagus was placed in the water. Peter knew it was a sarcophagus because the top had been slid open. Due to the angle the photo was taken at, the contents inside remained obscure. Nothing else really jumped out at Peter about the photo.

Peter lifted his eyes up to look at Boyd. "Looks like an impressive find. One would think if they found a body, which could possibly be Osiris' corpse, they would want the world to know. Interesting!"

Boyd stood up and retrieved the photo. Returning to sit down, he held the photo in both hands which rested on his lap and stared at it. "What's interesting, Mr. Knowles, are the hieroglyphics on the columns."

"Looks like Egyptian writing to me, which means I have no idea," Peter replied with a chuckle.

"Resurrection!" Boyd grinned at Peter. "It's about bringing someone back to life."

Peter heard Boyd. And of course, it sounded preposterous. He squinted his eyes a little at Boyd as he leaned back against the couch and threw his right arm to rest on the back.

"The photo alone wouldn't have gotten me interested in any of this," Boyd began again. "However, my knowledge of the contents which were stolen from the Iraqi Museum..." Boyd began to smile big as he looked at Peter. "...made this photo very interesting to me."

"What knowledge?" Peter asked inquisitively.

"That Nimrod's treasures held at the Iraqi museum were saturated with hieroglyphics detailing the resurrection process," Boyd stated matter of factly. "Do you understand now, Mr. Knowles?"

"Understand what? That the 'others' want to resurrect a dead Egyptian god?" Peter chuckled. He could hardly believe he even said it. He began to shake his head in disbelief.

Boyd now sat on the edge of his seat with eagerness, "Is it so hard to imagine? Really? All the things I have told you about cloning, DNA sequencing, programming, preparing the masses..."

"Stop! Just stop!" Peter said sternly with a raised voice as he stood up.

"You've looked behind the curtain, Mr. Knowles! The truth revealed! There are powers out there far more powerful than you or I, and they just so happen to be puppet masters! They pull the strings, control the governments, and even more disturbing is the fact they keep it all in the dark while we sheeple just play their game!" Boyd exclaimed with all seriousness letting Peter know it wasn't a joke. "It's a very dark curtain."

The room went quiet. Both men stood thinking and waiting to see if the other would say anything more. The only noise was the crackling of the fire. Peter looked up and glanced around the ceiling as he thought. *Crazy, crazy, crazy!* He didn't fit anywhere into any of this equation. He was a loner. It was him, his truck and his RV. What part could he possibly have in mass population control, conspiracies, and secret societies? He wanted to get back to his life and leave all of this behind him. It wasn't intriguing anymore. His curiosity was abated and he wanted to leave this part of his life far behind him. Deep inside, Peter was afraid of the potential truth and what it could really mean. He didn't want to face any of it. He wanted to return to reality, even if it had all been orchestrated somehow. He turned and looked at Boyd.

"I just want to get my life back," he started solemnly. "My truck, my RV, the road!" He rubbed his face with both hands as if trying to wake up. "How do I do that?" he asked with all sincerity.

"One way is hope and luck," Boyd responded and then sat down. "You can walk out of that door right now and, with a little bit of hope and luck, you can live your life as you were. But how much trust are you willing to place in hope and luck? Who knows, maybe these 'others' have forgotten all about you. Maybe they realized you weren't really a threat to their agenda and would leave it at that." Boyd couldn't help but smile a little sarcastically.

"What's the other way?" Peter asked quickly as if the first option wasn't an option at all. After all, these 'others' had tried to kill him and the woman he had come to know.

Boyd's smile widened. "Help me fight against them. I need you to do something for me, something which will require risk."

"And in return for this risk?" Peter asked.

"A new life for both you and Miss Fisher," Boyd stated calmly. "I can't get you back your old life, Mr. Knowles, but I can give you a better one. One with a nice, discreet home anywhere you like. One with a new name and a new bank account. Even a new truck and RV to go along with it, if you like!"

What other choice did Peter have? Of course, he would need to think about this as well as talk it over with Sam. What would she say? What alternative did they have?

After a few seconds of contemplation, Peter looked back at Boyd and said, "What exactly are you wanting me to do?"

"Clean floors and take out trash," Boyd casually stated as he sat down. He extended his palm towards the couch indicating Peter should sit down.

Peter raised an eyebrow questioningly as he sat and was about to say something, but Boyd continued talking.

"When I heard about this archaeological find and surmised certain entities may be involved, I hired someone to investigate more and gather information. It only took him a trip to Egypt and a couple of weeks to find enough information to convince me they were!" Boyd explained.

Curiously, Peter asked, "What did he find out?"

Boyd was happy Peter was listening. "He found the dig site, but it had been placed off limits to the public. Additionally, there were several security personnel guarding the entrance which prevented access. Turning to alternative means, he inquired with several Egyptian vendors which had set up shops to trap tourists. Of course, they didn't provide any additional information as to what could have been found inside the tomb. But what they did provide was eye witness reports of large trucks with trailers parked near the entrance. A large curtain, as they described it, had been placed around the opening which prevented anyone from seeing what was being loaded into the trailers. They described the trucks and trailers as white with no identifying logos or markings. They were there only three days before departing," explained Boyd.

"And you think this loading activity into these white trailers is proof the 'others' were involved?" Peter inquired.

"Who else?" Boyd asked. "If it were only an ancient tomb, archaeologists would have taken years to completely excavate the site. Using brushes and chisels, they would have meticulously removed each piece and certainly wouldn't have used large trailers to haul their findings in."

"Okay," Peter agreed as he thought. "Let's say your assumption is correct. Unless you know what they loaded or where they went, it is still all speculation."

Boyd nodded in agreement. "It would be. But there's more!" Boyd said with eagerness. "Two large, white trailers were loaded into an American C-5 cargo aircraft on 14 January 2015 headed for Nellis Air Force Base. That was the critical piece of information!"

"How so?" Peter asked skeptically.

"Know of any secret bases around here, Mr. Knowles. Perhaps a base I have been employed at before?"

"Area 51? You think they took whatever was in the back of those trailers to Area 51?" Peter inquired as his interest was growing.

Boyd nodded quietly and gave Peter a few more seconds to contemplate what he had just been told. Then, he continued, "I no longer have access there, obviously. However, I need to find out what they took there from the tomb. That's where you come in Mr. Knowles," Boyd smiled as he finished his sentence.

"I can't help you there. I'm retired. Furthermore, even if I was still active duty, only a few select airmen get selected to work there. It isn't exactly a base where they allow you to park your RV overnight!" Peter contested.

"I can get you in," Boyd stated matter of factly.

"I don't feel like getting shot! In case you have forgotten, it's a shoot on site type of place," Peter responded, shaking his head.

"Let me explain," Boyd responded. "When I discovered something had been moved from that tomb to here in Nevada, I knew I had to find out what it was. Their cyber security systems are such that my skills and knowledge are useless. As a result, I had to think of another way. So, to make a long story short, I created a janitorial business and began bidding for a contract with the base. Well, I funded it anyways, it's actually Tony who runs the business. Of course, I underbid every competitor which allowed me to secure the contract."

"Haven't we talked about curiosity before? You see where it has gotten me and yet here you are, determined to find out what they have to satisfy your curiosity. Even if you do determine what they found and brought there, what good is it going to do you?" Peter asked.

"I have my reasons, Mr. Knowles," Boyd responded. "I've had years in seclusion to think about all I've done in the past and what I've been a part of. Perhaps it is time to tear down the dark curtains and show people what's really going on."

"Alright. I still don't see why you need me. Just get Tony, who heads this business you talked about, to go in and find out," Peter threw back.

"Running a business with a contract is completely different than getting access. They would never expect the business owner to clean toilets himself. Furthermore, a background investigation check is required for anyone obtaining access and that wouldn't be good for Tony. Being the business owner and not having access keeps him from unnecessary scrutiny," answered Boyd. "And of course, I'm not going to rely on one of the janitors to find out what I need. They are not trained in how the military works, the jargon, protocols, et cetera."

Peter understood what Boyd was explaining. A lot of time and effort had been spent planning for this. Had Boyd been waiting for someone to come along? Someone with a military background and nothing to lose? The thoughts in Peter's head began to swirl in a continuous loop which spawned question after question. He decided to stop thinking to clear his mind.

"Did you somehow lure me into all of this?" Peter asked with all seriousness.

Boyd could see the sternness in Peter's face. "Of course not!" Boyd rebuked. "I've been looking for prospects for some time now, but my efforts have proved futile. You were a welcomed coincidence. It was your intuitiveness and analytical skills that led you to me, remember? It didn't take me long after meeting you to figure out you could be of assistance to me. But it had to be your choice. It will always be your choice, Mr. Knowles."

Peter had to agree it was he who found Boyd and not the other way around. The thought calmed him a little. But now, he had a choice he was going to have to make.

"So, you were serious when you said earlier you wanted me to clean floors, huh? Besides this cleaning, what specifically are you wanting?"

Realizing he was making progress, Boyd continued, "I want you to immerse yourself into the life of a janitor. Follow the schedule, do your duties and let people get familiar with your face. Granted, it will take some time, but I believe it's worth it. Listen to conversations, peek inside doors, and try to decide where they may be keeping whatever they found. When you feel the time is right, do what you have to do to find out what they retrieved from that tomb."

"I can't make a decision until I speak with Sam. This involves her just as much as it does me," Peter informed Boyd.

"Of course," was the reply. "Know that I'll take care of her if you choose to do this task for me. Take a day to think about it. Tony and I have some things we need to take care of, but we should be back by tomorrow evening. You and Sam enjoy the evening. Mi casa es su casa!"

Peter nodded and continued to sit as Boyd walked away and up the stairs. *Area 51!* He had a lot to think about.

Chapter 15

With the exception of Sam sleeping upstairs, Peter had the house to himself. He had warmed up some leftovers from the night before and had even walked through the entire house since Boyd and Tony had departed two hours earlier. He had convinced himself to walk around the house and, in particular, check out Boyd's bedroom. A crazy thought of a sleep preservation chamber from some science fiction movie had entered his head which led him there. Of course, there was no such contraption. Rather, it was just another rich, fancy room devoid of personal enhancements, such as pictures and paintings. He knew it was the right room, because he noticed the clothes Boyd had worn the previous day, folded up and placed on a chair beside the bed. By the end of his trek through the house, Peter realized there was nothing which could indicate whom the house belonged to. *Simple and smart.*

Although he had peeked in on Sam sleeping during his walk through, a couple more hours had passed so he figured it was time she ate something. He headed upstairs and quietly walked to her bedroom door. She was still sleeping. He briefly thought of the struggle leukemia had placed on her life. It saddened him. He didn't understand why such a wonderful person had been afflicted with such a terrible cancer. He watched her sleep a little more before walking over to sit on the edge of the bed.

"Sam," he whispered, not wanting to startle her.

After no response, he tried it a second time a little louder, "Sam."

He was relieved to see it work this time as she rolled over gently and slowly opened her eyes.

"What time is it?" she asked through a raspy voice.

Peter grabbed the bottle of water on the nightstand and unscrewed the lid. Handing it over to her, he replied, "It's about three o'clock. Thought I would let you get your rest."

She reached out for the bottle of water and consumed most of it. She looked around the room and then back at Peter to whom she handed the bottle. "Thanks."

He placed the bottle back on the nightstand and then offered Sam, "Hey, there's some leftovers downstairs. What do you say I heat them up for you? You must be starving. Want me to bring them up here to you?"

"Please. I should be able to take care of myself by tomorrow," she responded, indicating she was very familiar with what had happened to her. "Can you wet me a washcloth so I can wipe my face before you go?"

"Of course," Peter replied as he hopped up and retrieved what she asked for from the bathroom.

"Don't be too fast heating the food up, please. I need to pee and brush my teeth too," she spoke with a little smile.

"Sure, no problem," Peter answered as he headed downstairs. As he approached the door, he paused and turned around to say, "I'm glad you're awake."

He missed me. She could tell. Although she had only known him face-to-face for a short time, she could read his eyes as if they spoke his thoughts. She only wished she was in a better condition and under different circumstances. *Uggh! I look awful!*

It was about fifteen minutes before Peter returned with the food on a tray. Sam had finished her business and even managed to brush her hair.

"You look great!" he voiced as he placed the tray on the bedside for her to eat. He walked over and sat on the chair which had previously served as his bed.

Sam looked up sarcastically with her eyes. *Really?* She was about to take her first bite when she paused to ask, "Where's Alfred and Tony?" She continued with her bite.

"They had to take care of some business or something. They will be back tomorrow evening," he answered.

After a few moments watching Sam eat, he said, "I found out what he wanted."

Sam stopped chewing in anticipation with her eyes locked on Peter. "And?" she managed to ask, pushing the food in her mouth into her jaw.

Could she be any more attractive! Peter told her of his conversation with Boyd while she ate. He provided every detail he could remember and the choices they would have to choose from. All the while, she ate and listened. She would raise an eyebrow, let her mouth fall open, and even throw her head back in disbelief every so often while Peter spoke.

"So that's it! I told him I had to speak with you before I did anything," Peter explained to her.

Sam had finished her food by the time Peter finished explaining. After taking a final sip of water to wash her meal down, she placed the water bottle on the nightstand and looked at Peter seriously.

"So, let me get this straight. I have a choice. I can either leave and try to recover the life I had, or, I can sit here with Alfred while you're away at Crazy Land in hopes of a big house and bank account. If I go back to what I had, there's a possibility someone may kill me. If I take the second option, I forfeit my old life. Sound about right?" she summarized.

Peter realized how absurd all of this sounded, but all he could do was pull in his lips, raise his eyebrows, and nod.

Sam had been sitting up to eat. But after the nod from Peter, she fell back against her pillow and began to laugh. Peter couldn't help but join her. There they were, right in the middle of the world's largest conspiracy, and all they could do was laugh. The longer they laughed, the harder they laughed. It was a while before they stopped.

Peter was the first to speak, "Do you have any family in St. George?"

Sam had stopped laughing but still had a smile on her face. Peter knew it wasn't a joyous smile, but rather one of those smiles people give when they don't know what else to do. She looked over to Peter.

"Family? As in family I may have an emotional attachment to which might prevent me from starting a new life?" she asked a little sarcastically.

"Look," Peter stated and paused for a short moment. "I don't know what the right answer is. I still can't believe this is all happening! Maybe I'm losing my mind! I can't seem to think straight, I don't know what's after this, and I really have no idea how far into this hole we are. That's why I'm up here with you, Sam. I need you to help me realize this is all happening, if it is, as well as help me make sound choices for what's best for us."

Sam could see Peter was at a loss. Perhaps, he was even more at a loss than she was. He didn't have the answers to the question they both had, which was how were they going to get their lives back and get out of this unbelievable situation. They both sat quietly contemplating what was happening.

"Do you really think someone wants us dead?" she asked in a calm voice.

Peter looked back over to her and replied, "I'm not sure. There are so many possibilities. I know two fake FBI agents visited and stole from me. I know Tony shot two men at the restaurant. I know Alfred Boyd is alive."

Sam lay quietly to let Peter continue. She could tell he was trying to figure it out as he spoke.

Peter continued, "As far as all of this conspiracy stuff, it could all just be coincidence, I guess, with Boyd just playing a game with us.

But, I have to admit, that type of control sounds logical based on my military intelligence experience."

Peter paused for a moment. His brows had squinched together indicating he was in deep thought. Sam remained silent. She knew she didn't have the answer, so her best choice was to let him figure things out.

"On the other hand, a lot of this stuff sounds like nonsense! Fallen angels, a very old guy that looks half his age, mega corporations controlling the public with subliminal messages..." Peter went on while shaking his head. "But the numbers add up and it is Alfred Boyd we found." He looked over to Sam. "There's so much I've heard which sounds unbelievable and even crazy. Strangely enough, I can put a finger on all of it."

"Sounds like you believe it then," Sam offered.

"Based on what I have learned compared to what I can find? Yes!" he answered. "If I had to give an intelligence analysis on the current situation, logic would dictate my recommendation to believe it."

"If that's the case, then you also believe Alfred when he says our lives are in danger because of what we know," she surmised.

Peter nodded slowly. Both sat quietly as their minds wrapped around their conclusion.

After a few minutes, Sam spoke, "My mother died when I was four. We used to live in Maine, but my father moved us to St. George when she died. I went to school, and he worked. It was just the two of us, really, and a few friends I made. As he grew older, he started to forget things and, eventually, I had to place him in a home. My sickness prevented me from taking care of him the way I wanted to. I still visit him once a week, but at this point, he doesn't even remember who I am."

Again, Peter felt sadness for Sam. He didn't know what to say, but he knew she was telling him in response to his earlier question about her family.

"How old is he?" Peter asked.

"Only seventy-eight," she answered solemnly. "He has always been a good man, taking care of me and all. Funny thing is, he's probably going to outlive me. Considering his condition, I guess it's kind of a good thing that he won't remember that the girl who visited him once a week was actually his daughter."

Peter recognized what was happening as one of those times people went over and placed an arm around a person for consolation. And, for once, he felt like doing it. Repositioning himself beside Sam, he placed his arm around her the best he could. He wanted her to know he was empathizing with her.

"I'm sorry," was all he could manage to say in her ear.

After a minute, Sam held her head up. Her eyes were red and the bags beneath them were swollen. "Can you get me that washcloth out of the bathroom, please?"

Peter stood up and did as she asked.

After wiping her face and eyes, she sat up straighter and said, "Enough of that. I'm sorry."

"It's okay. I understand," replied Peter.

Sam took a deep breath and said, "Well, the way I see it, if we have to make a choice, I can go back to St. George and die from a bullet or sickness. Or, I can die with a new life, house and large bank account somewhere else. Doesn't sound like much of a choice."

Peter hadn't realized it before. *How stupid!* Sam really didn't have a choice at all. There was no new life for her. Either way, she was going to die, and she knew it. He felt so selfish and ashamed.

Sam saw the look on Peter's face. Again, his eyes told her everything he was feeling. It hadn't been her intention to make him feel that way.

"It's not your fault, Peter," she expressed with concern. "And I know you never intended for any of this to happen to me."

Something was wrong. Peter felt something in his guts tightening. It was a physical manifestation of his emotions and it hurt. His hands began to shake and his breathing quaked. He felt as if his muscles were shutting down along his upper arms, back and legs.

Sam was looking straight at Peter. She noticed a rigidness all about his face and body. He was staring straight ahead and refused to blink. As his face started to turn solemn, she felt the bed starting to vibrate softly from the slight convulsions going on in Peter's body. Then, a couple of tears rolled down his face. She could tell Peter was uncomfortable with crying and that he was trying to hold it back. The fact he was crying now confirmed her thoughts. *He truly loves me.* She scooted next to him on the edge of the bed and pulled his head into her chest. She gently ran her fingers through his hair and whispered, "It's okay. It's okay." Holding him there in her arms, she realized Peter no longer had the life he loved with his truck and RV. She knew, in his mind, he had nothing now...except her.

Chapter 16

Peter remembered he had observed a pizza place in the small town of Mt. Charleston during his last walk, so he decided to head there now. He and Sam had consumed more of the leftovers the previous evening, but they wanted something different today. Besides, Peter needed to walk to think a few things over. It was only yesterday he realized he couldn't control his emotions when Sam was involved. He couldn't have helped it. His feelings for her were strong, and he knew it. Moreover, he knew she knew it too. She was a different story, though, since Peter couldn't tell exactly how she felt about him. Sure, she seemed to really enjoy his company during their initial, face-to-face meeting. But then, everything had turned to chaos and out of his control. She had expressed her anger at being forced into a car and driven out of the state. Then, she was so stressed, the leukemia had gotten the best of her. Was there any way she could have feelings for him after that? If it had not been for him, she would still be in St. George managing her bike shop. Of course, she did comfort him yesterday, but that really didn't mean she had feelings for him. It could have just been to show empathy. It was all new ground for Peter.

After a twenty-minute wait, Peter had the pepperoni and jalapeno pizza in hand. *Jalapenos?* He had been surprised when Sam asked for them, as most women, or other people for that fact, didn't really like spicy foods. *Well, we have that in common.* He smiled at the thought as he walked back towards the house.

It was quite chilly outside, but he was enjoying the fresh, mountain air. It seemed to clear his mind. He felt well rested. He should be, since both he and Sam had fallen asleep on the bed after he lost control of his emotions. The running of her fingers through his hair was like a prescription strength, sleeping pill. That, and the strain of the emotions which he felt had knocked him right out. He had gotten up later and fixed some of the leftovers. It was late after they ate, so they both decided to get more sleep. *Never knew I could sleep that long.*

Although he had awoken early this morning, he didn't do much of anything. A shower, a cup of coffee, and a quick perusal through an unexciting book in Boyd's bookcase. He was relieved when he had heard Sam call for him from upstairs. Boyd had stocked some bagels in the cupboard, so Peter had taken one with some cream cheese upstairs to her for a small breakfast. There, they talked more about their choice and had come to a decision. The more he talked to Sam, the more he understood her and the more he grew fond of her.

Peter was about to open the front door when he heard a car approaching. Turning around with the pizza in his hand, he saw Boyd and Tony pulling up. He couldn't help but notice how the car seemed as if it had just been cleaned even though they had been gone for a while. *Does Tony just clean the car when Boyd is occupied?* Boyd smiled through the windshield and threw up a quick hand as they parked. As the doors opened, he stepped out and peered over the car with the continuing smile.

"Pizza! I love pizza," he exclaimed as he started to walk towards Peter. "Tired of leftovers, eh?"

"One can only eat so much duck," Peter replied. "We were about to start quacking," he added with a half smile.

"How's Miss Fisher?" Boyd asked as he stepped in front of Peter and opened the door for him.

Peter started in the house and answered, "Better! And hungry, too!"

Tony followed the two men inside, closed the door and then proceeded up the stairs. Boyd and Peter headed for the kitchen.

When the two were almost in the kitchen, Boyd paused. "I apologize. I didn't even think this pizza may be just for the two of you," Boyd stated apologetically.

Peter saw the quaint, little smile Boyd had when he said it. "No, no! Nothing like that. Please, join us. I must warn you, though, it has jalapenos," he informed Boyd as he placed the pizza on the counter.

"Need me to get Tony to get the plates and napkins, or can you handle it?" Peter asked in a sarcastic, yet jokingly way.

"I never knew you were a funny man, Mr. Knowles!" was the reply followed by an obvious, exaggerated laugh.

"I'm going to check on Sam and find out if she wants to eat upstairs. She was feeling better earlier and was thinking about getting up to move about. Perhaps she'll join us downstairs," Peter said as he headed out of the kitchen.

"Splendid!" replied Boyd.

The door to Sam's room was shut when Peter arrived. She was obviously up and walking about since he had left it open when he left. He knocked lightly on the door and then heard footsteps approaching the door.

Sam opened the door with a smile. "Hey! Pizza here?" she asked.

She looked much better! She had combed her hair and put on the clothes Boyd had previously provided. The sky-blue hoodie and black jogging pants looked great on her. Peter surmised Boyd had been careful when finding something for her to wear. Women were peculiar with their clothes. Even more, they could always seem to psychoanalyze what a man thought of them based on the clothes the man recommended or chose. If too much skin showed, she would think the man thought she was a hooker. Too conservative, and he would think she was old. Boyd had been smart with his selection.

"Yes, the pizza is here," Peter answered. "And so is Tony and Boyd."

Sam cocked her head to the side and asked, "Why do you call him Boyd? Why not Alfred, since that's his first name?"

"It's the military in me," Peter answered with a smile. "I usually refer to people by their last name."

"Oh! That's odd," she replied. After a couple of seconds, she asked, "Wanna eat downstairs?"

"That's exactly what I came to ask. Do you feel up to it?" he asked.

"I feel like getting out of this room! Let's go!" she said while slipping by Peter and heading for the stairs.

I think she is in a good mood...maybe?

As the two of them walked downstairs and entered the kitchen, Boyd was looking through the cabinets. Three white plates had been placed on the counter beside the pizza box.

"I'm not sure where the napkins are," Boyd voiced over to them as he closed the cabinet doors. "We'll just have to use some paper towels, if that's ok?"

"Sounds fine to me!" Sam answered as she sat in one of the four chairs around a small, glass table near a window. "I'm so hungry!"

"That's a good sign. I can only imagine how draining your ordeal must be. So sorry you have to go through that. Seems like bad things tend to happen to good people," said a sincere Boyd.

"Ordeal? Oh, you mean the shootout, the kidnapping, and conspiracy theories!" Sam responded sarcastically.

Boyd walked over and sat in the chair across from Sam which left it up to Peter to get the paper towels and serve the pizza. Before long, the three of them had an open pizza box in the middle of the table and were filling their stomachs. They were quiet to start with, preferring the pizza over conversation.

After Sam finished her first slice, she broke the silence, "So, you want Peter to go to Crazy Land."

Boyd was caught by surprise. He stopped chewing, glanced over to Peter, and then back to Sam. Was that a statement or question? He started chewing again in order to swallow and reply.

"I see the two of you have talked," he replied, looking over to Peter.

Peter wasn't going to help him. He rather enjoyed watching Sam converse with Boyd. He decided to sit back and listen, once again. Sam was still waiting for an answer as she reached for a second slice.

"I do! I expect he filled you in on all the details?" Boyd asked Sam.

"You know you are asking him to put his life on the line, right? I've seen those TV shows about Area 51, and the thing that comes most to mind are those signs warning people to keep out or be shot on sight," she informed Boyd and then took a bite of pizza.

"Of course, there are risks, Miss Fisher, but I assure you, steps have been taken to mitigate them," Boyd replied seriously.

Sam swallowed and responded, "Miss Fisher...mitigated...you sound like a lawyer."

Peter was smiling inside. If Boyd couldn't have an intellectual, jousting conversation with someone, then he was handicapped. He was out of his league with Sam. *Note to self...don't use 'mitigated'.*

"Would you rather I call you Sam?" Boyd asked apologetically.

"I'd rather," she answered. "And, just to summarize, in return for Peter doing this, you offer us a new life, a house and a very large bank account, right? I'm assuming it's a house for each of us." She took another bite.

"That was the offer. Though, large bank accounts are relative. Wouldn't you agree?" Boyd smiled as he answered.

"Your 'large' is bigger than my 'large'. Let's keep it relative to you if you're serious about all of this," she answered.

Peter saw the large smile on Boyd's face. Both men were fascinated with Sam. She was exciting, to the point, and had the type of charisma that just mesmerized others. *I bet she gets good deals on buying vehicles.*

"So, can I assume you two have agreed to my offer?" asked Boyd as his face changed back to one of seriousness.

Sam looked over to Peter. Both knew the answer as they had discussed it earlier in the morning. They agreed to take Boyd up on his offer, but that was about the extent of it. They figured they would wait till later to look at the rewards in more detail. The choice had to be made now, though.

"You realize it's a lose-lose situation for Sam. Whether she walks out of the door now or starts a new life, ..." Peter answered but didn't finish the sentence.

It was easy for Boyd and Sam to see the emotion in Peter's response. Sam wasn't expecting him to say that.

"The loss would be ours, Mr. Knowles," he answered in a comforting tone. "But one never really knows how long we have. Look at me." Boyd glanced over towards Sam to make sure she heard him.

"Before I agree to your terms, I need to know Sam will be taken care of," Peter finally answered. "Will she stay here? And I want a doctor that will be able to respond immediately and not have to drive from Vegas."

"She will be under my protection, right here," Boyd answered with a small smile. "And getting a doctor up here will be no problem, I assure you. Let me get Tony so we can discuss the future..."

"And one more thing," Peter interrupted. Sam stopped chewing and Boyd raised an eyebrow. "Her father is at a nursing home in St. George. I'm pretty sure they have surveillance cameras installed and I would like Sam to be able to see her father whenever she wants. I'm sure hacking into their systems will be no problem for you."

Sam looked over to Boyd and he looked back at her. "Not a problem at all," he said. "Anything else I can do for you, Mr. Knowles?"

"If I'm unsuccessful and something should happen to me..." Peter started.

"Sam will be given what I've promised whether you succeed or fail. I just ask that you try," Boyd finished the statement.

"Before you go, I've got to know something else. Why are you so curious about what they took to Area 51? Are you seriously planning to expose them?" Peter asked seriously.

Boyd paused for a second to think, then responded while shaking his head slowly, "Lies! It's all lies. They used me to further their plans and then tried to kill me after they disposed of my colleagues. Expose them I will! I'll expose the whole lot of it to the entire world! With you, the opportunity has finally arrived. All we have to do now is find out what they are up to and then I'll expose myself and what they are doing to the public."

Peter could see the seriousness on Boyd's face. "Then I'll do it, or at least try to," Peter concluded.

Boyd relaxed a bit. "Excellent! Why don't we all meet by the fireplace in a few minutes," Boyd offered. "I'll bring Tony."

Sam and Peter nodded in agreement. Boyd finished his last bite of pizza and stood up.

"Thanks for the pizza," Boyd said graciously. "Now, if you two will excuse me?"

Both Sam and Peter nodded and then watched Boyd walk out of the kitchen. From the sound of the fading footsteps, they could tell he went upstairs. The two looked at each other.

"I think I've lost my mind," Peter put out there with a blank expression on his face.

"That makes two of us, then. Are you sure you want to do this? I mean, if you get caught, there's no telling what would happen to you," Sam replied.

"I imagine I would either be shot or locked up for a very, very long time," he answered.

"Well, if anyone could pull it off, it's you Peter," she said. "Your intelligence background in the military, your logical way of thinking and your meticulous analysis of people have prepared you for this. Don't you think?"

Peter looked impressed. "That's quite an assessment for only having met me for a few days," he stated, waiting for a reply.

"I've known you for a while, Peter. Reading your emails provided great insight. Your grammar and formatting are almost always perfect when writing and you never misspell a word. Plus, it doesn't take a genius to figure out someone who served in the military is going to be disciplined. As for the meticulous analysis, your eyes are always looking around. When I see you looking at someone, you're not just seeing their face and clothes. No, you are seeing the way they comb their hair, the condition of their hands, whether their shirt is tucked in, that kind of stuff," she summarized.

"I'm impressed," Peter submitted. "Not many people know me like that. For that matter, not many people know me at all. I'm almost embarrassed to admit it, but you are the only person I've really conversed with on a continual basis."

"I can tell. You should socialize more when all of this is over," Sam encouraged with a smile. "You have a lot to share with the world."

"Do you think you'll be okay here?" Peter inquired. "Boyd seems weird and all, but I think he will stick to his word and look after you. Will you be comfortable is probably the better question?"

"Only one way to find out, I guess. I can tell you I don't plan on just sitting around. I plan on keeping myself busy," she answered. "How long do you think it will take you to do what Alfred wants you to do?"

Peter shook his head slowly as he thought about the question. "I'm not sure, to be honest. It may take a while," he responded.

"Like a week, or a month?" she asked, trying to narrow his response down.

He continued to shake his head and honestly answered, "I really have no idea, Sam. I mean, it depends on the security measures and if I can garner trust with some of the workers there. On top of that, there may be nothing there to start with, you know?"

"Well, I hope it doesn't take too long," she stated as she stared more intently at Peter.

Peter could see the true meaning in what she said. He surmised the doctors had probably given her a prediction on how long she would live. From the way she looked at him now, he imagined it wasn't far away.

The two finished eating and then headed upstairs to their rooms. They were going to shower and get ready for the meeting downstairs.

An hour passed by. Peter knocked on Sam's door and spoke through it, "You ready?"

The door opened. She was in the same clothes but her hair was still wet from the shower.

"I guess," she said.

As the two walked down the stairs, they noticed Boyd and Tony waiting for them over by the fireplace. Peter noticed Tony was standing in front of the fire with a folder while Boyd was sitting with his legs crossed in his polio chair which he had moved to beside the couch. He had decided to call it 'the Polio chair' based on the story Boyd had told him when they had arrived. He and Sam continued and took a seat on the couch.

"Everything has been arranged," Tony started. He handed the folder he had over to Peter. "Here's your security badge, passport, driver's license, birth certificate, social security card and debit card."

Peter opened the folder to find the aforementioned. It was his face on the identity documents, but the name was different. *Peter Norris?* All of the documents looked real.

"Where did you get these and how did you get them so fast?" Peter asked.

"The little day trip we took, Mr. Knowles," Boyd answered from the side. "Your picture wasn't hard to acquire."

"So you knew I was going to agree?" Peter asked, looking over to Boyd.

"I had to be prepared, either way," was the only answer Boyd provided.

Peter closed the folder and handed it over to Sam who began to inspect the documents as well.

"You will be staying in a small house on the south side of Alamo. The address there is the same as what is on your documents," Tony continued.

"Wait!" Peter exclaimed. "Alamo? That's on the other side of the Nellis training range. It's like a three-hour drive from here. I thought I would be staying here."

"That wouldn't work," Tony answered. "Although there are Janet flights between Las Vegas and the Ranch, they are reserved for military personnel and government employees. All of the janitorial contracts hire from the closest towns, with Alamo being the biggest supplier."

Sam realized she probably wouldn't understand a lot of the conversation before she even sat down. She had never been associated with military or government work. Rather than interfere with questions, she decided to sit and listen. If she needed to understand something better, she would ask Peter afterwards.

"I understand," Peter reluctantly answered. "This task may take a while. Am I going to be able to come here and see Sam?"

Boyd and Sam turned to look at Peter.

"To make sure she's okay, and all," Peter clarified. *My cheeks feel red.*

Tony pulled a cell phone from his back pocket and tossed it over to Peter.

"You can call her whenever you like. I have a phone upstairs for her," he stated as he quickly glanced over to Boyd who nodded.

"I assured Tony you two would be smart enough not to make calls to known relatives or friends. Please don't make a fool out of me," Boyd informed the two. He smiled knowing the decision would please them.

"And, if something were to happen to Miss Fish…," Boyd cut off his statement. "Sam, then we would alert you via the cell and arrange to pick you up at the small airport just west of Alamo. Does that make you feel better?"

Peter nodded.

"Also, make sure not to discuss anything associated with your work, its location, or your true identities." Tony added. "Agreed?"

Peter and Sam nodded.

"I'll provide you more information on the company you'll be working for as well as some dos and don'ts on our ride to Alamo tomorrow. Any questions for right now?" Tony asked in conclusion.

Peter realized this little briefing was more for Sam than himself. He surmised there were parts of the briefing for his ears only which he would get during the ride.

"I'll be riding with you and Tony tomorrow," Boyd put in.

Again, Peter nodded in agreement. During the drive, he would have about three hours to pick Boyd's brain on how to best blend in at Area 51.

"Sounds like a plan," Sam cut in. "I assume I'll have the house to myself? It will give me a chance to be nosy and look around," she said jokingly.

"I have something for you too, Sam," Boyd smiled at her in return. He reached into his pocket and pulled out a plastic card. Getting up to hand it to Sam, he added, "I'm going to provide you with a computer and access to the internet so you can shop online and not have to be bored to death around here. Same rules apply as we just discussed concerning contacting others or using your real name. Use this card to order what you like. Clothes, movies, books, and other things to keep you occupied. If the funds run out, and they shouldn't, just let me or Tony know. I'll provide the address for the card and shipping as well."

Sam accepted the card and looked at the men. "Do you know what you're doing?" she asked with a wry grin.

A woman with a credit card and freedom to use it at her will. All three men knew what she asked and they just smiled and laughed in return.

"Sam, I truly mean it when I say my house is your house. Make yourself at home!" Boyd politely said to her.

The gesture made Peter and Sam feel more comfortable with all that was happening. Boyd had done what he could to make her feel welcomed while reassuring Peter she would be taken care of.

Boyd stood up. "I think I'll retire to my room as it has been quite a day. I must admit, I'm excited the opportunity has presented itself. There's been a lot of planning and anticipation for this to happen. Together, maybe we can shed some light on what's really happening to the rest of the world," he said to the others and then went upstairs.

Tony followed after him. Sam and Peter looked at each other for a moment waiting to see what expression the other one would show. Sam finally smiled. It made Peter feel better. Sure, she could be smiling just to make him feel better, but he felt she truly meant it.

"Going to do some shopping, huh?" Peter asked, smiling back.

"Oh, yeah!" Sam replied. "You heard him say his house is my house, right?"

Again, Peter smiled back at her and threw in a nod.

"I'll make the best of it here. Sure, it's not really my life and all. But, considering the circumstances, I just as well make the best of it," Sam reckoned. "You just make sure you do what you need to do and get out of there, okay?"

"As fast as I can," he replied. "If all of this is true, and the American people have been deceived, then I need to do what I can to help reveal it. I didn't serve my country for so many years just to have these 'others' take advantage of it."

Sam nodded in response showing she understood his commitment to his country. She also understood she might never see him again after tomorrow if something went wrong.

"Peter," she started but then paused.

Peter waited for her to finish.

"I know you didn't mean for any of this to happen. I also know you care about me and I truly appreciate that. Get this done so we can get back to the restaurant and continue what we started. Okay?" she said in a sincere manner.

Peter was smiling wide inside. *Hope.* Maybe he hadn't screwed things up so badly there was no recovering from it.

"I will," he answered.

Chapter 17

Morning came early and started with a quick breakfast Tony had prepared. After the meal, Peter and Sam exchanged goodbyes and wished each other the best. Before Peter had gotten in the car, Sam walked over and gave him a hug without saying a word. It was their first real hug, so Peter decided to cherish the moment. He remembered the look in her eyes, what she was wearing, and the way she had crossed her arms together afterwards to block the morning chill. He didn't say anything, either. Sam watched the three men depart.

Heading down from Mt. Charleston, Peter looked over to Boyd who sat in the rear seat with him. "I'm going to need some clothes, toiletries, and a few other household items. Think we can stop at a shopping center on the northside of Vegas?"

"Of course," Boyd answered and nodded to Tony who was looking at him in the rearview mirror.

"I appreciate the care you have shown Sam. She is a wonderful person deserving of better," Peter then threw in.

"She is indeed," Boyd answered. "Hopefully, when this is all over with, you two can continue your relationship. I can tell you have deep feelings for her. I think she knows it too!"

Peter didn't reply to the statement. Rather, he decided to go ahead and garner some information.

"So what can you tell me, from your experience, about Area 51?" Peter asked.

"I can tell you the people there don't refer to it as Area 51. They prefer to call it the Ranch. Tony can correct me if he knows something different as I'm a little out of date," Boyd started. "It's not what you are used to either, in regards to military bases. With the exception of the security forces, the military personnel assigned there wear civilian clothing and refer to each other on a first name basis. No one salutes. There's also a sense of pride in each person there, knowing they are part of an elect group lucky enough to work at the Ranch. They get excited when a new project has arrived with each of them eagerly awaiting their first glimpse of something new."

"Something new? What exactly do they work on there? All I've ever heard is they have top-secret aircraft there," Peter inquired.

"They do have aircraft there they experiment with. You already know the capabilities of one as I recall from our initial meeting back on West Side Road. However, as I have told you, there's more there than meets the eye. Most of the people that work at the Ranch believe they only test top-secret aircraft and reverse engineer foreign equipment they acquire. What really goes on there eludes most of them," Boyd explained further.

"Project UGEN," Peter chimed in.

"Yes, Mr. Knowles. Project UGEN," Boyd replied.

"Based on what you've told me, Project UGEN is a huge conspiracy to control people," Peter elaborated.

Boyd nodded in agreement.

"But there's more to it than that, right? Something you haven't told me," Peter asked inquisitively.

Boyd just sat there not answering. It was obvious to Peter the man was hesitant to answer.

"I've been able to wrap my finger around a lot of what you've told me. But there's still one thing I haven't figured out," Peter said. "The top-secret document I discovered at Mule Peak said you had been injected with UGEN. I assume whatever was injected into you caused your body to age at a slower rate than the rest of us. I just can't figure out how you would inject a conspiracy into someone. Care to elaborate? I mean, I'm heading directly into the lion's den, so don't you think it's time you shared a little more with me?"

Boyd turned his head to stare out of the window, but he remained silent. Peter decided to sit quietly to give Boyd some time to think.

After a long minute, Boyd turned to look at Peter and spoke, "Remember when we first met, I asked you if you knew the truth would change your view of reality, would you want to know it?"

Peter nodded.

"Well, I ask you again, Mr. Knowles. Do you really want the truth? You've already seen what can happen when you peer behind the curtain," Boyd said as he looked Peter in the eyes.

Peter didn't know how to respond. His life, and Sam's, had been turned upside down because he had wanted to satisfy his curiosity. If he looked further behind the curtain now, what would he see and what would the outcome be? Could he complete the task at hand without knowing more of the truth? The real question was, did he want to know because it could help him or to satisfy his curiosity.

"I want the truth," Peter answered. He noticed Tony glance at him through the rear-view mirror upon his response.

Boyd gave a slight smile. "As you wish," he responded. "On the fourth of May, 1912, the New York Times published an article claiming archaeological excavations near Lake Delavan in Wisconsin had found skeletons of extraordinary dimensions. Their skulls were elongated, they had two rows of teeth, and had six digits on both their hands and feet."

Boyd paused to read Peter's face who only raised an eyebrow and lowered his head slightly to indicate he was waiting to hear more.

"According to the article, these bones were sent to the Smithsonian, which, of course, is operated by the US government. Needless to say, the Smithsonian denies any such claims," Boyd added with a sarcastic facial expression. "The story was truthful. And, let me also add, these were not the only giant skeletons unearthed which were quickly confiscated and hidden away. Of course, inquirers looking into these matters were dismissed as conspiracy lunatics."

"Nephilim?" Peter questioned. Although he was skeptical of what he had learned from reading the Book of Enoch and the Bible, the story Boyd was telling didn't surprise him. He remembered the conversation he had with Dristan Cavanaugh. Although there was no real proof, the man had truly believed it.

Boyd was impressed as he nodded toward Peter. "Yes, Nephilim," Boyd said. "My former colleagues claimed they were extraterrestrial. The truth of their origins was never revealed to us; only their existence. Perhaps the nephilim discussed in the Bible were actually extraterrestrial beings. It is easy to understand how primitive cultures could have mistaken them for gods, angels, and nephilim."

Once again, Boyd paused to see if Peter had any questions. After none came, he continued, "Needless to say, scientists carefully studied the bones, but were unable to extract significant data. However, years later in 1944, Hungarian biochemist, Erwin Chargaff, had discovered the double helix structure of DNA. With this new medical breakthrough, scientists successfully extracted DNA from the bones and were able to synergize it on a genetic level with human DNA."

"You were injected with it," Peter stated more than questioned.

"Yes, as were several of my colleagues," Boyd answered.

"What exactly did it do to you?" Peter inquired.

"At first, nothing. We didn't start growing to become giants," Boyd said with a slight smile. "But, as we were physically and mentally tested over a course of several months, we began displaying increased intelligence. There were some physical differences as well. We never got sick and didn't have allergic reactions when tested for such. It took a few more years to identify a resilience to aging as well."

"So that's your secret?" Peter asked sarcastically, referring to Boyd's appearance.

Boyd's eyes stared out of the window behind Peter as he reminisced, "It was an amazing time and I had never felt more alive. All of those events and discoveries in 1955 I spoke of, new technologies, the money...the possibilities were limitless!"

"So, what happened? Why were your colleagues killed?" Peter asked.

Boyd turned to look back at Peter. "We each had made significant contributions to the project, and had started to focus more on our civilian lives. The Gen6 corporation I began took most of my time. Others had their interests and investments as well which put us squarely in the public's eye. Inevitably, that became a problem," Boyd answered as his face turned to a frown.

"You weren't aging," Peter surmised.

Nodding, Boyd added, "Proof of a higher intelligence was in our blood and we were not aging. As a result, the powers that be decided it was time to eliminate us to prevent exposure. Unlike the rest, I managed to escape and disappear," Boyd summed it up. Exhaling deeply, he leaned back in his seat. "Now you know, Mr. Knowles!"

"So why haven't you exposed them?" Peter asked. "You have the proof inside you. Why do you need me to infiltrate Area 51?"

"I'm the last one that I know of," Boyd answered. "Without additional proof, I would be nothing more than a genetic abnormality which could easily be written off. The real world doesn't have anything to compare my abnormality to. All evidence of superior intelligence has been kept classified at the highest levels."

"So, you think whatever they're keeping at Area 51 will help you expose them?" Peter followed up.

"It has too!" Boyd exclaimed.

Peter didn't respond. Rather, he thought of what had just been exposed. His reality had changed in the fact he now knew there was a higher intelligence out there. Whether it was biblical or extraterrestrial, the implications were astounding. *God? Aliens?* He preferred extraterrestrials over the existence of God. With God, there were two possible destinations and he knew his would be a lot warmer than the other. Peter could feel the gears churning inside his head. For every thought, two more would pop up. It was an endless loop! With his chest feeling like it was sinking, he decided to gain control over his thoughts by changing their direction.

"So, tell me more about working there," Peter requested, getting back to the mission at hand. "And, what will happen if I get caught?"

"Don't get caught!" Boyd replied, welcoming the change in topic. "Most people who get detained are just ordinary people trying to sneak close enough to see the base. They get held up for a day or two, fined, and then released. However, if you get caught, you will be viewed as intentionally trying to damage our national security. You would get around twenty years in prison, if you're lucky!"

Twenty years in prison was a long time. Death would be far worse. The risk of what he was going to do was really starting to sink in. No wonder Boyd offered such a reward.

"I'm not going to get caught," Peter said confidently. "Will I have access to the whole base, or is it like most janitorial contracts where the members are assigned to specific buildings?"

Tony responded to the question, "There are twelve janitorial teams, each with three members. Four of those clean the living quarters for the workers that stay a week at a time. The other teams have between two and five office buildings each to clean. During their cleaning window, an escort is assigned to each team to watch them until they are done. Once done, they are escorted back to the building where the bus drops them off and picks them up."

"And no one has access to the whole base, not even the workers themselves," Boyd added. "I'm sure you are familiar with compartmentalization. Each top-secret project and their buildings are designated by their own identifying codewords. That way, no one person can have all the information."

"The custodial workers have top-secret clearances, just like you, but it's for getting them access to the base. None of you have access to any of the special projects, which is why an escort is assigned," Tony inputted.

"I'm familiar with how it works. We always knew when the cleaning crews were coming and had to make sure all classified paperwork was put away. We called it sanitizing the area," Peter replied. "While the area was being cleaned, we had to assign an escort and were told not to discuss any classified information around them."

"Your knowledge of how things work is why I've asked you to do this," Boyd said with a smile.

"So, I assume you have me assigned to clean the building where they are supposedly hiding whatever they found in the tomb?"

Tony looked up at the rearview mirror towards Boyd and then put his eyes back on the road. From that, Peter knew his assumption was wrong. He looked over to Boyd.

"Not exactly," said Boyd. "You are assigned to the building which we think will get you access to where you need to go."

Peter looked confused.

"Think of the Ranch as a hub, Mr. Knowles. As we've already discussed, the base itself and the experimental aircraft serve as a cover. Please note, a lot has changed since I was last part of the project so we are led to speculate on some things based on what we have gathered. We believe the real work goes on beneath the ground, only accessible via an underground rail system," Boyd said, trying to get Peter to understand.

When Peter nodded that he understood, Boyd continued, "We didn't have tunnels at the time when I worked there. However, before I left, plans were being created for them. A lot of planning occurred to keep the digging secret."

"I imagine," Peter interrupted. "As an intelligence analyst, I looked at a lot of satellite images of enemy territory where they were building underground facilities. It was easy to find them, just look for large piles of dirt outside of a cave entrance. The caves were easy to find. All we had to do was follow roads till it looked like they just ended at the mountain. We could tell how large the underground facility was based on the amount of dirt hauled out."

"The planners digging these tunnels knew that too, Mr. Knowles," replied Boyd with a smile. "In their plans, they were going to construct a large hangar which would fit right in at the airfield. However, this hangar was not for planes. Rather, large trucks would pull in and become obscured from any overhead imaging systems. Inside, the excavated dirt would be loaded and then hauled off. They wouldn't just dump the dirt somewhere, either. They were too smart for that. They would haul it over to the Nevada Test Site, where all the nuclear tests occurred, and dump it to cover radioactive waste barrels lined up in revetments. There are tons of radioactive waste sites around here, you know!"

"Wow! They really wanted to hide the fact they were digging tunnels," Peter replied, showing he was impressed with these planners.

"Yes, they did!" Boyd returned.

"So, you think what we are looking for is at the end of one of these tunnels they planned to build?"

"I do," answered Boyd. "It's not just a guess, either. In May of 1989, one of the workers from the Ranch, Bob Lazar, went public when he was interviewed by a Las Vegas news reporter. During the interview, he recalled working on UFOs and seeing photos of what he thought were extraterrestrial bodies. He spoke of knowledge the rest of the world didn't have. However, a lot of it was familiar to me. He spoke of working at an underground facility known as S4 which was a few miles southwest of the Ranch."

"So, when the opportunity arises, I should try to find out if there is a tunnel leading to the southwest? Supposedly to a place known as S4?" Peter asked.

Boyd nodded and answered, "Yes. That is where I would start. Remember to keep your ears open, too. You never know what you may overhear at lunch which is always a hotspot for workers trying to talk around classified information."

Many miles had passed during their conversation. The desert vegetation and distant mountains on either side started to seem monotonous. Although Peter had always thought the landscape was beautiful in the southwest, the awe of it seemed to wear off after a few days. There wasn't much to see in this part of Nevada. Most of the land belonged to the Bureau of Land Management or the Nellis Training Range. Only a few ranchers and people wanting to get away from everything lived out here.

After a while, they drove into the Alamo city limits. The entire town was situated adjacent and west of US Highway 93. Although the population was probably around five hundred, it was really the only sign of civilization they had seen since leaving Las Vegas. Peter noticed a small grocery store, post office and library as they drove through. It was peaceful enough, and for that, Peter was thankful. Once again, he would have time alone the way he liked it. *Wonder what Sam is up to?*

Tony headed for the south side of town. It only took a minute before they entered a conglomeration of houses which formed a small neighborhood. Eventually, Tony pulled into the driveway of one of the houses and stopped.

"This is it," Tony said as he opened the door and stepped out.

Peter went to open the door, but Boyd reached over and held his arm. "Let's wait till Tony gets inside with your bags of clothes and things. I don't like to be in the public as I'm sure you understand," he explained.

"Public?" Peter looked back and asked. "This is about as far from public as it gets!"

The two men sat in the back seat and watched Tony open the trunk and retrieve all of the items they had bought earlier. Then, after he entered the house, Boyd took a look around to make sure no one was around, and then exited the vehicle to enter the house.

Peter got out of the vehicle, too, but didn't enter the house right away. After a quick stretch, he looked around. The big, open sky and fresh air were a delight. Looking up at the sky, he was sure the stars would be really bright out here in the middle of nowhere. Looking over towards the house, it wasn't anything special. It was tan with black trim and came complete with a desert tile roof. A few desert bushes and a decorative cactus had been planted in the yard years back, but had not been maintained. There was no grass, just rocks and dirt. Peter thought about how he hadn't lived in a real house for a few years, preferring his RV. But, for the meantime, he would have to call this home so he decided to make the best of it.

Tony greeted Peter as he stepped into his new home, "You should have everything you need. Everything works and the television will even pick up a couple of stations. I'm going to head over and pick you up some groceries while you two talk."

Tony tossed a key down on a wooden coffee table and walked out. Boyd sat in a corner chair as Peter walked around slowly inspecting his new dwelling. The front door had opened up into the living room. There was a small hallway on the left wall which led to a full bathroom and a single bedroom with a queen-sized bed. Across from the front door, on the backside of the living room, was a bar separating the kitchen. A couple of wooden stools were pulled up against it on the kitchen side. The kitchen wasn't the prettiest thing Peter had ever seen, but it had the manly essentials of a microwave and coffee pot.

"Will this do?" Boyd asked.

Peter was in the kitchen, but looked back to Boyd over the bar. "Nothing to complain about. Still, I would prefer my RV," he stated with a smile.

"It should suffice till this is all over with," said Boyd.

Peter walked back into the living room and sat on the couch near the coffee table. He picked up the key Tony had left behind, held it up for Boyd to see, and then asked, "Only one key? There's no truck in this deal?"

"We didn't see the need for one," Boyd answered honestly. "The bus which takes you to the Ranch circles this neighborhood picking up and dropping off riders. Everything else is well within walking distance. If you insist, though, I can get you a car."

Peter considered the offer for a second, but then replied, "That's okay. I guess it would be a waste anyway, right now. Depending on how this evolves, I may ask for one near the end. We'll see, I guess."

Boyd nodded in response.

"Here's a question," Peter started. "These 'others' know what I look like. Are they not going to recognize me walking around the base?"

"Not likely," Boyd answered. "They are not confined to a single base, you know. The ones working at the Ranch are concerned with what goes on there, while the rest take care of other matters, such as tracking down those who stick their noses in too far."

Peter snickered at the comment and then asked, "What if I don't find anything?"

"Then you don't find anything," Boyd replied quickly. "I haven't known you long, Mr. Knowles, but I consider you an honorable and truthful man. You've told me you would do your best to find out, and I believe you!"

"How do I contact you?" Peter continued to ask questions.

"You don't! Tony will visit you every Saturday at noon. You can disclose any information you may have discovered to him and keep him apprised of your progress. When you feel you are about to complete the task, we'll accommodate as necessary with whatever you need," stated Boyd.

Peter sat calmly on the couch with his hands clasped together resting on his stomach. He was trying to think of any other questions he needed to ask. So far, it appeared everything had been taken care of and was falling into place.

"When do I start and what will my first day be like?" Peter asked.

"You start Monday, but I don't know the exact details. Tony can fill you in when he returns," Boyd replied. After a brief pause, he continued, "I'm sure I don't need to say this, but I'm going to say it anyway." He looked over to Peter more directly.

Peter nodded and listened.

"I'm really not sorry you got involved in all of this. I'm sorry that Sam did, but not you. You just may be the person I've needed for years.

If you are successful, I may just have my best shot to take these 'others' down for good. Or, at least, expose them for who they are and what they have done," Boyd admitted. "And let me say another thing. These people will stop at nothing to get their hands on me, and we can't let that happen. I know you don't have the whole story, Mr. Knowles, but trust me when I say it's critical they don't know my whereabouts. Understand? Even if they capture you, threaten you, or even offer you everything you've ever wanted, you can't let them know where I am. Tell me you understand!"

Peter saw how Boyd leaned up in his chair and his expression became intense as he spoke those words. "I understand!"

"Good, then. It's not just for my protection, either, believe me!" Boyd finalized and then relaxed back into his chair realizing he had gotten intense.

"And you make sure Sam is taken care of. No matter what happens to me, her safety is paramount to me. If anything happens to her, I'm holding you responsible. Just want to make sure you are clear on where I stand," Peter let his concerns be known.

"I've actually grown pretty fond of Sam. She will be protected and cared for, I assure you," Boyd replied.

Before long, they heard Tony pulling up in the driveway. As he promised, he had bought a few bags of groceries which would last at least a week. Peter was quite impressed at the selection. It was mostly items to make sandwiches, but Tony had also bought some cookies, chips and other snacks, too. He had to make a second trip out to the car to fetch two cases of bottled water.

Once the groceries had been put away, Peter looked over to Tony and inquired, "So, what time will the bus be by on Monday and what do I need to know on my first day?"

Tony grabbed a bottle of water, opened it to take a drink, and then replied, "It will be here at seven in the morning and will pick you up in the evening, on the base, at five o'clock." He took another drink of water and continued, "There's a woman, Yana Conners, who will be your supervisor. She also serves as site lead. I've already called her to let her know you are a new employee and will be there Monday. She will meet you at the drop off location on base. She's in her thirties and has long, dark hair with brown eyes. From there, she will take you everywhere you need to go and show you what to do."

"I'm thinking she has no idea why I'm really here," Peter asked for certainty.

"To her, you are just another employee. She doesn't need to know anything more," answered Tony. "Work hard, blend in, and don't let anyone on to what you are really doing."

"Got it!" Peter confirmed.

"One last thing. Don't take your cell phone. They're not allowed. Anything trackable isn't allowed at all," Tony informed.

After an affirming nod, Tony and Peter walked back to the living room to where Boyd was still seated.

"Wouldn't it have been easier to make me a scientist or engineer. At least then, I wouldn't have to scrub toilets," Peter said with a little chuckle.

"Toilet scrubbers have the doors opened for them, Mr. Knowles. Scientists and engineers have to submit to biometric scans to open doors. Besides that, and I'm sorry, but you wouldn't pass for one of them," Boyd replied with a big smile.

It made sense to Peter even though he had been joking. His true identity would be known if he had his fingerprint or iris scanned. Truly, Boyd had spent a lot of time considering every detail to best accomplish this. The thought made Peter feel a little safer.

Boyd and Tony departed soon after, and Peter finally had some alone time. He decided to walk through the house again and take a closer look. When he walked into his bedroom, he noticed Tony had provided a week's worth of uniforms and had them neatly hung in the closet. On the bed were five khaki pants and five red, polo style shirts. The company's initials, CYN, were etched in black over the left breast. *Nice.* It was a typical house for this part of the country and provided everything Peter needed.

There was still plenty of time in the day, so Peter decided to walk through the town. In doing so, he figured there would be a need for some cash in case he wanted to buy lunch at the Ranch. Using the new card at an ATM in the grocery store, he pulled out a hundred bucks. *It works!* He looked at the name on the card and read the name out loud, 'Peter Norris'. He took his time looking around other parts of the town before heading back to his house. He realized he was going to have the upcoming evenings to himself, so as he walked, he looked in the distance at the mountains to see if he could spot any hiking trails. He also thought of other ways to occupy his time.

Back at the house, he sat on the couch and pulled out the cellphone. He took a few moments thinking about what Sam might be doing and then decided to shoot her a quick text:

Peter: *Hello, SF! I'm here.*

It took less than a minute to receive a reply.

Sam: *Hey Papa Bear! Good to know. See you soon!*

Saturday and Sunday were uneventful. Peter had walked the town over and even explored a few desert trails. All in all, it was a boring town, which was just fine with Peter. He welcomed it knowing it had been a while since he had been relaxed. Plus, it provided time for him to contemplate a course of action.

Chapter 18

Monday arrived. A full eight hours of sleep felt great. Peter rolled over and placed both his feet on the floor. It was odd to wake up in a new place, but he was used to it. He had been assigned to fourteen duty stations during his service, not to mention having stayed in over a hundred hotels. Still, it felt odd. As he looked around the room to give himself time to adjust from the sleep, he realized it hadn't been long ago that he had been in the Sacramento Mountains where he had met Ahanu. He actually chuckled at his experience with the man whose name means 'He Who Laughs'. However, he quickly shook off the thoughts knowing he had a big day ahead of him. Up he stood and headed for the shower.

It didn't take Peter long before he was standing outside waiting on the bus. His new clothes were crisp, and he actually felt like a civilian contract worker. Earlier, when he was tucking his shirt into his pants, he wondered if he should just leave it out. Stereotyping, he wondered if the other janitorial workers left theirs untucked, in which case he didn't want to stand out in any way. In the end, he decided to tuck it in to present a good impression on his first day. If everyone else was more casual, he could always untuck it.

The bus was right on time as Peter saw it round the corner at the end of the street. It was large and boxy, resembling Air Force buses he had ridden on in the past, except this one was white instead of blue. He wasn't sure if the bus knew to stop at his residence, so he decided to encourage it by walking out closer to the street and then threw up a hand. Sure enough, the bus came to a stop. The driver slid open the window to his left and looked at Peter.

"I think this is my ride," Peter said, smiling at the driver.

"Where's your badge?" the driver asked.

Peter reached into his right pocket, retrieved the badge, and held it up.

"Get on!" the driver instructed.

Peter walked around and heard the familiar squeaking of a bus door opening. Climbing up the three steps, he got a better look at the driver. He appeared to be a mix of Caucasian and Native American with short, black hair and dark eyes. He probably weighed in at nearly three hundred pounds as his belly actually pressed against the steering wheel. He too, had on slacks, but instead of having on a red polo shirt, his was black. There were no markings on the shirt to indicate which contract company he belonged to.

"First day?" the driver asked while holding out his hand towards Peter.

"Yes, Sir!" Peter returned, handing over the badge for inspection.

After a quick glance, the driver handed the badge back, closed the doors, and then pressed on the gas. Peter almost lost his balance and figured he had better find a seat pretty quick. Looking for a seat, Peter noticed there were five other men and three ladies on board. None seemed to take interest in him, preferring to just stare blankly out of their window. The fourth seat back on the left was open, so Peter flopped down. His heart was racing, but he had anticipated the excitement. Not a fun type of excitement, but rather the type appearing when you are doing something illegal.

The bus made about six more stops, sometimes picking up multiple people at one. Once they got on the road, Peter counted thirty-five people, including himself. The majority were wearing red, CYN shirts like his. By the way they had gotten on the bus and found their seats, Peter could tell they all probably sat in the same seats every day. Most threw a smile at the person they were going to sit with and would immediately start a conversation once they sat down. Peter overheard several conversations near him, but they just pertained to family or what they had seen on television the night before. No one talked about work.

Ten miles must have passed when the bus took a left onto US Highway 375. After driving a mile on the new road, Peter noticed a fork coming up. A sign indicated US Highway 375 was left while US Highway 318 split off to the right. In between the split, a car was parked with a man and woman walking around. As the bus passed, Peter noticed the man had a camera while the women went over and leaned against a sign. The sign read 'Extraterrestrial Highway' and was covered with all kinds of stickers. Peter realized this area must be a hotspot for UFO fanatics and tourists. *Crazy Land...here I come*!

Heading west, the bus continued along the lonely, desert highway. Eventually, after about fifteen miles or so, the bus took a left onto a dusty, dirt road. Looking up the aisle and through the windshield, Peter saw the road extended as far as he could see and disappeared into the mountain range. It wouldn't be long now as Peter figured they had to be about there. The road was actually quite smooth revealing it was well maintained. It seemed to take forever to reach the mountains, but soon enough hills began to rise on both sides of the bus.

Off to the right and sitting on top of one of the first hills, Peter noticed a white truck parked facing the road with two men inside. *Security*. Looking ahead, he saw an area off to the right where vehicles could pull off the road and park. Beside the road ahead and at the end of the parking area were government warning signs. Peter had seen signs like these before in the service. There were several warnings listed to include no trespassing, no photography and no drones. The realization he was too far to turn back crossed Peter's mind as the bus crossed over the line. It slowed down a little to meander through the hilly terrain just ahead. It turned right, and then left, as it followed the curvy road through the natural valley. As soon as they were past the first hill, the road became paved. For sure, Area 51 was just ahead!

Within another minute, a security checkpoint came into view. It was a remote outpost, probably serving to ensure anyone who dared cross the line a few thousand yards back wasn't going to get any further. The other people on the bus started retrieving their badges from pockets and purses, so Peter did likewise. The bus slowed and eventually stopped at the checkpoint. Everyone grew quiet as a uniformed soldier carrying an M4 assault rifle stepped onto the bus.

"Good morning," the driver greeted the soldier.

"Good morning, George!" the soldier answered.

Starting at the front, and one-by-one, each person handed their badge to the soldier for inspection. When it came to Peter, he remained calm, and handed the badge over. After a quick look on the front and back, the soldier looked directly at Peter.

"Mr. Norris, I don't remember seeing you before. Are you new?" the soldier asked.

"First day!" Peter replied with a smile.

With that, the soldier kept the card and stepped off the bus. He went inside the security building. Peter was about to get nervous, but as he looked around, everyone seemed to be calm as if everything was normal. A minute later, the soldier stepped back on the bus.

"Welcome aboard, Mr. Norris," the soldier greeted and then handed the badge back before proceeding down the aisle.

It worked! The soldier probably went inside the guard building to run his name on the computer to see if he would show up in the manifest. It must have been there. Peter knew he had gambled when he had placed his trust and his life in Boyd's hands. But so far, everything was going as planned. Moreover, he felt more relaxed than he had expected. *Almost there.*

The bus continued on after everyone had been checked. After a few more hills, the desert basin opened up to reveal Groom Lake. It was a large, dry lake bed and took up most of the viewable basin. On the other side of it, Peter could see buildings and hangars which would have to be base. *I'm really here*. The bus continued along for another four or five miles before they reached the actual base.

The first thing Peter took note of was the lack of civilian vehicles. As a matter of fact, there were none. Almost every vehicle he observed was white and had government license plates. The predominant features were the large hangars to his left and a water tower to his right. A large and mounted parabolic dish, pointing straight up, passed by on the left. Other than that, the rest of the buildings looked like the ones you would see on any base.

A few hundred feet after the parabolic dish had passed by, the bus came to a stop with a large building to the right. Three people in CYN shirts stood and got off. Noticing a softball field and tennis courts, Peter surmised it must be the gym. As the bus pulled off, he started to wonder where he was to get off. He had no idea.

The bus made a couple more stops behind the housing area. More people got off. The bus took a left and headed in the direction of the flight line. Peter was just about to inquire where he should get off from one of the other passengers, but didn't get a chance to.

"This is your stop, bud!" the driver said loud enough to get Peter's attention. Looking up at the large, rearview mirror, Peter could tell the driver was talking to him. After a complete stop, Peter stood up and approached the exit while stooping down a little to see outside. Luckily, to the right side of the bus, a lady matching the features Tony provided stood just outside. Peter stepped off the bus.

"You must be Peter!" the lady stated as she held out her hand. She, too, was wearing a CYN shirt. "I'm Yana! I was told you would be arriving this morning."

Peter extended his hand and gave a shake. "Please, call me Peter!" he urged.

"Okay, Peter. Follow me so we can get started," she said and turned to head inside the building.

Peter gave a final glance over to the white bus pulling away and then followed after Yana. She was physically attractive which surprised him. Most cleaning ladies he was familiar with were older and not as pleasant to the eyes. From her grip and figure, he also figured she worked out often in order to stay in shape. Hopefully, she would be a good boss which would make his life here a lot better.

Inside, she continued to walk down a center hallway which separated offices off to the left and right. Each door had a placard with either a business icon or initials on it. The third door on the right had CYN written on the placard. Yana pointed at it but kept walking.

Without turning around, she said, "That's our office and where you'll find me if you need to."

As they neared the end of the hall, she stopped at a door which had BRIEFING ROOM on the placard. She opened the door and gestured for Peter to enter, which he did. Peter recognized the room immediately.

"Let me guess, death by PowerPoint?" he asked knowing he would probably have to sit through hours of slideshows and briefings. In the center of the room, ten chairs had been lined up to face a projector screen. The projector, with an attached computer, was placed along the back wall.

"How'd you guess?" she asked in return and with a big smile.

Peter grimaced. He really hated briefings like these. He dreaded the fact he was about to get another big dose of how to keep secrets as well as a generic history lesson of the base. These were routine during in and out processing of a base. Maybe this one would be more interesting though.

"It's not too bad," Yana cut in to interrupt the dread. "This base has an interesting history and you're one of the lucky ones that get to sit through these briefings!" She couldn't help but smile, noticing his face was grimaced up.

She motioned for Peter to sit down and then walked back to the computer where she started up the slides.

Peter was already looking up at the screen watching the projector's make and model flash across the screen while it booted up.

From behind, Yana added, "It's just procedure. These briefings help a little, but myself and your team will teach you everything you need to know to stay out of trouble. Lucky for you, us janitorial types don't have to sit through the multitude of briefings like the other people that work here."

"Then let the fun begin!" he murmured loud enough for Yana to hear.

After getting the first briefing ready, she walked back over to Peter. She bent over slightly to take his badge out of his hand.

"I have a gift for you," she said as she reached into her pocket and pulled out a lanyard. Connecting it to the badge, she handed it back to Peter. "Harder to lose if it's around your neck!" she said smiling.

"Thanks!" Peter replied.

"Okay, Peter. I think you're ready. I'll come back around lunch and show you where we eat. The bathroom is directly across the hall. When a briefing finishes, just walk back here and start the next one. They're labeled numerically. If you need something else, just come down to the office," she finalized.

Peter nodded. *I'll be nodding a lot today!* On her way out, she started the slide show and dimmed the lights. Over the course of the following three hours, Peter learned not to talk about anything he saw on base. Stiff prison sentences would be imposed on anyone disclosing classified information. He was briefed on how to handle outsiders if they started asking him about his job and where he worked. The last briefing of the morning explained what to do if he found he needed to get off the base for some reason. It also informed him how his family could contact him should the need arise. A number was given which would put them in contact with the security forces' First Sergeant, who could find you and relay the message. Peter didn't write the number down. There was no need to. *Sam*

At around noon, the door opened. Peter turned around and saw Yana enter smiling.

"Are you at a good stopping point?" she asked.

"Sure," Peter replied as he got up and walked over to the computer to pause the briefing.

"Did they tell you about the aliens, yet?" she asked with a smile.

Peter turned to look at her seriously.

"I'm just kidding! There's no aliens here if you haven't figured that out yet," she said joking around.

"What do they do here?" Peter asked.

"Well, they use the bathroom a lot and never clean up their offices," she answered joking around again. When she saw Peter was smiling back, she added, "But, in all honesty, I have no idea. They keep tight lips on everything. Of course, they work on top-secret aircraft, but we never get to see them. They wait till it's dark and no 'normal' people are around." She held up two fingers on each hand to make imaginary quotation marks when she said 'normal'.

Peter smiled then and said, "I'm just glad they use the bathroom a lot and leave messes! Gives us a job, you know?"

Yana nodded. "Let's go get something to eat!"

It was a quick walk to the dining facility which was just across the street. Looking at the parking lot, Peter saw nothing but white government vehicles. Unlike most air bases, this one was unusually quiet. Peter had neither heard nor seen any flight activity since he had arrived. Looking towards the flight line, he did observe two passenger jets with Janet logos. He figured they must have arrived with passengers before he got to work.

The dining facility, or chow hall, as Peter liked to call it, was almost full. The only uniformed soldiers Peter noticed were seated at the table closest to the door. This was normal on most military installations in case an emergency arose and they had to respond fast. Their guns were in a rack not far away. Other than the soldiers, people were dressed in normal, casual clothing. Peter could differentiate between the support personnel, who wore mostly jeans and t-shirts, and the ones there actually working on special projects as their attire consisted mostly of slacks and tucked in shirts. Additionally, he noticed how the better dressed people had vegetables on their plate and drank water versus sodas and mashed potatoes. Peter thought of how a lot of people would frown on him for stereotyping. But he didn't care. He considered it analytical. There were fifteen other people who stood out from the rest. He figured they were scientists since they wore white lab coats and half of them had on glasses.

Yana led him through the lunch line and then to a table. He could tell this was routine for Yana as she headed over to the table where a bunch of redshirted people were. *Birds of a feather flock together.* Yana gave a brief introduction of her new guest which led to a bunch of 'hellos' and 'welcomes'. Peter wasn't surprised when the majority of conversation was about utter nonsense. Some spoke of sports while others talked of how lazy their spouses were. He would smile ever so often and even nod his head. He marveled at how much people could talk about nothing significant. He understood most people were uncomfortable with silence and would talk about anything to break it. However, Peter just sat and listened. Well, he pretended to listen. His real ears were turned into other conversations at tables near his. It was his first day on the job, though, so he didn't overhear anything of substance.

As Yana and Peter exited the chow hall, she stopped him with a serious look on her face.

"Listen. This is important," she started.

"Okay," he replied.

"This is the only place we are authorized without an escort. Our office building, the dining facility, and the space in between. Anywhere else requires an escort. The different offices on base have a schedule of when we arrive and leave. Each one will have an escort waiting on you when you get off the bus. That escort will lead you to the next building and hand you off to the next. At the end of the day, the last escort will walk you to the door and watch you get on the bus. We've lost a lot of employees because they have messed it up. Got it?"

Peter looked at their office building across the street and back over to the chow hall. "Got it! No worries."

As they returned to the office building and neared the briefing room, Yana said, "The bus arrives at five o'clock. I'll come get you a few minutes before then, since it's your first day."

"Thanks. I hope the next briefings are more interesting than this morning's, or you may have to wake me!" Peter said, smiling.

Yana smiled back. "See you then!" she replied and headed back down towards her office.

Peter let out a sigh and then headed over to the computer to unpause the briefing. When it began, he dimmed the lights and took his seat.

The briefings were more interesting. He learned the history of the U2 spy plane, the SR-71, and the F-117 stealth fighter with which he was familiar. Nothing was briefed on an aircraft capable of disappearing from both radar and optical detection. Neither did any of the briefings mention Project UGEN. Peter didn't figure they would.

It took forever for five o'clock to arrive, but it finally did. Peter had finished his last briefing about thirty minutes prior, but not knowing what to do, he just sat in the room patiently. As promised, Yana arrived at five minutes till five.

"Hey there!! You finish them all?" she asked.

"Yep," Peter answered. "And I didn't even shoot myself!"

They both laughed at the effect briefings, like these, could have on a person.

As they walked down the hallway to exit their office building, Yana grabbed her office door handle and wiggled it to ensure it was locked. Seeing that it was, they continued out to the bus stop. At exactly five o'clock, the white bus rounded the corner.

"See you in the morning, Peter!" she said.

"You're not coming?" he asked surprised. "Are there more buses?"

"This is the only bus. Being the site lead, I get a room here Monday through Friday. When the weekend comes, I fly back to Vegas."

"Oh," Peter replied. "Lucky!"

Yana smiled. "Tomorrow, I'll introduce you to Mr. Mop and Mrs. Bucket!"

The bus came to a stop in front of them. Peter extended his hand and stated, "Thanks for helping me today. I really appreciate it!"

Yana shook his hand and nodded. "No problem!"

The same faces from the morning gradually filled the bus as it made its way around the base. Before long, it started the trek back to Alamo. When they crossed the security line on the way out, Peter let out a quiet sigh. *So far, so good.* Even though he had a successful day, he knew his work was cut out for him. He would have to look for opportunities whenever and wherever they presented themselves. Having to be escorted around everywhere meant one thing, doing anything not related to cleaning toilets was going to be difficult. *This may take a while.*

***

Peter stood outside and looked up at the stars which were just starting to appear. It was quiet, peaceful and even made him think of how things used to be. However, in truth, it wasn't as enjoyable as it once was. Something was missing. He reached into his right pocket and retrieved his cell phone.

Peter: *Hello, SF! Today was a good day. Kinda boring, actually. How are you?*

Sam: *Hey Papa Bear! Glad it's all going good so far. I'm good. Daddy Warbucks walked with me today. He's not so bad when not talking about sci-fi movies.*

Peter chuckled. He loved the way he and Sam communicated so easily. Their new text names and the new reference to Boyd showed they had a lot in common. He missed her already.

Peter: *Wish I had brought a book. I was getting used to having people around.*

Sam: *Papa Bear, if I didn't know better, it sounds like you are lonely. It's only been a couple of days. It'll be over in no time!*

Peter wasn't so sure about that last sentence, but he smiled all the same.

Peter: *Talk again tomorrow. Goodnight!*
Sam: *LOL! I love the way you change subjects to avoid attention to yourself. Until tomorrow then...*

Chapter 19

The next day, the bus arrived on time and delivered Peter to the Ranch. He had made it to his second day now, so he felt more comfortable on the ride. The guard at the security checkpoint didn't need to check his name against the register and even threw a 'good morning, Mr. Norris' his way. Today, Peter was going to discover exactly what his job entailed and, hopefully, give him a little more insight on the challenges ahead pertaining to his real mission.

As the bus approached Peter's stop between the chow hall and the building with the CYN office, he didn't see Yana standing outside. It wasn't a concern, though, as Peter knew what to do. Getting off, he realized two other CYN employees, a male and female, were following him. The three of them walked into the building and then on to the office door which was already open. Inside, Yana sat at her desk and was typing on her computer. She turned to see who had approached.

"Good morning, Peter! I thought that might be you when I heard the door open and close at the end of the hall," she greeted him. "Have you met Bob and Cindy?"

"Mornin!" Peter replied as he turned to look the other two in the face. He extended his hand to Cindy and then to Bob for a shake. "Nice to meet you."

"You'll be working with them. They've been here for a while, which is why I was asked to put you with them. They will show you what to do today. Be careful, and don't get into any trouble please," Yana finished and then picked up the phone.

After waiting for someone on the other end to answer, she spoke into the phone, "Hey! Good morning! Did you get my email yesterday?" There was a pause as she nodded her head in silence. "Yeah, I'm ready for you. Come on over please. Thanks!" With that, she hung up the phone.

"The coffee house is sending someone to escort you," Yana spoke to Bob.

"Okay," Bob answered. "You need him to catch the bus from here or from the ops building?"

"The ops building is fine," she replied and then looked at Peter. "Enjoy your first, real day, Peter," she said with a smile.

Bob and Cindy walked out into the hallway and then headed for the door at the end of the hallway. Peter fell in behind them and stood with them at the door.

"Coffee house?" Peter asked inquisitively.

Cindy was the first to answer, "Yeah, that's what we call it. It's just next door. Used to be a hangar or something, but they converted it into something else. Since we really don't know what to call it, we just say coffee house since there's a coffee shop inside. You'll see."

Peter liked Cindy already. She was a little older than he was and had hair pulled back in a ponytail. She had colored her hair blonde to hide the gray, but it must have been a while since she last had it done. Her face was a little rugged and the wrinkles around her lips indicated she was a heavy smoker. Her voice was a little course for a woman. However, she had a sincere and humble look about her, too, that grabbed Peter's attention. The kindness she showed in her facial expressions were indicative of motherhood. He could also tell she wasn't confrontational and probably tried her best not to bother anyone. He liked that in her.

Bob, on the other hand, was short and stout. His upper lip supported a thick, black and gray moustache which hadn't been trimmed in a while. On his right forearm, a tattoo of a woman riding an anchor was faded and almost covered by arm hair. Peter couldn't help but notice the gray hairs protruding from his collar on the front and back of his shirt, too. On the top, the sun had taken its toll on his head as that was the only area on his body that wasn't completely covered by hair. Since he didn't even try to answer Peter's inquiry on what the coffee house was, Peter figured he was more of the quiet type. Peter liked that, too.

After a minute passed, the door opened up to reveal a guy in his late twenties. Peter figured he was probably the youngest person in his office which is why he was probably chosen to escort. Usually, the junior person is the most expendable. His security badge was attached to the left breast pocket on his shirt which was neatly tucked in. His hair was neatly combed to the right. His skin was pale, which told Peter he wasn't from the desert. *Recent college grad.*

Jeffrey M. Scott. That was the escort's name according to his badge. Peter also noticed something else on his badge. Unlike the CYN worker's badges, which had TOP SECRET in the upper right-hand corner, the escort's badge had TOP SECRET//RUBY. Peter had never heard of that clearance level and figured it was some sort of project.

"Good morning! Is this the new guy?" Jeffery asked.

Again, Cindy was the first to respond, "It is. His name is Peter."

"Nice to meet you," Jeffery greeted looking over to Peter. "I'm Jeff!"

"Nice to meet you," Peter responded casually and with the expected return smile.

The three of them then headed out of the building and started walking toward the flight line. Peter could tell they were headed for a large, white hangar style building just east of their building. However, there were no large hangar doors which indicated it must have been converted at some point. A medium sized parking lot was on the north side which they had to walk through to get to the door.

Jeff opened the door for them to enter. Once they were all inside, Jeff flicked a switch which turned on three red flashing lights positioned around the ceiling.

"Uncleared!" Jeff exclaimed in a very loud voice. Peter knew it was standard protocol to announce when uncleared personnel entered a secured area.

The inside area was large and not what Peter had expected. The first thing he noticed was a large, black F-117 suspended from the ceiling. It was probably serving as a commemorative for the old project. The floor was also very noticeable. The entire thing was solid red. Up above, large metal beams were also painted red. These large beams supported the hanging F-117. The walls were white with large pipes extending from the floor up into the ceiling area where they intersected and crisscrossed one another. Peter imagined a lot of fiber optics running through them. Sporadically spaced over the floor area, six-foot-tall plants added a hint of greenery to the area. Surprisingly, the color scheme of the whole area blended quite well.

Besides the hanging F-117, there was another predominant feature which grabbed Peter's attention. About thirty feet directly in front of them and centered between the right and left hangar walls, a downward, sloped walkway had been cut out. It was about thirty feet wide and extended to the rear wall area which was about another hundred feet away. The end of the slope descended to at least thirty feet below floor level and then ended at two large, metal doors painted white. Peter noticed what appeared to be a security badge reader attached to the wall to the right of the doors. To the left of the doors, an armed guard stood in a uniform keeping watch. *This must be the building.*

Around the upper edges of the sloped walkway, preventative measures had been taken to keep people from falling down into the walkway. Metal rails had been placed along the edges and were painted an obvious white. Two conversing men stood near the railing and peered down into the sloped walkway.

To the right about fifty feet, and along the wall, was a coffee shop. An older lady was behind the counter and was brewing a cup for a customer. Three round tables were nearby, but only a couple of people sat at them to enjoy their coffee. Peter thought it a little odd to see them reading something, but then he realized there were no cell phones. Peter liked that they were forced to read instead of wasting their lives on social media.

Along the left side of the building, male and female restrooms had been constructed. One of the large plants in a pot was placed between the male and female doors. Another door was further to the left and had no markings. That door, too, had a large plant placed near it probably in an attempt to obscure it. Further along the left hangar wall and near the rear, another office had been constructed. There was only one door with a security badge reader next to it. Peter couldn't ascertain what purpose that office served, but figured it was probably where Jeff worked.

After giving Peter a minute to look around, Bob and Cindy started walking towards the restrooms. Peter took in after them. Jeff didn't follow them. Instead, he walked over to the coffee shop. Peter knew being an escort was boring. Being routine, Jeff probably figured there was no need to keep a meticulous eye on the cleaning crew while they performed their duties. Rather, he would probably get a coffee and just walk around on the floor appearing to watch them. *Typical escort.*

"Neat place, huh?" Cindy asked as they walked towards the door left of the male and female doors.

"Grandiose, I would say!" Peter responded. "Please tell me we don't have to clean the entire floor here. This place is huge!"

Opening the door to a janitorial closet, Bob stepped inside and started pulling at something to his left. Out came the buffer! He smiled at Peter as he pulled the all-to-familiar device over to Peter. Cindy had stepped into the closet as well to retrieve a spray bottle. Bob placed the buffer in front of Peter and Cindy handed him the spray bottle.

"The whole floor!" Bob exclaimed with a slight chuckle. "You're the new guy!"

"You don't have to strip it. Just keep spraying some of this in front of you and go over with the buffer to make the floor shine," Cindy informed Peter as she handed him the spray bottle. "Know how to use it?"

Unfortunately. "Sadly, I do," Peter answered with a frown. "But I'm getting paid, right?" he said as he turned his frown into a smile and reached for the buffer.

Cindy and Bob returned to the closet to retrieve yellow buckets and more cleaning supplies. Peter decided to start on the opposite side of the walkway and work his way around. Pulling the buffer, Peter glanced at the few people on the floor to see if any were paying special attention to him. His assumptions were correct. He was a janitor and therefore invisible to them.

It took Peter almost an hour as he worked his way back towards the front near the coffee shop and another hour to buff the other side. It wasn't hard buffing the floor, just monotonous. However, it gave Peter time to observe what was happening around him. Jeff mostly just walked around the floor but still didn't pay much attention to the cleaning crew. He would enter the unknown office occasionally, but never more than a minute. More interesting to Peter, though, were the people utilizing the sloped walkway. Over a thirty-minute period, people would filter in and stop to have coffee. Then, on the hour or half hour, they would all leave the coffee shop and head down the walkway. Soon after they entered the doors at the end, other people would exit the doors and proceed up the walkway and then out the building. Some of them wore lab coats, while the others wore the more common slacks and tucked in shirts. They weren't in large groups, either, but rather two to five people at a time.

Peter kept an eye on the time. It was approaching noon which meant it was almost time for lunch. He worked his way over to the top of the walkway to coincide with the top of the hour. He noticed Bob and Mary had finished the restrooms, watered the plants, and wiped down the guard rails. Now, they were drinking coffee at the coffee shop while waiting for him to finish.

As expected, three people left the coffee shop and headed down the walkway. As they passed, Peter noticed the names on their badges and started committing them to memory. A minute later, a larger group exited the doors at the end of the sloped passage. Peter was right to think lunch time would bring more people out. As they passed, Peter grabbed as many names as he could and started memorizing them. In addition to the names, he was able to grab their clearance levels as well. Everyone that passed had RUBY on their badge, but they also had another designator: KGEN.

Finishing up, he placed the buffer back into the closet and then walked over to Bob and Cindy.

"Took you long enough!" Bob stated a little sarcastically.

"Sorry," Peter apologized. "But you only get one chance to make a first impression, right?" he threw back.

"Well, I'm starving!" Cindy cut in as she waved over Jeff who was conversing with the lady behind the counter. "Let's get something to eat!"

Shortly after, Jeff had escorted them over to the chow hall and left them. Of course, there were menial conversations again about nothing, but Peter did his best to look interested and even participated a little. All the while, he kept reciting the names he had learned in his head.

An escort arrived at their table near the end to take them over to the ops building. Once again, the red light was turned on and people were notified of the uncleared personnel in the building. It was set up like a traditional operations building Peter was used to when he served in the Air Force. However, there were only two or three people in the entire building. At first, he thought the lack of people was unusual. But then he remembered that most of the flights would take place after dark which is probably when the pilots would arrive. As he worked his way down the hallway between offices, he took a moment to stop by the operations desk. The operations desk normally had either white boards or flat screen televisions depicting the day's flights, aircraft, and pilots assigned to each. Not surprised, he found large white sheets draped over the desk area and the monitors were off. Obviously, the escort had sanitized the place in order to hide anything classified. Unlike Jeff at the coffee house, this escort was serious about his duties. He kept all three of them under his eye the whole time with the exception of the restrooms. On several occasions, they would have to wait till everyone finished in an office before they could move on to the next.

A little before five o'clock, the crew returned their cleaning supplies to the closet and were then escorted outside. The escort remained with them until the large, white bus pulled up. Although a little uncomfortable, Peter was happy to see the escort had taken his job seriously. *I'd hire him!* Moreover, he was glad this escort didn't work at the coffee house!

During the ride home, Peter kept going over the names in his head. He intended to provide them to Tony on Saturday to see what Boyd would dig up on them using his abilities to hack people's computers. Hopefully, he'd be able to discover a great deal about each of them which could provide insight and help Peter plan the next course of action. He also thought about the security level KGEN. Was it related to UGEN? In his gut, Peter felt that whatever he was looking for was behind the doors down the sloped passage.

***

Before going to bed that night, Peter retrieved his cell phone. Once again, he texted Sam:

Peter: *Hey SF! Another day making donuts. Getting better at it though. How's your end?*

About thirty seconds after he sent the text, the phone rang. It startled Peter! He wasn't expecting a call. The number on the screen revealed it was Sam calling. He pressed the button to answer the call.

"Hello?" he spoke into the phone.

"Hey you! I'm not in the mood to text tonight, so I thought I would give you a call. Is that okay?" Sam asked.

Peter coughed off to the side to clear his throat. "Of course. How are you?"

"As good as can be. I don't think Mr. Warbucks thought anyone could talk so much. I can tell he isn't used to having people around. And Tonto, he rarely talks. That man is all business, you know?" she said into the phone.

Peter laughed. He was genuinely entertained at the names Sam had chosen for the two men. "Yeah, Tonto's not the talker!" After he stopped chuckling, he asked, "They are treating you okay, right? Be honest."

"Papa Bear, there's nothing to worry about! They do their thing and I do mine. By the way, I got you something. Going to have Tonto take it to you this Saturday," she replied.

"What is it?" Peter asked.

"It's a secret! You'll just have to wait and see," she said in a fake motherly tone.

"You sound good," Peter said. "I'm glad to hear you in this spirit again."

"Well, shopping can do that to a woman. I'm not even going to tell you what all I've bought. You'll just have to wait and see for yourself," Sam returned excitingly.

"I can only imagine," Peter replied. Again, they both chuckled a little.

"Enough about me! All joking aside, how are you doing?" she asked.

"I'm good, really. It's not exactly my forte, but I'm glad I don't have to do this all the time," he explained. "I'd much rather be cruising down the road somewhere."

"Well, I know you're not a talker, so I'm not going to keep you. Just wanted to say hi outside of texting all the time," she said.

"It's good to hear your voice. I'm glad you called! Really!" Peter said to her.

"Thanks! Alright then, I'm going to let you go. Talk to you later. Goodnight Papa Bear!" she concluded.

"Goodnight," Peter responded. He waited to hear her hang up and then he put the phone down on the table.

He was glad she had called. Somehow, he knew he would sleep better that night after conversing with Sam. Before going to sleep, he picked up a sheet of paper he had written on earlier and read over it. *Ronald Dawson, David Tompkins, Shannon Spivey, Luke Reynolds, Jennifer Lovato, Jason Collins, William Peterson, RUBY, KGEN.*

***

Over the next few days, Peter completed the same routine. Head to work, clean the buildings, and then head home. Although Bob had offered to take turns buffing the floor, Peter insisted on doing it himself. Bob was relieved and accepted graciously. While buffing, Peter noticed the same people coming and going that were on his list. Furthermore, he noticed the guard at the end of the sloped passageway was the same guy. Jeff continued to escort them at the coffee house and then hand them over to the ops building escort, who remained committed to his job.

Before Peter realized it, Saturday had arrived. He didn't have to work again until Monday. Earlier in the morning, he went for a walk through the desert towards the western mountains, but realized they were further away than he thought. Still, he enjoyed being outside. After his walk, he just hung around the house. He even managed to take an hour nap after lunch. After he woke up, it was almost two o'clock. He almost picked up the phone to see if he could find out when Tony would arrive, but then a car pulled up. Looking out through the window, it was Tony in the same car he had used before. Peter opened the door and waited for Tony to come inside. After retrieving a box from the backseat, Tony walked over and entered the house.

"Hey!" Peter greeted.

Before saying anything, Tony walked over to the table near the couch and placed the box down. Turning around, he asked Peter, "How was your first week?"

Tonto. "It went smoothly," Peter replied. "What's in the box?"

Tony remained emotionless. "It's for you. Sam asked me to bring it to you. You can open it later, if you don't mind. I have to get back soon.

Find out anything yet? The building you work in, think it has a railway beneath it?"

"What's the rush? You just got here," Peter inquired.

"It's pizza night," Tony answered. "Sam made me promise to be back in time."

Peter started smiling. He was about to ask how she was doing, but now he knew. He also knew she was the type of person who loved life and found joy in it. She's probably thinking Boyd and Tony could use a little joy, hence, the pizza night. He liked that about her.

"Well," Peter started. "I think I'm in the right building. I've already gotten into a routine and have noticed a few interesting details. First, the building is large enough to have once been a hangar, or, at least a building large enough to conceal trucks being loaded with dirt. There's a sloped passageway in the middle of it that leads down and terminates at two doors. The doors are about thirty feet below the floor level. Furthermore, the people entering and leaving through those doors do so at thirty-minute intervals, on the hour and half hour."

Tony processed what Peter was telling him and then stated, "So you think there's probably a rail car operating on a thirty-minute schedule?"

"I do," Peter answered. "Aside from that, the escort at that building is pretty lax and doesn't keep a keen eye on us. And, there's an armed guard at the end of the passageway. He just stands beside the doors watching people badge in."

"Have you figured out how to get through the doors?" Tony asked.

Peter shook his head. "Not yet, but I'm working on it."

"Anything else?" Tony asked.

"Yes," Peter replied as he reached down and grabbed the paper on the table. "A list of names and a couple of security level designators I'm not familiar with. Figured you and Boyd could look into it. Some of those people wear white lab coats, so knowing their area of expertise could help ascertain what's behind the doors." He handed the paper over to Tony who folded it up and placed it in his pocket.

"Are you in need of anything?" Tony asked.

"I've had a few thoughts running around in my head. I may need a camera. One that is really small and can be concealed. I was wondering if you could have one made that could fit into a keychain or something. If I go behind those doors, there's no telling what I'll find. Having a camera would make things easier," Peter explained.

Tony nodded. "I think we can manage that."

"Also," Peter continued, "take a look at my badge." He walked to his bedroom and retrieved the badge. He handed it to Tony. "It would be good if we could figure out whether or not we could create one of these. All the badges seem to be the same on base, but I see some scanning them at badge readers leading me to believe they have a chip in them."

"Not sure I can help you there," Tony replied while looking at the badge. "If the other badges have a chip in them, then they are directly linked with a specific individual, I would imagine. Not only would you need the chip, you would need to be the person who the chip is assigned to."

"I figured as much," Peter admitted. "That's how our badges worked when I was in the military. Figured I would ask all the same."

Tony handed the badge back over to Peter.

"That's it," Peter said. "Need water for the road?"

"I'm good. I'll pass along the information. See you next Saturday," Tony stated before he turned and opened the door.

"Give Sam a big hug for me, please," Peter threw at Tony as he walked through the door. He couldn't let an opportunity for another inside chuckle pass. Tony turned around and eyed Peter who was smiling. Then, without a word, he shut the door behind him, entered the vehicle, and departed.

Now that the visit was over, Peter walked over to the couch and plopped down. Reaching over, he reached for the box and sat it on his lap. After wrestling with some tape, he managed to get it opened. He smiled. The first thing he saw was four books. He remembered telling Sam he wished he had something to read to make the time pass, so she had delivered. Next, there was a large bag of Skittles candy which made him keep the smile going. *She's amazing!* Peter then noticed a polaroid picture at the bottom of the box. Taking it out, he turned it over to see what was on it. He couldn't help but laugh out loud! Sam and Tony were in front of the fireplace which meant Boyd must have taken the photo. Tony had the same serious look on his face with his arms hanging by his side. Sam stood to his left and was trying to imitate Tony's expressionless face. Her right arm hung straight down, like Tony's, but she had bent her left arm across her waist and was pointing at Tony. *She knew this would make me laugh.*

There was nothing else in the box. Even so, receiving the package made Peter feel alive! He could feel the extra energy in his body. He placed the candy on the table and then took the books and polaroid to his bedroom and placed them on his nightstand. Peter positioned the photo so it would face the bed. Standing up, he stared at the photo and smiled. *I have a photo of her.*

Chapter 20

The weekend passed by quicker than Peter had thought. Mostly, he hung around the house or took a quick stroll to the store to pick up a few things. On Sunday, he had walked through the desert again just to get out of the house for a while. Before going to bed, he texted Sam to thank her for the gift and to share laughs over the photo. He was thankful to be able to communicate with her. It was a relaxing couple of days.

But today was Monday. He had just retrieved the buffer and was about to pull it to his normal starting point.

"Hey, Peter!" Cindy called out to him from the closet as she pushed the yellow mop bucket out.

He stopped and turned around. "Yeah?"

"Based on the time it has been taking you to buff the floor, we didn't tell you the slope has to be buffed too!" she said smiling. "Now that you know what you are doing, you may want to speed it up a bit to make sure you get it from now on."

"I'm sorry, I didn't realize we could go down it. I'll get it today," he returned with an apologetic smile.

As Peter pulled the buffer by the coffee shop heading for the back corner, he heard someone calling his name. It startled him, because whoever was calling out to him sounded like they recognized him. Continuing to pull the buffer, he slowly glanced over at the coffee shop where it had originated. There was a tall guy looking directly at him who smiled when Peter made eye contact. The man had a coffee in his right hand, but threw up his left to wave. Peter wasn't sure what to do. Should he acknowledge the guy? Not wanting the man to make a scene, Peter stopped and looked at him. The man looked a few years younger than Peter. He was dressed nicely in dark blue slacks and a white buttoned up shirt with no tie. Before Peter knew what to do, the man started walking in his direction smiling. Peter threw a quick glance over towards the bathroom and noticed Bob and Cindy had already entered the bathrooms. They had placed the yellow cones in front of the doors.

"Peter!" the man greeted and he walked right up. "Never thought I would see you here!"

Peter squinted his eyes a little trying to figure out who this guy was. There was something vaguely familiar, but Peter just couldn't put a finger on it.

"You don't remember me, do you?" the man asked, smiling all the same. "It's Rob, man! Rob Simmons!"

At that moment, the gears in Peter's brain started working. He and Rob had been stationed together at Osan in South Korea back in 1994. He remembered being assigned as Rob's supervisor. They had worked together for about five months before Peter had completed his tour and left. As he recalled, Rob had been a hard worker and never got into any trouble.

"Rob! From Korea!" Peter replied. "Yeah, I remember you. Long time!"

"How's life? Did you ever get married and have kids? When did you get out? Man! We've got a lot to catch up on!" Rob said excitedly.

"Looks like we do," Peter responded. "What do they have you doing here? Are you still in the Air Force?"

"I am! I'm the Security Forces Chief here. Been here for about two months now," Rob explained.

"So you made Chief Master Sergeant, huh?" Peter asked. "I'm not surprised. I remember you used to always be a hard worker."

"It wasn't easy. Heck, you should know. Last time I spoke with Sara, she said you were a Chief at Creech Air Force Base working on them drones," Rob stated.

Peter remembered the Sara he was referring to. She had been stationed in Korea with them. "I was, but decided to push the button and see what the civilian world was all about," Peter explained with a smile.

"Shoot, I remember how smart you were. And always serious too! Figured you would work for some big intelligence contractor after you got out!" Rob admitted.

Peter noticed how Rob looked down at the buffer and then back up. The picture in front of Rob wasn't what he was expecting. It was when Rob started looking at his badge that made Peter grow nervous.

"Who's Peter Norris?" Rob asked.

Peter stood motionless with a blank expression on his face. He had to think fast!

"Shhh!" Peter whispered over to Rob. "It's who I am now."

"What the heck are you talking about?" Rob asked with his face growing more serious.

Peter realized he was not only talking to an old friend, but also a leader in the security forces squadron. His brain was churning for answers.

"It's a long story," Peter answered. "I can explain in more detail at another time, but let's just say I completed a mission that got me into some hot water before I retired. I wasn't married and had no children, which is why I volunteered for it."

Rob's face grew even more questioning. "What are you talking about, man?"

"I helped stand up the new drone program for the Air Force. Drones were becoming a big thing, you know. One day, I was pulled aside by an agent who needed help south of the border. The cartels were using drones to fly drugs over the border. Long story short, the Air Force released me for a while to help. The FBI knew the cartel was actively seeking someone knowledgeable of drones, which is where I came in. Before I knew it, I was teaching the cartel how to fly drones while helping set them up for the FBI."

"Are you serious?" Rob asked, growing excited. "Don't tell me the drug cartel is after you now."

Peter shrugged. "Here I am, Peter Norris. The FBI hooked me up with this job. Figured no one would be able to find me out here. I insisted on working somewhere. I'm one of those that needs to work, you know?"

"That's the craziest thing I've ever heard!" Rob said. "I've always dreamed of being picked for an assignment like that."

"No one else knows. The FBI had a hard enough time getting me a job on this contract so I don't want to screw it up," Peter continued to lie. "Keep it a secret, will you?"

Rob thought for a second, but then nodded. "I know you, brother. We go back a long way. You're safe with me." Rob started to smile again. "Jeez, man! Talk about crazy!"

Peter was able to relax a little seeing that Rob had bought his lie. He decided to get off the subject. "So, did you switch from intelligence to security forces, or what?"

"Well, we were kinda overmanned for Chiefs in intel. They offered me this job, so I took it. Figured I might start my own security business once I retire," Rob explained.

"How many more years do you have?" Peter asked.

"Four!" Rob answered.

Peter nodded. "Cool! Hey, listen, I really need to get back to work. I don't like to draw attention, you know?"

"No problem, Mr. Norris," Rob said with a smile while emphasizing the name. "I'll keep stopping by so we can talk about some old times!"

"Sure thing," Peter replied as he reached for the buffer.

Peter took a quick glance at Rob's badge. *TOP SECRET//RUBY//HUMID*. Peter had never seen HUMID before, but recognized there was no KGEN either. Obviously, his old pal didn't know what was on the other side of those doors either.

Rob nodded as he turned around and walked out of the building. It had been a close call. Peter never imagined running into someone he knew here. At least he was able to lie himself out of it.

An hour later, Peter found himself nearing the doors at the end of the slope. He looked over and nodded at the guard who was looking back at him. The guard nodded back. As Peter unravelled the buffer's electrical cord so he could plug it into the outlet, the guard walked over a few steps in his direction.

"You know the Chief?" the guard asked.

Peter was a bit surprised but answered calmly, "I do! We go way back." The guard was in uniform and was wearing Staff Sergeant stripes which meant he had probably been in less than six or seven years. "I imagine you were still in elementary school," he added with a smile.

The guard smiled. "So, you retired from the Air Force?"

At that moment, Peter's brain jumped into overdrive with thoughts exploding. So many ideas went through his head in a flash, he could barely make sense of them. But then his eyes widened a bit as he found clarity.

"Who said I'm retired?" Peter asked while raising one eyebrow.

"Oh! I'm sorry. I just figured..." the guard let his words drop off as he looked over at the buffer.

The guard was easy to read for Peter. He was a young, junior security forces guy with lots of enthusiasm. He had probably asked if Peter knew the Chief in efforts to somehow gain an advantage at work. Even more, Peter could tell this guard was an overachiever based on how well his boots were shined and the closeness of his haircut. Peter had met security forces personnel like this young man before. And most of them aspired to become an agent in the OSI. It was the Air Force's special investigation unit where agents took on different identities to blend in and get the scoop on any criminal activity which might be happening on base. Hopefully, by choosing the right words and actions, Peter could convince this guard he was an agent working for OSI!

"It's okay," Peter replied calmly before throwing a quick wink at the guard. "You should know not everything is as it seems."

The guard's face scrunched up a bit as if in confusion, but then his face brightened up a bit as he looked back at Peter.

"Shhh!" Peter whispered quietly. "I'm just a janitor cleaning this floor." He plugged the buffer in and stood back up. "What's your name, son?"

"Staff Sergeant King, Sir," he answered proudly.

"Okay, Staff Sergeant King, I'll be seeing you around. By the way, what we discuss stays between you and I. Got it?" Peter ensured. After a nod from the guard, he turned on the buffer and started working. Taking a quick glance at the guard's badge, he noticed it lacked the KGEN security clearance. *Even he isn't cleared for what's beyond those doors.*

The day had barely started, and already Peter had lied multiple times to keep his real mission secret. However, those lies may have opened up opportunities. Knowing his old friend, Rob, gave him credibility with the guard. With the guard thinking Peter was in OSI, it would allow Peter more flexibility. When Peter decided it was time to go through those doors, having an ally like the guard could prove beneficial. However, Peter knew lies only lasted so long. By lying to them, Peter put a severe time limitation on what he needed to accomplish.

Peter whistled as he buffed. He could tell from his peripheral vision the guard kept looking over at him. At one point, Peter let go of the buffer and stretched his back. This stretch just happened to coincide with three men walking down the slope. Peter watched carefully as each man held his badge in front of the security badge reader and waited for a green light to come on. When it did, they placed their right index finger on a small piece of glass located on top of the reader. *Biometrics.* Once it beeped, they opened the door and walked through. When the door opened, Peter took a quick glance at what was behind the doors. It was a white hallway that extended beyond Peter's line of sight. If there was a rail system beyond those doors, it would have to be further down that hallway.

Peter remembered what Cindy had told him, so he worked a little faster in order to completely buff the entire floor. He completed the job just in time. Placing the buffer back in the closet, he walked over to join Cindy and Bob who were standing near the door with Jeff.

"Man, I'm sure glad you like that thing. I can't stand it!" Bob stated with a grimacing face.

"Keeps my upper arms strong!" Peter answered with a smile.

"Well, more power to you!" replied Bob as he followed Jeff outside.

***

Over the next three days, Peter thought about how to get through the doors at the end of the sloped passageway. Sneaking into the security office to make a badge, when no one was looking, was impossible. He didn't even know where the badge office was. Furthermore, even if the guard thought Peter was OSI, he would never just open the doors and let Peter walk through. However, Peter surmised there was only one way to walk through those doors without being arrested. He needed someone else's badge and fingerprint. If he walked down the slope and badged in, the guard would have to assume he was cleared. As for the badge and fingerprint, Tony would have to do some of his magic. Peter had provided a list of people who had badges, so hopefully, Tony could figure out how to obtain one as well as a fingerprint to go along with it. It seemed to work on television and spy movies, so there was a chance it was possible.

How to handle Cindy and Bob was the next dilemma Peter thought through. If they were to observe Peter walk through those doors, red flags would go up. It didn't take him long to figure out what to do. Again, Tony would have to take some action. Peter would have him pull them out of work to attend some training somewhere. With them being out for the day, Yana would probably insist on someone helping

Peter. He would have to refuse if she did and convince her he could handle it alone.

That left the escort, Jeff. Although he didn't keep a keen eye on them, he stayed in the area where he would occasionally glance over to see what they were doing. If, for some reason, Jeff wasn't able to escort, another person would be appointed or the cleaning would be cancelled. Peter thought through several ideas on how to overcome this problem, but there was only one viable solution. Somehow, he would have to debilitate Jeff and possibly leave him in the janitor's closet.

The red CYN shirt wasn't going to work either. Once he got through the doors, he had to look like he belonged there. Peter concluded the best option would be to bring a change of clothes. When he debilitated Jeff in the closet, he would change into a pair of slacks and a different shirt.

Thinking over the different scenarios, Peter knew a million things could go wrong. The spies on television always made it look easy, but Peter knew better. Real life was different! Everything had to work precisely. He wished there was an easier way, or another way at all, but realized this was probably the only solution.

Two other problems remained if he did get lucky enough to get through the doors. One of the problems pertained to the other side of the doors. Although he suspected a rail system, he really had no idea what was down the white hallway beyond the doors. On top of that, people beyond the doors wouldn't be familiar with him. In every classified environment, people were trained to challenge anyone they didn't know. Also, even though the janitors cleaning the floor were all but invisible, it was possible someone would recognize him as the buffer guy.

The other problem, which remained unsolved, was how to get off base if he did manage to pull it off. The bus didn't come until five o'clock, which left way too many hours to spend on base waiting for the alarms to go off. Peter would have to figure out how to get off base quickly!

At least the pieces were starting to come together, even though they were loosely connected. For now, Peter just needed to stay focused and figure out the two remaining problems. Once he figured them out, he could complete his mission and get out there for good.

***

It was Friday morning, now, and Peter was tackling the floor as usual with his buffer. He was thinking about the upcoming meeting with Tony, when he saw his old friend, Rob, walk in. Thinking on his feet, he switched off the buffer and walked over to meet him. Of course, he happened to intercept him at the top of the sloped passageway just so the guard would see the two talking together.

"Hey Rob! Haven't seen you in a few days," Peter greeted.

"Yeah, we've been kinda busy. Getting ready for the big DV visit. You know how that goes," Rob replied.

A distinguished visitor? "I thought that everyone that came here was a DV!" Peter chuckled in response.

"No, no! The BIG DV," Rob corrected as he glanced around to make sure no one was close by. "The new SECDEF is paying us a visit. And can you believe it, they want me to give a briefing to him?"

Even though Rob's face appeared to be upset at the fact he had to brief, Peter saw it for what it was. It was pride. He wanted Peter to know how important he was on base. Normally, a base doesn't speak about DV visits and keeps them classified. Rob probably wasn't supposed to say anything, but figured Peter could be trusted since they knew each other. *He trusts me.*

"Sorry, man! I feel your pain," Peter consoled haphazardly. Peter threw a glance down the slope to see the guard looking up at the two of them. Seizing the opportunity, Peter threw his arm out and pointed at the guard.

"Your guard down there should be commended. I see him every day, and you're lucky to have him on your team," Peter told Rob as they both looked down at the guard. Peter saw the guard straighten up a bit.

"That's Michael! One of my best Staff Sergeants. Walk with me," Rob said with a smile as he headed down the slope.

Peter wasn't expecting this. He was just trying to build trust with the guard, not have two people he lied to talk together right in front of him. He had no choice, now, so he left his buffer behind and followed Rob down the slope. The guard looked nervous. It was a common reaction when a Chief approached.

Before they even arrived, the guard greeted them, "Good morning Chief, good morning, Mr. Norris!"

"Good morning!" Rob returned in kind. "My old buddy here was commending you on how well you do your job."

"I'm just guarding the door, Chief," the guard answered humbly.

"You're doing more than that," Peter cut in. "The Chief, the people on this base, and the American people have placed their trust in your hands. You're not just guarding a door, son. You're guarding your country. I appreciate that!"

The guard smiled and said, "I appreciate that, Sir. Thanks for the kind words."

With that, Rob reached into his pocket and pulled out a coin. It wasn't a coin of monetary value, though, but rather a Chief's coin. They were rarely given out and only on special occasions deemed worthy by a Chief. He handed it out to the guard who received it with wide eyes.

"You won't see many of those around," Rob informed the guard as he handed him the coin. "Keep up the good work!"

"I will, Chief!" the excited guard replied.

Rob turned to walk back up the slope. Peter threw a quick wink at the guard before following.

As they walked up, Peter decided to bolster Rob's ego a bit. "Looks like you've grown to be the type of Chief we all like. Your troops look up to you," Peter stated seriously.

At the top of the slope, Rob turned to face Peter. "Just trying to take care of my troops is all."

"Listen, I'm sure my site lead is going to make us clean extra hard in preparation for the upcoming DV visit. I'd like to get a head start and make a good impression on her, if you know what I mean. When is the visit?" Peter asked. The wheels in his head were turning again.

Rob hesitated for a brief moment, but then smiled. "You old dog! I know your site lead. Well, I don't know her, but the guys on base know who she is. Quite the eye candy!"

Peter just shrugged.

Rob was smiling big and patted Peter on the shoulder. "I'm just kiddin' with you! I know what you mean, man! He'll be here next Friday. Heck, you'll probably get to see him. I brief him at nine in the morning and then he's coming over here at ten," Rob informed Peter.

"I don't know," Peter returned. "I always cleared out the cleaning crews when people like that were coming through."

Rob scrunched up his lips and replied, "SECDEF visits are a norm here, even if this is a new one. I doubt they'll pull you out."

Peter nodded. "Either way, thanks for the heads up. I'll keep the info to myself, too."

"Thanks!" Rob nodded in agreement.

"Well, I better get back to it. Bob and Cindy will start calling me lazy if I don't!" Peter smiled as he turned to his buffer.

"Alright! Talk to you later," Rob concluded as he threw up a quick wave bye and then walked over to the coffee shop.

As Peter buffed the floor, numerous ideas began to formulate. Could he somehow take advantage of the Secretary of Defense's visit? He would have to think about it. Hopefully, he would have a plan when Tony arrived on Saturday.

Chapter 21

Peter was outside when Tony arrived. However, as the car pulled up, Peter realized he had a passenger. *Sam!* Peter grew excited and walked over to the passenger side to open the door for her.

"Hey!" Peter greeted her. "Wasn't expecting this surprise!"

"Hey, you!" Sam replied with a smile as she exited the vehicle. "The house was starting to get stuffy, so I insisted I come with Tony." She looked over to Tony who had gotten out of the vehicle. Tony didn't look amused. Sam turned back to Peter and giggled a little.

"Let's get inside, please," Tony encouraged as he headed for the door.

Peter and Sam smiled at each other, once again, and then went inside. Even though he felt like it, Peter wasn't sure if he should hug Sam or not. What if she was growing disgruntled hanging around the house with Boyd and Tony. Perhaps she had enough time to think things over and wished she would have just left when she had the chance. Currently, however, she looked quite happy. Regardless, the time passed as well as the opportunity.

"Help yourself to the fridge. It has some cold water stocked if you're thirsty," Peter invited.

"I'm going to check out your pad!" Sam answered as she started strolling through the house.

Tony had sat on the couch and was looking at Peter. Surprisingly, Tony wasn't dressed as usual. Rather, he had on shorts and a t-shirt.

"Never thought I would see you looking casual like this," Peter said smiling.

"It was Sam's idea. She wanted me in shorts. When I refused, she said wearing my normal attire would draw attention. Considering the people in this town, I decided she was right, so I'm blending in."

"Don't forget to smile once in a while!" Sam exclaimed from down the hallway.

Peter chuckled and then sat down in one of the chairs opposite the couch.

"Were you able to figure out if you could get that camera I asked for?" Peter inquired of Tony.

"Yes. There's a guy working on it in Vegas. I will pick it up this Tuesday," Tony replied. "I also checked in on getting a badge made. Needless to say, I couldn't find anyone that could replicate one."

"That's okay," Peter said. "I think I have found a solution around it."

Tony raised an eyebrow waiting for Peter to elaborate. However, Sam entered the room at that time and sat in the chair beside Peter.

"Not bad," she said. "Could definitely use some personality, though!"

"How's your dad?" Peter asked.

"He's good," Sam answered. "Boyd finally installed the software on my laptop after I threatened to steal the car and drive to see him." She smiled wryly.

"How are you?" he asked. "Any more episodes?"

"None," Sam answered. "I actually feel good. Boyd had a doctor come visit this past Wednesday, who said I was as good as could be expected."

Peter nodded. "So, what have you been doing besides threatening to steal cars?"

"Well, I ordered some supplies and started drawing and painting a little," Sam answered while thinking. "I've read two novels. Oh yeah! I tried a couple of new recipes I saw online. Alfred and Tony seemed to like them."

"Good. Imagine if you were stuck here!" Peter chuckled.

"I don't think you'd like it if I were here with you!" Sam replied with a chuckle. "You'd probably send me back to Alfred for talking so much!"

Not a chance! "Hey! I ate all those Skittles you sent me," he said smiling.

"Good! Maybe they'll brighten you up!" Sam replied. "So, on a different note, when are you going to be done with all of this?"

"We were just about to discuss that," Peter replied and then turned to look at Tony. "Find out anything about those names I gave you?"

"We did. Mr. Boyd has quite a talent when it comes to finding things through the computer," Tony answered and then pulled a piece of paper from his shorts pocket. After unfolding it, he read the contents, "Ronald Dawson graduated from Duke University with a doctorate in microbiology. David Tompkins and Jennifer Lovato both graduated from Johns Hopkins. Each has a doctorate in neurosurgery. Shannon Spivey graduated from Penn State with a doctorate in archaeology. Jason Collins served twenty years in the Navy as a linguist. And William Peterson graduated from NC State with a doctorate in cloning technology."

"That's a lot of brain power!" Sam exclaimed. "That place is crawling with a bunch of fifty-pound heads."

"Hmm," Peter chimed in. "Appears Boyd may have been right in his assumptions. If something like he explained was dug up in Egypt and brought here, this would be the group of people I'd have working on it."

Tony nodded. "Mr. Boyd thinks so as well."

"Do they all reside in Vegas?" Peter asked.

"Yes," Tony answered. "In very nice houses."

Peter sat back in his chair. "Well," he started, "I have somewhat of a plan. The first thing I have to do is get behind those doors at the end of the sloped passageway I told you about. I think I have it figured out, but I'm going to need a badge from one of those gentlemen doctors. I plan on using their identity to get past the security badge reader. However, it's impossible for me to swipe one while at work." He looked over to Tony.

Tony raised an eyebrow. "You need me to get the badge?"

"If you don't mind," Peter answered. "But that's not the hard part. I need to be able to use their right index fingerprint as well. I don't know if that can be done, or not, but I've seen them do it on TV, so I thought I would ask."

"It's possible," Tony assured. "You just have to know the right people."

"Good! Next, I'll need you to pull out my coworkers, Cindy and Bob. Send them to training somewhere, or something. I just can't have them around when I do this," Peter explained.

Tony thought for a second and then responded, "I can make that happen."

"Then there's Jeff. He's our escort at the building. I need to get him out of the way somehow. I was thinking I could drug him, or something, and then leave him in the janitor's closet."

"Propofol," Tony interrupted. "An injection of propofol in the neck will make him go unconscious immediately. It'll last at least four hours."

"It's scary you know this!" Sam exclaimed to Tony. "I knew you killed people, but injecting drugs into necks? Who have I been living with?"

Tony looked back over to Peter. "I can get it for you."

"Good. Once I get Jeff out of the way, I'll change clothes and then head towards the doors. There, I'll use the badge and fingerprint you obtain. The guard already thinks I'm an undercover agent, so I don't think it'll be a problem when I open the doors," Peter explained. "The barista is an older lady and can hardly see. I'm not worried about her at all."

Tony nodded to show he was understanding the plan so far. "Okay, that takes care of people on this side of the door. What about the ones behind the doors? Won't they challenge your identity?"

"Well, the key to avoid being caught behind the doors is to show I belong behind the doors," Peter smiled. Tony shook his head showing he didn't understand. Peter explained further, "If I were to just go back there and walk around, the people behind the doors would know I didn't belong back there. I'm pretty sure everyone behind those doors knows one another. Even if I claimed to be new, they would have been notified of a new arrival."

"So, what's the solution," Sam asked, obviously interested in how he was going to overcome this obstacle.

"The SECDEF!" Peter replied.

"The who?" Sam asked, confused.

"The new Secretary of Defense is coming for a visit. He'll be in our building at ten that morning, and I suspect he's going behind those doors," Peter revealed.

"Okay. But you're not the SECDEF," Tony replied.

Peter smiled. "No, I'm not. But the SECDEF will be expected back there. Everyone working there will know he is coming. And everyone knows he doesn't travel alone. He'll have one or two aids with him."

"Yes, but he'll know you aren't part of his crew!" Tony stated.

"Yes, but he doesn't know I don't belong back there. The SECDEF will just think I'm part of the team that normally works behind those doors. The actual people working back there will have to believe I'm with the SECDEF. I'll stay away from where the SECDEF is, so if anyone asks who I am, I'll just explain I'm with the SECDEF. This will help because I can then ask the workers about their projects and just tell them the big man wants to know."

"I'm not sure that's going to work," Tony said skeptically.

"It has too! It's the only opportunity available," Peter replied.

"Wait," Sam cut in again, "I thought you were going to be one of those doctors."

"I'm just using the doctor's identity to get through the doors. Once I'm through them, I'm going to be someone working directly for the SECDEF," Peter elaborated. "If I get back there and see it's not going to work, I'll have to abort."

Tony then asked, "Which badge are you going to wear back there? If the workers see your badge, they'll know you don't belong back there."

"True. But I'm guessing the Ranch treats the SECDEF like other military installations do. Never would they ask him or his team to wear a badge. His identity should be well known to everyone working in the Department of Defense, so asking him to wear a badge would be considered an insult. He and his team will not have badges, or at least I don't expect them too. If they do, I'll just put on the stolen badge and avoid inquisitive eyes."

The three sat quietly around the wooden table between them. They each were going over the plan in their minds.

"Now," Peter started again after letting them chew on it for a bit. "Let's say it all goes as planned and I get out with no one knowing the difference. I still have a problem. I'll need to get off base immediately."

"There's only one bus, right?" Tony asked.

Peter nodded in affirmation.

"Well, there are three options the way I see it," Tony continued. "A person can fly out, walk out, or drive out. I don't think flying out will work. Walking out isn't an option either. There are sensors all over the base and desert around there, so you wouldn't get far at all on foot. Looks like you just have one option. You're going to have to drive off."

"Do you have a car there you can drive?" Sam asked.

Peter shook his head. "Guess I could steal one. Of course, I have no idea how to steal a car!" he said, a little concerned.

Once again, the three sat around the table thinking.

"Maybe I could have Yana arrange for transportation. I'll tell her to close down early and have everyone attend a CYN social here in Alamo," Tony pitched. "Maybe the base will provide a bus for her."

Peter was nodding. "That would probably work. Think she can pull it off?"

"Only one way to find out," Tony replied. "When does the SECDEF arrive?"

"Next Friday!" Peter answered. "I'll need the badge, the fingerprint, the injection, the camera and a planned ride off base by Thursday evening. Is that doable?"

"I'll make it happen. Anything else before we leave?" Tony asked.

"Not that I can think of," Peter answered.

Tony stood and headed for the door. Sam stood up and said, "I'll meet you in the car."

Tony nodded and walked out of the house.

Peter stood up beside Sam.

"This is scary, Peter," Sam confided. "And I know why you are doing this." Her face was one of endearment.

"I'm doing this because we don't really have a choice," Peter replied.

"That's not true," Sam answered. "You could've left this all behind. You could have started a new life all on your own with a new truck and RV." She smiled gently. "But you didn't. You knew I didn't have a way out."

Peter stood quietly. He didn't know how to respond.

"Get this done with," she urged. "Get it done and then come get me." She leaned over and kissed Peter on the cheek. "Be careful," she said and then started to walk towards the door.

"Wait!" Peter said hurriedly.

Sam stopped as she was reaching for the door and turned around. Peter walked up to her and threw his arms around her. It was a heartfelt hug. He wanted it to last forever, but after a few seconds, he let go and took a step back.

"See you soon!" he said. Sam nodded with a smile and walked out the door. Peter watched them drive off.

Chapter 22

Monday rolled around quick enough. Now that Peter had a plan, he kept churning it around in his head. He was going to have to execute everything perfectly while being able to adjust to unexpected situations. Luckily, he had a military background which might prove useful in a sticky situation. As he rode the bus to work, he thought about Staff Sergeant King. He needed to gain more trust if he was going to walk through the door.

Soon enough, Peter was hard at work in the coffee house building. Jeff was over at the coffee shop, again, while Cindy and Bob were cleaning the restrooms. Peter worked the buffer from side to side as he made his way to the end of the sloped passageway.

"Good morning! Have a good weekend?" Peter asked Staff Sergeant King.

"I did! I actually got to go home over the weekend and hang out with some friends. We went and saw one of those Cirque du Soleil shows. You ever see one?" Staff Sergeant King asked.

"Can't say I have. Thought about it once, but those tickets cost too much for an old janitor like myself," Peter answered with a wink. The wink showed the guard he was joking around about the price.

"Well, it was awesome. I recommend you check one out," Staff Sergeant King stated.

Peter took an obvious look around to make sure no one was looking, and then he moved closer to the guard. "Quick question for you, if you don't mind?" Peter asked in a lower tone.

"Sure, what's up?" Staff Sergeant King inquired.

"First, I never spoke to you about this. Got it?" Peter insisted. After seeing a response nod, he continued, "There's a gentleman that passes by you every day, Dr. William Peterson. Know who I'm talking about?"

Staff Sergeant King squinted his eyes a little to think harder and then nodded. "Yeah, I'm familiar with him."

"I've been watching him, trying to figure out a few things. You've been here longer than I have, and I know you do your job well. Ever see him carrying in a briefcase or backpack? Maybe something not as big, but different from the rest?" Peter asked knowing it would spark interest from the guard.

Peter already knew the answer. Over the past couple of weeks, he examined the people walking through the doors for anything that stood out. William Peterson stood out. He never stopped for coffee in the mornings, but he always carried a thermos with him. The thermos was white with a picture of Darth Vader on one side, and JOIN US OR DIE on the other.

"Hmm," Staff Sergeant King started and then paused to think. "Never seen him carry a backpack or briefcase. They're not allowed behind the doors. He does carry a Darth Vader thermos with him though."

Peter raised an eyebrow inquisitively. "Has he always carried it with him?"

"As long as I can remember," Staff Sergeant King answered.

Peter nodded and thought. He knew the guard would think he was contemplating the thermos. "Thanks for the info," Peter said as he grabbed hold of the buffer again.

Staff Sergeant King was showing excitement. "You want me to check the thermos next time he passes, and say it's just a random check?"

"No, no, no! Don't do anything. Don't say anything, either," Peter demanded. "You know how difficult the legal system can be, and he's a civilian. Just let things play out and let me handle the rest."

The guard nodded. Peter started the buffer again and finished the sloped passageway. *Poor kid.* He liked the guard and hated manipulating him. However, Peter saw no other way. Hopefully, the guard would just keep performing his duty as he always did.

Peter had finished buffing the entire floor and had put the buffer back inside the closet. Walking over to meet Cindy and Bob, he noticed Yana was talking with them. He moved in to join them.

"Hi Peter!" Yana greeted Peter with a smile. "I was just telling Cindy and Bob that we were going to have a social this Friday."

Peter raised his eyebrows and replied, "A social, huh? Sounds fun!"

"Yep! And it's going to be a half day, too! I'm arranging for a bus to pick us up at noon that day," Yana explained.

"It's not a half day for us," Bob injected.

Peter put a look of confusion on. "You're not going to the social?"

Cindy and Bob looked at one another smiling and shook their heads. It was obvious they knew something which tickled them.

Cindy couldn't contain it! "We're getting the whole day off!" she almost screamed. She and Bob looked like they were about to start jumping with joy.

Peter looked over to Yana who was smiling with them. Looking over to Peter, she explained their excitement for them. "Bob and Cindy have been recognized for their outstanding work. It appears the powers that be have been putting in some good words. As a result, the company has presented them, and their families, with a weekend getaway. They each have a three-day reservation at Caesar's Palace in Vegas, in a penthouse. And, to help them enjoy themselves, they're each getting a thousand bucks spending cash!"

"Can you believe it?" Cindy exclaimed rhetorically while grinning from ear to ear.

Seems like Tony came up with a better idea than training! "That's awesome! Congrats!" Peter said supportively. He was happy for them.

"Don't worry, Peter," Yana said to grab his attention. "I'll make sure someone is available to help you here."

Tony had done his part. Now it was his turn. "No need for that. I can handle things here," he replied.

Cindy and Bob were paying no attention. They were talking to each other about the upcoming weekend. Yana scrunched her brows together. "This is a big place, Peter. You're going to need some help."

"How about this," Peter offered. "Send whoever you were going to get to help me over to the ops building. That way, both places get cleaned since it's only a half day. I assure you I can get things done here!"

Yana thought for a second and then began nodding. "Okay, then. I'll arrange for ops to have an escort ready Friday morning. You just make sure you get this building cleaned!" she answered in a woman-in-charge type way. Peter smiled and nodded.

Jeff walked up then and said, "You guys look extremely happy today."

Yana summarized Cindy and Bob's reward to Jeff. Jeff was almost as excited as they were. After the excitement passed, Yana headed back to the office building while Jeff escorted the three of them to the ops building. *So far, so good*!

The next three days evolved as normal. Lunch was more exciting, though, with the CYN employees discussing the upcoming social and formulating plans to earn rewards like Cindy and Bob. It was obvious nothing like this had happened in the company before.

Peter and Staff Sergeant King only exchanged nods. Peter was happy the guard didn't draw unwanted attention to him. As for Jeff, Peter kept a more watchful eye on him. He didn't have a routine, but rather just roamed around. Sometimes he spoke to people, and sometimes he just walked around thinking inside that head of his. Basically, Jeff did what he could to make the escort time pass by quickly. Peter's old friend, Rob the Chief, came in once on Wednesday morning for a cup of coffee. He was in a hurry, though, only throwing a simple greeting towards Peter. As for William Peterson, he kept bringing the same Darth Vader thermos with him...every day.

The evenings provided quiet, ample time for Peter to rehearse the upcoming mission in his head. Over and over, he thought of the many different ways events could unfold. He had to make sure he was prepared. There was no room for failure. If he failed, he would probably spend the rest of his life in prison. In the worst-case scenario, the 'others' would get him.

Before bed, he exchanged casual texts with Sam. Mostly, they pertained to making fun of Mr. Warbucks and Tonto. On Wednesday night, she texted Peter to confirm that Tonto would be going for a horseback ride on Thursday evening. Sure enough, he did.

***

At around seven o'clock on Thursday evening, Tony pulled up in the driveway. Peter greeted him at the door and then the two of them sat down on the couch for final preparations. Tony had brought a briefcase with him.

"Did you get everything I need?" Peter asked.

"I did," Tony answered as he popped open the briefcase.

Peter immediately picked up the badge and looked at it. "Ronald Dawson?" Peter asked. "Now that I think of it, I didn't think he might be staying at the Ranch during the week. Looks like he must fly home every day instead of staying up here. Can't believe I overlooked that."

"He does stay up at the Ranch," Tony cut in a little sarcastically. "After staking out his residence for a couple of days, I realized he wasn't coming home. That meant I wouldn't be able to get the badge."

"Well, how'd you get it then?" Peter asked curiously.

"We remembered you said you wouldn't be able to steal a badge. So, Mr. Boyd did some digging on his computer. He found that Mr.

Dawson had provided an emergency contact number to different businesses like power and water. The prefix in the phone number belonged to the Ranch. We also knew he was divorced when we originally researched him. With that, I just made a simple phone call last night pretending to be with the Las Vegas Water and Sewer department. A First Sergeant answered and said he could deliver the message and a contact number I provided. Within thirty minutes, Mr. Dawson called back. I explained how we suspected a pipe had burst at his residence due to the amount of water being consumed."

"That was smart!" Peter cut in. "But what's keeping him from coming back to work? Surely, he'll find his badge missing when he goes to get it!"

Tony looked Peter in the eyes, "He flew into Vegas this morning. I was waiting for him. I'm sure he wasn't planning on going back to work today."

"Well, he will tomorrow morning and that's a problem!" Peter replied, getting anxious.

"He's not going to work tomorrow, either," Tony answered.

Peter showed serious concern after that statement and inquisitively stated, "Please tell me you didn't..."

Tony shook his head, "I didn't. He's safe and doesn't even realize his badge is missing."

"What did you do with him?" Peter asked.

"Is it important? You have the badge and he won't be a problem tomorrow. Trust me," Tony insisted.

Peter looked back into the briefcase trying not to think about what happened to the man. "Were you able to get his fingerprint? This badge is useless without it," Peter asked.

Tony reached over and grabbed a small box from the briefcase. It was metallic and about the size of a ring box. Flipping it open, he held it out to Peter. Inside, a skin-colored material with a fingerprint was pressed flat against a piece of glass.

"When you are ready, just peel it off the glass and place it over your right index finger. It should work," Tony explained.

"How'd you get it made so fast? You only came in contact with Dawson this morning," Peter inquired.

Tony's face showed he was growing impatient answering details. "I lifted the print on Monday from his residence. I didn't wait till today."

Peter understood and nodded.

Reaching into the briefcase, Peter pulled out a keychain. It was rectangular with a picture of the Vegas Strip on it. Even after flipping it over a few times and examining it more closely, he couldn't figure it out. Tony reached over and took the keychain.

"Here, let me show you. You have to put a lot of pressure on it and slide it open," Tony said while placing his thumb over the Vegas image and pushing. The top of the keychain slid open to reveal a small lens in the center and a small button in the corner. "There's a microSD card inside which will store all the pictures you take. Sliding it open like this and pressing the button is all you have to do. Got it?"

Peter nodded and was impressed. He slid the cover back up and then attached it to the ring his house key was on. "It'll blend right in!"

There was one last item in the briefcase. Peter reached in and pulled out the syringe. It was a normal looking syringe with the typical orange cap over the needle. Inside the tube, a clear fluid was noticeable. "Propofol?" he asked, turning to look at Tony.

Tony nodded. "Just get behind him and inject it in the base of his neck," he instructed as he took his index finger and placed it on Peter's neck. "Right here."

"Will it take a few seconds or will he just knock out?" Peter asked.

"You're injecting it into his neck, so it will be immediate," Tony explained.

Peter nodded and looked over what Tony had brought. He had everything he needed. Now, he just needed to do his part.

"That was really cool, what you did for Bob and Cindy," Peter stated.

Tony just simply replied, "It was easier than sending them to training somewhere." After a few seconds, he continued, "There's something else I need to tell you."

Peter grew concerned immediately. "Is Sam okay?" he asked.

"She's fine," Tony answered quickly to relax Peter. "But the two of you have been placed on a missing persons list back in St. George."

Peter's eyes widened.

"After the incident at the restaurant, police showed up and interviewed witnesses. Seems they told the cops you two were kidnapped, and the kidnapper shot the two men. Your vehicles helped them identify both of you very quickly."

"Were you identified?" Peter asked.

"Not directly. They don't have my name, but they were able to draw a sketch from witness accounts. Luckily, there were no cameras in the place," Tony explained.

"At least Sam and I aren't wanted for a crime," Peter stated, seeming to relax a bit.

Tony sat quietly for a minute and then told Peter, "Some agents visited Sam's dad."

Again, Peter grew concerned.

"He's safe. However, the agents were a male and female from the FBI," Tony elaborated. "Probably the same two that gave you a visit."

"What did Sam say? What are y'all going to do?" Peter asked.

"Sam doesn't know. We didn't tell her. And we're not going to do anything. Seems the agents realized her dad was of no use. However, it tells us the 'others' haven't given up looking for you two," Tony stated as he watched Peter contemplate the information. "Don't let this get in the way of what you need to do. Stay focused."

Peter nodded. For now, they were still safe. He had already come to the conclusion he could never return to his truck and RV. The whole purpose of what he was doing, from his and Sam's perspective, was so they could start new lives. He was determined to successfully execute his plan.

"So, the social is tomorrow, here in Alamo," Tony continued. "The park beside the store is where the bus will take all the CYN employees. Once you get off the bus, you'll see a gray colored Nissan Altima parked at the store across the road. The doors will be unlocked, and the keys will be beneath the driver's seat. Take it and drive it to the Aliante Casino Hotel on the northside of Vegas. You know where that is, right?"

"I do," Peter answered.

"When you arrive, I'll pick you up at the front entrance and take you back to Mt. Charleston. Got it?"

"Yes. Take the gray Altima and drive it to the Aliante Casino. There, you'll pick me up at the front doors and take me to Mt. Charleston," Peter recapped.

Tony nodded, "Good. Need anything else?"

"A drink!" Peter answered. For the first time, Peter saw Tony smile.

"You've got this," Tony replied as he stood and headed for the door. Before walking through the doors, he turned and said, "See you tomorrow, Mr. Knowles!"

Chapter 23

Peter opened his eyes. Before getting out of bed, he lay still and stared up at the ceiling. *Today's the day*. So much was at stake. He wanted to make sure his mind was in the right place before he put his feet on the floor. Looking to his right at the nightstand, he looked over at the polaroid Sam had given him. She was beautiful. Today had to go perfectly if he wanted to see her again. Peter thought about what Sam had said to him before she left last Saturday. He knew she was right, and that he was doing all of this for her. *I will not fail*.

A new thought crossed his mind. If he were to get caught, it would be considered disgraceful. Rob, Staff Sergeant King, and all of the old friends he knew while serving, would consider him a traitor. More than two decades of serving his country honorably would be forgotten. *I will not fail*.

Peter knew everything was ready. He had packed a backpack the night before. Inside, he placed the badge and syringe in a hard-to-spot side pocket located in the interior of the main storage area. The fingerprint box wouldn't fit in the pocket, so he had wrapped it up like a gift just in case someone decided to check it. This would be his first day bringing a backpack. Of course, he had seen others bring them. Unlike his backpack's contents, the other ones usually contained a packed lunch or good book to read while on the bus. The last thing Peter had placed inside was a long sleeved, button-up white shirt. He really had no idea what to wear in order to look like he belonged with the SECDEF's team, but he figured the white shirt was his best bet. As usual, he would wear slacks to work which would go well with the white shirt. Of course, he would choose his dark blue slacks today. Beside his bed, he had placed the black, dress shoes he had purchased the day before at the small clothing store in town. He was counting on no one noticing them. *I will not fail. I cannot fail. I've got this!*

Peter sat up and swung his legs over to put his feet on the floor. Taking a deep breath, he stood up, stretched as usual, and then began getting ready for what would turn out to be a successful day. Everything seemed amplified to Peter. The combing of his hair, the brushing of his teeth, and even the way his CYN shirt had felt when he pulled it over his head. He didn't take for granted the freedom in doing such menial tasks. He paid extra attention to the taste of his coffee and how it felt as it went down and warmed his throat. Many people took these things for granted, but not Peter. Not today.

Grabbing his backpack and slinging it over his shoulder, he walked out the door and headed for the bus. He was calm. When the bus stopped, he stepped on with his usual greeting to the bus driver and then took the same seat he had always taken. Of course, there was more talking on the bus than normal with CYN workers discussing the upcoming social. Some thought it was weird they were having one at all, while others were thrilled. Needless to say, everyone was cheerful about only having to work a half day.

The bus ride to the Ranch was uneventful. Due to their excitement about the social event, more CYN employees than usual seem to happily greet the soldier at the security checkpoint. The soldier was happy for them as he checked everyone's badge and even wished them a good, long weekend.

Upon arrival, and as Peter stepped off the bus, he noticed two female CYN employees stepped off with him. Peter figured Yana had tagged those two for the ops building today, since Cindy and Bob had the day off. As usual, it was about nine in the morning. Briefly, he imagined Rob must have started briefing to the SECDEF by now. *One hour to go.* Looking towards the CYN office building, he noticed Jeff and the ops escort waiting for them. Peter slung the backpack over his shoulder and headed towards them.

"Good morning, Jeff!" Peter greeted as he always did.

"Morning, Peter!" replied Jeff. "A backpack, huh? That's a first!"

Peter was in mission mode. His brain was crisp and ready. Without missing a beat, he responded, "Yeah, I thought I would bring a little snack today since we aren't going to eat till the social. I'm going to have to eat something before then."

Peter noticed the other two CYN employees shaking hands with the ops escort, who, of course, didn't even smile. He motioned for them to follow and then headed for the ops building. The two ladies shrugged it off and followed after him.

"I'm happy for you guys! More people should appreciate the work you all do. No one else wants to do it, that's for sure!" Jeff complimented.

"I like you, Jeff! I like the way you trust us to do our job. The escort over at the ops building is quite smothering," Peter threw in after he saw the ladies and the ops escort were beyond hearing distance.

"Some are like that. But I have a good sense of people. I find them easy to read. You, Bob and Cindy don't raise any red flags at all. Besides, it isn't like you're going to see anything you shouldn't in this old building," Jeff said as the two of them walked over to the coffee house. Peter was glad no one noticed the dress shoes.

"Maybe I'll share one of my snacks with you later!" Peter told Jeff. "I'll call you over when I decide to eat something."

"Alright!" Jeff replied as he opened the door for Peter. "Hope it's something sweet!"

After entering the building, Jeff broke off and headed for the coffee shop in the corner. Before heading for the janitor's closet, Peter looked ahead and towards the end of the sloped passageway. He made eye contact with Staff Sergeant King and gave a more serious nod than usual. Staff Sergeant King nodded back. Peter turned left and headed for the janitor's closet. Opening the closet, he knew he needed to set up in order to be ready when the time came. He pulled the door almost completely closed behind him and then took the backpack off of his shoulder. Unzipping it, he carefully retrieved the syringe and badge and placed them on a shelf to the right. He then placed an orange cleaning rag over them for concealment. Next, he pulled out the wrapped box and tore the paper off. After placing the paper in the waste basket beside him, he set the box on the shelf near the orange rag. Lastly, he pulled out the white shirt and hung it on a hook which had been placed on the wall to hold jackets or coats. He took the time to unbutton it so he would be able to put it on quicker. Satisfied, he grabbed the buffer and started his normal routine.

He had only been buffing about fifteen minutes when Jeff walked over to him. Peter stopped the buffer and raised his eyebrows questioningly towards Jeff.

"What's up?" Peter asked.

"Just found out we have a DV coming through in a few minutes. Can't have you buffing the floor when he comes through, you know?" Jeff stated.

"Okay! What do you want me to do?" Peter inquired.

"Umm...just go clean the restrooms really quick. Try to be done by nine forty-five 'cause the DV is coming at ten sharp," Jeff explained.

"Not a problem! Want me to just hang out in the janitor's closet till the area is clear?" Peter asked, hoping Jeff would agree.

"You don't have to do that, bud! You can hang out at the coffee shop if you want," Jeff replied, being nice.

"It's okay," Peter returned. "I'll hang out in the closet. It'll give me time to eat some of my snacks!" Peter was smiling.

"Up to you! I'll come get you afterwards," Jeff promised.

Peter nodded as Jeff turned to walk off. Grabbing his buffer, he headed back towards the janitor's closet. *This is going better than I expected.* Soon enough, he had exchanged the buffer out for the yellow bucket Cindy and Bob normally used. Peter glanced over to the clock hanging on the wall behind the coffee shop. *9:17 a.m.* He entered the restrooms and began to clean. At 9:25 a.m., Peter stepped out to exchange a bottle of cleaner. However, the real reason was to scout the area. As expected, and as normal, William Peterson entered through the front door carrying his Darth Vader thermos. *Right on schedule.* Peter had been watching the guy over the past few days and realized he always arrived at the same time. Satisfied, he returned to cleaning the restrooms.

At 9:37 a.m., Peter exited the men's restroom and headed for the sloped passageway. Looking around, he didn't see Jeff and figured he was in the office. Continuing on, Peter walked down to where Staff Sergeant King was standing guard.

"Looks like Mr. Peterson brought his thermos again today," Peter said seriously.

"I noticed that, too," replied King, showing a little excitement. "He's brought it every day."

"I'm pretty sure today will be the last day he brings it," Peter said confidently. "Just got to get the final straw to go on the camel's back."

"Final straw?" Staff Sergeant King asked curiously.

"More evidence. And, today's the day," replied Peter.

"Do I need to do anything? Call someone or something?" asked Staff Sergeant King.

Peter shook his head sternly. "No. I want you to do absolutely nothing. Do everything as usual. It'll take a few hours, but by this evening, Mr. Peterson isn't going to be a happy man."

With a nod from the guard, Peter turned to walk back up the slope. Before getting too far, he turned around and said, "Thanks, Staff Sergeant. I know it isn't easy keeping secrets. I'll be sure to put in another good word for ya!" The guard nodded in appreciation. As Peter walked away, he was thankful the walls, which the slope made, were high enough to obscure the guards view of the floor except what was directly ahead.

It was 9:40 a.m. when Peter got back to the janitor's closet. Before entering, he took another quick look around the floor. There were three familiar people, two men and one woman, drinking coffee. All three normally walked through the doors at the end of the sloped passageway at 9:57 a.m. Peter expected they would today. He figured the SECDEF would probably arrive about the same time. Behind the counter, the usual barista was cleaning the cappuccino machine. The only other person on the floor was Jeff, who must have just exited his office in the corner. He was headed towards the coffee shop.

Quickly, Peter opened the janitor's closet and placed the yellow bucket down. He reached under the orange rag and retrieved the syringe. Peering back around the doorway, he attempted to get Jeff's attention. "Psst!" Peter sounded towards Jeff, who looked back at him. Peter jerked his head twice towards the closet indicating Jeff should come over. Jeff shot over a quick smile and then turned to walk towards Peter. *Come get your snack.*

"We've got to hurry! It's the SECDEF that's coming and I don't want to miss him," Jeff informed Peter as he got closer.

Peter nodded and took a quick glance over to make sure no one at the coffee shop was watching. Then, he stepped out of the closet and motioned Jeff inside. Without hesitation, Jeff walked right into the closet.

"Get that bucket off the back shelf for me, please," Peter requested as he pulled the door quietly shut. Jeff went for the bucket and raised his arms to retrieve it. *This is it.* Peter took a step forward and lifted the syringe. Quickly, he injected the needle into the right side of Jeff's neck, right where Tony had told him, and quickly shot the Propofol in. Jeff jerked violently pulling his right hand down to grasp the side of his neck. Turning around with a very angry look, he opened his mouth to scream. Before any sound emitted, his eyes rolled up into his head as he fell forward towards Peter. Peter caught him and gently helped him down to the floor to avoid making any noise. It was then Peter noticed a small drop of blood on Jeff's neck and realized the needle had broken off. Looking closer, he could see the end of the needle protruding a little. Carefully, he reached over and was able to extract it. He reached up and grabbed the orange rag to wipe away the trace of blood. Standing back up, he decided to take a quick look out the door. Silently, he inched the door open and looked out. No one was reacting and probably hadn't even noticed Jeff enter the closet. *Clear*. The clock on the wall now displayed 9:46 a.m.

Peter closed the door once again and pulled off his red CYN shirt. *Breathe*. He tucked it into his backpack and then grabbed the white shirt. He worked to control his breathing and heart rate as he buttoned it up. *Relax*. Afterwards, he sucked in his breath and used his hands to tuck the shirt neatly into his slacks. Looking down at his clothes, he figured he looked like someone who belonged beyond those doors. He then looked over at the body lying on the floor. Detecting the slight rise and fall of the chest, he felt a little more comfortable. *At least four hours*.

Peter reached over and grabbed the box off the shelf. Opening the box, he gently peeled the fingerprint off the glass. Carefully, he pressed it over the tip of his right index finger. Fortunately, it blended right in. Unless someone were to examine his finger closely, they would never know it was there. Next, he retrieved the badge of Ronald Dawson and slipped it into his left pocket. He then walked over to the door and took a deep breath.

Peter exited the janitor's closet at 9:52 a.m. No one noticed. The three people were still at the coffee shop minding their own business. Peter headed a few steps to his left and entered the men's restroom. He figured if he exited the restroom, it wouldn't draw as much attention if there were more people on the floor when he did so. Patiently, he waited and listened behind the restroom door.

About three minutes later, Peter heard voices echoing around outside. Listening carefully, he was able to make out someone say 'Mr. Secretary'. He heard several sets of footsteps, but couldn't make out exactly how many people were out there. He estimated two to five.

As the voices faded towards the sloped passageway, Peter heard a few more footsteps. *The three workers*. He waited until they almost faded away as well. Taking one last deep breath, Peter casually opened the door and stepped out. The barista was the only person he noticed remaining on the floor, but she didn't pay any attention to him. She was writing something down on a piece of paper and had her back turned his way. Confidently, he headed for the sloped passageway. As he approached, he couldn't see the end of the sloped passageway from his vantage, but he did hear the tail end of a conversation between Staff Sergeant King and probably the SECDEF. He continued to walk but slowed a bit.

"Thank you, Sir! Have a great day!" he heard Staff Sergeant King say.

Looking to his right, Peter observed the barista still writing as he arrived at the corner where the sloped passageway began. He eased up to glance just over the wall, which the slope made, and saw three men in suits near Staff Sergeant King. One of the men placed his right index finger on the security badge reader. It must have been the head guy who worked here at the Ranch. He was probably escorting the SECDEF, who stood just behind him with one of his aides. They waited for the doors to open. The SECDEF threw a final nod at the guard as the three men in suits walked through. *I should have brought a suit top*. Peter figured the three workers that were previously at the coffee shop must have gone ahead and entered while the SECDEF greeted the guard.

Peter rounded the corner and began walking down the sloped passageway. Staff Sergeant King noticed him immediately. Peter began to smile slightly as he approached.

"What are you doing?" Staff Sergeant King inquired.

"Today is the day! Getting that final straw I need," Peter answered as he approached.

There was a questioning look on the guard's face. Peter reached into his left pocket, retrieved the badge belonging to Ronald Dawson, and then held it slightly up to indicate he had a badge. He had positioned his fingers to obscure most of the badge.

"Just hope this thing works!" Peter said to the guard as he walked up to the security badge reader. "Weren't expecting this, huh?"

"Not exactly," answered Staff Sergeant King. Peter noticed the guard's face had changed from questioning to surprise.

Here goes nothing. Peter placed the badge near the reader which let out a beep. Then, he pressed his right index finger against the glass on top and waited. It seemed like an eternity, but then a red light came on. There was no click indicating the door had been unlocked. Peter's heartbeat went into overdrive. He noticed the guard turn to face him more squarely.

"Great!" Peter responded. He repositioned the badge to make the reader beep again. Again, he placed his right index finger on the glass. He figured if it didn't work this time, he would be detained. Thankfully, a green light came on and then there was a single click coming from the door.

Peter smiled and said, "Second time's a charm!" He pulled the door open and walked through. The guard didn't stop him.

"Sure you don't need me to do anything?" the Staff Sergeant King asked from behind.

"I've got this," Peter answered without turning back to look. Confidently, he began his walk into the unknown. *I've got this.*

Chapter 24

When Peter had walked through the doors into the hallway, he noticed a door shutting at the other end. The SECDEF's team must have just gone through. Everything, to include the floor, walls and ceiling was white in the hallway which continued to slope downward. It extended another hundred feet or so and seemed to be an extension of the sloped passageway he had initially walked down. *How far down does the rabbit hole go?* Peter walked a little quicker figuring the rail cars, if there were any, would be leaving soon. It had to be about 10:00 a.m. by now. Arriving at the end, Peter listened carefully at the door. Somewhere off to the left, beyond the door, he briefly heard voices, but then they disappeared. Peter stepped back and looked at the wall around the door. There was no security badge reader, so Peter pushed the door open and walked through.

Peter's assumptions were correct. He had stepped through the door onto a platform. Four railcars, without windows, fit nicely into cutouts along the platform's edge. The platform's floor was white and extended approximately fifty feet forming a semi-circle against the wall behind him. Directly to his left, a white railcar with yellow trim had SOUTH

1 painted on the front. Its rails led off to the east. Forty-five degrees to the right of it was another railcar with SOUTH 2 on it whose rails headed southeast. Directly to his right, another railcar with the same colors had SOUTH 4 with its rails leading west. SOUTH 3 was painted on the remaining car and its rails led to the southwest. *SOUTH 4...S4?*

The platform's walls were white and followed the semi-circle pattern around the floor. They extended upwards about thirty feet. On the wall directly in front of Peter, a digital display was counting down from 20. He remembered hearing voices to his left before he came through the door, so he figured he would get on one of the railcars to his right. But which one, SOUTH 3 or SOUTH 4? If SOUTH 4 did translate to the S4 Boyd had spoken of, it would probably lead Peter to something associated with Project UGEN. Peter headed for SOUTH 4. As he arrived, he heard a computer voice announce the doors were closing. He quickly stepped through the doors.

As Peter had surmised, the SECDEF and his team were not on this railcar. However, two of the workers who had been at the coffee shop were! They were seated across and to the right of Peter, and both of them were staring up at him. *Just great!*

Peter smiled at both of them and then sat down directly across from them. He had placed the badge back into his left pocket, so he knew the two of them would be curious. Taking a quick glance at their badges, the woman's name was Kathleen while the man's name was Andrew. Although he had seen them before, he had never noticed their names.

"Who are you?" the woman asked. Both of them had puzzled looks on their faces.

"I'm Donald," Peter answered quickly. "I work for the Under Secretary of Intelligence, who wanted me to come with the SECDEF today. This is my first trip here, so I'm a little anxious." Peter had assumed correctly that no one ever paid any attention to the janitorial staff. These two, based on their appearance and demeanor, probably couldn't identify any of the support staff on base.

The man beside the woman nodded. But the woman had another question for Peter, "Why aren't you with the SECDEF? You guys aren't supposed to come to our section until 12:30."

"We may have to leave a little earlier than expected, so he wanted me to come on over, just in case," Peter answered without hesitation.

"We have an update briefing. Are we supposed to give it to you, then?" she asked.

Peter knew why she was asking. In his past life, he hated having to brief something more than once, especially if it could have been avoided. It wasted time and resources. From the questions this woman was asking, she was like Peter and didn't want to waste her time.

"No, no!" Peter replied, waving his hand left and right. "This is more of an orientation for me. I'm just to look around and see things. Nothing more."

The woman looked somewhat relieved. "How long does this ride last?" Peter asked in an attempt to play the part.

The man answered, "Not long. Four minutes or so."

Peter nodded and then decided to just wait till the ride was over. In the meantime, the man and woman had a conversation which grabbed Peter's attention.

"I think this is the first day Dawson has ever missed," the man said. "Must have been some serious damage to his place." Peter figured they were referring to the story Tony had told him.

The woman shrugged and replied, "And of all days, too! I wonder who in S3 is going to have to fill in for him and brief the big guy." She looked over to Peter and smiled.

The railcar started slowing down and eventually came to a stop. The man and woman got up and started for the door which opened automatically.

"When will this go back?" Peter asked them as he stood up to follow.

"It'll go back in twenty minutes. It always arrives at the main platform five minutes before the hour and half hour," the man answered. "As you look around, come to me if you have any questions."

Peter nodded as they exited. They had stepped off onto a rectangular platform. It wasn't large at all, and had a single door fifteen feet in front of them. Again, there was no security badge reader. However, painted and centered on the door was KGEN. *This is the right place.*

Following the man and woman, Peter walked through the single door on the other side of the platform.

Holy Cow! The man and woman stopped to view Peter's expression. Obviously, they enjoyed watching people who entered this area for the first time. Peter's eyes were wide.

"What do you think?" the woman asked, smiling.

"I'm blown away!" Peter answered. He was excited and he was blown away. In all his life, he had never seen such a thing. He felt like a kid in a candy store as he just stood there and looked around.

"Have fun!" the man said before he and the woman walked off.

They had entered into a large, underground hangar! It had to be at least two football fields long and almost as wide. The floor was a dark gray color. The large wall, to Peter's left, was carved out of the earth. To the right, the wall must have been made out of some metallic substance. It was shiny, like it had been polished from the floor to ceiling, and no apparent doors or seams were visible. Overhead, the ceiling extended upwards at least seventy-five feet with bright metallic lighting structures hanging down. A group of offices were off to the left and were butted up in the corner against the wall with the door Peter had just walked through. More lights, on stands and pedestals, were placed around the floor for more illumination. Peter couldn't really see the opposite side, but figured it's where the hangar doors would be. He couldn't see the other side, because the most impressive attraction, the two triangular shaped aircraft, was blocking his view!

These were not the usual aircraft Peter was familiar with! They didn't have normal landing gear, but rather four black, metallic legs which were extended from the bottom of the aircraft. The entire craft was a dull black and didn't have any observable windows. Each side had to be at least a hundred and fifty feet long. Its profile was flat, with the exception of a bulbous area in the center which extended above and below the craft. There were no visible numbers or letter designators. There were no beacons or landing lights. Peter could tell they were built to be invisible! These two aircraft were the most amazing technology he had ever seen!

After a few moments, he was able to peel his eyes away from the aircraft. Looking around, he only noticed four people on the floor who were beneath the aircraft. The woman he had ridden with had entered one of the offices. He began walking slowly towards the right and then on around the side of the closest aircraft. The metallic looking wall to his right grabbed his attention again. Walking up to it, he wondered how it was made. There were no seams. Was it possible to create such an enormous wall without having to put it together? Peter extended his arm to place his right hand on it. He just had to feel it. To his surprise, his hand went completely through the wall! He quickly retracted it and took a step back. *It's not a wall at all*! Taking a deep breath, Peter realized what the wall was and took a few steps through it. His eyes were filled with scintillating lights which dissipated as he made it through to the other side. He was now out in the desert! Peter almost lost his breath! He had stepped out onto a dry lakebed. Mountains were all around him beyond the lakebed. He figured he was somewhere on the Nellis training range which surrounded the Ranch. Looking back from where he came, he didn't see the hangar he was just in! The illusionary wall depicted a desert landscape ascending up the side of a small mountain. He took a few steps back the way he had come. As expected, he walked through the hologram and was back inside. Peter was blown away!

From his right, the man who had ridden with him on the train was approaching him smiling. "What 'cha think?" he asked.

"I'm blown away!" Peter replied truthfully. "They told me this place was cool, but I never imagined anything like this."

The man let out a small laugh and said, "Yeah, I was blown away, too! It's an honor to be part of something like this."

Able to regain some control, Peter remembered his mission. "Tell me they didn't find these two aircraft buried in Egypt!" he inquired jokingly as he pointed at the aircraft.

"No, no, no, no!" the man replied quickly. "We built these. I mean, our predecessors did anyway. We maintain and work to enhance them here. What you are talking about is over in S3."

"Are all these areas associated with KGEN?" Peter asked, keeping the conversation going.

"Of course," the man replied. "These aircraft were designed based on the knowledge we have discovered."

The man spoke as if Peter should know whom he was talking about. Peter worked hard to maintain his composure and keep his thoughts controlled. He figured this wasn't the time or place to start asking questions concerning that topic.

"Man! I could spend all day here. I feel like a kid again!" Peter stated. "So, those aircraft are stealth, huh?"

"They're more than that! They go completely invisible. Naked to radars, infrared, optical, all of it! They don't even have engines, per se. In simple terms, there's a chamber inside filled with a heavy metal. We superheat and pressurize it which, in turn, distorts gravity. Anyone or anything on board becomes virtually weightless. G-forces have no effect on anything inside. As a result, they have no problem escaping the Earth's atmosphere or turning on a dime at high speeds."

"So, they're spaceships, too?" Peter asked, smiling.

"Like I said earlier, they're more than that. The TR-3B is the most advanced aircraft ever designed and built. But I've got to get back to work. It was nice meeting you. Hope I was able to help!" the man said, smiling as he turned and walked over to join another man under one of the aircraft.

Peter knew time was passing by quickly. He had to make sure he was on that railcar when it departed. As he walked back towards the door, he reached into his right pocket and pulled out his keys. Carefully, he felt for the Vegas keychain and slid the cover open. As he walked, he discreetly aimed the camera towards the aircraft and began pressing the button. He tried to capture as much as he could before he reached the door he had entered through. Satisfied, he slid the cover back closed and walked through the door. A digital display was counting down and indicated Peter had less than two minutes to wait. Before long, he was headed back to the main terminal.

Peter stepped off the railcar which had brought him back from S4. All the other railcars had just returned as well and their doors were opening. Three people were waiting near the S1 railcar and another person waited by S2. From his view, he couldn't tell if anyone was waiting on the S3 car, so he started walking in that direction. He noticed the other workers had stepped into their respective railcars. As he rounded the S3 car, two men almost bumped into him. He had to dodge right to avoid hitting them.

"Sorry!" Peter let out apologetically, and he continued for the doors of the S3 railcar.

"Badge!" one of the guys said loudly.

Peter had heard that many times throughout his career! It usually came in a demeaning tone and really meant 'put on your badge, stupid!' He stopped quickly, reached into his left pocket, and retrieved the badge. To let them know he got the message, he held it up to his left quickly, letting his fingers obscure the picture again, and pulled it back down to clip it on his shirt. It must have worked as Peter heard the two continue walking. He stepped into the S3 railcar, removed the badge, and sat down.

Chapter 25

T he ride on S3 took a little longer and seemed to go around more curves. During the ride, Peter could feel a slight pull to his left indicating the railcar was probably descending. It wasn't much, but it was enough to notice. Peter had no idea how far below the surface he was. Luckily, no one else was on the railcar which gave Peter some time to relax and focus. So far, he had been successful, but he knew he couldn't let his guard down or let his mind start to wander.

The railcar eventually came to a stop. If it had left at exactly 10:30 a.m., Peter deduced it was probably around 10:40 a.m. now. When the doors opened, Peter stepped out. Again, the platform was rectangular and wasn't that large. Unlike S4, the door across the platform had been constructed to allow passage through a wall which slanted upward and away from the platform. Since it angled away at about forty-five degrees, the door had to be positioned further back inside the wall. Again, KGEN was painted in the center of the door. Peter walked up to the door, took a few breaths, and pulled the door open and entered.

Peter had stepped into a giant pyramid structure! The wall he had just walked through continued up over him at an angle and met the other three walls in a pinnacle about two hundred feet overhead! The floor area was a giant square. *Did they dig up an entire pyramid?* The area was dimly lit. Peter felt uneasiness about him and tried to shake it off. Once again, though, the structure wasn't the main attraction.

Centered on the floor was something Peter had seen before! Four enormous, black columns extended upward. Hieroglyphics had been etched all over them and were filled with a gold metallic substance to highlight them. They were placed in the same manner Peter had seen them in before in the photo Boyd had shown him. Centered between the four columns, a large area had been cut out of the floor and filled with water. A large, black sarcophagus was horizontal and centered in the water. Half of it was below the waterline. A seam along the top edge indicated it had a lid. Boyd was right! They had dug up a tomb and transported it all the way out here.

S3 was busier than S4! Peter counted fifteen people in his immediate view. Five of them were huddled together to the left of the sarcophagus area and columns. They were looking at a computer monitor which had been attached to a projector screen. On the screen and centered, Peter read:

PROJECT KGEN
STAGE 3

Obviously, they were reviewing a briefing prepared for the new SECDEF. To the right side of the floor, a man and a woman were seated in front of computers while six others hovered around a lighted, glass top table. Papers were scattered all over the top of it. Another guy was seated off behind them and was flipping through a document which had been stapled together. The last guy was swapping out bulbs in a stand used to highlight one of the black columns. Peter recognized most of them as the ones whose names he had written down. Most of them were in lab coats.

No one seemed to pay any attention to Peter. But there were enough people in here he didn't want to stay any longer than he had to. It was easier to fool a couple of people than it was a roomful. He reached in his pocket and retrieved the keychain camera. Making sure no one was watching, he held the camera down to his side and began pressing the button as he started walking to his right. He moved casually and tried to make it look like he was examining the columns. He knew he couldn't walk behind the computers and glass table to the right, because it would obscure the view of the columns for the camera. He wanted to get pictures of all the hieroglyphics. Bravely, he headed more towards the right-side columns. He managed to take a few more shots without anyone noticing.

As he walked past the two computers on his right, he had to step over some cables which connected the computers to the four columns. Several of them had been run up the sides and were attached somehow to the tops of the columns. As Peter walked towards the rear side, he noticed the guy who was seated and reading, was staring at him. Peter continued his stroll as the guy stood up and walked towards him.

"Excuse me," the guy said. "Who are you?"

"I'm with the SECDEF. Are you guys ready?" Peter asked like he was somebody important. *Hope this works.*

"Of course we are," the man answered but still maintained a look of confusion.

Peter had to think fast to prevent further inquiries. "Listen, I wanted to come ahead of the big man to make sure you were ready. He's on a tight schedule and is a little stressed. He's in one of those moods today where he snaps at the smallest mistakes. I figured I would make sure you guys were prepared and ready to brief him. Just get straight to the point and be ready to start the brief when he enters. I don't want you all to think the new SECDEF is a prick, which is why I want things to go smoothly to avoid him snapping," Peter explained. He had done something like this before, going ahead of one of his old commanders to warn the troops.

The man's face seemed to calm. "I understand," he replied. "I'm going over the briefing now and can assure you I'm well prepared."

"Is everything working properly?" Peter asked, still maintaining his composure.

"Yes! We've triple checked everything," the man answered.

Peter looked over to where the five people were around the computer. He noticed there wasn't a chair in front of the projector.

"You expect the SECDEF to stand the entire briefing?" Peter asked, a little condescending.

"I'll fix that," the man answered.

"I would appreciate that," Peter remarked.

With that, the man placed his briefing papers back on the chair and went to retrieve a chair from somewhere. Peter walked over to the chair the man had been sitting in and picked up the briefing. He knew he didn't have enough time to read the entire thing, so he flipped through it trying to garner what information he could.

The first page contained STAGE ONE. It described the site in Egypt, excavations efforts, and transport of the sarcophagus to the Ranch. The next page was STAGE TWO which had a chronological diagram of how the columns were placed, how the floor was dug out and filled with water, and how the sarcophagus was placed. From the diagram, precise measurements were used for placement of each object. Complex mathematical formulas took up a lot of the paper.

Peter flipped another page over. STAGE THREE pertained to power requirements and tested measurements of electricity. Peter got the idea they were trying to power the columns in efforts to charge the water somehow. He didn't understand everything and knew it was way over his head. As Peter flipped the page, he saw STAGE FOUR on the top. But his eyes were glued to a photo in the center of that page. It was Alfred Boyd! Below the picture, Peter started to read more closely:

STAGE FOUR still on hold. Efforts to locate and retrieve the UGEN have failed. STAGE FOUR can't commence until the UGEN has been obtained. A recent development...

"He's got the most comfortable seat in the house," Peter heard a voice interrupt him. He looked up from the paper and saw the man had returned.

"Good!" Peter replied sternly. "Still no luck finding him, huh?" Peter asked, holding the briefing up and then handing it over. He decided the risk was worth it.

The man started shaking his head as he replied, "No. But there's a new development. We heard he may be helping a man and woman in Utah. Our teams are on it, but that's all I know. At least it's something! First time in a long time we've had some good news. When, and if, we capture him, we can proceed to the next stage."

"Good luck with that," Peter stated as he moved to walk more around the area.

"Are you staying for the briefing?" the man asked.

"No, I'm going to make my way over to the other sections and give them a heads up too!" Peter answered. He continued to walk away.

Peter kept pressing the camera button as he walked around and thought. No one seemed to second guess the keys in his hand. *Boyd has the UGEN? Is he the UGEN? What don't I know? Why do they need him? What the heck are they trying to do here?* Peter then realized his attention to the mission had drifted away. His thoughts had returned to churning a multitude of questions which clouded his mind. He forced himself to maintain discipline and stick to the plan.

No one else approached Peter. With the other people seeing the one guy converse with him, he figured they didn't think he was a threat. He made his way around the room taking digital images of every side of the columns, the sarcophagus and the entire room. With this part of the task complete, it was time for Peter to move on. The most important part of the mission was still ahead. He had to make it off base with the information! It was time to leave this area.

Peter had timed it perfectly. As he stepped out of the room and back onto the platform, he looked at the digital display showing how much time remained before the railcar departed. He had forty-seven seconds remaining. Soon enough, Peter stepped into the railcar, sat down, and tried to remain calm. *I still don't really know who Alfred Boyd is.* The doors to the railcar closed. As it ascended back up the rail line, Peter thought of Sam. He needed to! Thinking of her would keep him more focused. She was the one that would get him out alive. She was the reason Peter was on this railcar. She was what motivated him. *She was the centerpiece!*

When the doors opened, Peter remained seated for a minute. He could hear talking from outside:

"They're doing great things, Sir. As a matter of fact, they are ahead of schedule in that area," a man's voice said.

"Are we going to S1 now?" another man spoke. Peter figured it was the SECDEF.

"Yes, Sir!" the other male replied.

Peter kept listening to their footsteps. He heard the SECDEF say something else, but figured he had already entered the S1 railcar since he couldn't make out what he said. After not hearing any more footsteps, he stood up and looked out at the wall with the digital display. *One minute, twenty seconds.* He stepped out and headed for the doors. He was ready to get out of this place! As he neared the door, he stopped. It was only eleven o'clock. The bus leaving for the social wasn't due to leave until noon, which meant Peter had an hour to wait. If he hung out on the coffee house floor, one of the workers walking out might recognize him. He could stay in the closet, though, and just wait. He almost walked through the door, but didn't.

Looking back at the digital display, he had fifteen seconds. Peter made up his mind. He walked briskly and stepped onto S2. *What am I doing?* Peter thought of the curious cat as the railcar pulled away from the platform. It was too late to get off!

Peter figured it took about the same amount of time to reach S2 as it did S3. Once again, he stepped out onto a rectangular platform which had a door directly across from him. It resembled S4 in that it didn't have an angled wall. Confidently, Peter walked up to and through the door.

It wasn't just a room that Peter entered. It was a warehouse! No, it was more than that. Peter had never, in all his life, seen an inside area this large. It extended as far as Peter could see. The ceiling, walls and even the floor were painted white. Even so, a blue hue filled the entire area.

From the left wall to the right wall, and as far down as Peter could see, rows and rows of cloning vats filled the entire area! They were stacked three high and were filled with a bluish liquid. White, plastic lids connected to tubes sealed the vats on top. Inside, human-like forms were suspended in the liquid and appeared to be mature specimens. Their skin was pasty white and hairless. Chills went up and down Peter's spine! Directly in front of Peter, between the vats, a walkway had been left open and extended beyond Peter's view. Off to the right, where the walkway between the vats began, a small pedestal held a whiteboard which read: WE WELCOME YOU MR. SECRETARY!

"Hey!" a voice shouted from Peter's left.

Peter heard footsteps approaching rapidly. Turning left, he saw William Peterson! He had a serious scowl and looked like he meant business.

"How'd the visit go?" Peter asked.

William cocked his head as he stopped beside Peter.

Peter saw the confusion. He added, "The SECDEF asked me to come back so you could answer a few questions he forgot to ask. He was thoroughly impressed with you!" Peter was trying to massage the man's ego.

"Really? The SECDEF asked you to come back here?" the man replied sarcastically. "Did he also tell you to leave your buffer behind?" He raised his eyebrows to let Peter know he wasn't fooled! *Not good!*

Peter's heart rate accelerated and his breathing became shallow. Perspiration was already beading up on his head. He knew there would be no fooling this guy. He looked around to see if anyone else was in the area. There wasn't. Peter faced the man and looked him square in the eyes without any emotion showing on his face.

William Peterson obviously recognized the look Peter was giving him. His eyes widened a bit, and he took a couple of steps back. On instinct, Peter had already sized the man up. The man was shorter and rounder. He was slower and not skilled in the art of combat. Seeing the fear grow in the man's face, Peter lunged forward.

William Peterson turned to run! He was heading toward a small office in the corner which was probably where he sat most of the day. He made it halfway before Peter leapt on his back and knocked him to the floor. Both men skidded to a stop. Peter grabbed the back of the man's hair, lifted up his head, and then rammed it against the floor. Before he could repeat the bash, the man began fighting back violently and rolled over knocking Peter off in the process. Before the man could get both legs under him good, Peter jumped to his feet and rammed into him again. It was a hard hit, knocking the man against the wall. Peter followed through and placed his left forearm on the man's chest. Repeatedly, Peter punched him in the face with his right fist! After three punches, William Peterson stopped struggling. His nose was broken and he had a deep gash over his right eye. Blood was pouring from his bottom lip. Peter let go of him to watch the man slide down against the wall.

Peter felt awful! William Peterson had done nothing wrong. On the contrary, he did what anyone in his position would have done. But now, he was slumped against the wall bleeding and holding his arms up in defense of his face. Peter had done that to him! Peter held his fists up in front of him to see they were covered in blood. His left shirt sleeve had blood all over its cuff.

"Please, stop," William Peterson managed to beg.

Peter took a step back. His hands were shaking from all the adrenaline pumping through his veins. His breathing was shaky and forceful.

"What is this place?" Peter asked forcefully.

William Peterson didn't reply.

"Tell me, or I'll finish the job!" Peter yelled.

The man slowly looked up at Peter and stated, "I may be weak, but I'm not a traitor!" He placed emphasis on the last word.

The words cut like a knife down to the center of Peter's heart! Usually, Peter was a master at hiding his emotions. But so much was happening, and he had just severely beaten an innocent man. His emotions got the best of him.

"You think I'm a traitor?" Peter shouted as tears filled his eyes. "Are you kidding me? You're the one down here growing these things. I bet the American people don't know about this! You think you're a patriot? You have no idea what a patriot is! Have you ever been shot at? Have you ever been somewhere where everywhere you looked, someone wanted to kill you? Do you wake up in the middle of the night screaming thinking rockets are about to fall on you? Don't call me a traitor! I've served my country!" Peter paced back and forth rapidly. He knew he had lost control. He didn't care. He just wanted to get it out!

William Peterson was cowering against the wall.

"Don't you ever call me a traitor! You think I want to be here? You think I don't care about national security? Well, I do, and this isn't it! What you are doing down here is wrong! You're misleading the people that put their trust in you! You're the traitor!" Peter couldn't control himself. He took a step over and kicked the man in the gut.

Sam. The image of Sam popped into Peter's head then. He didn't want it there! He didn't want her to see him like this! As a final outburst, Peter threw his head back and yelled as loud as he could. It emanated from his inner, mortal coil. It was every ounce of hatred and anger he could muster, and he screamed it out like an erupting volcano. He screamed a second time to make sure he got it all out.

Almost out of breath, Peter let his legs fall out from under him as he fell to the floor on his bottom. Both of his arms slumped down into his lap. *Sam.* There she was again. He imagined her smiling at him from across the table they had sat at during their first meeting. He imagined her looking up from her bed when she was sick. *I've got to get to her!*

Peter managed to stand back up. He walked over to the small office William Peterson had run for. Opening the door, he saw a computer chair pulled up in front of a computer. To the right of it, the Darth Vader thermos sat on top of a coaster. Peter rifled through a few drawers before he found some duct tape. He made his way back over to the bloody man. He rolled William Peterson onto his belly and then proceeded to duct tape his wrists together behind his back. Then, he wrapped it around both ankles. He then moved over and lifted both legs so they bent at the knees. Holding them up with his shoulder, Peter used the duct tape to hogtie the wrists to the feet. Standing up, Peter looked over his work. There was no way William Peterson was going anywhere. He tore off one more strip of duct and tape and kneeled down beside the man.

"I'm not normally like this, really," Peter whispered into his ear. "You left me no choice." Peter placed the duct tape on the man's mouth.

Peter had gained back control over his breathing. *Sam.* He unbuttoned his cuffs and rolled them both up carefully to hide the blood. Then, he walked back over to the office. Looking at the reflection in the glass of the door, Peter straightened his hair as best he could. He moved inside and pulled out several tissues from a box on the desk. He wiped the sweat off his face and then did his best to get the blood off his knuckles. Spitting on them a couple times helped. He balled up the tissue and stuck it in his right pocket. He felt the keys which made him think to take an image. Pulling the keychain out, he took several shots of the cloning vats. Now, it was time to get out of there! Before leaving, he walked back into the office and grabbed the Darth Vader cup.

More time had elapsed than Peter imagined. The doors to the S2 railcar were about to close, but he made it on just in time. He took a seat and continued to try and completely regain his composure. By the time the railcar reached the main platform, Peter was breathing normally. His heart was still beating a little fast, but he was confident he could finish the job. As the doors opened, Peter stood up and walked out. Looking around quickly, he noticed two people entering the S4 railcar and three others entering the S3 one. He was glad it was only 11:30 a.m., since most people would leave their areas at noon for lunch. Peter walked across the platform and exited through the doors. A little further, and he came to the double doors where Staff Sergeant King would be on the other side. He walked through.

The guard was looking at him inquisitively after he exited. Peter looked around to make sure no one was in the area.

Holding up the Darth Vader thermos, he whispered over to the guard, "Got the straw. Now, I've just got to go and check it out. If my guess is correct, I'm going to find a thumb drive inside."

"I have to be honest," Staff Sergeant King replied, "I never would have suspected Mr. Peterson."

"That's why he's been successful. But not anymore," Peter said. "If I don't see you again, I wish you the best of luck in all you do. Rob is lucky to have you on his team."

Before Peter could turn to leave, Staff Sergeant King asked, "Hey! Did you get to meet the SECDEF?"

Peter shook his head. "Nah. We didn't want to alert him to this. He might think we are incompetent, you know?"

The guard nodded he understood before Peter headed for the janitor's closet. Peter felt more comfortable on this side of the doors. As he walked, he thought about how no one had gotten on the S2 railcar when he stepped off on this end. It would be at least another thirty minutes before it would make the return trip again. From what Peter could tell, William Peterson was the only one in that area. Maybe luck would be on Peter's side and no one would find him until much later.

Peter closed the door behind him as he stepped into the closet. He still had about twenty minutes before the bus was going to leave. Once again, luck was on his side, and nobody had discovered Jeff passed out on the floor here. Peter checked again to make sure Jeff was still breathing, and he was. He unbuttoned the white shirt and shoved it in the backpack before putting on his red, CYN shirt. Next, he placed the empty syringe, the fingerprint box, and extra badge inside. He was ready.

Eventually, the clock over the coffee shop showed it was 11:55 a.m. Peter stepped out of the closet with his backpack slung over his shoulder. Walking towards the exit, he took one last look around. *Glad I'm not going to see this place again.* Before he could reach the door handle, the door opened up. His old buddy Rob walked through.

"Hey, man!" Rob greeted with the usual, cheerful smile.

Peter figured Rob's briefing to the SECDEF must have gone smoothly. "Hey!" was the only response from Peter who wanted to keep the conversation short. Over Rob's shoulder, Peter noticed two men walk away from the coffee shop and head down the sloped passageway. Looking further, Peter noticed Staff Sergeant King looking at him and Rob. *He'll just think I'm telling Rob what happened.*

"See the big man?" Rob asked, not letting Peter get away so soon.

"Oh, yeah. He walked through at ten this morning. I just stayed in the restrooms till he passed," Peter lied. "Hey, I'm sorry, but I've got to get going. The bus is leaving soon to take us to a CYN social."

"No problem!" Rob replied. "I'm giving myself a half day, too! Told everyone I had a dental appointment in Vegas. But honestly, I just wanted to start my weekend a little early. I don't feel guilty, either. I put a lot of extra time into preparing for the briefing I gave to the SECDEF."

Peter just nodded with a smile.

Chapter 26

The bus seemed to take forever as it meandered through the desert. It passed by the security checkpoint on the way out without being stopped. Obviously, no one had alerted them of anything. The CYN employees onboard were excited. Their conversations were loud. One of the employees had even managed to sneak a bottle of Jack Daniels on board and people were taking turns to chug some down. Yana sat in the front seat. Every so often, she would turn around and tell the employees not to get too crazy!

About midway down the unpaved road, before reaching US Highway 375, a black helicopter flew over the bus. It was extremely low and had the occupants on the bus scrambling to a window to check it out. Out of the left window, it made a sharp bank and headed back towards the bus! Within seconds, it was flying beside the bus about fifteen feet above the ground. The helicopter's door, which faced the bus, slid open to reveal a uniformed soldier sitting behind a mounted, 50-caliber machine gun. They meant business.

Before anyone knew what was happening, a security truck flew past them to only stop directly in front of them. The bus slammed on the brakes sending CYN employees flying! Behind them, another security truck pulled up and stopped. Armed soldiers exited the vehicles with weapons aimed at the bus. The helicopter hovered with its huge gun ready to blast holes through the bus. It was the end of the road!

***

Peter's ears felt like they were about to melt. It had been a long time since he had heard anyone talk so much! Not even Sam could compete in this verbal marathon. Looking to his left, Rob had his jaws flapping in the wind. The left window of the white security truck was rolled down, and Rob had his arm slung out like a Texas cowboy. He was even gracious enough to roll Peter's window all the way down. Peter was starting to regret his decision to accept Rob's offer to give him a ride off base so he wouldn't have to sit on the bus. Since Rob had planned to leave early that day, he had scheduled to drive a security vehicle to Nellis Air Force Base to drop it off for repairs. He was then heading down to the strip to gamble his money away. Peter initially felt lucky after he informed Yana he was taking a different ride. By the looks of it, it was going to take the bus another ten minutes before everyone was loaded. When Peter added that time to the 45 miles per hour the bus moved at, he decided it was better he not spend any more time on base than he had too.

Rob's mouth didn't stop! Since they both got in, Rob had been talking and Peter was having thoughts of reaching over and slamming Rob's head against the steering wheel. He heard about old girlfriends from the base till the end of the long dirt road. After they turned on to US Highway 375, he listened to Rob talk about his climb to becoming a Chief Master Sergeant. At one point during that conversation, Peter reached up to see if any blood was coming out of his ears. Now, they were about five miles away from Alamo. Rob had started comparing his leadership abilities against other chiefs. However, he was interrupted when the security forces' radio came on:

'Alarm Red! Alarm Red! Suspect is white male wearing a red CYN shirt. Middle aged. Last observed in Building 17. Goes by Peter Norris. Suspect is considered dangerous.'

For the first time during the whole ride, Rob stopped talking. Peter turned and looked at him. Rob kept driving and looking ahead.

"What did you do, Pete?" Rob asked in a serious tone while keeping his eyes on the road.

Peter shrugged hard enough he knew Rob could see it through his peripheral vision. "I have no idea, man! I've been cleaning the floor all morning. They must be mistaken!" he exclaimed.

"They've got to be!" he replied as he turned to look quickly over to Peter. "Here, I'll clear this up," he stated as he reached over to grab the mic.

This isn't going to be good! "Please, don't do that," Peter requested calmly.

Rob looked hurt as he pulled his hand back. He turned to look at Peter and screamed, "Are you kidding me!" he asked, banging both hands hard against the steering wheel.

At that point, Peter's instincts started to kick in again. Unlike William Peterson, though, Rob was a threat. He was taller and more muscular. Still serving in the military, he was in great physical shape. Peter was outgunned if a fight were to ensue. Looking at Rob, Peter knew the man was contemplating his next course of action.

Peter tried to interrupt Rob's thinking. "Come on, dude! You know me!" Peter pleaded.

"Then tell me what happened! What did you do?" Rob asked angrily. "And don't lie to me! I'll know if you are!"

Peter took a few breaths and looked out the window. He needed to pass the time. After a moment, and right before Rob was about to say something else, he said, "Alright! Alright! I'll tell you what happened!" For effect, he bent his head down and placed it in his hands. A bit later, he took a deep breath and sat back up. "Do you know what's beyond those doors where I work? Down that sloped passageway?" Peter asked.

"How would I know that, you idiot? I'm security forces! I guard doors, not pass through them! You of all people should know that!" Rob replied angrily.

"I love my country, Rob!" Peter said loudly. "Don't ever question that! But what's going on beyond those doors goes against everything I believe in!"

"I don't give a crap!" Rob yelled back. "You know our government does some stupid stuff. They keep some of it secret so our enemies don't find out. And sometimes, they keep things secret because the American people don't want to know about any of it! It's better that way! Always has been!"

Time was ticking and Alamo was less than a mile away now. Peter looked over at the side view mirror and didn't see any cars behind them. "Trust me, Rob! What they are doing behind those doors endangers all of us!" Peter explained. "I'm sorry!"

"Don't be sorry to me, bud! You can be sorry to the base and the American people!" Rob stated as he lifted his foot off the gas pedal. He was looking ahead to find a place to turn around.

"I'm not sorry for what I did," Peter explained further.

"Then what are you sorry for, man?" Rob responded.

"This!" Peter answered as he reached over with his left hand and unfastened Rob's seatbelt. Simultaneously, he grabbed the steering wheel with his right hand and pulled as hard as he could!

Rob started to react, but it was too late. The security truck was already spinning towards the right side of the road. With the truck out of control, Peter quickly braced himself for impact! Rob fought against the steering wheel, but to no avail. It was too late! Once the truck slid over the edge of the road, the two wheels on Peter's side left the ground. The truck began to roll violently while bouncing down a small ravine! Glass flew everywhere! Peter's chest felt like it was being ripped apart from the pressure of the seatbelt restraining him. His head was jerked from left to right.

Everything stopped. Peter's ears were ringing. Aside from the ringing, he could make out the squeaking of rotating tires. They were upside down and swirling dust filled the cabin. Slowly, Peter looked over to see Rob unconscious and laying on the ceiling of the truck. There was still immense pressure on Peter's shoulders and chest from the seatbelt holding him in place. Carefully, he reached over and braced himself against the ceiling with his left arm. With his right hand, he unfastened the seat belt. His left arm slowed the impact, but he fell pretty hard nonetheless. Watchful of the broken glass, he positioned himself to sit on the ceiling between Rob's legs. Then, he reached forward and pulled the door handle to open it. It was stuck. Peter drew in his legs and kicked against it. On his third attempt, the door swung open. Before climbing all the way out, Peter grabbed his backpack and looked back at Rob. There was a lot of blood! A huge gash had opened on the left side of Rob's head. Peter felt for a pulse and found one. *You'll survive!*

Standing up and getting his bearings, Peter realized the truck had flipped several times. Now, he was in a small ravine about thirty feet off the highway. As fast as he could, he climbed up the bank back to the road. There was a sharp pain in his chest, but he just ignored it. He could see the Alamo gas station and market ahead about a quarter of a mile. Walking at first and then speeding up to a jog, Peter ran towards the town. At one point, he thought the old white bus might pass him with all the CYN employees. But then, he realized that wasn't going to happen. The bus would have already been stopped and everyone detained. He was out of breath and felt like he was about to pass out! Only one thing kept him going. *Sam.*

Peter welcomed the shade from the trees near the road as he walked into the town limits. Immediately, he checked to see if the gray Altima was where it was supposed to be. It was! As he walked over to it, he noticed a bright colored, bouncy house had been erected in the park where the CYN social was supposed to be held. Several green topped tents were also set up to provide shade. They covered about ten plastic tables with plastic chairs pulled up to them. It actually bothered Peter a little that the CYN employees weren't going to enjoy the social they were longing for. Peter opened the driver's door to the Altima and got in. Reaching beneath the seat, he grabbed the keys and then started the vehicle. Quickly, he drove to his house, ran inside to grab his cell phone and the picture of Sam, and then returned to the car. Hurriedly, he drove out of town and headed south on US Highway 93.

It had only been about five minutes when Peter noticed two Blackhawk helicopters out of his right window. They were low and moving fast in the same direction as Peter. As they passed by, Peter realized what could be happening. He suspected they were going to drive ahead and block the road off. It was smart, since US Highway 93 continued on for about seventy more miles before it hit Interstate 15 on the east side of Las Vegas. There were no paved roads exiting off, either, between where Peter was and the interstate. They would know he was heading south after discovering the wrecked security truck. Peter figured a Blackhawk had already located and landed near the wrecked truck. That would explain why Peter only saw three of them pass by. Normally, they flew in groups of two or four. Three indicated one was missing.

He reached over into the right seat and grabbed the cell phone. There was no signal. Peter flung it back into the seat. As he thought about it, they were probably intercepting every phone call in the area. He was probably lucky there was no signal. Peter kept driving south, keeping an eye ahead for roadblocks. He knew he wasn't going to make it to the casino today. If he kept driving, he was going to get caught!

A few minutes later, after he ensured no cars were around, he turned left off onto an old dirt road. He had driven down many dirt roads in the southwest like this one. Typically, cattle ranchers used them. Sometimes, people would take their dirt bikes and four wheelers out on them. Other than that, no one ever really used them. Hopefully, this one led to nowhere important and would provide a spot for Peter to hide. At least he hoped so!

The dirt road led Peter deeper into the desert landscape. Huge power lines ran adjacent to it for a while, but then they turned away and headed off into the distance. Peter continued. After about three miles, he was in the middle of nowhere. He pulled the car off the dirt road onto a dry riverbed and then followed it another fifty feet. There, he stopped and got out. It was quiet. Not even taking time to take a deep breath, Peter walked around the desert floor looking for uprooted brush. It took him about fifteen minutes to gather enough to cover his car. Walking up the riverbed and back to the dirt road, he looked to where his car was. It was camouflaged! Satisfied, Peter walked back and entered the car. It was hot. Peter was thirsty and hungry, but there was nothing he could do about it. Exhausted, he let his head fall back against the headrest. It was going to be a long evening and night. But Peter knew he would make it through it. He had to! *Sam.*

***

Sam was excited! She had wanted to ride with Tony to pick up Peter at the Aliante Casino, but he wouldn't allow it. Alfred didn't think it was a good idea either. After watching Tony pull off, she returned inside the house and joined Alfred in the kitchen.

"You seem excited!" Alfred said as he pulled out the leftovers from Sam's meal she had prepared the night before.

Sam walked over and sat at the table. "I am," she said calmly. "Peter's a good man and I hate that he's having to risk himself. It's time he gets out of that place."

"You have feelings for him, don't you?" Alfred asked as he started scooping out some of the chicken alfredo onto two plates. "And you know what feelings I'm speaking of!"

Sam didn't reply. Instead, she leaned back in her chair and looked through the window at the mountains.

"Your silence tells me all I need to know," Alfred added. He walked over and put Sam's plate into the microwave. "You know, I'm going to miss all of this home cooked food after you leave." He smiled over towards Sam.

"I don't know. I mean, I'm not sure," she said, still looking out the window. "I've thought about how I feel about Peter, but there are some uncertainties."

"Well, I'm certain he cares a great deal about you!" Boyd injected. "I see the smile on his face when you enter the room. There's an eagerness about him when he knows you're around. I'm pretty confident when I say he's quite smitten with you!" Again, Boyd smiled over at her.

"I know. I can feel it from him," Sam replied. "He's caring, knowledgeable, doesn't impose, and isn't overbearing from what I've seen. He's got a lot of great qualities that I've always looked for."

After waiting for Sam's plate to finish heating up, he removed it from the microwave and placed his inside. After getting it started, he retrieved a fork from the drawer and delivered the meal to Sam. Placing it down on the table, he asked, "And? What are you uncertain about with Peter?"

Sam looked over to Alfred. "You misunderstood me, Alfred. It's me I'm uncertain about, not Peter."

Alfred then realized her concern. "You know," he began, "I grew up during hard times. My family was poor and we worked hard in Mr. Dawsy's fields. From dusk till dawn, we tilled his land and harvested his crops. I guess I must have been around fourteen when, on one particular day, I saw the most beautiful girl I had ever laid eyes on. I remember it like it was yesterday!" Alfred stopped for a minute and closed his eyes. "She had on a sky-blue dress with white lace around the edges. She was out gathering some roses behind her house. All I could do was stand and stare. She knew I was staring too!" Alfred said with a wry smile. "Anyway, over the next week, I made sure to be in that same field at the same time each day. And each day, she would come out and pick roses. One day, I got up enough nerve to walk over to her. When she saw me approaching, she just smiled. When I got up to her, she handed me the rose she had just picked. I was so nervous, and I was covered in dirt. But it didn't matter. For a brief moment, I lost my mind! I put my arms around her waist and pulled her against me. We kissed, closing our eyes just before our lips met! I've never experienced anything like it since." Alfred just stood there, beside the microwave, with his eyes closed. He was holding on to the memory.

"Wow, Alfred! I never imagined you were the romantic type. I'm glad you told me that," Sam told him.

He opened his eyes and looked over to Sam, "You didn't let me finish!" he said as he retrieved his plate and walked over to join Sam. "You see, it was Mr. Dawsy's screaming that stopped our kiss. As he ran over to us, he bent down and grabbed a small tree branch. I remember hearing that beautiful girl crying and begging her daddy to stop beating me. Her dad beat me, and beat me, and beat me some more! He hit me so hard on the right side of my head, it almost tore my ear off. My back was bloody as I limped away. It took me over an hour to walk back home, which wasn't but about a half mile away. There, I told my dad what happened. Then, he too, began to beat me. All my wounds were reopened, and the blood began to pour down my back again. I suffered all that because I kissed Mr. Dawsy's daughter. I never even knew her name."

"That's so sad!" Sam said comfortingly. "I wish you two could have been together. But I see your point. Sometimes bad things happen which prevents something that could be amazing."

"It is you who have misunderstood me this time, Sam," Alfred said looking at her. "My point is that I would have suffered those same beatings every day of my life if it meant I could be close to the girl again! To have the feeling I had for that brief moment in time, when our lips connected, I would choose to suffer again."

Alfred looked over to Sam who understood what he was saying. "Even though Peter may feel the pain of your loss, don't take that brief moment of happiness he could have with you away from him!" he advised.

Sam felt the tears starting to swell in her eyes. She leaned across the table and punched Alfred gently in the arm. "You old fart! You didn't have to make me cry," she managed to say before letting out a half cry and half laugh sound.

She understood what Alfred was saying. He reminded her of her father when he used to comfort her after something bad had happened. Still, even after all that, she needed to think. However, this time, she was going to think of how a relationship with Peter could work rather than why it wouldn't work.

A few hours later, around five in the evening, Sam and Alfred sat by the fireplace. On several occasions, she had texted Peter's phone, but received no replies. She was the first one to hear a vehicle door shut. She jumped up and hustled to the door. She opened it just as Tony stepped up. He stopped and looked at her. Not seeing Peter, she stood on her tip toes and looked over Tony's shoulders towards the car.

"Where's Peter?" she asked.

***

The sun was down. Peter awoke and quickly realized he had slept longer than he expected. Quickly, he picked up the cell phone to check the time. It was already 9:00 p.m. His body was sore all over. After opening his door so the interior light would come on, he then lifted up his shirt and looked down at his stomach and chest area. As expected, he was badly bruised which made his breathing difficult. Not wanting to move just yet, he sat still in the car. *Sam.* He wondered how Sam had reacted when Tony didn't bring him home. Were they all still at the house? Maybe they figured their location would be discovered, so they had left by now. Peter didn't know, and there was no reason to worry over it. He lowered his shirt and shut the car door. Leaning his head to the left in order to rest it against the window, he peered out and up into the night sky. The stars were bright. He loved nights like these. He thought about what he would be doing if he had his RV here. Were those days over?

His stomach and mouth demanded attention. He could actually hear his stomach growling and his mouth felt as if he had been chewing on cotton balls. Carefully, he slowly opened his door and stepped out. Immediately, he knew he wasn't going to stretch. The pain was just too great. Holding the cell phone out for its light, Peter moved it left and right to scan over the desert landscape. He didn't see anything to eat or drink. He licked his lips and was barely able to wet them with his tongue. He had to find something. Even though his body didn't want to move, he started hobbling further along the dry riverbed. About a minute later, he noticed a cactus. Kneeling down beside it, he grabbed a stick and started wiping away the thorns. It was harder than he imagined, but he managed. He cleared an area on the cactus large enough to dig at it with two fingers. Soon, he had green, gooey cactus slime over the tips of his fingers. He knew it wasn't going to taste good, but it would serve as sustenance. *Where's my jerky when I need it? And my water?* Placing his fingers in his mouth, he sucked off the slime. It was disgusting, but it was also wet! Repeatedly, he kept digging at the cactus and forcing himself to swallow it. When he had finished, he was still hungry and thirsty. However, the cactus had satisfied him enough to get his mind off his hunger and thirst. Afterwards, he limped back to the car and crawled inside.

Sam. Peter wondered how long any roadblocks, if they had been set up, would continue. He really had no answer. Either way, he was going to have to leave in the morning. It was leave, or die of thirst! Peter sat back in his seat and waited for the night to pass by.

As the light began to crawl through the windows, Peter opened his eyes a little. He was still tired and sore. He had hoped he would feel less sore and more rested by the time morning arrived. He sat up in the car. Then, it struck him! It wasn't morning at all and it wasn't sunlight that woke him. Looking through the back glass and scattered brush covering the car, he saw the headlights moving slowly down the dirt road. *Please drive by. Please drive by.* As he continued to watch, the vehicle moved slowly past his location. It was too dark outside to make out what type of vehicle it was. Luckily, whoever it was didn't seem to notice him.

***

Tony continued to creep down the dirt road. According to the coordinates Alfred had provided, he was at the location where Peter's car should be located. Not seeing anything, he continued to drive down the dirt road, thinking the coordinates he was given were not as accurate as expected.

He had to give it to Sam for thinking of the idea. After she had discovered Peter wasn't with him, she began thinking of ways to find him. Alfred had turned on the television to watch the local news channels while surfing the internet for any relevant information. Sam had asked him to check Aliante Casino one more time, just in case Peter arrived later than expected. He did as she asked, but to no avail.

At nine o'clock, the local television news channel put up a picture of Peter. They described him as dangerous and called him Peter Norris. Additionally, they reported he had escaped from the maximum-security prison where he had been locked up for murdering his mother. Anyone with information on his whereabouts should contact the authorities via the number listed on the screen. It was only then they realized Peter had not been captured.

As soon as the news of Peter passed, Sam thought of something. "Wait! I've got an idea!" Sam screamed, grabbing Tony and Alfred's attention. "Doesn't his car have a GPS?"

When she saw Alfred smiling in response, she exclaimed, "He does!" Tony was impressed.

But now, Tony was driving through the desert. Already, he had driven through the coordinates and was well beyond any margin of error. Still not seeing anything, Tony turned his car around and headed back the way he had come.

***

Once again, Peter had gotten relaxed inside the car. He had just closed his eyes for sleep, when the inner parts of his eyelids started to brighten. Alerted, he opened them to find the bouncing lights dancing in his car again! Looking left through the window, he saw the slow-moving vehicle headlights again. It didn't take a genius to figure it was the same car that had passed earlier. They didn't see him the first time, so Peter thought they wouldn't see him this time either. To his surprise, the car stopped where he had turned off the road into the dry riverbed. It was too close!

Tony stopped at the coordinate location. He decided to look around one last time. He switched off the car and got out. Slowly, he turned to his right scanning for any signs of a vehicle. Making it all the way around, he didn't notice anything. Peter's car was nowhere to be found.

Peter sat as quiet as he could. He heard a car door shut behind which meant someone had gotten out of the vehicle. Slowly, he turned around inside his car and peered through the back window. Through the glass and vegetation, he could make out a single silhouette, probably male. Additionally, he could tell the vehicle wasn't a truck, but rather a car. A thought crossed Peter's mind. He had remembered seeing a navigation button on the car's steering wheel. This car had GPS!

Tony was about to open his car door when he heard a click behind him. It sounded like another car door opening. Turning around, he quickly noticed a light. He then heard a car door shut and the light disappeared.

"Peter?" Tony called out into the darkness.

Peter heard the call. Although the cactus had helped, his throat and lips were still parched. He did the best he could when he responded, "It's me!" through a raspy voice.

The response focused Tony's eyes in Peter's direction. After a few seconds, he saw Peter's silhouette against the background, and it was hobbling. Quickly, Tony walked over to meet Peter.

"Was hoping I would see you again," Peter managed to rasp out. He was about to collapse when Tony threw his arm around him to help him stay up.

"I've got you!" Tony comforted as he all but carried Peter back to the car.

Chapter 27

S am was sitting on the edge of Peter's bed when he woke up. The last thing he remembered was Tony finding him in the desert. He moved his eyes around to examine his whereabouts, and soon realized he was back at the house in Mt. Charleston. Then he realized who was sitting on the bed next to him. His eyes widened a bit when he saw her. *Sam*. She was smiling at him.

"Hey, sleepy head," she softly spoke. "Glad to see you back with us." She took her right hand and gently ran her fingers through Peter's hair.

His lips opened a bit, and he was able to push out some air. But that was it, he couldn't push the air hard enough to speak.

"Shhh," she indicated for Peter to remain quiet.

Peter saw her look away and motion for someone to come over. A few seconds later, a man walked over and stood beside her. He had a stethoscope around his neck.

"Let me get there," he told Sam.

Sam stood up but remained standing close by. The man sat down and positioned the stethoscope in his ears. Peter could feel the cold piece of metal touch his chest in several places. Then, the doctor held up a finger in front of Peter's face and moved it left to right. Peter instinctively followed it with his eyes.

He could tell his body was still sore from the wreck, but he didn't feel as much pain as he had before. Although he didn't lift his head to see, he could tell something was wrapped around his chest. He felt something wrapped around his head as well. Looking with his eyes further to the left, he saw a bag of clear liquid hanging on a metal post and realized he had an IV stuck in his left arm.

"He's recovering just fine," the doctor said to Sam. "He needs more rest, of course, but he should be on his feet in no time."

Sam nodded as the doctor stood up. Before leaving, the doctor added, "Give him a couple of those painkillers twice a day until he doesn't need them anymore."

Again, Sam nodded and watched the doctor walk away. Then, she sat back on the edge of the bed with Peter. "You're going to be just fine," she said while looking at Peter.

He could feel her fingers combing through his hair again. *Sam.* But the sandman was knocking, and Peter let him in.

***

It was dark outside when Peter woke up again. In front of the bedroom window, and curled up in a ball, Sam was sleeping in the chair beside the bed. He knew he must have been out for a while, so he didn't attempt any sudden movements. Rather, he wiggled his fingers and toes at first. Then, he pulled his right hand up to his face and rotated it a bit. He turned his head left and then back to the right. He felt much better.

"Sam," he was able to speak. It was almost inaudible, though. After a few breaths, he forced more air through. "Sam."

Sam's head popped up and she let her feet hit the floor. Peter was smiling over at her.

"Hey!" she answered. "You feeling better?"

Peter nodded slightly and replied, "I am. Please tell me you have some water."

"You know I do," she said, reaching over to the nightstand and grabbing the bottle of water.

She was able to place her hand behind Peter's head to help him lift it, but he held up his right hand indicating she should stop. Slowly, Peter took both hands and placed them flat against the bed. Pushing with them while simultaneously pulling his legs up, he scooted himself up so that he was sitting up. He leaned back against the headboard and smiled. He reached out and took the bottle of water. He drank the entire bottle and let out a sigh of satisfaction.

"Careful, now. You don't want to overdo it, Mister," Sam said to him with a big smile and she retrieved the empty bottle.

Peter was now wide awake. Whatever sleeping drugs the doctor had given him were starting to wear off. There was some pain, but it wasn't debilitating at all.

"How long have I been out?" he asked Sam.

"Two days," she answered. "Tony brought you home about three in the morning yesterday. It's now eleven at night."

Peter took his right hand and scratched through his hair. He felt a bandage and looked over to Sam. "Didn't even know I had hurt my head," he informed her.

"The doctor put a couple of stitches in it. You must have hurt it during the crash," she replied. "You also have two broken ribs and some cuts on your arms and legs. Other than that, you're just fine."

Peter figured his adrenaline had been working overtime during the escape. It must have masked a lot of the pain. He was very familiar with what adrenaline could do. On many occasions, the body releases so much that it makes a person vomit.

Sam reached over and held Peter's hand. "I'm so glad you made it back!"

"Me, too," Peter replied. "The past few weeks went by so slowly."

"Same here! But I passed the time the best I could," Sam stated as she began to smile. "I can't wait to show you what I've done with the place!"

"I can only imagine," Peter replied smiling. "I'm thinking bright curtains with flowers!"

Sam laughed. "You'll see!" After she finished laughing, she asked, "Do you want to sleep some more?"

Peter looked at her and answered, "Are you kidding me? I've been sleeping for two whole days." After seeing Sam nod, he asked, "How's your dad?"

"He's fine. He sits in his room most days, but the staff there takes good care of him. I've realized he really likes to watch Wheel of Fortune," Sam laughed. "I miss him a lot."

"Did I make the news?" Peter then asked with a smile.

"Do you really have to ask that?" Sam asked with an exaggerated face. "Just in case you didn't know it, everyone is looking for you since you escaped from the maximum-security prison where you were serving a life sentence for killing your mother!"

Peter's eyes widened in disbelief. But then, he started smiling and almost laughed.

Sam's face took on a more serious expression then. "Alfred and I talked about it. How you served your country honorably all those years. The sacrifices you've made and the wars you helped fight. And now, your face is splattered across the news as a murderer," she said sadly. "It's not right."

Peter squeezed her hand a little and looked her in the eyes. "It was worth it. I knew I would be sacrificing my honor," he explained. "Even if I could go back, I'd still sacrifice it if it meant you would be safe."

Sam thought of the story Alfred had told her about the girl he had kissed. The tears burst out from her eyes and she fell into the bed holding Peter. He gently placed his arm around her. He held her until they had both fallen asleep.

***

Sam woke up to find she was alone in the bed. Sitting up, she looked towards the bathroom to see a light emanating from the bottom edge of the door. Sliding off the bed, she headed for her room to take a shower and get ready for the day. She felt good and she was glad Peter had found his legs.

Peter placed his hands against the wall and let the water just run down his back. It felt refreshing. His body was still bruised up, but most of the pain had dissipated. He had started off making the water as hot as he could stand it. But, as the time passed, he kept turning the shower knob to the right, making it colder and colder. By the time he was finished, there was nothing but cold water coming out. Peter knew it would work his muscles well while giving his body a good shock to wake up. Afterwards, he examined himself in the mirror. He hadn't realized how much damage his body had endured from the wreck. But he was recovering, and it wouldn't take long till he was back to one hundred percent.

He took his time to finish getting ready for the day. Either Sam or Alfred had made sure there were plenty of clothes for him to choose from. He chose to put on a long sleeved, red t-shirt and a pair of tan cargo pants. He grabbed a pair of socks and slipped them on, but didn't bother to put on shoes. Once dressed, he ran a comb through his hair again and walked back into his bedroom in time to hear the knock on the door.

He opened the door to find Sam waiting. Her hair was still wet from showering. She had put on a pair of blue jeans and had an oversized, black sweater pulled over a white t-shirt. *You're beautiful.*

"Ready to start your day?" she asked with a smile.

Peter nodded as he smiled at her. He liked the way some of her hair dangled in front of her eyes. Even more, he liked that she didn't have any socks on, preferring to go barefoot. The two of them walked down the hall and to the top of the stairs. As Peter looked down, he noticed Boyd and Tony were sitting by the fireplace. They started down the steps.

"Good morning, Mr. Knowles!" Boyd greeted him before he reached the bottom of the steps. "Welcome back!" he added as he and Tony stood up.

Peter and Sam walked over to where they were. Boyd extended his hand to shake Peter's. Peter returned the gesture and shook. "It's good to be back," he said.

"And good morning to you, Sam!" Alfred greeted Sam. "It's good to see you, too!"

"If you two will excuse me, I'm going to make us some breakfast," Tony informed them as he started for the kitchen.

Before Tony made it too far, Peter called after him. Tony stopped and turned to face Peter. "Thanks, Tony. I know you saved me out there, and I truly appreciate it," Peter said sincerely.

"I'm just glad I found you. Welcome back," Tony answered and then headed for the kitchen.

Peter smiled as he turned to face Boyd. "That guy is all business. You should send him on vacation or something," Peter stated with a chuckle.

"I'm sure he could use one, too!" Boyd responded. He then motioned towards the couch, "Please, have a seat."

Peter and Sam sat down on the couch. Peter liked the way Sam sat next to him. Boyd walked over and sat in the Polio chair. For a minute, no one said anything. No one really knew how to start.

Peter decided he should start. "So, I made it out alive! That last day was something else, though," he said, lifting his eyebrows to emphasize the point.

"You've been through quite the ordeal, Mr. Knowles. Yes, I'm eager to hear all about it! But it's more important you tell me when you feel up to it," Boyd replied.

"I feel fine," Peter stated as he began looking around. "Please tell me you have the backpack and the keychain."

Boyd smiled and answered, "I do. After Tony found you out there in the desert, he placed you in his car. Then, he went back to your car and retrieved all the items you had. I've already downloaded all of the images you took, and, let me say I'm quite impressed!"

Peter relaxed after he heard Boyd had the keychain. He leaned back on the couch. "They are looking for you," Peter informed Boyd.

"I know. They've always been looking for me, ever since I left," Boyd responded.

"More than that," Peter said seriously. "They need you to complete whatever project they are working on. According to them, you are the UGEN. They can't proceed without you." He emphasized the word 'you' when he said it.

"I know y'all have talked about it before, but what is UGEN?" Sam asked, looking over to Alfred. Peter looked at him too.

"It's best to keep some things behind the curtain," Boyd replied.

Peter didn't respond. Sam turned her head and was looking at him now. "What's behind the curtain?" she asked.

"Honestly, I still don't know what all is behind it," Peter answered sincerely.

"Well, I want to know!" Sam replied. "I want to know what this is all about. I want to know what you risked your life for, Peter!"

Before she could continue, Peter held up his hand indicating she should stop. She did. Still, she had a confused and surprising look.

"Sam," Alfred called to get her attention. "Sometimes it's better to not know the whole story."

Peter spoke up to Boyd and asked, "Now that you know what they have, what are you going to do?"

"I'm going to stop them!" Boyd was quick to respond. "Far too long have they manipulated society. It's time to end this."

"How?" Peter further inquired.

"I still know people in high places who will trust me, once they know I'm alive. I'll tell them everything and provide the evidence you obtained," Boyd explained. "It may take some time. And, honestly, no matter how much evidence and proof I give to some, they just will not accept it. But others will, Mr. Knowles. Others will believe it and take the necessary actions to expose all of it. Working with them, we can expose all of it and pull down the curtain. We'll put the power back into the people's hands."

"I hope you are successful. I fought hard for my country and still believe in it," Peter responded.

"What about us?" Sam asked. "What happens to us?"

Tony walked over to the three of them at that point. "Breakfast is ready," he alerted them.

"Let's eat breakfast, shall we?" Boyd offered. "Tonight, at dinner, I shall tell you what happens with you two."

Together, all four of them walked into the kitchen and enjoyed breakfast. Boyd told Peter stories of how Sam had entertained himself and Tony. Peter could hardly wait for breakfast to be over so he could see Sam's bedroom, which she had supposedly redecorated completely. Sam and Peter told the two men what names they had been using for them. All throughout breakfast, they laughed and enjoyed the meal together while unwinding all the stress which had accumulated over the past few weeks. They all knew they would be parting ways soon enough, and decided to focus on their friendship rather than events related to Peter's adventures at the Ranch. Tony laughed once.

***

It was evening time with the clock showing the time was eight o'clock. Tony had prepared the dinner, but then returned upstairs once everyone was situated around the table. Alfred sat at the head of the table with Sam to his right. Peter was on the left. Once Sam finished saying grace, they all began to eat.

After they all took a few bites, Boyd had something to say. "Well, I have something for both of you, as promised." He stood up and retrieved a folder and laptop which had been placed on the kitchen counter earlier. He opened the laptop and let it begin to boot up before he continued. Opening the folder, he handed each of them a new passport, driver's license, social security card, and birth certificate. "Here are your first rewards." He had a big smile on his face.

Sam looked over to Peter. "You first!" she insisted, smiling gently.

Peter looked down and opened his passport. "Adam James Livingston," Peter said, looking up to see Sam's reaction. "I'm Adam Livingston! And who might you be?" he asked with a sophisticated voice looking over to Sam.

"Well," Sam almost giggled. "Since you asked, I'm…" she paused to open her passport. "Evelyn Rose Summers. Yes, I'm Evelyn Rose Summers!" she said with a smile. Looking over to Alfred, she added, "I like the Rose in it!" She remembered the story Alfred had told her.

"Adam and Eve," Boyd cut in. "I thought it appropriate." After a brief pause to smile, he continued, "Now, time for the next rewards!"

Boyd began typing on the laptop. Then, he asked, "Adam, can you please give me your identification number?"

"Of course," Peter answered, looking down at his card. "It's 77345284!"

Alfred typed as Peter read off the numbers. A second later, he turned the laptop around and slid it over to Peter. Peter ran his eyes over the web page and recognized it as a bank account under his new name. Moving his eyes further down, he saw the account balance. His eyes widened.

"Are you serious? That's a lot of zeros!" he asked looking up to Boyd who was nodding. He looked over the laptop at Sam. "There's a lot of money in my new account!" His mouth gaped open.

"I've got my social ready!" Sam screamed!

Alfred took the laptop back and pressed a few keys. "Shoot!" he said, ready to capture the numbers.

"77539112!" Sam read off rather quickly.

Alfred turned the laptop and pushed it over to Sam. She was still long enough to read the screen. She, too, had more money than she expected in her account! She exploded with screams and began jumping up and down. She bounced all the way over behind Alfred and threw her arms around him. "Thank you! Thank you!"

"I'm not the one you should be thanking!" he responded.

He and Sam turned to look at Peter. Sam walked over behind Peter's chair and pulled hard, sliding him from beneath the table. When his legs were clear, she walked over and plopped down right in his lap to wrap him in the warmest of hugs.

"Careful!" Peter whelped. "I'm still a little sore."

She almost got up remembering he was bruised, but he held on to her. "I didn't say get up," he said with a smile.

"As for the house, I figured the two of you could cover that with your new bank accounts. Besides, you two may not want to have two separate houses!" Boyd explained as he grinned at them both. Sam reacted by leaning over and picking up a napkin to throw his way!

After a moment of smiles and laughs, Sam stood up and walked back to her chair. She was still smiling, but, behind her eyes, she was thinking of something else. Both Peter and Boyd detected a change in her demeanor. They both knew she was thinking about how she probably wasn't going to be around much longer. The men grew quiet and Sam noticed they had stopped smiling.

"This has to be one of the best nights of my life!" she exclaimed as she watched both men remain somber. "Come on guys! Why the serious faces?" she said in hopes of cheering them up a little. Her fake smile began to fade and her face grew red seeing the men were saddened. "Don't do that!" she exclaimed loudly while banging her fist down on the table.

Alfred sat quietly. Peter looked over to Sam who looked furious. "Sam," he said in a gentle voice trying to calm her.

"Don't...!" she began as her voice erupted into crying. The tears came flowing out.

Peter stood up and walked over to her. He was about to place his arm around her when she threw out her arm to keep him away.

It was Boyd who then cut in. "She's right! What's the need for these serious faces?"

Peter looked over at Boyd who motioned for him to take his seat. Sam still sat with her head hung down. With a napkin, she tried to dry away her tears as she got control over her emotions. Peter walked back over and sat down in his seat.

"Sam, look at me," Alfred said to her. "Look at me."

Reluctantly, Sam held her head back up. Her eyes were red but she had managed to stop the flow of tears. She sat quietly looking over at Alfred.

"You have changed my life, my dear. I've never met someone as kind and gentle hearted as you, and I've lived a very long time," he said with a slight smile. "You have filled my days with brightness and laughter. You stayed with us, even though you thought we had lost our minds. And now, Sam, it's time for me to brighten your day."

Alfred reached down and pulled a rectangular, plastic case from his pocket. It was leathery brown with two gold hinges on the side. He placed the case on the table and kept his fingers on top of it.

"I have one last gift for you. Within this case, a new life exists. I've never offered this to anyone, but I'm offering it to you now."

Sam and Peter looked at the case as Boyd pushed it over to Sam.

"What is it?" Sam asked before reaching for it.

"Life," Alfred answered. "There's no need in you believing everyday may be your last. You are a bright and beautiful person, Sam, and the world needs more of you around."

Sam opened the case. Inside was a syringe filled with a red liquid.

"The UGEN," Peter surmised, looking over to Boyd. "You're offering it to her."

Boyd simply replied, "Yes."

"What will it do to her?" Peter asked with concern.

"Like I said earlier," Boyd answered. "It will give her life."

"Are you telling me this will free me from my sickness?" Sam asked as she carefully retrieved the syringe from the case and held it up.

"Oh, yes! You'll never get sick again, Sam." Boyd honestly answered.

Peter was excited, yet cautious. Something in his gut told him to stop her from taking it. But in his mind, he imagined Sam free of sickness. She would have all the time needed to travel and see the world. She would be free from fear and worry. Moreover, he would no longer have to feel the pain and sadness he had felt at the thought of losing her. Thinking about it, did he even have a right to tell her what she should do?

Sam looked over to Peter who only said, "It's your choice, Sam."

Sam looked at the syringe again. She thought about Peter. *How to make it work, and not why it won't work!* Having made up her mind, she looked over to Alfred and simply stated, "I want to pick more roses."

Chapter 28

The North Carolina senator sat quietly in the waiting room. Already, the crew had styled his hair, dabbed on a little makeup, and briefed him on how the next few minutes would unfold. He glanced up at the wall clock across from him. It was 8:53 a.m. He was just a few minutes away from executing what he had been planning to do for several weeks now. He carefully pulled his right hand up to his neck and wiggled two fingers behind his buttoned shirt collar in efforts to breathe a little easier. Closing his eyes, he began to recite in his mind what he needed to say. He didn't get far before the door to his left swung open.

"Senator, they're ready for you," a petite lady wearing a tan skirt and black top announced to him as she held the door open. While holding a computer tablet in her left hand, she extended her right arm and hand through the door indicating the senator should pass through.

Letting out a long exhale, the senator placed his hands on his knees and stood up. Standing up tall, he gently tugged at the bottom on his jacket to pull any wrinkles out. It was time. Walking through the door, he noticed the three news anchors standing in front of their couch waiting on him. Four television cameras were on mounts with wheels and were being repositioned. Lights beamed from the ceiling and several pedestals positioned around the floor. He composed a slight smile as he approached the set.

"Good morning, Senator!" the blonde female anchor greeted him as she extended her hand to shake. "Please take a seat on the couch. We have fifty seconds until we are back on the air."

After shaking her hand, the two male co-anchors greeted him likewise. He exchanged pleasantries and took his place on the couch. He pulled up his left arm to glance at his watch. It was 8:55 a.m. The three co-anchors each took their place on the couch as well as they shuffled through a few notes they had placed on the table in front of the couch. As the time neared to go on air, they placed their notes away, straightened their posture and put on the expected smiles. The man beside one of the television cameras began the countdown and went silent for the last three numbers.

"Welcome back!" one of the male co-anchors stated while looking into a camera. "Joining us now is North Carolina Senator Jason Steinbeck." He then looked over to the Senator, "Good morning, Senator."

"Good morning," the senator replied.

The same male co-anchor continued, "We have a lot to talk about this morning. But first, you said you had a special announcement you would like to make."

The senator looked down at his watch again. It was 8:57 a.m. The three co-anchors stared at him intently waiting to hear what he had to say. Not only that, he knew there were millions more waiting on the other side of the cameras. He took a deep breath.

"Good morning, and thanks for having me on," he replied.

Before he could continue, the female co-anchor spoke up, "Are you going to run for President, Senator? Is that what you are going to say?" Her smile was wide as she anticipated his message.

Shaking his head, the senator replied, "No. I'm not running for President." He returned the smile. "I'm here on a more serious matter.

A matter that involves everyone watching." His smile faded as did the smiles of the co-anchors.

Turning his head towards the camera with the green light, the senator spoke directly to the millions of viewers, "In about two minutes, at 9:00 a.m. eastern time, everyone with a smart phone or internet connection will be receiving evidence of a global conspiracy. Like me, several other senators are simultaneously on other major news networks delivering this same message. Within twenty-four hours, the whole world will be enlightened."

"Senator," one of the male co-anchors interrupted. "This is unexpected. What global conspiracy are you talking about?"

The senator looked over at the anchor and then back to the camera as he continued, "Alfred Boyd, the founder of the largest computer company in the world, has emerged from hiding. A select few congressmen, military leaders, and governors have been working with him on the best way to divulge and handle the information about to be released."

"Senator," the female co-anchor spoke up. "This is quite alarming."

"Yes, it is!" the senator responded. "Alfred Boyd has proof of this global conspiracy. At this moment, steps are being taken to not only expose the truth, but also to expose those in power that are behind all of it. The world as we know it is about to change."

***

Peter and Sam listened intently to the radio as the news broke. Neither one spoke. Instead, they peered out ahead as the miles rolled by. Sam had her window down letting the wind dance through her blonde curls. Peter glanced over to each side view mirror to ensure the RV was stable. He couldn't help but smile. *No people, no worries, just us!*

Taking his foot off the gas pedal, Peter began slowing to make a right turn. Once on the new road and accelerating, he looked over to Sam and asked, "Wonder where this road will take us?" He really didn't know where it would take them. All he knew is they would have many, many more days and roads ahead of them.

End

About the Author

Cecil Nobles knew there was more to the world than tobacco farming in rural North Carolina. As a result, and upon graduating from high school, Cecil enlisted into the US Air Force to see what the world had to offer. His naivety transformed into an awakening over his honorable 22-year service performing duties as an Intelligence Analyst with top-secret clearance. Highly decorated, one of his milestones was helping to lay the foundation for the Air Force's remotely piloted aircraft (drone) operations as a Sensor Operator stationed in the Nevada desert. Upon retirement at age 41, Cecil returned home to North Carolina and earned his Bachelor of Ministry degree with Summa Cum Laude recognition. Having experienced the world, he now spends much of his time exploring the Bible which he believes contains the answers to life. Aside from the hobby of writing, Cecil enjoys spending time with his wife, two children, and Enoch, his dog.

www.ingramcontent.com/pod-product-compliance
Lightning Source LLC
Chambersburg PA
CBHW032138190626
46814CB00005BA/1743